# Inspector Bucket

# and the Beast

## Peter Cooper

# Inspector Bucket

# and the Beast

## Peter Cooper

First published 2012 by Dahlia Publishing Ltd
6 Samphire Close Hamilton
Leicester LE5 1RW
ISBN 978-0-9566967-2-4


© Peter Cooper 2012

Printed and bound by Berforts

A CIP catalogue record for this book is
available from The British Library

To The Lady Vivienne

# Chapter 1

The mortuaries were full that year. In Limehouse, bodies of young girls were laid out on slabs. The surgeons scratched their heads at seeing street girls dressed up like daughters of Lords and Ladies. At the Christ Church mortuary in Belgravia the surgeons were similarly bemused. The clothes were identical in both places: the gauze dresses and crinoline frocks, the hoops (in imitation of their elders' fashions), the frills and the white drawers reaching to the knee. In both places, the tiny faces and bodies were pricked over with knife wounds like smallpox scabs. It was expected that there would be evidence of abuse but the surgeons were shocked by the precision of the mutilations. They had been made by an instrument that left fine, almost bloodless pin pricks, as if the killer might have been one of their own.

Such was the summation of my reading matter as I travelled on the train from Chatham towards London Bridge Station. Below me, the gritty streets of London unwound themselves like a grey snake, leering at me through the stifling fog. And somewhere in those dark alleys and courts, amongst the shadows and in the darkness, there dwelt a killer. A killer who raped children. A monster that raped and murdered and mutilated. Girls. Small children. Children of the rich. Children of the poor.

The newspapers had named him 'The Beast of London Town'. *The Morning Post* insisted he was a Lord or a Baronet; a surgeon was what *The Times* had; *The Standard* decided the Beast was an opium-eating Chinaman. *The News of The World* had it on good authority that the murderer might actually be a *murderes*s, a woman in a man's clothes.

Of course, I was unqualified to come to any such conclusion. I was merely a poor boy, once from the streets of London myself.

But it occurred to me even then that it might have been the rapes of the daughters of the aristocracy that inflamed the ire of the press. After all, the children of the poor were dying *all* the time. Nevertheless, the papers all agreed on *one* thing: Inspector Bucket of the Detective was the man to catch the killer.

Back then in the 1850s, all of thirty years ago, Inspector Bucket was a sensation. These were the days when London was alight with rumours of Bucket's activities: the Bucket who arrested Charles Gill for firing an ounce of powder into the skull of Lord John Russell at 10 Downing Street; the Bucket who had investigated the disappearance of an actress from Drury Lane only to find she had eloped with the Duke of Devonshire; the very Bucket who had arrested Robert Pate for striking Her Majesty the Queen on her crown with his cane. It was Inspector Bucket who had solved the mystery of the murder of Lawyer Tulkinghorn and the scandal that afflicted Sir Leicester and Lady Dedlock. Such was the reputation of Inspector Bucket of the Detective. There had been rumours abounding that Bucket was due to retire from his position in the Detective Branch and that he would soon be opening up his very own private bureau. And here was I, William Aloysius Jakesbere, full of enthusiasm to meet him and hoping that it would be he who would help me make my fortune as a Fleet Street reporter.

It was early in the January of 1851 that the events recorded herein occurred. I remember I commenced the New Year with a resolution to return to London, hopefully to take up employment as a reporter for *Reynolds' Weekly*. London then as now was ever the heart of a young man's ambitions and where his fortune might be made. Consequently, I had not been pleased when my mother and father had removed me from the joys of the Great City when I was merely a child. I had felt aggrieved by thoughts

2

that I should be excluded from all the pleasures and excitements of the metropolis when I came of age. Now that I had reached that milestone, and my parents had passed away, my Uncle Silas had encouraged me to return to the seat of my birth and to learn to be a Londoner again. In addition to this, at the time of my return, there was the expectation of the Great Exhibition to look forward to.

'The World's Fair', as it was then called, was due to be opened by His Majesty Prince Albert on May 1st in that very year. London would be the centre of the world. Anyone who was anyone would be in London in that spring and summer of '51 and I wanted to be there amongst the notables - to see them, to meet them and to write about them. What's more, Bucket of the Detective was obliged to be on show. Important officers of the law (such as he was) were to be deployed by the government to ensure that the streets were free of criminal incident. I was determined that I should be the one to describe the adventures of the great Bucket, and that this would make my fortune and reputation as a writer.

I remember I made my way along from Chatham with only a small leather bag containing the few belongings that I had not already been wearing. Amongst these were my father's fob-watch (with a little pen-knife he had bequeathed me) and a testimonial of good work from my Uncle Silas. This had been my first railway journey by steam locomotive. However, I recall, I was too excited to be apprehensive for long. I felt I had joined the modern world at last. I became even more stimulated when I alighted from the train to renew my acquaintance with all the sights of old London Town. It was, I remember, its sound that impressed me to begin with - for indeed the bedlam of the city had almost a physical presence that one might feel or see like a cloud hovering above the church roofs and domes. However, the sense of hearing was soon overcome by that of smell - for I fear mire, muck and manure were everywhere in those days, even more than today.

Nevertheless, it was all a delight to me on that golden day. I remember I had my mouth wide open in anticipation simply in observation of the heaving squash of humanity all around me. The roads, alleys and courts were overflowing with crowds, carriages and cattle. The weather was just as I had remembered it too. The sea air of Chatham was replaced by the yellow fog of London and, of course, it was raining. Despite the warnings given by Uncle Silas to watch my purse and to be sure not to make myself look foolish by putting up a 'boom shooter' nor to go in, by the by, for anything that would make me 'look like a molly', as he put it, my first commercial transaction was the hire of an umbrella from a station stall. I remember the gay abandon with which I strutted towards St Giles, Cripplegate, oblivious to the looks of contempt from street beggars and the missiles of street urchins, secure as I was from being wetted by the London squall.

I had written in advance to secure a room in a cheap lodging house just adjacent to Boziers Court, in the parish of St Giles. It was a rather down-at-heel area, to be truthful, but at least the houses there were not quite as maggoty as those at nearby Seven Dials. At St Giles the street stench did not insinuate itself into one's nostrils quite so powerfully - although the air was ripe enough as it was with the aroma of hops from the nearby Meux's brewery.

The landlady of the lodging house was named a Mrs Peckers. I do not hesitate in recalling that she was a thoroughly dislikable harridan with eyes like slits and a nose like a walnut. She informed me with some severity that she ran a "respecrable house" and that I would be required to be on my best behaviour from the beginning.

Despite the unprepossessing nature of the area and the lodging house, I looked forward with pleasure to exploring the famous parish of St Giles, not least because the Cripplegate Station House was Inspector Bucket's favoured haunt at the time. The headquarters of the London police detectives were at Great Scotland Yard by Whitehall - but I was not so naïve as to think I would find Bucket there. He would more likely be found around such dens of iniquity as the gin palaces of St Giles where the criminal classes might converge. As with all Metropolitan detectives, Bucket had licence to practise his trade anywhere in the city and to go without uniform. He might be anywhere in the city at this moment, I remember thinking, anywhere where crime and poverty were companions. As they so often were.

Cripplegate was indeed an area of shocking wretchedness - even for a boy who had seen the squalor of the Woolwich dockyards in his youth. My senses, as well as my sensibilities, were offended by the manner in which the broken houses and fetid streets, their gutters clogged with filth and abandoned children, could sit side by side with the gaudy opulence of the glass palaces known as gin houses. I recall being drawn to the door of such an establishment just across from the station house. It was partly the cold that gnawed through my gloves and partly the shining lights reflecting from the ground glass windows and their sparkling invitations to the "Gin Emporium" that attracted me. The gas lights in their ornamented burners lit up the insides like a theatre. The elaborate interior seemed at odds with the grubby customers who supped inside.

On the occasion of which I speak it was still only early evening but trade was brisk. Old washerwomen, itinerant Irish labourers and young men without coats or expectations seemed the chief clientele. I watched through the distorted glass as a dispute simmering inside boiled over. The door flew open and a gaggle of wrestling, swearing men - and young women too - rolled out to continue their altercation in the mire. A pot-boy followed who raced off around the corner to the station house, returning in a moment or two with a half dozen constables, truncheons at the ready. As they arrived I made a discreet retreat to the shadows of a broken-down house. From here I observed the proceedings.

After a brief struggle, several of the disputees were borne off to the Cripplegate lock-up and the remainder returned to their glasses or their wretched hovels. What took my eye, however, was a face I recognised: a beak-like nose and freckles that, even in the fog, glittered on his face like dust motes in a shaft of light. It was my old friend Archibald Sparrow. I had not had the pleasure of his company since our childhood, yet here he was in full fig. His lanky length was all dressed up in the uniform of a *policeman* no less: swallow tail coat, dark blue trousers, chimney-pot hat and a boldly numbered E63 on his collar to round off the picture. Here he was, brushing the dirt from his topper in the light of a gas jet, as his companions escorted away the last of the complainants. Still wondering whether it was really he, I continued to observe for a moment as he took up station under the warm light of the gin palace. He listened with a pained face as his superior gave him fresh commands. It was clear that Sparrow did not relish his designated duty: to be sentry against further drunken incursions into the street. I hallooed him as soon as he was alone in exactly the old way we had used in our Woolwich days.

"Sparrow, old bird!" I called in my youthful brogue. "I can't believe it!"

He looked at me as if he had seen a ghost - but now I knew it was him, by the distinctive way his lower lip hung like a loose flap.

"Don't you know me? It's Jakes, from Woolwich! And what's this I see?" I continued, according him a thorough examination. "You're not, you're not *really* a Bow Street Runner, old beak, are you? *Please* say you're not, it's too much!" My friend looked quite the man with his bright and shiny buttons and his broad belt with six-inch buckle.

"Jakes! Blow me down with a ... is that you, Jakesy?" he said out of the corner of his droopy mouth before looking up and down the road with some anxiety. "Well, if it is you or if it ain't, lay off, can't yer! You can see I'm on duty. The sergeant'll have me swabbing out the cells if he catches me with the likes of you. And *don't* call me a Runner, they don't like it. I'm a Metropolitan *Police* officer to you!"

I had known Archibald Sparrow from the days long ago when he would steal veal pies from Woolwich Market and rollick and rifle through the dockside storehouses for easy pickings. That was the sort of character he was. And now here he was, a China Street pig, as we used to say. Sparrow had a good trick with a bent pin in those days too, I remembered. He would utilise the iron pin to ease open a lock-up, and he had passed this dubious ability on to me. I had not put that talent to much use since those old times - although I would do so in the days to come. Now, of course, we were all more serious and law-abiding and such behaviour was beneath us. Even so, I remember thinking, '*Him* - the old bird, the old villain, *truly* become a *Runner*?' It did not seem quite credible.

"Get away, Jakesy!" he was saying. "I can't talk to you now. My sergeant'll think I'm takin' back-handers from a fogle-hunter if he gets an eye-full of you - go on, clear off, or I'll 'ave to arrest you for lurking like a shoot-flyer." I thought this ironic – being accused of looking like a thief by somebody who had been a pick-pocket himself in his wild days. Nevertheless, I was not to be put off.

"Come, come Archie - you haven't forgotten your old pal have you?"

"Clear off, I say Jakes! If I don't get cracked across the knuckles for not arrestin' you as a gin-bibber they'll think I should have had you for a dipper." He looked up and down the street again as he spoke, although there was little chance of anybody seeing who he was talking to in the fog. "I'll talk to you when I'm off duty, ten at *The White Lion*," he whispered, but added by way of explanation, "they're all nervy at the minute, see, worrying about thieves meetin' up at beer shops and gin houses and makin' plans for a spree when the exhibition's on. I suppose you've heard about Crystal Palace, haven't you? Well, there are villains about and my sergeant has…"

"Well, you're just the feller for me, Sparrow old bird," I interrupted, "and that's just the sort of talk I want to hear! If there's a hunt on for villains, then Inspector Bucket is bound to be in it and he's the man I'm looking for and wanting you to give me news of!"

When the name of Bucket was mentioned Sparrow made a grimace as if I had uttered a taboo word. He obviously thought Bucket might pop out of the gas-lamp like a jack-in-a-box. But it was Sparrow I saw jump when the very sergeant he had been wary of materialised from the fog like a great hulk. His eyebrows were as broad as broom brushes, as if to make up for his lack of a moustache, I supposed. I made a hasty retreat, affording Sparrow a friendly cuff on his neck as I made my exit. I remember I bruised my hand on the leather stock he wore beneath his collar, to ward off garrotters, as I did so. I ran off into the fog towards Boziers Street, sucking my fingers like a child and wondering in my youthful way about the transformation in Sparrow from crook to copper.

# Chapter 2

When I returned to my lodgings, Mrs Peckers was in the doorway jangling her keys and making a face of reproof, one of the many faces I would become familiar with. This one, I recall, was a countenance so sour that it near made my eyes water. She kept a grandfather clock decorated with a figure of St. Peter, pointing to heaven, or hell, in the hallway, and by the face of this she timed the entrances and exits of all her clients as a way of monitoring their respectability. As the minute hand frowned on its way past six o'clock, I knew I was late for tea, and had already been consigned to the hell side. She and St Peter both made their faces at me as I climbed the rickety stairway to my room like a child sent to bed without any supper.

Fortunately, there was a little house-girl who had already taken a liking to me, and it was my good luck that she was on the landing as I climbed up. With a conspiratorial hiss and a finger to my lips, I gave her a wink and a penny to fetch me a muffin or two from the larder. After charring these over an ashy fire on a rusty toasting fork, I took my clandestine tea with delight and had a light nap.

After a refreshing sleep I shook myself awake a minute or two before nine o'clock by my fob-watch and, after preparing my toilet, vacated my lodgings to face the world again. I was looking forward to making a tour of the hostelries of Cripplegate and to finding out what my old friend Sparrow knew about Inspector Bucket. There was only the grandfather clock to chide me when I crept into the hall, chiming a quarter past the hour. I thought myself lucky to escape a wigging from Mrs Peckers but when I stepped out into the street I saw that my relief had been precipitate; looking up at the lighted landing window I saw a curtain pulled back and her nose squashed up against it like an over-ripe tomato. She was squinting down at me through the slits she had for eyes, wondering if I was "respecrable", I supposed. She obviously did not approve of my going out into the streets at all hours. Still, I headed off cheerfully enough into the fog, pointing my nose in the direction of the public house. My plan was to eat a proper supper before I met up with Sparrow, not liking the look of the greasy mess Mrs Peckers had been serving up.

I remember, I had a thirst on me that needed quenching and three pennies in my waistcoat pocket that wanted spending. Since my mother and father had died, one of the dropsy and the other of palsy, I had been left alone with my old Uncle Silas and felt that I had spent too long at the font rather than the fountain. Silas was a kind old gentleman but a little too churchy for the taste of the young man that I then was. It was he who had introduced me to literature and imbued me with some of the manners of a gentleman. It was Uncle Silas, too, who had provoked the idea that I might one day make my way as a writer, once having been a scribbler himself on *The British Press*. In fact he had presented me with my first Keswick pencil, so that I could write on the run, so to speak, and follow the exploits of the famous Inspector Bucket.

Like Bucket himself, my father had been a Bow Street Runner as a young man. When my mother had first met him she had not thought it quite a genteel enough profession. And so it was that Pa had given up policing for a position in insurance in Greenwich. Bucket, however, was made of more determined mettle. He had *policeman* running all the way through his bones. He couldn't help himself. Bucket went to join what they used to call the *New Metropolitan Police Force*. At first he had been posted to the Greenwich Division when he, like the century, was in his mid thirties. He had been a regular visitor to our house in those days and a regular sight on the streets when I was a young boy in Woolwich. One might see him around the Arsenal or down by the docks. I confess I was wary of him then, of his great bull neck and his thick police collar. I would creep out the back door when he came in the front for fear he might arrest me for having stolen a radish from Woolwich Market.

I first became aware of Bucket's fame when the case of Eliza Grimwood became well known. In our innocent Woolwich days it seemed a very sensational tale indeed. Eliza was a pretty young woman who had lived in Wellington Terrace and who had disappeared in mysterious circumstances. Her family feared that she had been murdered. Although they were a poor family, and such disappearances were common, they had connections with a wealthy and influential tradesman in Greenwich who had been able to exert some pressure on the police to take some strenuous action. Eliza had last been seen with a man twice her age, who had dual guild membership as a bricklayer and cheese-maker, a strange combination of professions which turned out to be material to the case. Just as the investigating officers were about to leave the bricklayer's house with their enquiries no further advanced, Bucket noticed that, amongst the rounds of piled up cheese, there was not a cheese-cutter to be seen. He had observed, too, that the cellar had been freshly furnished with a new but rather shabbily built wall. He pointed out to his superior officer that such a wall was hardly commensurate with the work of a master craftsman, especially in his own home. He politely proposed that the wall might be disassembled. The Inspector in charge at the time was resistant to such drastic action and thought Bucket something of an upstart, with his reliance on new fangled observational techniques to solve crimes. Nevertheless, Bucket had something about him, even then, that would not be denied. The wall was taken down and Eliza's body was discovered, the cheese-cutting wire lying beside her. The brick-layer had garrotted her with the cheese-cutter and bricked her body up behind the wall.

Bucket's fame grew from that day. It was at that time that Uncle Silas had found a position for Pa in Chatham and, because Ma liked the sound of the address, I had said goodbye to the London of my childhood and forgot all about Bucket. The night when Uncle Silas said it was time I should do a little swimming in the world rather than drowning in the offices of Marine Insurance, I realised that my scheme to be a writer and my memory of the famous Inspector Bucket might be drawn together. It was Uncle Silas who had encouraged me to return to London and had furnished me with a testimonial to give to the famous sensationalist writer and radical, George Reynolds, whom he once knew.

I hoped that my experience as a junior copywriter and the shorthand I had learnt from Uncle Silas might qualify me to be a 'penny-a-line man' on *Reynolds' Weekly*. Reynolds rented a crumbling, red-painted building in Fleet Street, next to *The Morning Post* and squashed in by *The News of the World*. I remember vividly how I strode up the steps to the heavy doors of Reynolds' offices and how the rusty old grille had rattled up when I knocked. I remember, too, the ugly eye of the doorman regarding me as a vagrant. I held up my testimonial to this bloodshot eye before it could turn into an arm that might throw me back down the steps. Fortunately, the eye recognised the scrawl of my Uncle Silas and I was let in.

"Young Jakesbere, is it?" Reynolds said when I was shown into his busy office and he had finished reading my testimonial.

"Yes sir," I said.

"You know shorthand, do you?" he asked, and then addressed himself to some or other of the half a dozen bustling figures in his office without waiting on my answer. "Mr Martin, the galley proofs, please," he said to one, and then, addressing another, asked, "What's the latest on the Exhibition?" He didn't wait to receive an answer to this question either but instead continued to issue instructions and demands. "Barney, take that pile of quarto to the newsroom. - Makepiece, where's the Chancery docket?" After this, at last, he returned to me for a moment. "And your Uncle is old Silas Jakesbere, is he? How is the old hack? Still got religion bad? Pencil out your ear, Snoops!"

"Yes sir," was the only answer I could think of, because I was too confused to know which enquiry to answer first. Reynolds became distracted again then with some other newspaper business, perhaps not being overly impressed with my monosyllabic answers. I knew I had to say something to get his attention again. And so it was that something made me blurt out that I had once known Inspector Bucket of the Detective.

There was a sudden silence.

"Bucket?" he exclaimed with interest. "You tell me that you actually *know* him?" He sounded quite incredulous.

"Yes sir," I said, with all the bravado of youth.

"Then if you can get me a story, boy, you're engaged!"

That was the end of the interview, if I remember it at all correctly. But I was employed as a reporter at last. Except, of course, that I wasn't, for I had nothing to write about. George Reynolds would pay me a penny-a-line but only for material about the famous Bucket, and as yet I had not seen even a shadow of him.

# Chapter 3

This was the thought that had kept me awake during my first week back in London. I had wandered up and down outside St Giles Police Station until I thought they might hook me up and deposit me in one of their lock-ups. I had martyred myself in all the ale houses and gin palaces from Drury Lane to Whitechapel. All this in hope for word of Bucket. And word there was none.

After a week I had still not heard a whisper. It was my ill-fortune that I had not discovered Sparrow earlier, but he had been completing his probation in Deptford. Now, however, fortune was smiling on me. Sparrow had a placement in St Giles - the home of the great Bucket. And now here I was, waiting to keep my appointment with my old friend. He was bound to have a tale or two he could tell me about Bucket. And I might be able to write a few lines for Reynolds before he gave up on me and ended my days as a reporter before they had even begun.

And so it was that I was reading *The Standard* that night whilst I supped my half and half, waiting for Sparrow. There, next to all the news and complaints about what *Punch* called The Crystal Palace, was yet another murder story. It talked, in sensational terms, of a *Child Killer, the Rabid Raper* and *the Beast of Old London Town*. There was a report of a body that had been fished up from the Thames. Usually a corpse discovered in such a way would merit hardly a line but the fact that the Great Exhibition was coming up, and a murdering monster was on the loose, meant that any body that was dredged up was put down as the work of "The Beast." Dead bodies had been given a new lease of life, so to speak. *The Standard* said that a girl of eight years of age had been reported missing and that a search of a nearby river bank had been undertaken. There was a long report of all the lurid paraphernalia of the search: the barge and pole; the drag and net; the men with jackboots and hatchet and spades; the ropes and the dogs. However, what had inflamed the ire of the writer was that the child whose poor white body was eventually hauled up was the daughter of a *respectable* family. The daughter of a gentleman from the upper classes was what was meant by this euphemism. *"Kidnapped whilst out walking with her nurse,"* it maintained. *"Abused, murdered and dumped in the river."* The correspondent went on to say that the work of The Beast was *"obvious by the markings on the body, for he always left his victims with fine incisions to the flesh as if pierced by a surgical instrument."*

Inspector Bucket was described on his visit to the Dead Houses, where the swollen bodies were laid out for the coroner and the police. The writer's tone implied that Bucket was little less than a beast himself, describing him as a *"ghoulish be-cloaked figure searching for signs in the shadows, executing macabre river-side autopsies."* Bucket had appointed divers to search for clues amongst the grisly detritus of the river-bed, the report said. The Inspector had been *"foiled yet again"* by a lack of clues - as if it were all his fault.

This was grim fare to be reading but it was sweetened by the hearty meal I had been served by *The White Lion*'s girl, Alice. I had consumed a crusty piece of eel pie and tuppence worth of mash, and was sitting back enjoying my ale when Sparrow finally appeared. He was still in his police uniform, carrying his chimney-pot hat under one arm and mopping his brow with the other, as if he were fresh from the pursuit of some villain.

"Sparrow, old man, on the dot as ever," I remarked, tapping my watch. "As good as railway time, old beak. Now come and rest your size 13s," I said cheerfully. Policemen were not supposed to sup in the ale house, but as *The White Lion* was only a stone's throw from the Police Station a blind eye was often turned. Nevertheless, Sparrow was still anxious and was feeling his wrist to ensure he had removed the band that indicated he was on duty.

"I shouldn't be in here at all, Jakesy," he said. "If I gets caught by the sergeant I shall cop it something chronical!" He stole a sup from my tankard and coiled his bean-pole body over a stool. "But I didn't want you to miss the chance," he gasped, licking his lips and giving Alice a sideways smile.

"Chance for what, old bird?" I said.

"To go out on a trawl with Inspector Bucket, o' course!"

"Tell me more!" I said. Just then Alice staggered past, carrying a bowl of empty shells and a basin of fish skeletons. I called her over. "You'll have a bumper of your *own* half and half now, won't you?" I said to Sparrow. "Instead of filching mine, I mean. Fetch us two jars of your best foaming, my girl," I said, like a man-about-town. Alice and Sparrow grinned at each other and I realised with disappointment that Sparrow had stolen a march on me already.

"Can't," Sparrow grunted again, finishing off my beer in one gulp. "Got to be on the out. But *you* can come along, Jakes. Now, don't look so gormless! I thought you *wanted* to meet him. Didn't you? Inspector Bucket I mean." I was in mid-gasp at this offer but Sparrow gabbled on while buttoning up his tunic. "He's hot with another body that's been found, don't yer know? Put down to that Beast. It's in the rag you're reading as a matter of fact," he said, noticing the paper and giving it a tap. "On top o' that, one more girl 'as been attacked today around Seven Dials. The papers won't report that o' course, her just bein' a poor mite from the slums, but, listen to this, Jakesy. Rumour has it Bucket's

17

got a smell of the chase." He touched his nose. "There's a trawl on tonight!" I was open mouthed. "Don't you worry, Jakes, he's *always* 'aving people tagging along. Oh yes - gen'lemen and the like, - those who want to see a bit of the *low life*, so to speak. Sometimes 'e's 'ad famous writers followin' 'im and writin' it all up for the *Chronicle* and such." Sparrow gave me one of his sarcastic grins. "Why, *you're* a writer now. A penny-a-line man for *Reynolds' Weekly*, ain't yer? Or *so* you tells me! As long as you don't get in the way and does as I say, you'll be all right, Jakesy."

"You're a brick, Sparrow!" I said, refusing to rise to his sarcasm. "Now, when do we start?"

"I just want a word with Alice," he said, standing up suddenly and acting quite coyly as he made for the corner where Alice was waiting. When he returned, after an interlude of whispered words, he was buttoned up, with his duty-band on and his truncheon properly straightened. Alice followed on a moment later bearing two heavy grey oilskins.

"Thank you Alice," he grinned, his bottom lip drooping.

"Now, you make sure you wrap up warm, Archibald," the girl replied.

"Pull on this cape, Jakes," Sparrow said, when he could tear his eyes away from Alice. "Follow me down into the station yard. In this fog no one'll notice one more Runner, policeman I mean, as long as you keep mum. Keep that cape fastened tight. It's a dirty night, Jakes, and it'll be filthier still where we're goin'!"

I tossed a few pence onto the table for pretty Alice and followed my friend down a set of maze-like stairs under the low beams and out into the alley at the rear of *The White Lion*.

When my eyes had adjusted to the dense fog, I saw that the station house yard was full of flickering figures.

"Make way, Mr Martin!" a voice called. Someone appeared out of the dark like a giant fire-fly lit up by a barrow-full of lanterns. The flapping figures looked like bats and appeared to catch fire as they picked up their lamps. As the wicks were turned up, their flames flared out and scattered like Catherine wheels. Each policeman stood with his bulls-eye lantern bright. As they did so, a corpulent man in a pot-hat and a grey greatcoat appeared out of the yellow smoke. The constables turned at the sight of him but promptly looked away as if they were under orders not to look at him directly. For, of course, this was Inspector Bucket of the Detective. Fastening my oil skin, I tagged on behind Sparrow and out we marched into the dark, grey parish of St Giles.

Once we had left the junction with Arthur Street and had crossed to the end of the High Road we soon became lost in a maze of alleys and courts. I tried to keep a watch on Bucket as he marched at the head of the line but he kept veering off without warning to the right or the left before vanishing into the stew of the fog, only to reappear a moment later as if conjured up by magic. Any policeman we met continued to look away as if Bucket were the Sultan of Siam whose very sight would cause him to have his head chopped off. Some, Bucket would tap on the shoulder and they would melt away into the mist.

As Sparrow had warned, the night had become a filthy one and, apart from the spectral figures appearing and disappearing in the yellow smog, all I could see were the sickly swaying lanterns. I tried to communicate with Sparrow but either his regard for his professional responsibilities, or the fact that he had Inspector Bucket close by, rendered him deaf. My thoughts were interrupted when a voice called out a halt. We had stopped outside a crumbling night-house looming out of the fog like a prison hulk. Bucket swept in, followed by his favoured few. They called out "Make way! Make way!" as they did. I swept on too.

It was a bulging beer-shop wedged in the crannies of Seven Dials. The fog outside was replaced by the fog within, of tobacco smoke mostly from old pipes and rotten cigars. A group of customers was swilling around where the beer was being served. Up until this point I was only familiar with comfortable taverns, the likes of *The White Lion* in St Giles or *The Wig and Pen* in Fleet Street. There was nothing comfortable about this den, squeezed up as it was under the eaves of the old rookeries. When we burst in, every face turned - but the flash-house's clients were clearly familiar with Bucket's courtesy calls and the broken-toothed, weasel-skinned customers returned to their beer almost immediately. Bucket was soon making himself intimate with the governor of the house, a blinking figure behind the serving table.

"Evenin', Mr Bucket," a drinker called, making Bucket look up from his enquiries. "Still trying to catch Spring-Heeled Jack are you?" His cronies roared. Spring-Heeled Jack had been famous since the Thirties. He was supposed to be a fire-breathing demon with eyes like coals who could leap thirty feet in one bound. Jack was famous for molesting young girls. However, Bucket did not rise to this mockery and, after another word with the proprietor, he passed on with a smile.

"Top o' th mornin' to you, Inspector," came a sarcastic greeting from another figure, muffled up in a fancy, spotted cravat. "Come to wet your whistle now, have you?" Despite these instances of conviviality, I noticed that several drinkers consumed their porter in haste before making an exit, not relishing the chance of conversation with Bucket of the Detective, I supposed.

Bucket himself greeted this ironic crew by name and just as cheerfully, calling out a 'Davy' or a 'Michael' as he mingled with them. The nub of his enquiries always seemed to be about a gentleman buying unusual clothes from the rag or pawn shops thereabouts, or regarding surgical instruments or jewellery that the same man might have purchased from the neighbourhood stalls or barrows. One of Bucket's favoured lieutenants took his place in the interrogation whilst he moved on. He was in conference longest with a thin figure who had been skulking in the shadiest corner. This was a sunken-faced body of one who might have been mistaken for a gentleman himself, given the rich if faded quality of his clothes. He might have been one of the swell-mob, I considered, a confidence trickster in the guise of a gentlemen; one of the tribe of those who worked their dodges amongst the places where the upper classes might linger. He looked ravaged with laudanum.

Although Bucket clearly had serious business in mind, these interviews were carried out as if they were friendly conversations between pals over a jar of ale. Two spectral-looking creatures talked quite freely to Bucket about the prison hulks that had clearly recently been their home. One of the two had a face like a skeleton under his billycock hat, and eyes that stared permanently; the other seemed to have no eyes at all. Their figures were skinny and somehow stretched. It was as if they had spent too long on shot drill at Pentonville and the like, passing the cannonball up and down the punishment line.

"Yers, well," said one, "the geezer I'm talking of gave the beak short change, din't he, Ralph?"

"Inda digging party, you see, Bister Bucket," said the other through a blocked-up nose.

"If you want to spring yerself that's one of the ways see - digging graves in the marshes."

"Grim that is, Bister Bucket. I'd sooner do the shot drill."

"Well, most gets drownded trying to skulk off under cover of dark, don't they?"

"An 'orrible death, that is, Bister Bucket."

"But there's some that does get away 'cross the marshes."

I pictured the dark and boggy marshes near where I played as a youngster and a shiver came over me.

"Well, this covey as I'm telling you of - a nasty brute he was, wasn't he, Ralph?"

"Very dasty."

"Talk was he'd got himself some work with a swell like what you've been askin' about round Belgravia and those ways, so they said…"

Although I was listening to the talk, it was Bucket himself who took my eye. This was my first chance to really observe him. He was about five feet ten inches in height, corpulent but steady-looking and sharp-eyed. He carried his head well back on his bull-like neck. He was about fifty years of age, but seemed ageless. His eyes were somewhat heavy-lidded, as if he had suffered a deal of anxiety in his life, but they were always animated, making him look stern but kind. He was dressed all in black beneath his greatcoat, apart from a note of flamboyance in his faintly speckled cravat. He wore his pot-hat high up and carried a thick stick. I noticed that he wore a plain mourning-ring on his little finger. He toyed with this absent mindedly as he talked or listened. Apart from the way he looked at you as if he was going to take your portrait, there was nothing remarkable about Inspector Bucket. Except, of course, his ghostly way of appearing and disappearing, for when I looked away he was gone, back out into the Rookeries.

# Chapter 4

"Is he on the trail of the Beast, then?" I muttered to Sparrow. We were stepping carefully through the refuse-filled alleys of Seven Dials, a few minutes later.

"That's right, Jakes. They say the Beast's been hunting after girls as young as six and seven. He likes them best if they're daughters of the toffs but if he can't find one o' them to prey on he'll take a slum child and have her dressed up as he wants. He ain't content with poor thirteen year old girls from a case-house. No, he likes 'em young!" Sparrow breathed out in a cloud of steam. "Bucket's had a tip-off from one of his blowers."

"Does Bucket know who the Beast is then?" I asked, straining to see Sparrow's pale face in the yellow fog.

"No. He goes in disguise, see. He seems to like it. Sometimes dressed as a gen'leman, sometimes a labourer or some sort of man-servant, or someone from abroad. Some say he's a bedlam case escaped from his chains or some sort of medical man turned nasty. Some've told tales of a little feller with a big head that goes ridin' on wild horses and swingin' about a sword like a scimitar! All just fairy tales, ain't it? But if anyone can catch him, Inspector Bucket can. He don't mind shoot-flyers or cracksmen or *any* of the thievin' types but Bucket won't abide 'arm to no child. You should hear him going on about child prostitution and that. Really gets his mad up!"

"Make room there, draw off a bit. There's a fever gang coming. Step back now!" Sparrow was cut off by the man himself.

As I looked, I noticed the blood-red braziers on the corners burning in a futile attempt at cleaning up the noxious air. Then a group of scarfed men came between us, pushing a broken-down cart. In the see-sawing lantern-light I could see the outlines of a disease-riddled face. I looked away quickly, covering my mouth for fear of breathing in anything contagious. Sparrow passed me a handkerchief that had been soaked in vinegar. I held this to my mouth and nose in imitation of the others in our party. The old Rookeries were due to be pulled down because of the nightmare of the fever but there was no sign of it happening yet. Here the alleys were built on alleys and muck on muck. It was a nightmare true enough: grey figures in grey doorways; grey mothers with grey babies; three-legged dogs and one-legged children. I might once have been in terror of such ghastly figures and indeed Uncle Silas had warned me to watch out for garrotters who might haunt the back alleys and courts of London. He had told me, only half-joking, that I should make sure that when I ventured out at night I wore a spiked collar as protection against strangulation. Wise advice, I am sure. But these poor souls looked like they had barely enough strength in their bodies to stand, let alone throttle you for Fourpence.

However, Bucket kept stopping in his perambulations and it was making me nervous. He stopped to speak to an old blind woman with a toothless mouth. After a second or two he moved on, squeezing a coin into her hand. He stopped to talk to a half-naked young woman with a gash across her forehead and then with a soot-faced child who hobbled on a broomstick for a crutch. As he did so he would be turning over a pile of coppers he kept in his pocket. This seemed a habit with him, to turn the coppers in his pocket as if they were some sort of rosary. Sparrow nudged me back into awareness of my surroundings and pointed into the ruins:

"Fever houses," he said. "The fever struck 'ard 'ere a couple o' years back. Lots of deaths, Jakes - dropped like sheep with the rot they did!"

"Come along wi' me, young 'un," a voice suddenly called out of the fog. To my astonishment it belonged to Inspector Bucket. I thought the game was up when he lifted me by the elbow. I imagined myself spending a night in Pentonville for impersonating a Police Officer. Instead, he led me toward the houses. I don't know if I reeled from the stench of sulphur coming up from these or from Bucket's sudden attention. Sparrow looked after me, gaping. Leading me on, Bucket tapped the shoulders of various constables who vanished as if they had all been the vaguest vapours.

"You look a bit poorly, young feller - Jakesbere, ain't it? I'd know that face anywhere." I looked at him in amazement. "Don't look so shocked," Bucket said, "you'll come to no harm, my lad. The fever that was here has waned and there ain't so many deaths now – not from that anyhow. The cold weather's done for it. But since you're here, there's a little job you can do for me, in remembrance of my friendship with your old pa, shall we say. Dead spit of him you are, my boy." And with my heart banging away with shock he led me into the first of the broken-down hovels.

He pushed open a half-unhinged door that had been hacked about for firewood. It was a dark and stinking space heaving with shadows. Eyes looked up towards us from dirty beds. I ducked through the doorway into yellowy candle light. The human termites crammed together here were only divided from each other by filthy hanging sacks. The tallow light spluttered. It gave the eyes that peered out the look of corpses. We stepped over sleeping bodies until we came to some crumbling steps. The brick and plaster gave way as we went down into a deeper dark, over more sleeping bodies and crawling vermin, until we found ourselves in a low ruin of a cellar buried in the bowels of the building. The space hummed of decay and disinfectant, of rot and the stink of boiled food, boiled clothes and boiling fever. Next to a stinking glim there were the remains of water in a chipped bowl. There was a rusty pail, and rolled-up cleaning rags. Someone, it appeared, was still attempting a losing battle with dirt and infestation, as the floor was crawling with black beetles. A family seemed to live here. There was a bluntly-built man slumped at a table and a weary-looking woman stooped over a low bed upon which a small body lay groaning in the gloom. There was a baby too, gurgling quietly in a wooden box stuffed with rags. Despite the filth, these creatures had won a kind of grim privacy and this hole was their reward. It was clear that the slumped man was responsible for this victory, his bare hard muscles being testimony to his power. He looked up as I regarded him. His mouth and face were wet, his eyes bloodshot and angry. He gazed at Bucket as if he knew him, gave a contemptuous look and then slumped down again.

"Mrs Naiskins?" Bucket called out gently. The woman stooping over the low bed turned for a moment. Bucket drew nearer and I followed, getting a whiff of the vinegar and camphor that had been splashed about the bed by way of disinfectant. A thin grey boy of about nine years of age lay there, his head boiling with fever. I am afraid to say I stood back. She held a chipped pot of water to his blue lips.

"How is he, ma'am?" Bucket whispered.

"Bad. He's had the runs all day and I just can't get enough water in 'im. He seems ever so thirsty." She covered the child when he had quietened, at last, and turned to face us. "I've not been able to raise myself from this stool since yester-night for worry about the child." Under her weariness and the old scars of small pox I could see she must have once been pretty.

"John's still gettin' some work so we can eat, but as you see we're brought t' this," she said looking around her, "and the burden's taken its toll on him." She smoothed back her hair and secured her shawl as if suddenly aware that she had company. "I'd send out Nancy for more medicine only … the *other* business, as you know, 'as been keeping her in …" Her voice faltered and she turned back to the sick-bed.

"Aye and I'd a' killed him if I could!" said her husband, so suddenly it made me jump.

"Oh, hush John!" she said quite sharply. "Don't mind his snitherin', Mr Bucket. He gets angry because he can't feed us and look after us as well as he'd like, that's all."

"Angry is right! If it weren't for Mr Interfering Bucket here, I'd have 'ad some cash in my weskit *now*, cash enough to buy food for 'ungry moufs, stead of 'avin' nothink but rotten shellfish scavenged from the river or ole bones from the dust yard!" Fortunately this speech exhausted him and he slumped again with his eyes reeling.

"Is that right, Mr John Naiskins? And what good would you be doing your family stuck behind bars at Her Majesty's Pleasure, eh?" Bucket rebuked. "That's where you'd have been if I hadn't stopped your thieving! What good would you have been to your missus and your little ones then, eh?"

"He don't mean nothin' bad by it sir," said Mrs Naiskins. "Only he takes it all to 'eart so."

"Well, my dear," said Bucket, turning back to the wife. "You know why I've called. I must speak to your little girl while she might still remember what befell her."

"She won't come out, sir," Mrs Naiskins said, turning to see to the sick boy again. "I 'ad to send her to beg some colic for the baby from Miss Alice - nor I won't drug the little mite with

27

Laudanum or Dover's Powders - but Nancy come back tremblin' and a-feared afore she was half way … and now I've not the 'eart to send her out again." My ears pricked up at mention of the name of Alice, of course.

"Be that so, ma'am, but I must try her to see if she'll speak to me," said Bucket.

"You can try, but as to whether she will, I can't say. She's 'ardly spoken a word since it 'appened, you see."

Bucket nodded and then moved quietly to the end of the room where a great heap of rags was piled up. He cleared his throat and, when ready, began a strange little speech. At first I thought he was still talking to Mrs Naiskins but soon I realised he had another audience in mind, or had succumbed to some sort of private reverie.

"I had a child myself once - passed away … pretty little thing. A bit like your Nancy I'm guessing. Ribbons she had in her curls. Loved to play, she did. A good hopper an' all. And a skipper." He stopped and felt for his mourning ring. "Dear me, the hours that Mrs B would spend brushing that little girl's hair. Good heavens! Like gold it was. And nattering on they'd go - like two old housewives." There was a shuffling in the heap of clothes - like a mouse - but Bucket continued regardless. "I'd come in for supper sometimes and I'd say, 'Where's my pie? Where's my pie? A man needs his belly filling when he's come home from catching villains all day!' Well, and my little girl'd start giggling then, wouldn't she? Mrs B'd scold me just like my old mum used to do. 'Pie?' she'd say, 'pie?' How can I be doing you pies when I've got this little angel here just dropped out of heaven, just landed this minute and is wanting some ribbons in her pretty little curls - and you is askin' for pies! Bless me! You shall have to wait, my man!' she'd say. 'I don't care if you are Inspector

28

Bucket of the Detective, I don't care if you're the Emperor of *China* still dressed in his under drawers - you shall have to *wait* for your pie, won't he my ducks? He'll have to wait till we have got your lovely ribbons in place."

Suddenly a voice like a flute piped up from behind the mound of rags.

"What colour wibbons?"

"Red 'uns," said Bucket without a pause, as if he'd been in conversation with this party all along.

"Shiny 'uns?" the piping voice added.

"Oh yes!" said Bucket, looking up for the first time and turning behind him. A thin stick of a girl had popped up through the rags. "Oh yes, as shiny as the golden earrings on the ears of a Princess."

"What else she like to play at? Tha' girl?"

"Oh, she liked to play with Patch," went on Bucket, very serious, "our little dog. She'd walk him and teach him tricks. Fierce little soul my Beth was. Wouldn't let no one stand in *her* way. Oh no, not she! If she'd a message or an errand to take for her daft old dad or her loving ma she'd be out there as brave as a tartar, with our little Patch yapping at her feet like a tiger." There was a silence and then looking at the Naiskins' child he said, "I expect you'd like to be out and about again wouldn't you, eh? Runnin' errands for your brothers and your ma and pa, wouldn't you?"

The child crawled further out from behind her pile of rags. About seven years old she was. Pretty, if thin, with blonde curls and a few dark and crooked teeth.

"But we'll have to catch that bad man that wanted to hurt you first, shan't we?"

She ran to her mother and leaned against her skirts.

"You tell Mr Bucket what he wants to know, Nancy."

The Inspector turned to me now, whispering. "Have you got your writing tackle with you, Mr Jakesbere?" I looked blankly at him. "Oh, come on lad! I think you'll find you'll need something to scratch on if you're going to be a scribbler like your Uncle Silas was." He sighed when I failed to move. "Well, in the meantime …" He plunged a beefy hand into the deep pocket of his coat and brought out a black note-book with a stub of a Keswick pencil stuffed in its spine.

"We shall need to write down every word, my angel, won't we?" he said, smiling at the child and handing the book to me. "Now my dear," he began, kneeling down and brushing aside a crawling beetle. "This man, the man who stopped you, do you remember where it happened?"

"The alleys," she replied, her thumb jammed in her mouth.

"You'd got lost 'adn't you, Nance?" her mother said, dividing her attention between the child and the man. "She'd been to see our friend Miss Alice at *The White Lion*, you see, Inspector. Alice told you to run straight back home and show me your dress, didn't she Nance? But some boys teased her and took the little bag Alice gave her. That's it ain't it Nance? She chased after them all the way to Drury Lane by the sounds of it."

"And that's when the man stopped you, eh?" said Bucket.

"He give me my bag back."

"I think this man must 'ave seen 'er chasing after the boys," Mrs Naiskins said. "He must have mistook her for a proper little lady, I think. Gave the urchins a clout you said, Nance, is that right?"

Nancy nodded, twisting her thumb in her mouth.

"Said I was pretty," she mumbled.

"Well, so you are!" Bucket smiled. "I expect you was wearing

30

something nice?"

"You were all dressed up, weren't you Nance?" said Mrs Naiskins. "Miss Alice liked to play dressin' up with you, didn't she? She had some fancy-dress stuff you see, Inspector. Alice always liked her fashions. She made you look like a proper swell didn't she Nance, eh?" Mrs Naiskins looked up at the Inspector. "I didn't think there was no 'arm in it, sir."

"No, ma'am. Not in the normal run of things there's not," said Bucket quietly. "And what did this man say to you, Nancy?"

"Asked me if I was on me own…"

"And what did you say?"

"Tha' I was lost."

"Did he take you somewhere?"

"Tried to … in the alley…"

"Where it was darker?"

She nodded.

"Got angry," she said.

"Why was that?"

"'Cos I wouldn't go."

"Well, you're a brave girl, Nancy Naiskins! I knew you were. Now, tell me, can you remember what he looked like?"

Nancy shook her head. "It were dark."

"I expect it was! But you might have seen how big he was, eh? Now then, was he as big as me, say?"

"Bigger. But not fat," I couldn't help but give a splutter. Bucket gave me a look.

"And was he as tall and funny as Mr Jakesbere here?"

"Tall. But not so skinny," she answered like a shot.

"And how old might he have been? As old as your daddy, or as old as an old fellow like me, or …?" The girl didn't answer.

"No? Never mind. Do you remember anything *at all* about

31

him, say, his face? You might have got a look at that, eh, even in the dark. Its shape, say?"

"Powd'ry…"

"Powdery? You mean on his hair, my dear? Like some old gentlemen wear sometimes?"

"On 'is face. Like stuff in Miss Ali's box. All cakey on 'is face… on 'is nose…"

"You mean make-up, I expect, don't you, love?" Mrs Naiskins said. The little stick nodded.

"I see," pondered Bucket, "but what about his hair, could you see its colour? Was it like Mr Jakesbere's, or…"

"Blacky. More blacky. He 'ad more'n yourn." I couldn't help another splutter.

"And what else can you remember about him? Could you see the colour of his eyes? The shape of his nose? Was it a big one?"

Nancy shook her head again.

"What did he sound like? Can you remember that? Did he have a low voice? Like a gruff old man, or was it a high voice, like a lady's perhaps?

"Squeaky."

"Squeaky, eh? Anything else?"

"Out of breath."

"Like he was poorly you mean? Or because he'd been running?"

The girl looked blankly up at him.

"All right, my dear. What about his clothes? I expect you can remember that, eh?"

"Like a gen'leman."

"A gent, eh? Was he dressed like a rich gentleman my dear? Have you seen such a person?"

"Yeah. I seen 'em in the streets. He 'ad a stick," she said

looking up at Bucket and giving *his* stick a spin. "Like this 'un, but all silv'ry…with a dragony face. Like in a picture book that Miss Ali' read me once."

"Was he wearing any jewellery, my dear? A pin in his shirt, like mine? Or perhaps a ring on his finger…?"

The girl looked up tearfully.

"A wing. It 'urt. He 'ad me by my neck. It dug in my chin … and 'e dug his other hand…" Stopping, she turned her head into her mother's skirt.

"And is that when your daddy came, eh? And the man ran off?"

"Yes it was, as well you know it!" came the father's sour voice. He'd appeared to be asleep through all of this but he had been listening all along.

Bucket looked at him sharply. "And if you'd have been less in a funk from so much drinking in a Drury Lane gin-palace, p'raps *you* could have been telling me the answers to these questions, instead of me having to ask the child!"

Naiskins scowled and Bucket turned back to his daughter.

"Well," he said softly. "We'll let your daddy 'ave a proper rest, shall us? He's getting angry with old Bucket, ain't he? But just before I go, I've just got one more question, if your mum'll let me. This ring, did the bad man see you looking at it?" She nodded. "And what was it like, my dear? Was it pretty or was it a plain ring, my girl. Like this one?" he said, holding his finger out for her to see.

The girl looked hard at Bucket's mourning ring, turning it around on his fat finger with her own little ones.

"No. Yourn ain't got a picture on it," the child muttered.

"A picture, eh? Might it have been a letter?"

"Don't know," she answered bluntly.

"A clever girl like you, eh? I expect you know a letter or two?"

33

said Bucket. "If it *was* a letter could you tell me what letter it was?"

"She don't know her letters, Inspector," Mrs Naiskins said. "She's 'ad no schoolin'. Miss Alice promised to learn 'er when she's time."

"Ah well, I bet you're a clever girl who could learn her letters as quick as a stick if you had someone that could teach you, eh? Why, pointing out a letter is nothing to you, is it, my sweetheart?" Bucket smiled. "They're just like little pictures as you said, ain't they?" The little twig nodded and grinned. Bucket looked up at me. "Mr Jakesbere, write us some letters in our book won't you - then Nancy and me'll play a game to see which letter was on that ring, shall us, my dear?"

We all knelt down together as if we were in the British School and one of the monitors was about to teach us for our allotted fifteen minutes. I began an 'A' as big as I could. A big black mark against the white page.

"That one, my dear?" said Bucket. She shook her head. "No, we knew it wasn't that one." I wrote a B. "That neither? No? Of course not! Try another, Mr Jakesbere."

I went through the whole alphabet. Her sharp little eyes watched closely as I drew every curve and line. But she shook her blonde head at every one.

"Not that one neither, then," Bucket sighed. "Well then, Mr Jakesbere, you can't be making those letters *clear* enough, can he, my dear?"

"I think she's tired now, sir," Mrs Naiskins said.

"I expect she is. Well, you've told us enough for now," said Bucket standing up and giving Nancy a smile. "P'raps we can visit you another time, eh? And you can see funny Mr Jakesbere again. I know," he said, bending to her again. "I'll bring you a red ribbon like *my* little angel had! How about that?"

Nancy smiled. But as soon as Bucket drew himself up to his full height, she pulled him back down.

"That wing 'ad wibbons ... sort of wibbons."

"Ribbons?"

"On its face. Not a letter. It were a face!"

Bucket looked up at the mother, still nursing her baby, and then at me.

"Would you draw it for us, eh? In Mr Jakesbere's book, would you? I expect you're good with a crayon, ain't you?"

I held out my pencil for her and once more we all got down on the floor with the crawling things. The girl was all fingers and thumbs with the stumpy stick of pencil (for she'd probably never held one before) but she drew a shaky circle right enough. Inside this she drew an O for a face and then added girlish topknots and circles for eyes. But she wasn't done yet. She drew more little circles, like stones, around the circle she'd drawn for a face.

"And what were *these* little things?" Bucket said, pointing at the outer circles.

"Shiny things."

"And did they have a colour?"

"Red."

"Well of course they were. Didn't I say to you, Mr Jakesbere, that this clever girl would know all her colours all right?"

"I think she really is tired now, Inspector Bucket," said Mrs Naiskins, before I could comment on the quality of Nancy's art work. The child sat among her mother's skirts, her thumb in her mouth again.

"Of course, ma'am," agreed Bucket, standing up to his full height but giving a little wink down at the child for one last time. "I wager you'd like to see funny Mr Jakesbere jiggle his ears before we go, wouldn't you though, eh?"

I looked at him, not for the first time, with my mouth open in astonishment. Nancy gave a nod.

"Mr Jakesbere?" he said, looking at me with expectation.

Well, what could I do? I *had* been a bit of an ear-jiggler as a lad, as it happened, and perhaps Bucket had remembered seeing me doing it once on a long ago visit to our house. It was a special talent I had. There are some in life that can roll their tongues; there are some that can show the whites of their eyes. I was one of those blessed by Mother Nature with the capacity to set my ears doing a jig. I still had the memory of the beatings I'd suffered at the British School when I'd been ear-jiggling instead of reciting the liturgy as I ought. Well, I was in a cornet right enough - as my father would have said. Having no choice, I worked up the nerves and muscles in my neck and cheeks till a great jiggling and flapping of my ears came about as if from nowhere. Well, what a scream of laughter she gave! The little baby seemed to join in with the chuckling too. The fevered boy almost chortled in his sleep. The mother smiled, and even Naiskins grinned for half-a-second.

At this point Bucket made his exit, tossing a jingle of silver coins into the baby's cot as he went. I followed on out of the cellar and up the dark stairs. We came up for air at last, into the ruins of the streets with their crazy jack-knifed buildings. And I will confess that I was feeling a little red around the ears.

# Chapter 5

In the street the wind was blowing a storm. The capes of the constables were flying and the lanterns danced. For a moment, Bucket stood still amongst his officers. Sparrow was lit up like a goblin by the flaring lamps. He did not look at Bucket. His attention was on me, his eye-brows raised in astonishment, wondering what had happened. Indeed I wondered myself. Just then a cab leapt out of the fog like a ghost. It was pulled by a stout little horse so enveloped in steam that it might have just lifted its head out of a Turkish bath. It stuttered to a stop, wheels groaning.

"Well, Mr Jakesbere. We've not done so bad, have we?" Bucket said leaning against the door. "Little Nancy has helped us with a few things we needed to know about our man, eh? What do you think?" I was amazed at being asked but I attempted a reply.

"Well, she couldn't tell his age but we know about a walking stick with a dragon on it. And the ring of course - with a picture on it."

"You still think it a picture, eh? Not a letter?" said Bucket with interest. "Go on, what else?"

"Well, his voice." I considered for a moment. "Squeaky, she said. I expect she meant high."

"Out of breath too, she said. P'raps he was an old man or just someone with an illness. Or maybe he'd just been running. What did she say about his hair?"

"Black and powdery."

"I wonder if she just meant his face, or was it powdery hair she meant as well? An old gentleman might still be putting powder on, mightn't he, eh? And what of his build?"

"Medium, I suppose."

"Yes, all a bit vague. But what about his -" Bucket hesitated. "What shall we call it? His *tastes*?"

"Well, for young girls." Of course, I thought of the reports I had read in the papers. "Very young by the sound of it," I added, "and ones that might look like the daughters of the aristocracy."

"Well done, Mr Jakesbere. We'll make a detective of you yet - even if you don't make a scribbler. But, yes, we're surer now, I think. He attacked Nancy because he thought she was the daughter of a lady or a gentleman like himself, perhaps. A swell - if a swell is really what he is. He might just have been *dressed* up in fancy clothes eh? Of course, such a man could get himself poor girls like Nancy at any time he wanted, I'm afraid to say. But it's the daughters of the swell classes he seems to have a taste for. I think we're agreed on that."

As he spoke, he climbed into the cab and I realised my adventure might be over. But he had flattered me with his attention and treated me almost as an equal. I began to comfort myself with the thought that I had at least enough material for a sketch that I could compose to send to Reynolds.

"Inspector Bucket," I said as he settled himself, "don't forget your book!"

"You keep hold of it, lad. You'll need it where we're going." He looked at me quizzically. "Well, come on then boy - don't stand there gawping - get in."

And get in I did, finding my legs at last and jumping up lively-fashion beside Bucket in the police vehicle - and blessing my good fortune yet again.

"Away my lad!" he called to the driver before closing the door with a snap. The horse lurched away and I tumbled immediately on to the floor. Even when I managed to struggle back into a seated position it was of little relief to my injured feelings. The seat in question felt as if it had been stuffed with bricks. However, Bucket seemed not to be aware of any discomfort. He produced a plain silver snuff box and took a good pinch out of it, as if he were lounging in an arm chair in his sitting room with a bottle of brown sherry by his elbow. Meanwhile I slid from side to side like a madman. I considered what I ought to be saying to him. Although his face was directed towards me, its demeanour was unhelpful and somewhat severe - as if he were measuring me for a suit of clothes and didn't like the amount of material I would use up.

"They call *me* a detective lad," he said at last, ignoring my discomfort, "but it's *Mrs* Bucket who does the true investigations in our house. She said I'd find you under my nose in the end and, lo and behold, I did! Here you are!" He helped me up from the floor again. "She saw the clue in that letter from your Uncle Silas you see: '*Going with his testimonial to Reynolds' Weekly*', he wrote. Well, she saw that that meant you'd be trying to find *me*, don't yer know, because old George Reynolds, well, he's been trying to get stories about me all year. That's what all this is about, isn't it? You turning up at Cripplegate tonight, I mean? What do yer say?" I attempted to reply but the continued buffeting of the cab sides against my ribs was rendering me breathless.

"We'd like you to lodge with us, my lad. Mrs Bucket's been washin' and dryin' sheets for you specially. And the plum-duff! Well, I won't even mention the time and trouble she's spent on that! A remarkable human creation that is, my boy - Mrs Bucket's duff is always of a most remarkable composition!" After this reverie, he regarded me again. "But why didn't you show yourself *earlier*, eh? When I spied you out in the yard at Cripplegate I thought I was dreaming. I thought it was your pa I was seeing. The dead spit of him you are!" I continued to be dumbstruck and muttered something incomprehensible.

"My boy, my boy, there's no need to go on stuttering and stumbling. Didn't you *know* your Uncle Silas wrote a letter to Mrs Bucket? He told us you were coming up to London. He told us that you were hoping to work as a scribbler for Reynolds as well, and he asked us to look out for you."

I gaped, open-mouthed again and fell - for the fourth or fifth time - on to the floor of the cab.

"Blow me but you're a hard one to talk to. We shan't be able to converse if you keep jumping about, you know! I've never seen such a young man for jumping in and out of a seat." When I had retrieved my position and located a convenient strap to hold on to, he continued. "I hope you'll accept our condolences for your loss, my boy - on the death of your dear ma and pa, I mean. You know that me and your father was in the Runners together, of course, don't you? - Happy days! We were grieved to hear of his passing and of your mother, of course, pining away so soon after your poor dad died. Terrible. It must have been hard for you, my boy. I remember you from when we were in Woolwich, of course - when you were a little 'un – and my, you've grown, ain't you lad?"

I felt both pleased and anxious that the Inspector had remembered me - as it might have been for the wrong reasons - but he continued, apparently oblivious to my blushes. "Mrs Bucket wrote and told Silas that of course we'd look out for you when you came back to London. Mrs B's been worried that you might 'ave got yourself into mischief like you used to back in Woolwich Market in the old days." I reddened again, but he went on. "Oh yes, I remember that well enough," he grinned, adding, "You must have left Chatham before our letter got to

40

you, I suppose."

"I'm most obliged to you, Inspector," I said, finally finding my voice. "More than obliged, but I've already got some lodgings at Cripplegate, and Mr Reynolds..."

"Well," Bucket interrupted, "Mrs B will be sorry to hear that. *Already* made arrangements 'ave you? Oh dear me, what will she say, eh? I shall be in trouble now for not finding you sooner. Well, can't be helped. Still, at least I can help you with the other." I looked at him quizzically. "Old Reynolds, I mean," he said. "He'll have sent you on a hunt for me, won't he? Just like Mrs Bucket said he would. Well, well but, here I *am*, you see - the prey is already at your feet, my boy - and no need to get out the dogs and the horns. Here I am and at your disposal!" He clapped me on the shoulder and smiled. "Now, I mean to make our meeting an occasion for the benefit of us all. Mrs B and I want to be quite family-like with you, if you'll let us – and, well, you shall have more than just a *report* for Reynolds, more than just a page or two – you shall have the whole volume!"

At this point I could not refrain from opening both my mouth and my eyes to their widest extent yet. "What's the matter now, boy?" Bucket said with concern, "Do you want to take another turn around the cab? Why do you keep opening and shutting your mouth like you're trying to catch flies? Is it another one of the tricks you do - like the ear-jiggling? Very amusing, but you'll catch no flies in here. Look," Bucket said earnestly, "I'll be straightforward with you, boy. I aim to make you my scrivener."

Of course I reddened for the third time, but Bucket was looking out of the window. "Ah, we're nearly there. We'll finish this cheerful conversation at a more convenient time, shall us? We've work to do now, my lad, and we must be sombre. There's a gentleman to see who will be sore aggrieved at us turning up late, and distressed more at the loss of his child. The one that *The Standard* reported tonight. I expect you read it, eh? Not very flattering about me was it? Ah, here we are. Whelks!" he shouted and gave a thump on the roof with his staff. Whelks screeched to a halt. I flew on to the floor of the cab again. "Quickly lad, no jumping about now. Bring the book."

We had pulled up by a painted sign that announced Cheyne Walk, Chelsea. It was an avenue of very fine three storey houses nestled back just behind the river and the embankment. The rows of plane and cherry trees made it feel like a little country lane. Walking through a black gate under a gas lamp, we were met by a policeman guarding the door. Handing Bucket some papers, the officer turned to knock sharply. After an interlude an ageing servant appeared, uniformed in a black merino. She ushered us silently into a gas-lit hall where we were asked to wait. There were cupboards with shelves arranged for coats and a combined aquarium and fern case lodged against a window. I watched a goldfish swim mournfully in the green water. There were sounds of weeping from upstairs and a baby was crying fitfully, unattended, or so it seemed. After a moment a gentleman appeared. He was of late middle-age with thinning, peppery hair. What was remarkable about him, however, were his strangely white eyebrows, not in keeping with his complexion at all. He had dark rings around his eyes and whisky on his breath. He was clearly angry.

"Inspector Bucket, is it? You've come at last, have you, man? What took you so long? Is this the sum of the service we can expect from the Police? I shall be having words with the Commissioner's Office!"

"Yes sir, I'm sorry to have kept you waiting. But there was other urgent business to attend to, I'm afraid."

"Urgent was it? *Urgent?* More urgent than the murder of my child, was it?"

"No sir, of course not. But the matter I was engaged with was connected to the death of your child. Please accept my sincerest condolences, sir. I know what it is like to lose a daughter."

"Know what it's like, do you?" He stuttered to a halt. His albino eye-brows were raised as he noticed the mourning ring on Bucket's finger that the Inspector was even now turning around and around.

"But you see," continued Bucket, "there had been another sighting of the possible killer, and, while the scent was warm …"

"All right," the gentleman said, partially mollified. "Well, you'd better come into the drawing room. You won't be able to speak to my wife. She's had to be sedated." He led us into a large, high-ceilinged room where we trod on a thick Wilton carpet. There was a crimson couch and several ottomans. The gentleman leaned against the mantelpiece pouring himself a dram of whisky from a half empty decanter. "I've needed some sedation myself as it happens."

"I expect so, sir," said Bucket observing the gentleman closely.

He regarded Bucket more closely in his turn – and offered *him* a glass. It was declined. He tipped his own glass back in one gulp. "All right. Let's proceed, shall we? I was asked to wait up for you and I have. I've told the other policeman all I could tell him. It would have been a damn sight better if someone had taken action when we first reported the child missing!"

"That was yesterday afternoon I gather, sir?"

"Yes. It's been a damned mess. My wife was beside herself - rushing up and down the streets, and all along the river. The whole house was out searching. Making us a spectacle for our neighbours. It's been humiliating, man. And then being asked to

43

identify her body in the early hours, hauled down to the morgue with the whole street watching …"

"Yes," said Bucket dryly, "I expect that was very inconvenient for you, sir." Another whisky was poured and despatched in one movement.

"Well. What else do you want to know? What can be done to catch this woman?"

"Well, that's just it sir. I wanted to have a word with the child's nurse about that. She *is* still here then, only my officer led me to believe you might have …"

"Yes, she's still here," he said, pausing, "but against my will! She would have been birched and flung out on the streets if I'd had my way. She's been caterwauling ever since, so I'm informed by my housekeeper. As if that will bring my daughter back."

"May I speak to her then, sir?"

"*Speak* to her? Do as you want with her. Arrest her and throw her in Newgate is what you should do. But don't expect *me* to sit with you. If I see her face again I shan't be responsible for my actions."

"I see, sir."

"She's in the nursery; I'll have Peters take you up." The old servant appeared again. The gentleman returned to his decanter and we were led to a bifurcated staircase and up to the nursery on the topmost floor. Here, our guide knocked on a door. There was no response. The old woman shook her head and left us without a word. Bucket looked after her for a moment and then opened the door himself. We found ourselves in a poorly-lit whitewashed room. A mean fire burnt slowly in its grate behind a high fireguard and a gas light fizzed. At a little table under a barred window sat the nursemaid, a young woman of about my own age at the time. Her head was buried under her arms and pressed heavily against the oilcloth. In front of her was an opened bottle of Godfrey's Cordial. The baby in the cot was silent. She lifted her head at our entry, exposing a face lined with tears and eyes purple from constant crying.

"Don't be alarmed, my dear," said Bucket gently, "we just want to ask you a few questions."

"More ... questions ...?" she gulped thickly and laid her head down again.

"Just one or two, my dear," Bucket said gently. "I expect you might be frightened of all these policeman questioning you but you've no need to be wary of me, you know," he said with a smile. "As it happens, I've a niece who's a nursemaid. I'm very fond of her, you know. In service in Fulham she is. You might know her, perhaps? Might have seen her out and about pushing her perambulator, eh? Courting she is. Nice young feller." The young woman looked up. "Of course, it's 'ard for her, finding time to see her young man, I mean." The young woman began to come out of her stupor as she listened intensely to Bucket's words. "You know what she does sometimes, just between you and me? Meets him when she pushes the baby out." The girl sat up, now fully alert. "A bit wicked some'd say, but I don't think there's any 'arm in it. What d'you think?" The girl was still at a loss for words. Bucket hurried on. "Been a bit foggy o' late, of course, but I expect she met up with him a day or two back when we had a little bit of peace from the fog and the weather was a bit brighter. They like to go along the river when they can, you see. No 'arm in it, is there? No 'arm at all." The girl gave a great sigh, almost of relief. "The baby gets the air and my niece gets to see her beau," continued Bucket. "No harm in it at all. What do you think?"

"I didn't leave her long, sir, God forgive me!" the girl exclaimed earnestly.

"Of course you didn't."

"Only Agnes was crying so and..."

"Agnes was the little girl's name, eh?"

"Yes..."

Bucket pulled out his handkerchief and handed it to her. "And, of course, you couldn't talk to your young man with a crying little girl, could you?" said Bucket. "Stands to reason – so ...?"

"There was this old lady, see," the girl said hurriedly. "And when she sees Agnes crying she comes up to me. Well I was losing patience with the child, sir. Irksome little mite. I'm sorry sir. It's a terrible thing to say, I know ..."

"And why was Agnes crying?"

The girl looked behind her and at the door in case she should be overheard.

"Her father, sir."

"Yes?" said Bucket.

"Well. You know how young girls talk sometimes, sir." She looked up at Bucket again. "I didn't believe a word of it, honest sir."

"Believe what?"

"Well, the girl said her father'd been, well, touching her, sir. Touching her in a way as he shouldn't, I mean." She looked around anxiously. "I told you sir, I didn't believe her. I said to her, I said, Agnes, you stop that sort of talk. You stop it at once!"

"I see," said Bucket. "And she carried on crying, did she, when you were out pushing the baby?"

"Yes, sir. And, well, my, my friend, he was waiting for me by the wharf. The old woman had some sweet stuff in a little paper packet. She said the child could have some as she was upset. Well normally I wouldn't let her. Madam don't approve of sweet

46

things, you see."

"And what did this woman look like?"

"I've already said, sir," the girl cried out tearfully, "over and over again to the other policemen!"

"Just once more, for me, eh?" Bucket said.

"Well, she seemed old, but I couldn't tell properly," the girl considered. "She had a big hat with, like, feathers sticking out of it. I think she was wearing a wig. I think it was. It covered most of her up, if you see what I mean, sir. But, it didn't seem to fit her right, neither. The wig I mean. It was made of good hair. I could see that. She had a bit of it sticking out from under her bonnet you see, sir. It was knocked a bit sideways. She had a sort of birth mark under her hair, or her wig, and she kept scratching at it."

"A birth mark? I see," said Bucket with interest. "Was it on the right or left side of her head?"

"I, I don't know sir. I only know I saw it when she scratched." The girl considered again. "On the right I think. As I was looking at it, I mean.

"And did she carry a stick?"

"Yes, she did sir – being old I suppose."

"And could you describe it?"

"Just a walking stick, sir, like any other."

"No markings on it?"

"Markings?" Bucket ignored the question and carried on.

"Well, what about her hands?"

"Her hands, sir?"

"Any marks? Any hair? Any ornaments? Any rings?"

"I'm sorry sir. I only saw her for a bit and I wasn't really looking sir."

"All right," Bucket said with disappointment. "But what about

47

her face? You must have noticed that. Did you notice anything about her complexion, for instance?"

"Well, now you mention it, it was sort of funny – all thick with powder. She seemed to be covering up something but she hadn't quite got it smooth."

Bucket's eyes brightened. "Was it powdery?"

"Well, yes."

"Could she have been covering, say, hairs?"

"I don't know sir, but the mark I mentioned, by her temple here, she was trying to cover *that* up, I suppose."

"And are you sure she was actually a woman?"

"*What* sir?"

"I mean, could she have been a man?"

The girl gave a look of surprise.

"It's never occurred sir, but I suppose she wasn't very lady-like. Her arms *were* a bit, well, thick. She sounded a bit strange now you ask."

"Yes?"

"Yes sir, sort of wheezy like – as if she'd trouble getting her breath."

"Breathless perhaps? Would you describe her voice as squeaky?"

"Squeaky?" the girl repeated. "Well, it was sort of high up I suppose - and she *was* panting."

"And so you left the child with this old woman?"

"It was only a moment, sir." The girl seemed anxious again. "She said it'd be all right. She said she'd stay with the child while I spoke to my young -" she hesitated, "while I spoke to my friend. I wheeled the perambulator over with me and spoke to him. It couldn't have been more than a minute. He had to be back in his chambers you see."

"And when you got back?"

"She was gone. And Agnes gone with her. I shall never forget it, sir. It was terrible. I panicked and I ran around and ... there wasn't a sound. No crying of a child and no old woman. She'd just vanished. There was just the empty paper packet on the street blowing away. I ran back after Robert, my friend, and he helped me search. We looked everywhere – along the river, by the market. We asked at all the stalls. She was nowhere, sir. Nowhere ..." The poor girl broke down in tears at this.

"All right, my dear. You've told me enough. We'll leave you in peace," said Bucket.

"Peace, sir?" the girl cried. "I'll get no peace. The master thinks I've as good as killed her. No one will have me now. That's the end of me, sir. The end of me."

We left her and went downstairs to take our leave of the master - but he failed to answer when Bucket knocked on the drawing room door. Bucket pushed it open anyway, determined to have a word. The gentleman was slumped on the crimson couch with the empty decanter at his feet.

Back in the cab the fog swirled around us.

"What do you think, my boy?" said Bucket. "Was our killer a woman or a man?"

"There's many a woman that looks like a man, Inspector," I said, thinking back to some of my aged aunts in Woolwich.

"True, my boy. And many a man that might look like a woman too," he gave me a dry grin. "Now which paper was it that thought our killer was a woman? Was it *The News of the World*? It sounds like them." I suddenly realised how exhausted I was and struggled to stifle a yawn. "Tired, my boy?" said the Inspector. "Mrs Bucket will think I'm mistreating you."

"Not at all, sir. But, if you're done with me, p'raps I could start

49

making my way back to my lodgings. My landlady will be locking me out soon."

"We'll *take* you back, my boy. No need to fret. But I shall want your assistance again tomorrow so we'll make an appointment for then, shall we? We'll say eleven at St Giles?"

"You mean eleven in the morn..." I stuttered.

"No, my boy. At night. I think you'll find that's when the work of a detective gets done – and the work of a scribbler for that matter. But we must arrange for you to come out to see Mrs Bucket at a more civilised hour – and as soon as we can, eh - or I shall be in trouble!" Bucket banged on the roof. "Away, my lad. Back to St Giles."

When we returned to Cripplegate the fog was thicker still. Mrs Peckers *had* locked me out. I could not raise a soul. Bucket was obliged to send our driver, Constable Whelks, to try his policeman's knock. She opened up at last, wearing a dressing gown and a sour face. However, she didn't seem at all surprised to find me in the company of a policeman, only annoyed, perhaps, that I had been released rather too early from Newgate and had not thoroughly completed my shot drill.

"This won't do, Mr Jakesbere. It's not respecrable," she said. "Not respecrable at all."

Well, perhaps it wasn't but I had met the great man and, what's more, he had engaged to be with me on the morrow.

# Chapter 6

The cab was outside St Giles Station at eleven at night as promised. The comfortable Mr Whelks was already in position and giving me a cheery thumbs-up from his high seat under a fizzing gas lamp. Bucket appeared from his eyrie punctually too, dressed up like a Lord: top hat, tail coat and monocle. I hardly recognised him. "Put these on, my boy," he said throwing me a package of clothes bundled up in brown paper. "We're going to see how the aristocracy amuse themselves."

We climbed into the dim, sour-smelling cab and it rattled off into another night of fog whilst I used the cramped inners for a dressing room. Bucket looked the other way as I struggled to dress and to keep my seat at the same time. It took me the whole journey to make myself look presentable. When Bucket nodded as if to say 'you'll do' we had arrived at our destination.

I could not make out much beyond the dim shapes of trees looking like giants whose heads had been cut off by yellow vapours but when Whelks's lamp lit up a painted street sign I saw we were in Duke Street, St James. Whelks began attending to the steaming, tubby horse that had drawn us thither. Bucket began giving a word to the man and a sugar lump to the horse – though, in the mist, it may as well have been the other way about. Then, from nowhere two figures oozed out of the mist; one carrying a yellow bulls-eye that swung to-and-fro sending up shafts of eerie light. In this swaying arc I could see that he was apparelled in the same manner as Bucket and me. He removed his top hat, revealing a mop of blond hair that seemed luminous in the mist; his fellow was the thin, so-called gentleman I had seen the previous evening in the night-house by Seven Dials. He had been full of laudanum then. Now his twitching features and trembling pale lips just made him look as if he yearned to be.

"This is Sergeant Meehan, Mr Jakesbere," said Bucket, and I shook the muscular hand of the former gentleman who gave me a friendly wink. "He's acting in this little masquerade alongside of us. This other gentleman," he said bowing to the latter, "is known as Lord Murd." Murd gave a short, ironic bow in return. By contrast with ours, his outfit was shabby. He might have once been the real thing or a good counterfeit, a member of the 'swell mob' - but now he looked scarecrow-like and his wrists, I noted in the momentary glare of Meehan's lamp, were like twisted ropes. This was the sum of my observations, for Murd was restless and was soon absorbed in the fog as he moved off wordlessly.

"Stay close, Mr Jakesbere," said Bucket. I did. Sergeant Meehan took up the rear. As we were led up and across the high-road, I saw bobbing heads of half-hidden figures skulking in the topiary, but they vanished like rabbits at our step. We crept across to the painted sign that said Ryder Street and then up what turned out to be a blind alley. Here Murd and Bucket stood in quiet parley. Murd taught him some secret knocks, Bucket practising them on the open air. That done, Bucket palmed his Lordship a florin and Murd was off. In search of a dose of laudanum, I supposed. As I straightened my tail coat, I watched him scurrying away weasel-like and disappearing into the fog.

Bucket turned to me and said, "I suppose you've read of the Cave of Harmony, my boy? In the flesh-pots of Covent Garden, I mean. I expect that's been part of your journalistic education. Just the *reading* of, I hope! You'll know about the Bath Houses and Molly Dens as well, I suppose. Well, prepare yourself for stronger stuff still and don't tell Mrs Bucket! Now straighten your cravat. That's it. You'll be in the presence of Lords of the Realm and Ministers of the Church tonight!" So saying, he took a topper from Sergeant Meehan to complete my dress. "Put that on your noggin." The final touch was white kid gloves. "You'll do," he said with little enthusiasm.

At the end of the blind alley there was a silvery gas lamp and a red baize door. "Keep your eyes open, your pencil sharp and do what I say, Mr Jakesbere, all right?" I nodded. He inspected the door as if it was the porthole to Ali Baba's cave. I waited nervously for the *open sesame*. He knocked and there was the sharp ratchet of a viewing hole being opened. There was an eye. The spy hole snapped shut. From inside came the sound of an inner door being unchained. It opened and we stepped forward under a green light. The man who greeted us was dressed as a footman, but his square jaw and the heavy cosh he was carrying suggested a more violent form of employment. Once he had inspected us, he motioned us inwards with a bow, covering his weapon with a linen towel as if he were about to serve it up for supper.

We went up, past gilded picture-frames and over Turkish carpets, to the first floor, where we emerged into a room lined with silk paper and a stench of cigars and brandy. Crowds hovered around green and red gaming tables. A footman in canary yellow breeches took our coats and canes. Meehan slipped him a large coin and followed him to the cloakroom, engaging him immediately in a conversation about styles of walking sticks. Meanwhile, I was about to undergo a series of shocks. The first of these was the sight of the large lady who was exchanging money for gambling tokens. Her bosom was bare. Heavily made-up women decorated the corners of the room, lolling on chaises-longues, half naked. I confess that I did not know in which direction to guide my attention. Bucket hardly blinked. He joined a gaming table at once, ignoring the suspect charms surrounding us. I began gulping gratefully from a wine glass that one of the ladies had handed me.

When Sergeant Meehan returned, he passed a silent look of communication with Bucket, shaking his head almost imperceptibly before taking his seat at a black-jack game. I confess that I found it hard to avert my eyes from the exposed flesh, for I had seen nothing of the sort before. Eventually, a metallic rattle and a loud cheer drew my attention. Someone had won his bet on the *rouge et noir* table, or so I presumed. I had not much interest in gambling other than the 'penny drop' I played as a child in Woolwich. Some of the clients here looked as if they might be losing more than just a few pennies. There were dandies about sure enough, those who whooped at success as the gambling discs were scooped towards them, but other players looked less content. They were thin and haggard, with eyes that had seen little sleep. One player watched with a look of desperation as the next ball rattled its way around the spinning wheel. His fellow, a pock-faced player with bitten down nails, chewed up his bottom lip as the silver ball clattered into a red socket. His eyes showed equal despair. Despite this, however, I am ashamed to say that I could not tear my eyes from the magnetic attractions of the croupier and her heavily scooped décolletage, nor of the escorts who fluttered like phantoms around the tables. Bucket had warned me to expect strong stuff. Some of the escapades I had heard from the dockers in Chatham Yard had shocked me, but even my most shameful and dissolute fantasies were milder stuff than this. Gambling served up by half-naked wenches was not the only vice. I forebear almost to report such things but I was in a place where clearly prostitution took place, and, what was more, talk of the young children that might be hired for such purposes. Indeed, two military gentlemen were talking of just such a thing immediately before me as they lounged on a well-padded red Chesterfield.

"If you want to avoid the clap, have a young gal every time," one was saying. He leaned forward to his crony, waving a large brandy glass by way of emphasis and then smoothed his broad moustache.

"Wouldn't want one too young o' course, old fellow," replied his companion. As he did so he leaned over to light a cigar on a small gas jet protruding from the wall. "Best stay within the law!" He blew out a plume of white smoke and adjusted his heavy stomach into a more comfortable position.

"The younger the better, old bean and let the law rot!" replied the one with the moustache. He gave an ugly laugh that sprayed out brandy vapour. "Sir Henry says that a young gal will get you clear of siph. He should know. Five years in India and all that."

"Sounds better than a mercury dose at any rate, what?" said his large-stomached companion, jabbing with his cigar. I admit my pulse had raced at the salacious sights of the naked flesh about me, but listening to this talk had sobered me. I was shocked indeed when I heard another voice intrude.

"Couldn't help but overhear, old chap." It was Bucket, surprising me with the lordly tone he had taken on. He sat uninvited with the others, like an old friend. He had clearly been hovering near, alert to all. "Couldn't help overhearing. You mentioned Sir Henry? Cousin of mine was in Sir Henry's regiment, you know. Fine chap - Carter his name was. Did you know him at all? No? Well, look, I won't beat about the bush, but you were talking of young girls. I'm new here actually and I was wondering -" he paused, half whispering. "Is there an upstairs room, a little Corinthian nunnery where one might be entertained by such?" He was interrupted, however, by the appearance of a supremely buxom woman fanning herself with a black ostrich feather. The corpulent gentleman stood smiling, as did his colleague, and taking an arm each, escorted her, or were escorted by her, away. The one with the moustache touched his finger to his nose, glancing at Bucket. The Inspector watched them carefully.

"Why, gentlemen, you're not playing at the tables," another voice said. It was a much thinner girl leaning over us, with one breast almost bare beneath a string of glass pearls. Her face was heavily made up but it could not completely disguise a thin and pock-marked complexion, nor the rash on her lip that seemed to twitch as she spoke.

"You mustn't just sit here drinking of our wines and liquors now, must you, gentlemen? Won't you play at vingt-et-un or take another turn at the wheel?" I stared open-mouthed but Bucket ignored her, moving his eyes instead towards one of the footmen who was carrying out velvet bags of what may have been cash. He disappeared through a green door.

"No, my dear," Bucket said, rising, "we shan't be playing. We've other amusements in mind." Meehan appeared with our hats and sticks and the girl moved on as we did, though a little disgruntled.

"Now, my boy," Bucket whispered, "we must get a look at their visitors book to see what manner of person we have here. That's the door, I think. Stay close, lad." With a nod to Meehan we followed the footman. We walked straight through the door as if we were old friends of the management. It led to a darker passage-way, lit only by a candle fixed to the wall. Another bulkier door stood not six feet from the green one. Meehan pushed through this and it gave way onto a yet darker space lit by a green lamp and a low fire. There was a smell of perfume and hair oil. The club's proprietor jumped up violently.

"What the d..." he began. The burly footman who had been unloading bags of cash came towards us threateningly. For all his size, Bucket was quick - he side-stepped the attacker and pulled up behind him, holding his elbow behind his back in a fierce grip. He passed one side of a pair of stiff metal cuffs around the footman's wrist and the other to the leg of a heavy deal table, all in one fluid movement. The proprietor reached for a bell-cord. Sergeant Meehan stood by the window.

"I wouldn't advise that!" Bucket exclaimed. "No, I wouldn't advise that at all! Put your arm down quick! Quick I say! If you was to make a sudden movement toward that bell my sergeant would be forced to ring a bell of his own and then what a clanging of policemen's boots there'd be and turning of rattles. Your den would be surrounded by such a multitude of police officers in such double quick time that I don't know what embarrassment might be caused to your clients."

"What do you want? What's the meaning of this?" The fellow swept back his bouffant hair and jutted his square chin at us like a weapon. His face was sun-scarred as if from long exposure, leathery, scorched and incongruous against his effete clothes and hairdressing.

"Just a little pleasant conversation, Mr Dempster." The chin looked a little more tucked in at being granted a name, and the bouffant pile of hair subsided somewhat. "We can be civil, you know," Bucket went on, moving across to where Meehan was stationed, by a barred window. "Or not so civil." With his back to the window, Bucket gestured with his stick. "You are the proprietor of this establishment. Yes? You're responsible for all that goes on within it, ain't you? Might be a bit of opium smoking, perhaps some prostitution or unlicensed gambling or things much worse, eh? But all done, if done, in your house and under your name. So, as I say, you're responsible for all that goes off here - and your name is Dempster." The aforesaid looked dumbfounded. "Well, Inspector Bucket of the Detective is mine, as it so happens - and this is my rod of office." Bucket held out his stick like a challenge. "Dempster of the Hell Club, that's who you are. Of course you are, for my sergeant here's been keeping a friendly eye on you and your doings for some little while. Now, there's no need for us to excite one another, is there? Least of all to worry your guests out there, if there's no call for it. You wouldn't want to disturb their entertainments now, Mr Dempster, would you? So, shall us sit and be comfortable?"

He pointed towards two chairs in front of the fire. Dempster hesitated. His freshly cuffed servant began to rattle his wrists and curse.

"I wouldn't advise that neither, my man," said Bucket sharply to him. "You might have thought that *I* was a little fierce in my taking of your arm up behind your back, but *that* young man" he added, pointing to me. "*That* young man will be twice as furious and thrice as fierce should you make even the slightest little complaint. He could take your elbow on such a journey up your back that you would never want to venture it there again. Oh no, sir, I should desist from any more of your rattling."

The rattling promptly desisted. The footman slumped onto the carpet, eyeing me nervously. I gave him a theatrical scowl.

"I don't believe you about your policemen, Inspector," Dempster said, boldly jutting out his chin again, if less confidently.

"Well, that's a shame. I used to know a Dempster in

Camberwell, you see. A particular acquaintance of mine with that self-same identical name got 'imself transported to the colonies. Transported I say," Bucket said with sudden sharpness. "New South Wales, I believe it was. He probably got himself quite a suntan whilst he was lounging there. But apparently he managed to escape from Her Majesty's custody and made his way back to these shores." Bucket fixed his gaze on Dempster's. "Know him, do you?" Bucket continued when there was no answer. "Funny thing was, *he* didn't believe it when I said I'd introduce him to a *judge* I knew. Belief's a funny thing, ain't it?" Bucket said, sitting calmly in one of the chairs and picking up a decanter of sherry for inspection. "Oh, you don't mind if I do, do you Mr Dempster? The wine in your boudoir was not to my liking. A little on the sour side. Australian I expect, is it?" he added sharply. "But to be truthful with you, I've always been more partial to a sweet sherry. Or, then again, perhaps I should take a cigar?" Bucket lifted the lid of a mahogany cigar box. "Though that might mean I 'ave to ask Sergeant Meehan to bring a light for me as you don't seem to 'ave no fancy gas jet in here. He'd have to be lighting a lucifer right by that window whose blinds he is a-pulling back even now, ain't you Meehan?" Meehan nodded. "You see, Sergeant Meehan has a particular box of Congreves as he likes to use for his cigars, a very bright light they gives off. All that phosphorus, you see, tends to flame out a good deal. And he has a very large rattle in his armoury, don't you Meehan?" Meehan nodded again. "Such signals like those have the habit of telling the constables in the lane that they should start our little raid."

"Raid?" gasped Dempster.

"Yes, sir. Raid. Very noisy they'd be, Mr Dempster. And not one bit gentle with your guests. Tend to be ruffians, you know, policemen. Not from the gentrified classes that you cater for here, oh no. They might have to go arrestin' a Lord or two. And that might empty the upper chamber of the Houses of Parliament double quick, mightn't it?" Bucket smiled. "That might wake up two or three sleepy heads in their Lordships' House with a scandal they might lose some sleep over. God forbid that they might be implicated in such a scene," Bucket said sarcastically. "The Commons might be rocked a bit too. For I believe I spied one or two members of the Lower House communing with your free and easy ladies." He paused. "Now, what is it to be?" he said reaching into the cigar box. "What shall we choose? Sherry or cigar?"

"All right, damn you, take a sherry," said Dempster, his bouffant thoroughly collapsed under the weight of Bucket's rhetoric.

"Never did take to profanity neither, sir. I knew a gentleman once who was profane and he ended up in Newgate for six years. And besides, sir," Bucket said, pouring himself a long glass of sherry, "it might upset the clergy. I noticed there was one or two of the clerical persuasion in your establishment this evening. They were making themselves comfortable with one or two of your ladies as well. All that sort of thing'd upset their parishioners if it was known about, wouldn't it?" Bucket looked up after taking a sip of sherry. "By the way, you wouldn't be running a house of ill-repute, would you sir? As well as a spieler?"

"What do you want, Inspector?" our man sighed. "I'll cooperate. As long as you don't raise a hue and cry."

"I'm known for my discretion sir," Bucket said, taking a long gulp of sherry. "Very nice that. Had an uncle once in the gentlemen's clubbing line. Woods of Hanover Square, it was. A

60

most respectable gentlemen's club. I'm sure you aspire to the same, sir. Discretion is an admirable quality in a gentlemen's club." Bucket took another sip from his glass of sherry. "Now, we need to see your books sir. You'll have a list of punters. A list of guests, I mean, sir, won't you?"

"Good God. You don't think we sign them in do you?"

"No sir, but you'll have a *discreet* list now, won't you? A list of names that you can call upon, should you need to, in the way of establishing and safeguarding your business enterprises, I mean. Might even be in a code. *Very* discreet that sir."

"No. No code," Dempster said. "But a list, yes. Who exactly are you after?"

"A gentleman, sir. Of sorts. A knight of the realm, perhaps. A baronet or a Lord. You have many of that ilk here, I hazard a guess."

"Why come *here* for them? You'll find such in any gentlemen's club in London."

"I am reliably informed, sir, that the gentleman as we wish to speak to uses your establishment as his *particular* gentlemen's club. Perhaps you offer the sort of services he likes? He may even be here now - as we speak, perhaps in a discreet apartment set aside for the special entertainment he enjoys, eh?"

"Oh, you're after the child murderer, aren't you? The one the papers are calling the Beast," said Dempster. "Well, we've none of that sort here."

"I'm pleased to hear that, sir. Very pleased. As is Sergeant Meehan," Bucket continued. "He's been watching the comings and goings here for some while. As you mention it, he tells me he's seen some children being brought in here. Young girls, he tells me. Brought in by some back way that is cunningly disguised from the street. Now, why would that be? If you've

61

nothing to hide I mean?" There was no answer. "He tells me that he's seen some *very* young girls and gentlemen coming out by the same cosy little entrance and exit too. Coming in and going out by ways we can't quite fathom as yet. Sounds a bit beastly to me."

"No young girls. I swear, Inspector. No *very* young girls."

"None younger than 12 I take it you mean!" said Bucket with ill-disguised contempt in his voice.

"We keep within the law, Inspector. We *do* cater for some gentlemen's particular fancies but not younger girls. No. I've daughters myself, Inspector."

"I hope they are well then, Mr Dempster. I hope they won't end up in the same trade as your other young women. The ones pleasing the gentlemen's particular fancies in your apartments, sir. I hope they'll grow up with their father at home and not have to watch him off onto a crowded boat sailing to one of Her Majesty's overseas possessions." Bucket drained his glass. "Now to business. I think you have a list of names for me?"

Our man rose reluctantly from his uneasy chair and, opening a casement in the wall, revealed a safe. This he unlocked with a key that was fastened to his waist. He drew out a large red book. Bucket took it from him whilst Dempster retired forlornly behind his desk, scratching a sun-blister on his face that seemed to be irritating him more and more.

"Most accommodating of you, sir. Now, whilst my assistant runs a finger or two over your ledger, I'm sure your man here will gladly take my sergeant and me on a little tour of your more private rooms." He addressed himself to our prisoner in the Derbies. "You'd like to get yourself out of those cuffs, wouldn't you my man? And I expect you'd like to get out from under the eye of my tiger." I gave my growl again. "And as for you, sir,"

Bucket said, turning back to Dempster, "I'm sure you would like to be getting back to seeing to the needs of your guests. Eh?"

Dempster nodded with a sigh. Meehan unlocked the handcuffs. The quivering servant rubbed at the offended places on his wrists. He eyed me nervously before Meehan grabbed him by the elbow as inducement to move. But they were forced to wait a moment yet - for Bucket wanted a minute to scan the ledger himself first. There was obviously a name or two he recognised. He raised his dark eye-brows in wry amusement more than once. Satisfying himself at last, he passed the book to me for copying. With a short bow to our host, he made a shorter exit. Dempster ignored me, and I him. Once I was comfortable I began to copy the list of names.

I was not long, being accomplished with shorthand. I was only distantly aware of Dempster sitting there. He was slowly raising his hair into its earlier pyramid-like shape by regular sweepings of his hand. And then I forgot him as I concentrated on my chore. When I looked up again I caught him midways, so to speak; he was going out through a revolving door that had been cunningly built into a large book case. He was out, and at once in came Bucket, who had been watching all along through the key-hole, having sent Meehan on with Dempster's guard. "Come on, my lad," he called, and I was up. We pressed against the same bookcase and to my amazement it spun us around into a hidden passage behind the office. "I knew he'd lead us to some pretty little parlour if we gave him time to turn back into a spider again," Bucket said. "This way, my lad. I can still smell that cologne. Stay in the shadow and tread softly, softly my lad, oh and avert your eyes if you must. You might see some sights as'll alarm you."

The passage opened onto another room and we lost the scent

of our man. Perhaps he had some particular gentlemen he wanted to warn about us. We emerged into what might have been another place altogether - a club within the club, like a grub inside a festering sore. It felt like we were almost in a high-road - a road lushly carpeted - with the pedestrians moving up and down just as if they were in Regent Street. They paid us as little attention as shoppers in the High Street might. The silken walls were painted with harem girls and the activities they were engaged in were not for a Woolwich boy to describe. Oriental lanterns lit up lavishly coloured Arabian-style divans where half-dressed men and women lounged on silken cushions, most of them sucking on giant hookahs. The sweet stench of Arabian smoke was in the air, sweet, cloying and heavy. I had never seen an opium den, which I supposed this to be, but I had read of them in Mr De Quincey's book, and these sights accorded with that. Some were even more shocking. There were alcoves, and in each one a lascivious act was framed. In front of this series of alcoves the voyeurs promenaded, sometimes pausing to view their favourite scene. No one accorded us attention as we passed along; nobody seemed to mind us nor be ashamed to be seen. Indeed, it was as if they were out on their Sunday stroll.

Some of the voyeurs were serious in demeanour, as if they were connoisseurs of some fine art or sculpture, pointing out some special feature of the action displayed for them or commenting, without lewdness, on some item of physique. Some were laughing. Some sights were almost pretty. But most sights were cruel. In one alcove, a very thin naked girl was writhing on a carpet and a man with a whip was forcing her to swallow some evil smelling substance as if she were an animal. She must have been drugged or mad, for why else would she submit to being force-fed with I know not what - vinegar, mustard, pepper?

What pleasure the perpetrators of such violence and humiliation received from such acts was beyond my comprehension.

In the next alcove, a fat man with a red face, wearing only a bushy beard, was being flogged by a half-naked female dressed in spikes as he leaned over some stocks. Adjacent to this, a nude woman, heavily marked, sat over a man wearing nothing but a clerical collar. And so it went on. Bucket looked around at the moving crowd of voyeurs and quickly in at each alcove. Looking for the Beast, I suppose - for such a place might be to his taste.

Perhaps it was the heady smoke from the hookahs, perhaps it was the shock of the sights in the alcove shows, but I was soon overcome. Overcome by all this, and by the fact that I had seen a familiar face. A face I had seen only the day before. A face with blood-shot eyes, thin peppery hair and snow-white eyebrows. It was the gentleman from Chelsea whose child had been raped and murdered. He did not appear to notice me or Bucket for we were dressed in clothes quite unlike those we had worn yesterday. I observed him as he disappeared through another door in the labyrinth of chambers and corridors.

When I turned back to Bucket, impatient to tell him of what I had seen, he had gone. It was then that I saw the thick velvet curtain partly pulled across another alcove. My curiosity got the better of me and I peered between the heavy folds to see the back of a dark-haired man dressed in a loose linen shirt. The shirt exposed his arms and other places on his torso. Smallpox scabs indented this exposed flesh like little wounds. Black hair mottled with the remains of grey powder fell forward over his face, masking it. A young girl, no more than a child it seemed, was sitting on his knee dressed up like a princess. He was showing off some trick with a box and a very thin-bladed knife. Suddenly the girl squealed as if she'd been struck or pierced – and, cursing, he tipped her off, causing a gust of grey powder. The girl burst past me through the curtains and ran off sobbing, her tiny white legs disappearing into the shadows. She had reminded me of Nancy Naiskins. When I looked back, the curtain was wide open but the shirted figure was gone.

I felt someone grab my arm and I almost leapt into the air with shock. But it was only Bucket returned from wherever he had been spying. Without a word, he took my arm and led me through another porthole he had found. I meant to tell him what I had seen there and then, about the gentleman from Chelsea with the albino eye-brows and the man behind the curtain with the girl. I felt that either of these, or both, might have been our man - the Beast - but I was distracted by the sights of the next chamber we entered. Here, more scantily dressed women were acting out a mime on a raised platform. Bucket spent a good ten minutes here. He was scouring the figures in the audience of gentlemen lounging on the sofas. They were being entertained by more semi-naked young girls as they watched the masque on the stage. A few heads turned to look at us as we stood at the back of the chamber but Bucket was to be disappointed if he expected to recognise a face - for they were all masked, with visors of monkeys or lions or birds. I felt a chill. Once Bucket had seen what he had wanted, he tapped me on the arm and led me out. By now I was staggering under the shock, ashamed that I had not really averted my eyes at all. Still we moved on until Bucket found a door that took his fancy. This led to a wooden gallery, then to a stair-well and a gate that opened suddenly to the outside world. It was quite a shock to suddenly be in the open air and the black night. The mist had mostly cleared and a swollen moon looked down at us.

The sudden switch from the stuffy, smoky heat to the sharp

snap of the night was welcome - for a second at least - until it made me dizzy. And I felt dizzier still when I realised we stood at the top of a fire-escape. We seemed to have climbed high inside the building almost without knowing. We *both* swayed, to tell you the truth. But then Bucket pointed below; a dark shape was creeping across a walled-in square, hidden at the back of Great Ryder Street. This shape turned at once into a silhouette: a top hat, an opera cloak and then the full shadow of a man. He was tapping his way across the court with a heavy stick. I strained to see his face or his hair, to see black powdery hair or white eyebrows. His head was all topper and his face, all scarf. With a glance, Bucket indicated that we should go down into the dark. We had made it half way when the crack of a stick on the ground stopped us in our tracks. As we watched, the shape of a woman appeared. This shadow wore an enormous hat full of spiky shapes, perhaps feathers. Then two other figures emerged out of the darkness: two younger women. The one with the feathery hat was angry at the others, it seemed. Her voice echoed up to us as if from a stony vault, although the words themselves were inaudible at first. The moonlight caught the younger women, showing their dresses of rags, and they seemed to be carrying a bundle of rags too, like washer-women in want of a tub. But the rags they were carrying were alive. In the shaft of moonlight we could see clearly as a head of hair appeared and then, struggling, pale thin arms. It was a child. Next we heard a shrill cry and then another harsh, breathy but rather high-pitched voice and, this time, perhaps because we had adjusted to the night atmosphere, the words of the next speaker, the angry woman this time, were clear:

"Stop that, you wicious little wixen!" the woman was saying, "or you'll get a thrishing from me as *will* make you yilp! She's bin a scritching like a cat all the way, sir. Even took to biting me, had to give her a slap or two to make her stop sharpish or we'd have had the police upon us. Stop that, I say!" And she *did* give a slap, with a thick arm that set the child screaming. I sensed Bucket tense at this. "The gentilmin only wants to *look* at you, to see what a nice piece of summer cabbage you are, so shut it! She's been a dil of trouble sir. I shall have to ask you for another guinea for my pains. Shut it, I say!" she cried again to the child.

"Gently, gently," the male voice spoke, the words a little quieter but the voice still breathy. "Let me look. What a pretty one, yes." But then he was quiet as he uncovered the girl's features - he seemed suddenly displeased, for there was a change in tone. "What is this? I instructed you she was to be a child of a *Lady*, not a slum girl with bad teeth. I'm fed that fare by this damned club all the time! Look at her, woman! You've dressed her up like kid-leather from a brothel!" His voice rose into a shrill whistling, like steam coming through a too tight pipe. He raised his stick. Whether it was the woman or the child he was going to strike was uncertain, but Bucket clearly felt it might be the latter and his anger gave him away. His body lurched and his boots rang on the metal steps. The man looked up. He strayed for a second into the light and I caught a gleam of eyes, but his face was still muffled in darkness. Bucket *did* move then, hurtling and clanking down the winding staircase, for the chase was on!

Although Bucket moved at speed, for a man of his girth and age, his portly size was snagged by the narrow turns in the winding stair - and I, trapped behind him, could not get past to make up ground. Bucket gave a shout, a blast on his whistle and then let loose his rattle but our quarry, his victim and his accomplices, had already vanished into shadows like smoke. Down into the square we ran, chasing shades back out into Bury

Street. The street was alive with police with flashing lights and with voices shouting. Our man was nowhere to be seen but some sharp-eyed constable had managed to catch hold of one of the fleeing women.

"Get orf, get orff!" she yelled, kicking out.

Before anyone could move again a cab burst out of nowhere, clattering furiously on the cobble-stones and sending up sparks. The driver sat like a gargoyle bending madly as the cab turned, a billycock hat pulled down low over his face. Bucket leapt at it like a man possessed. He grasped the edge of the door and was dragged along by it dangerously till his grip weakened and he was thrown off like a doll, tumbling with a sickening crack on to the ground and rolling over heavily, almost under the charging wheels. An officer gave chase for fifty yards or more, screaming in vain for the vehicle to stop. I ran towards the fallen figure but Bucket was already struggling to his feet, gasping for breath and holding an arm and leg in pain. Seeing me he pointed down an alleyway.

"There, boy! Get the girl! Quickly lad!" And sure enough the other young woman was half-dragging, half-carrying the screaming child down a lane at the back of Boodles, keeping to the shadows but lit up by the halo of gas lamps even as she avoided the puddles of light. I leapt in pursuit. Whether she felt that her load was one not worth carrying or whether she felt convinced I would be able to catch up with her, she soon released the child and made her escape along St James's Street, her skirts hitched up and her bare heels flying. She vanished into the darkness of the courtyards and back-alleys.

I came upon the child sobbing in the street. She screamed as my shadow fell across her but, trying to run, she became entangled in her own bizarre dress, all hoops and petticoats, crinoline and lace.

"Shh, shh!" I called, holding on to a hand as gently as I could. "I'm with the bobbies. You're safe now! We won't let 'em hurt you." I held on to her tightly. She struggled at first but then the screams quietened to sobs again and I was shushing her for all I was worth. Soon, up came Bucket, limping, be-smirched with mud, clutching his arm and sucking at bleeding fingers. He held a small broken pen-knife in those same bloody hands. Police officers began to crowd around him with their bulls-eye lamps swaying.

"Well don't just stand there," he bellowed at them, brushing them off as they tried to administer to him. "Get after that cab, can't you! And get the other women, especially the one with the hat. I want her hunted down!"

The woman who had been captured was dragged before him. All the fight was gone from her now and she looked a pitiful sight.

"All right," said Bucket to his men. "No need to drag her along the ground. Take her over to Little Vine Street, book her and give her some gruel. She looks like she needs it. We'll speak to her by and by." Sergeant Meehan came up then. "Meehan," Bucket said with relief, "I want all the cab drivers' fares checked for tonight and all their vehicles inspected for knife scratches. Have you got that?" Meehan said he had and so, with orders given, Meehan hurried off with a group of bobbies, their lamps diminishing pin-points in the night, leaving us alone - all but for loyal Constable Whelks who was waiting on his master.

"Well done, my boy!" Bucket smiled at me as I stood by, the little girl cradled in my arms. She moaned softly as I shushed and rocked her.

"Are you hurt bad, Inspector?" I asked, noticing the edge of pain in his voice.

"Well, my lad," he grinned, "my copper's knife has suffered a grievous hurt and I might need to borrow sixpence to spend on a first-class hot wash at the public bath in Whitechapel - but apart from that I'm hurt just enough to make Mrs Bucket fret and fuss over me. The next time you see me, I'll look like a Turk, I'll warrant. She'll have me bandaged up tight as a mummy out of the British Museum. But how's the little girl, is more the question?" I laid her down gently and he knelt over her. "Now, my dear," he said, "you're safe now, ain't you?" He brushed a clump of dirty hair out of her eyes. "Mr Jakesbere is a-holding you like a daddy, ain't he?" I blushed and let go my grip but she quickly held on to my hand.

Now we could get our first proper look at her. She was aged about seven or eight, pretty but for the black colour of her teeth and gums. She was dressed in what might have been a ball-gown made for a lady.

"We'll get you into the warm and get you back to your mammy and daddy as quick as quick, won't we?"

Suddenly the little thing piped up, surprising us both. "I ain't got none, no ... wot you said. No mummy nor daddy, Mister. I on'y got Ma Baxter who lets me 'ave a bit o' bread."

"Well, we'll get you back to Mrs Baxter then, shall us?" said Bucket in some surprise at the child's perkiness.

"She won' wan' me," was the reply. We looked down at her, both a little lost for words.

"Mr Whelks!" the Inspector called, for want of any more conversation. Whelks's shell-like, wrinkled face appeared under its stove-pipe hat. "Get that carriage round here prompt, will you?" Whelks nodded and was gone. Bucket turned to the child again.

"What's your name then, eh? D'you have a name, my dear? What did Ma Baxter call you?"

"Gertyer," the child replied, staring at us.

"Gertrude?"

"Gertyer … don' wan' yer roun' 'ere agin."

Bucket was stumped.

"I should think I've a piece of something in my pocket," he said after a moment, fumbling for words and then in his pockets. "There's a nice lump o' sugar. I keep that to give to the horses so they'll fly fast for me. I should think you wouldn't mind that, eh?"

"I don' wan' no 'orse's dinner!" she said. "Why you givin' me 'orse's grub?"

Who would have thought that here was a child who only moments before had been in fear for her life? Whatever her objections to Bucket's offering, she snaffled the sugar anyway, nearly taking Bucket's hand off with it. Watching her chewing on the sugar with her black gums, I considered that the three of us must indeed have made a strange sight: Bucket standing on the left like an anxious, fat mother, me on the right holding her hand like a father and the little girl herself tucked away in the middle. The cab rolled up and Bucket lifted the child up onto the seat. Once we were all on board, she curled up and fell asleep between us almost instantly and the horse clattered away into the night.

# Chapter 7

That night, after Whelks had dropped me down at Bozier's Court, I lay in my bed thinking about the day's events. Now at least we knew that the murderer wasn't a woman. Or I suppose we knew that. And we knew that for all his attacks on the poor girls of the Dials and of the homeless and desperate children of the night in other places, it was the children of the rich he seemed to pine for. Gertyer or Gertrude, a girl of the slums, had been rejected.

And what dreams I had that night. Men dressed up as women and giant trees with fog for skirts; huge footmen carrying axes and waltzing through the park; naked ladies wrapped up in hookah pipes; snakes crawling down staircases; vicars with no breeches; cabs that turned into trains; hammering hoofs. Hammering, hammering, hammering.

I sat bolt upright in a sweat. Someone was banging nails into the door. But no, it was Mrs Peckers calling me to breakfast. She was not best pleased, if truth be told.

"I'm not well, Mrs Peckers!" I called out in a voice that came out thick and sick-sounding. "No breakfast this morning, thank you. I'm ill, I think. I'm sick!"

"Not well? Sick? No breakfast? Not respecable more like, staying out all hours. You came *in* at breakfast time young man, I'll have you know," she shouted, "an' it's nigh on *luncheon* time now! Not well, indeed! There's plenty askin' for your room you know, Mr Jakesbere, respecable folk an' all. Honest gen'leman who'll be wanting rooms soon when the exhibition starts. I shall be full with genteel gents, and *proper* gents they'll be! Don't think I shall put up with the likes of you when the season's in, Mr Jakesbere, for I won't and that's a fact!"

I knew, for a fact, that I was completely out of her favour now. Nevertheless, I was soon left in peace. I fell back on to the bed in relief and slept till late into the day. I slept through the letter-carrier banging on the downstairs door and I slept through the cries of the tradesmen delivering at the back, and I slept through till my stomach woke me with a hunger. When I did wake up, however, I could not face calling for anything from Mrs Peckers. Instead I called out to Milly, the little maid-of-all-work, as she passed by with a coal scuttle. I gave her tuppence as a tip to bring me a jar of small beer and a leg of boiled fowl from the *Lion*. Once refreshed, I was all industry, spending the whole of the rest of that day scribbling my story about Bucket, in case I should forget it all. *Reynolds' News* was waiting on me and I had much to report.

On the following day I endeavoured to make myself more domestic with Mrs Peckers. I woke up early and took all my meals with the other lodgers in the greasy dining room in an effort to be less bat-like in my time-keeping. But my fellow lodgers were no more inclined towards me than Mrs Peckers was. They regarded me with disdain over the butter, the bread and the muffins and muttered about me over the mutton and the roast guinea fowl.

By the noon of the next day, my story was done and so, wanting the exercise and the air, I made my way along Fleet Street. At the entrance, I tipped the door warden with a thrupenny bit to ensure my manuscript sped its way to Reynolds' snuffy before spending my last sixpence on refreshments in the *Wig and Pen*. After this, I felt sufficiently emboldened to face Peckers' walnut nose with fresh courage.

On returning to my lodgings I was surprised to find a letter under the door. At first I feared it was my notice to quit. But it was a missive from Archibald Sparrow, written in ugly British School spelling.

My dere Jakes,

Ware hav you bin? Wot hav you bin up to, you old thif? Wen I calls you are ether asleep or out on your wandrings. Wot a palaver yor cauzing! But now, I hav sum news! Wot do you think? You wont belive it! Just as the sarge was tering a strip off of me for having a dirty nap to my shert, who shud cum in and put them all in their usal flummox? Who do you think? Why, only Bucket of the Detectif, of course! I tell no wit of a lie, old Jakesy! Bucket hisself! He cums up to me and says *does I know Master Jakesbere, residing just orf Boziers Court?* Does I know him, sir, I sed, he's ony my childhood hoppo! The best pal a Woolwich grown boy cud hav. Tho I didn't quite say *that*, you unerstand, Jako. *Wood I conesend* he says. His very werds, mark you Jakesy. *Wood I conesend to take a message to the aforesed to meet him by the cab stand adjasaint to Little Vine St station at 11 o'clock this very evening?* I was getting reddy for another day keeping London safe from fogle hunters, I told him, but he sed *I was to be excused this charge as such comissuns were his to give and his to take away.* Wot do you think of that? He left me a Sovran to give you. Here enclosed, my dere Jakes. Now then Wot *do* you think of that my privy frend? Now dont let me down Jakes. Yor to be sure to meat him at the aponted time! <u>By 11 at Vines.</u> I feel the future of my polising kareer depends upon it! Oh and you *ar not to forget his black book,* Bucket seys. Now, what the devil ar you doin wiv *that*? You dident dip it out of his pocets for yor reportin malarky did you?
But I must stop scribling now Jakes. Im in the good books of the

75

sarge at last for being on such convivyial terms with a Bucket and a Jakes, I mean, an unholesome combinashun if you wos to arsk me but I feel that my affekztuynate sargant is simering inside and will be set to boyl over if I dont get out from under his feet and deliver yu this.

Yors in frendship,
Archibald Sparrow (Constable)
PS. Sorry for my speling.

PPS. Bucket had haf a doz of us scampring about all the cab stands after that nite you went off with him. We wos to make lists of the fares they took for the nite. We turned up nothing except bad tempered cabies.

PPPS. Now dont forgit, 11 at Vines - and yor to tell me all the latest.

PPPPS  Your landlady is a bit of a vulchure ain't she? I think she fort Id cum to arrest yu. When I pushed this under your door she fort I was posting a summens for yu to apeer at Newgate!

Sparrow.


I waited across from Little Vine Street Station at the appointed hour. Here I had to put up with the sneers of several policemen who were loitering in the road leading to the station doors. Then I had to suffer the miserable grumbling of the drivers at the adjacent cab-stand who complained I was putting off their clients and scaring the horses. They were indeed stirring rather restlessly in their kennels, but I thought this more to do with the way the water-man was neglecting them, sitting idly on his tub near the kerb-stone.

Bucket turned up just in time. He was limping a little from his squabble with the escaping cab three nights previously and I saw that he had his arm bandaged up under his coat, as he had predicted he would. All that showed outwardly of his injuries were the wrappings around his hand. Apart from this, he seemed fit. It was fortunate he arrived when he did for I was just about to be arrested for a vagabond on the say so of the water-man who didn't like the look of my face. I didn't like the look of his, to be honest. This habit Bucket had of floating in on the wind seemed like magic to me. Even the cabbies stood to attention for him, and the water-man was particularly obsequious, much to my annoyance. Bucket was pumping them again about the fares they might have taken or customers that seemed unusual on that fateful night. He came out even more disappointed, if the frown on his round face was anything to go by.

"All right then, my lad?" he said giving me a cheerful smile. "Where have you been hiding yourself? Mrs Bucket has been boxing my ears sore because I haven't brought you home yet. She says I'm to make arrangements pronto. We'll make them over a bowl of herrings when we've finished our business tonight, shall we? Now, follow me, my lad."

And so I did. Up the paved alley to a paved court and into the paved station past a blank-faced bobby standing like a wax-work on guard under the royal arms. A number of top-hatted and silver-buttoned policemen were drawn up in line just inside the doors. In what now seemed the customary manner, they looked the other way at the appearance amongst them of the great Inspector. However, as soon as we passed up the wooden steps into the outer police office, I could feel their eyes burning a hole in my back.

The walls of Little Vine Street Station were papered with the usual fare of police shops: peeling bills, legal rules and regulations, and posters - mostly with descriptions of "Wanted" villains. There was a dock with a height gauge standing in it as if it was waiting for someone to measure up for a prison outfit. Next to this, there was a desk where a rotund sergeant with bushy sideburns and a red nose was filling in his log book between alternate licks of a quill and of a giant aniseed ball. This stout Custodian of the Law was waited on by his opposite, a skinny officer with a badly-combed centre parting and popping-out eyes, who was chewing on a piece of liquorice with blackened teeth, the two of them looking like characters in a sweet emporium rather than peelers in a police shop. On hearing our heels rapping on the hard wooden floor, the latter looked up once, looked down and then, startled, looked again before giving an urgent nudge to his superior. The sergeant looked up in annoyance and repeated the same pantomime of expressions before realising who his distinguished guest was. He struggled in an ungainly wobbling motion to get to his feet, puffing the while.

"Good evening, Sergeant Blown," said Bucket, removing his coat with painful care and hanging it on a vacant peg. He would not be helped, of course. Mrs Bucket had certainly trussed him up, as could now be seen once he had his great-coat off. But he was all business-like, injuries or not.

"You've a young woman in your cells you've been holding for me, I fancy. If you'd like to tell me which one, I'd like a word."

The sergeant was all confusion and, not properly adjusted to having Inspector Bucket materialise in front of him, managed only to knock over a box of assorted handcuffs. They clattered to the floor and lay like open jaws. Both sergeant and constable bent down as one and, fishing for the spilt cuffs at the same moment, banged heads with an audible bonk. Bucket ignored them and decided to find the cell himself. After a second or two of rearranging bashed heads, the sergeant came after us and, after a moment, his skinny familiar followed on, holding up a bulls-eye to the metal viewing grids as the sergeant drew them back. The first cell was stuffed with customers large and small, old and young. Such an unpleasant odour emerged - even through the viewing slit - that I had to hold my nose. At the sight of the light in the chink, those inside began shouting and banging and abusing us and each other.

"This won't do, Sergeant. Won't do at all!" said Bucket sharply.

"I'll have Spike go in there with his cosh, Inspector. That'll quieten them," Blown replied, panting heavily with the exertion.

"No, Sergeant," said Bucket showing his impatience. "You're not getting the gist at all!" But he was cut off by Constable Spike.

"Ah," he said, "if you're inferring to the customers in the cells, Inspector Bucket, Sergeant Blown treats them particular well, don't he? Oh he's very considerate he is. Like a mother to them. When it's quiet they get an apartment to themselves, don't they Sergeant?" he added, showing his black teeth and giving a scratch to his centre parting.

"It's with the crack-down on pick-pockets for the Great Exhibition, Inspector Bucket," Blown put in quickly. "We've been calling in more of our regulars, you see - to have a word with them.

"Oh yes, Inspector Bucket, sir," added Spike ingratiatingly, his eyes popping further out. "No more than five to a cell is the general rule here, Inspector, sir." He held his lantern high so that his face became a menagerie of shadows.

"The child!" said Bucket, rubbing his arm and getting further out of patience by the second. "There was a boy in there, couldn't be more than seven or eight years old, buried under all those men!"

"Oh, 'im, Inspector. That's *my* doin' that is. I copped him with my own precious hands," said Spike proudly. "He *ain't* a child. Oh, no, nine years old if he's a day."

"Oh yes, a ripe felon that one," Sergeant Blown added, twitching his bulbous red nose, "in for stealing a pound and an 'alf of sugar out of a van and sleeping rough in Hyde Park."

"There's strong evidence of malice there, *strong* evidence," agreed Constable Spike.

"Get all your cells washed out by the morning and get that boy out to somewhere cleaner," said Bucket angrily. "Now show me where you've buried the woman I had brought in two nights ago, if you *know* where you've put her!"

The sergeant was agog. Spike had the presence of mind to scan down the chalk marks on the board above the cells. Upon this were scrawled the names of prisoners that had offended that day or in that week or fourteen days, if the magistrate was too busy to see them all.

"Meakin, Polly, number 18," he declared.

"That's the one. Now lead on, Constable!" said Bucket, and Spike led us through another doorway down foul-smelling, clattery stairs. Sergeant Blown stood fuming and scratching his nose, probably wondering how he was to get the boy out of the cell without being molested by the rest of the yelling inmates.

Most of the cells were on street level but there were others underground which the longer-term prisoners were privileged to fill. On opening the first of these, half-a-dozen or more women, separated from the men and in various states of imposed depravity, were revealed to us - a few were sleeping but one was screaming and two scratched at each other. Amongst these, a sodden limp figure with weeping face and gaps in her teeth was revealed by the shafts of the lantern. It was the young woman arrested as she attempted to make her escape from the yard of the Hell Club.

"Bring her out at once," Bucket commanded, pointing at her and hastening away and back up the stairs, out of range of the stench of unwashed bodies that had been released. Whistling for two other officers, Spike and his partners dragged her out, holding off the yells of the screaming harridan and the scratching pair with liberal use of their truncheons. Polly Meakin shouted out too - cursing and scratching - as she was bundled up the stairs to the main office. Here she was sat down roughly in a chair next to the sergeant's desk and in front of Bucket.

"Gently now, gently!" he admonished. "Bring us a basin of water and a bowl of soup and see that you bring 'em in that order!" he added, much to the constable's confusion. The girl quietened but sat twitching like a startled rabbit as Bucket freed her from her manacles.

"Here - have a wash," he said, when a basin was put down on the table top. Polly Meakins looked at him as he poured hot water from a pitcher. She still looked at him with bewilderment as he held out a piece of soap and a flannel for her. She looked down at these things wonderingly and then looked up at the guards suspiciously. Preferring the former things to the latter, she all but dived into the water, rubbing her face and hair as if she was standing under a pump in her own yard. Bucket passed her a towel and then called for the soup to be brought. Polly Meakin needed no introduction to this item. She dived in with even more vigour than that with which she had enjoyed her ablutions. Bucket watched her patiently. She was a prettier thing once a layer of dirt was cleared. Her eyes were child-like and her nose and ears like pink shells. However, her hair was close-cropped and uneven and her head scarred, as if someone had

81

taken a hasty blade to it. Her fingers were blunt - one index finger was a stump - and she had difficulty in gripping the heavy spoon. In the interim, Bucket took up a ledger from the desk, handing it to me and beginning to dictate a list of things for the station sergeant to correct in the morning. I was to head this list with the word "Reforms" and underline it twice. This was given to a purple-faced Sergeant Blown on his return from re-housing the boy. He sat in the dock for want of a chair and began reading the list, growing more and more grape-like in complexion.

The girl was scraping her spoon around the side of the soup bowl and dotting up bread crumbs with a moist finger by this time. As she licked the last dot, Bucket pulled up his chair so that it was directly next to her and he was under her nose.

"Now, Miss, if you're comfortable we can introduce ourselves properly. I am Inspector Bucket of the Detective...and your name is?"

"Polly Meakin," she blurted out before he could finish. And then gathering herself, "I ain't done nuthun!"

"Oh, done nothing, eh? Well then, there's nothing to ask and you may as well go back to your cosy cell."

"No, no. Don't!" she said urgently. "You can ask me questions if you've a mind to. Only, only, don't put me back in that stink 'ole!" she pleaded.

"You won't be treated badly, Polly Meakin," said Bucket, "but you didn't seem to mind treating that little girl badly, did you? The one we stopped you harming the other night, I mean!"

"I didn't 'arm her! I didn't sir! I didn't even mean for it to happen. Swear to God, sir!"

"No?" said Bucket sternly, "but what would have happened if we'd not been by? Eh? Your master would have hurt her sure enough, wouldn't he? That little girl might be raped and dead by now. Did you want that?"

"No, sir, 'onest to God, no sir!"

"Well, you're sounding more like a Christian *now*, Polly, ain't you? But Christian is as Christian does and you *were* going to give that little girl into the hands of that Beast weren't you, Polly Meakin?"

"Don't let 'em take me back to that cell, sir. Don't!" she pleaded again. "That man were no master o' mine! I didn't mean to do nothin' wicked. It were that old woman's doings, it were, so 'elp me God!" Bucket winced as if in pain or disappointment. "It's true! It was 'er doing, sir!" Polly Meakin's dark eyes narrowed as she looked up at him. "Molly and me, we didn't know there were any wickedness in it at first." She looked down again and gave a deep sigh. "We ain't been in London long, neither. We ain't, Inspector. We come up from the country to make us fortune, so we 'oped," she said with a sigh. "We thought there might be work. What with all the building and what not at Hyde Park. But we was turned away for vagrants. We ain't in the trade!" she said with sudden emphasis. "Not prostitutes, if that's what you're thinkin'!" she added indignantly.

"And because you found no work, you and your friend Molly decided to start a business in kidnapping, did you?" Bucket said angrily.

"No, sir. No, sir. We didn't mean to be doin' that." She looked at Bucket with pleading eyes. "We didn't, sir! It was all one thing following on another. The Bobbies shifted us on from Hyde Park as soon as they saw us. It's always 'Move on! Move on!' but they never tells you *where* to move on to, do they?" Bucket sighed heavily. "We went to Rotherhithe to try to get some factory work," Polly Meakin continued, "soap boiling or candle making or some such. *No hands wanted,* we was told. The foreman in the factories said they never take on girls who ain't been *properly* taught. Country hands are of no use to them, that's what they said." She looked at Bucket and then at me, to see if we believed her and then hurried on. "Bit by bit we pawned our clothes. All but for these few rags I sit in. We walked from place to place begging for work. We even cut all our hair off."

We both looked sadly at her ragged head. "Molly did mine," she continued, "then I did hers. We sold it to a man we met who told us there was value in it. He wanted Molly's hair you see, cos it was yellow and there's more of a price for that. We cut it off in front of him but he din't give much. There's no living in it, though, for it won't grow back as fast as your belly gets hungry, will it?" She looked up at us again pleadingly. "We found some short-time work, pickling in the Italian warehouses, but then it were a slack time. Always a slack time if you ask me. After that we got a position folding an' sewing."

"Vellum was it?" Bucket asked more gently.

"Yes, sir, we answered an advert. Molly knew some of 'er letters and could spell out what it said. They paid us a penny a hundred sheets. Near Fleet Street it was. Eight to eight with an half hour dinner."

My ears pricked up at mention of the street of ink. "Not so bad then," I said. Both of them looked at me in surprise.

"Oh no. Not if you like to forfeit yer wages. By eight o'clock my back had been bent over the foldin' table so long I couldn't straighten up. You couldn't walk upright in them foldin rooms, sir."

"I've a niece that works in folding and sewing the vellum sheets," Bucket said. "It's a hard line to be in to be sure, my girl."

"Laid us off on that as well after a few days," she continued. "We'd nothing in our pockets and nothing in our stomachs, sir.

84

On my mother's grave, blest if we didn't think it wouldn't be so bad after all to become frails, prostitutes I mean, sir. The next moment we might 'ave made a start in that trade even, joining the poor wretches outside St James's Park. But then that old woman comes up to us." Bucket nodded in encouragement. "We didn't think we was doing so much mischief by helping an old woman wiv' her granddaughter, or so she called her. The woman said we'd earn a sixpence each if we helped her take a naughty child back to its father. That was all it were." Bucket gave her a look, the look that makes you feel that you're being weighed up in judgement.

"All right, I knew it weren't true," Polly Meakin admitted. "But a coin ain't got no conscience when you're 'ungry, sir, and me and Molly *was* 'ungry . We 'ad no money. We didn't want to start on the trade, like some girls do when they're desperate, Inspector. We'd been livin' rough for four days." Bucket was about to speak but she hurried on. "And, oh yes, before you ask we *had* applied to the casual ward - but they had no room. We spent our last ha'pence on a nounce or two of bread from a street stall. We begged a cup o' gin and hot milk from the stall holder but the gin was sprinkled wi' Thames water and the milk were ground chalk dust. He said he'd give us real stuff if we'd give *him* something in return." Polly Meakin hesitated and looked up at us again. "Well, we weren't ready for that yet. At least he let us sit on the ground and eat our bread and sawdust. He 'ad eels and sheep's trotters on his stall an' all. He threw us an old cowcumber in the end - for he said we was spoiling his trade, sittin' and starin' and buyin' nothin'. That was when that old woman come up to us. We thought we could earn an honest penny and proper. Well, honest or not, we didn't ask no questions."

"Did you know who this woman was?" asked Inspector Bucket.

"I didn't know 'er. God's truth, Inspector." She spat on her hands and rubbed them together, crossing her heart as she spoke, looking him hard in the face. Bucket leaned toward her.

"My niece is a city girl and she's dear to me. It's a hard life, I know. But it would break her mother's heart to know that being out of work had made her stoop so low as to sell a child for a sixpence." He looked at her with his penetrating gaze once more. Polly Meakin wilted. "Now, this woman," Bucket continued at last, "you must know *something* about her!" Polly Meakin's dark eyes softened.

"We'd walked up by the omnibus drop. By the alms houses at Seven Dials. We thought we might be able to earn a penny 'elpin' some lady with her bags. We'd seen others do it. Well, she comes along, the old woman, I mean, draggin' the mite. It were like the little mite'd been given somethin' on purpose to make it sleepy, so she could be managed, I mean. She weren't makin' no trouble then. Not like she was when…" Polly Meakins looked down. "But you could see the old woman were fagged out wiv her. She told us, she said there'll be money in it for the both of you. She said all we had to do was help her wiv the child. All we had to do was to sit wiv her between us on the omnibus, as if she were our little sister. That's all it were, sir, I swear!"

"Go on," said Bucket coldly.

"She paid our fares from her purse. She said the child's father would give us a sixpence each if we stopped the mite from yellin' out and tryin' to get away when she saw 'im. She said the little wretch'd run away from home and we'd be doing a Christian service to be bringing the child back to her father. That's the 'onest truth, Inspector. We'd never seen her afore, honest to God!" Her voice was earnest enough and Bucket seemed to believe her.

"But you'd know her if you saw her again?" he asked.

"Oh yes. Nose like a needle."

"Yes?"

"I wouldn't forget her great big bonnet neither. And her hair. Well, she had funny hair. It didn't look real."

"A wig, eh?"

"Made from the hair o' some poor woman or child that had been attacked or from some poor souls like us that had cut their own off," Polly Meakin said. "Her bonnet kept getting knocked, when the child was strugglin' I mean. You see the old woman's bonnet weren't sittin' right. The girl had been a-scrittin' at her when she'd first found her, I s'pose. When she got knocked, I saw a mark on the side of her head. Here." She gestured to her temple. "All red and purple it was, like a birthmark. But she pulled her hair back and straightened up her bonnet. She gave the child a whack for that, I can tell you."

"And the man?"

"Never saw him, sir."

"But you *did* see him with the child?"

"Well yes, sir. But I didn't get a *good* look at him, if that's what you mean. He 'ad a silk cravat on. I saw that," the girl considered. "It covered him up to his eyes because he was wearing it like a mask. And he was wearing a topper so I don't even know the colour of his hair."

"Eye colour?"

"Too dark."

"Did you see if he was wearing a ring?"

"A ring, sir?" She looked up again innocently.

"Yes. Did you notice a ring?"

"I think I did, sir. Glinting a little bit. Or maybe I didn't sir. I don't know, to be honest. I saw 'is stick though."

"And what did you notice about his stick?"

"Expensive. Not like the ones you mostly see the gentlemen with. More fancy looking, with a decoration on it, like from a fairy-tale book. I remember thinking he must have a pretty penny and liked to show it, but I was lookin' at the child mostly, sir. I was wantin' to get away with the sixpence promised, so's we could get some food in our bellies." She looked Bucket in the eye. "He wasn't pleased. Well, angry, more like, as if the mite weren't really what he'd wanted. The old woman had got the poor thing all dressed up like a lady but she didn't *look* ladylike, if you know what I mean. That's all I can tell you. Really sir, it is!"

"All right, Polly Meakin. Perhaps that *is* all you have to tell. He stood up, leaning one arm on the chair to ease his leg. "Now we shall get your soup bowl re-filled and find you a better cell. Spike!" he called. Spike came running, his eyes like marbles. "More soup for Miss Meakins and then - where's your sergeant? Sergeant!" The fat purple head looked up from the dock where he was still sitting, all misery. "The sergeant here will send out an officer to find your friend Molly. I expect you know where she might be hiding." Polly Meakin looked worried. "You'll tell the good sergeant where she can be found, won't you, my girl? For the good of your conscience, I mean. And for hers. But, bide what I'm saying," Bucket said seriously, "she'll be questioned *alone*, my girl. So your stories' better *match*, or I shall be back to see you!" Polly Meakin looked sullen. "You'll both be before the magistrate for the afternoon sessions, either way. But we shan't forget that you have tried to be honest with us," he said more gently. "We'll send a report of your helpfulness and honesty and if Molly is as plain with us, you and she may find your punishment is not so bad - *if* you *have* been honest and stay so."

88

He limped to the passage-way watched by the irritated eyes of Sergeant Blown and the pop-eyed ones of Officer Spike.

Bucket called for all the statements that had been dragged out of the reluctant cabmen, although he had already realised there would be little comfort coming from that quarter - not least because he had noticed that on the Beast's cab there had been no number. While we waited for these statements, Bucket saw to it that cleaner accommodation was found for Polly Meakin till she met the magistrate on the morrow. When the paperwork was found he buckled up his great-coat. Blown watched us with his red nose glowing like a beacon. As we left the station, I couldn't help thinking that Bucket had made an enemy there.

We walked across to the Sportsman Inn and sat on a snug settle in an alcove. Here we shared a plate of pickled herring, beer, bread and red cabbage before pondering on the evidence so far. Sitting there, I was reminded of the alcoves in the Hell Club, the man with the smallpox scabs, and the gentleman from Chelsea, and I remembered I hadn't told Bucket what I had seen. But then the Inspector called for another bottle and we buried our heads in two bumpers of Bucket's favourite sweet brown sherry. As we drank, any pain he still felt seemed to be eased and any memories or intelligence I meant to share with him faded from my mind.

# Chapter 8

I was late in again that night. I seemed to be turning into a sort of vampyre in my night-time habits: sleeping in my coffin at Mrs Peckers' in the day and going out only at night at the whim of Inspector Bucket. The banging on my door the next morning felt like nails being drilled into my coffin. There then came the harridan cries of the angel of death herself:

"I don't say much, Mr Jakesbere!" she screeched through my door. "I don't say much, but what I do say is this, this is a respecrable house and those who can't keep respecrable hours for coming in or for meals should find rooms more fitting to their ways, as I've told you before! That's what I say and I don't mind who knows it!"

But morning had come and, as I had tumbled back into a fitful sleep, morning had gone (and Ma Peckers with it) leaving me in guilty peace. It was well after noon when I was woken again by more insistent banging. I tried to drown the sound by burrowing beneath my pillows, but to no avail. Still in a half-doze and half-clothed, I resolved to open the door and face the consequences. A police officer stood with truncheon up - about to bring it down on my door again. Behind him stood Mrs Peckers herself, arms folded, face more and more pinched, nose more and more nut than nose. Behind her stood half a dozen of my neighbours, some grinning, some gawping and some gurning at the fun. Clearly they thought they were about to witness the drama of my arrest.

"Sparrow!" I shouted, and with great relief I hurried my old friend inside, slamming the door on the leering crowd. Bending low to avoid the beams, Sparrow threw himself down at once on my jingling mattress as if the bed were his rather than mine.

"I say, Jakes, you old crook," he said, sitting up on his elbows and grinning at me, "you'll never guess who I've come from, only Inspector Bucket himself! And what's more Jakesy, he's only waiting outside to take you back to Vauxhall with him, to his own house of all places!"

"Well, Sparrow, old boy," I grinned back at him, "if I didn't know better I'd think this was one of your tricks just to get back at me for that day I pushed you into the river at Woolwich Ferry. But I *do* know better, for Inspector Bucket told me himself that he wanted me to stay with him!"

"Well then, if you do," said Sparrow, leaping up again and gathering my cap and coat, "why don't you get your skates on? Now that I'm in the Inspector's good books for being found out to be a pal of yourn I don't want him thinking I'm in dereliction of my duty by keeping him waiting!"

"Don't think I don't want to, old chap," I said with a frown. "Of course I do - but I've to settle with Mrs Peckers first. I don't suppose she'll shed many tears to let me go, she don't think I'm quite respecrable you see. But she'll want my bills settled and I'm afraid I've not got a bean to give her!"

"But that's why he's sent *me*, Jakesy!" Sparrow laughed cheerily and pulled out a fat bag from his pocket. "I was to bring you the good news and then sweeten the old lady with my charm and this bag of money Inspector Bucket has given me to save your bacon!"

And so it was that I was escorted from my chambers by a policeman, even if it was in the shape of Archie Sparrow, and I went out with a glad heart to face my public on the landing. I was met by volleys of cries and jeers. Down the rickety stairs we went, followed by the mob, as if my destination was to be Tyburn Hill itself.

"I always knew he was a rogue," opined Mr Crow, swaying from too much ale.

"Comin' in at all hours!" joined Mr Foxspit.

"Not respecrable!" a scratchily familiar voice agreed.

"Make way! Make way!" called Sparrow against the crowd and the whole circus of us tumbled out into New Oxford Street. On the corner, wearing his great-coat and reclining on his staff, Bucket waited. He tipped his hat to me as I appeared, which the crowds took as very policeman-like sarcasm and, despite his poorly arm, helped me take my seat in the cab.

"Plum Duffs await, my boy," he said, tapping his stick on the roof. The cab lurched off in the direction of Vauxhall, leaving Mrs Peckers and her lodgers in a lather of excitement. They called out curses and oaths as we wheeled away, one wishing merrily that the executioner might have a blunt blade. Another was agreeing that two blows to the neck was less than I deserved, whilst a familiar third, in deep conversation with Constable Sparrow and clutching a big bag of cash, was insisting for the umpteenth time what a very respecrable house she ran.

For the first time since I had been back in London, all was sunny and fresh. It gave me great pleasure to be travelling south of the river again, closer to my Woolwich origins, though I wondered why we hadn't taken the train. Vauxhall was only one stop from the new station at Waterloo. But Bucket said he preferred to see the streets and the alleys and courts of London as he rode along, not just the backsides of factories. We passed the old Pleasure Gardens and turned left into Vauxhall Street itself. At the end of this there was a little lane which led to Albion Cottages, where the Bucket family lived. Here, some of the smell of the country prevailed and it was quieter away from the bustle

92

of the river.

"Whoa, my lad," called Mr Whelks from the box above us and we skidded to a halt. All at once a little girl came dancing out from the end house. I could not believe my eyes. It was the little girl we had rescued only a few nights earlier. Bucket had said nothing about her since then, apart from using her history to admonish poor Polly Meakin. Now I realised Bucket had taken her to his house and had given her a home.

There had indeed been a transformation, for it was a giggling, jumping, happy little girl who came bouncing up to us. She was calling out my name: "Jakesbere! Jakesbere! Mr Jakesbere!" The last time I had seen her she was dressed up to look like the daughter of a Lord with only her black and broken teeth betraying her poor past. Now, she was looking more comfortably ordinary and like a little girl. Well, little *mischief* more like, for no sooner had she seen me than she forgot her manners and started pulling me out of the cab. This, however, was mild compared to the greeting I received from Ma Bucket. She squeezed me right up against the soft stuff of her bosom and started kissing me till I turned bright red.

"Ma, ma, it's Mr Jakesbere, he's come like you said!" the girl shouted, addressing Mrs Bucket as if she really was her *ma* and adding her slaps, affectionate I supposed, to Ma Bucket's squeezes.

"Yes, my dear!" she said, letting me breathe for a second. "And what a picture he is ain't he? Now let me look at you, young Will!"

"Here he is then, my love. Brought home as promised," said Bucket, limping around from the other side of the cab.

"Yes, but didn't it take you long enough, eh? Dragging him all round London with you, getting him into scrapes like I don't

93

know what before I've even had a chance to clap eyes on him! And look at you, Charlie - your bandages are all twisted up again! What shall I do with him, eh, Will?" Bucket looked quite admonished. She held me at arm's length and made an all-over study of me. I did the same to her.

She was indeed a fine looking woman. Her uncovered head showed thick blonde hair like a girl half her age; only the liver-spots on her hands evidenced a woman of fifty years plus. Although rather lopsided in her gait she might have come out of a picture by Rubens.

"Let me look at him! William Jakesbere! Well, bless me!" she began. "I can't believe it! Moira and Michael's boy all grown up and as tall as you could never guess. And been out and about getting into mischief with my Bucket. Well, young Will, but you and he *have* had an adventure, haven't you? I mean! Bringing home our little Miss Gertie here, and him himself coming in all smithered and smothered. What with his poorly arm and his bad leg that he got when he fell and his jacket and drawers all besmirched. I had to get some ox-gall and gin to sponge his silk cravat with, didn't I Gert? I'd have had his whole suit on the washing line now but for Phoebe. *'Oh don't ma, don't! It'll show us up!'* That's what Miss Fancy said, weren't it Gertie? But bless me, my boy, hark at me going on and on talking about dirty drawers and blistered bones and you standing here with your poor mama and papa just dead and you an orphan in the world! What must you think of me?" So saying, she tucked her arm in mine and led me around the corner to a freshly scrubbed front door step where a dark little maid, Hetty, stopped scrubbing and gave me an inspection. A curtain swung back from the front parlour and another blonde head appeared. I supposed this was the Phoebe who disapproved of underwear being exposed on a washing line. A tiny white dog came leaping out of a half-open window, running out and yapping at my feet ferociously while the little girl who had told us her name was Gertyer, happily rechristened as Gertrude, now danced up and down, screaming in laughter at the funny dog.

"Patch! Patch!" she yelled as we entered the hallway and the little wrigglesome bit of fur with a black patch for a face and eyes like charcoal rolled over twice and leapt up high into the air three times in a row!

"Oh stop it, Patch!" laughed Mrs Bucket. "He's just showing off again, ain't him, Gertie? He didn't stop the night you came in here and he ain't stopped since!"

We walked through to a bright parlour, all cosily set out with nice deep-piled chairs and little side tables covered in coloured cloth. "Now you sit there, Will, and Bucket can get himself comfy. Phoebe!" she called, and the blonde head bobbed in. "Fetch us up some tea and buns, oh and cream, my girl." The head bobbed back again. "We must have lashings of cream, mind you!" The shapely girl bobbed back for a third time, waiting for another order but, grinning at me instead, bobbed out again.

"Now, Mr Bucket is comfy there, ain't you, Charlie? And you, Gerty, what are you giggling at, child? You must sit on that stool between these two fine masters and keep charge o' Patch. Patch, you bad dog! Will you *stop* pulling at Mr Jakesbere's trouser bottoms! Just knock him off, Will, if he bothers you. He won't mind."

As we took tea, I admit I felt overcome. First Bucket, then his wife, and now Phoebe who was, well, quite handsome. I must have been staring, I realised. She started laughing at me as if to say, *who are you looking at then?* Gertie, meanwhile, kept trying to climb up on my lap and Patch was trying to jump up on *hers* whilst Mrs Bucket tried to keep them both down.

When our teas were finished, Phoebe cleared the things. We had not said a word but our eyes seemed to speak. I became confused. I turned around to look for Bucket but he had vanished and Gertie and Patch were playing tug o' war with my cap. For a second I was left alone as the tea things vanished. Suddenly my cap floated in front of my eyes. I looked and was swallowed up in the blue eyes of Miss Phoebe Bucket. She touched back two strands of hair that had fallen out of her mob-cap.

"This is yours I think, sir." Then she ran out of the room in a flurry of petticoats and aprons.

"A sweet girl that," said Ma Bucket sitting beside me suddenly.

"An angel!" I said.

"I meant little Gertie, young man, not that minx, Phoebe!"

I blushed. She laughed. "Don't mind me, my dear, I'm just teasing you! The trouble is, so's *that* little minx! You'll need to watch out for her tricks!"

She leaned towards me and placed her warm hands on mine. "You mustn't mind us, my dear. We want you to feel at home with us, Will, so you shall have to get used to being teased. We don't stand on ceremony here. We want you to think of us as family. We've no children of our own now you know, so we're forced to pick up what waifs and strays we can! I have to say we make a bit of a habit of it, don't we? But we mean well. This poor little Gertie you rescued is just the latest."

"Isn't Phoebe your own, then?"

"Well yes and no. Mr Bucket found her wandering lost after her mother had died in one of the fever houses in the Dials - five years ago now. Her dad had long gone to the drink and he died soon after. Charlie brought her back here rather than let her go to the workhouse. We've had others as well. But most of our waifs were claimed after a while, just like Gertie will be, I suppose," she said sadly. "Once Mr Bucket's made a few more enquiries. Good job too, eh?" she laughed. "Or we'd have had a barn-full by now! No, Phoebe's *not* our child, but we think of her as if she is. Maybe one day some relative will come and claim her too. But till then she's our own daughter, and we love her as much as we did our own Bethy."

"I'm sorry ma'am. I heard Mr Bucket talking about your child the other day."

"Did you, Will? Well. I'm glad he spoke to you about her. That's good."

"Well, it wasn't so much me he was talking to. He was asking another little girl some questions and he was telling her."

"Well I'm glad he did." And she looked away. "Well, hark at me, going on! You'll be wondering what you've let yourself in for, taking tea with us. But look, Will, we don't like to think of you in that lodging house at St Giles. I've been going on and on at Charlie about it! That's why I took the liberty of getting Charlie to pay off anything you might have owed your landlady. I hope you don't think we've taken a dreadful liberty? You are happy to stay with *us* - instead of going back there, aren't you?"

"Well, I don't suppose I'll be much missed by my landlady, as it happens. Not much anyway. Except she might miss having me to shout at for not bein' respecreble! Not that I'm not," I said in confusion.

Well, then of course I became flame-faced. Ma Bucket laughed again, a rich dark laugh that I was to grow used to. It did not take me long to say *yes, and that I would be very honoured to stay.* Ma Bucket pulled me to her bust again, saying, "Oh, Will, my boy, give me a kiss!" And I did.

At that moment the door burst open.

"Oh, you young devil, Phoebe, I couldn't keep you out if I tried, standing there ear-wigging at the door!" Ma Bucket scolded and laughed at the same time. Phoebe kissed me then. I blushed an even brighter red. I was rescued from further embarrassment by little Gertie running in and diving on me and then Patch leaping in the air by way of celebration.

"Come on, off with you!" Ma Bucket cried. "Mr Bucket'll be wanting a word with this young man. Come on all three of you, or you'll suffocate the poor boy!"

Bucket was taking forty winks by the fire in the back parlour when I opened the door. He had a decanter of brown sherry by his bad arm and a half-filled glass in his good one. I was about to leave when he stirred.

"Will? Is that you? Don't be backward coming forward, lad. Sit down. Have a sherry." He poured me a glass as I sat. "Is it all fixed then?"

"About staying, sir? Yes, sir."

"You can save your *sirs* for when we're working, and I'll save my Mr Jakesberes for the same."

"Yes sir."

"Well. Come on then. Will you do the job too then? The two ain't combined so to speak. You've a *choice*. But I should *like* you to do it for me. After all, you've begun already, ain't you? Making notes in my book, I mean."

"I'm sorry sir, I ..." I stuttered to a halt.

"Don't apologise boy. I want you to make a record, my lad. Careful notes, mind you. Nothing scribbled. A *scrupulous* account is want I'm wanting. A *minute* record of all my doings, of all my cases. That's what I mean." He took another drink. "You see, I'm reaching the end of my time as a paid-up member of Her Majesty's Police Force. I shall be wanting to catch this Beast." He sighed. "I shall be wanting him *well* put away. But after that, I'm planning to start my own agency."

"I don't think I'm quite cut out to be a detective," I stuttered again, groggy from the afternoon's adventures and woozy already from the strong sherry.

"Tush, lad. You've already proved yourself a star at it. And I *shall* want your help with my investigations, but it's more the *scribing* that I have in mind at the moment. *That's* what I shall want you to be doing. At least at first."

He rose and lit a cigar from the grate one-handed. "I'm a self-taught man. I had no learnin' as a child. I've learnt what I know through the *doing* of it. The rough and ready way. But I know the importance of words, my boy. I know the importance of order, of looking at the evidence and not jumping to conclusions, of following a clue, just like a bit of string that leads to your villain. I'm not a believer in feeling bumps or looking in a dead person's eyeballs to catch the shadow of the last thing the murdered party saw, like some people are. But the thing is, you see, I don't trust myself with writing things down. Words don't always mean the same as *things* do they? They're shifty. They put on disguises. Just like a villain does, eh? Well," he re-lit his cigar, "I've seen too many men undone by carelessness with what they've written down. Things they would have been better off *not* writing down, shall we say? Things that poked their tongues out at them later on, got them stuck on the wrong side of the Courts of Law. Are you following me? Pour us another sherry, whether you do or you don't. What I want to ask is, will you be my amanuensis? That's the word, ain't it? Will you be a Mr Boswell to my Dr Johnson? There, that's a literary reference for you from a self-taught man! Well? Come on boy. Don't expect me to get down on my knees as if I'm proposing to you! Come on, what do you say?"

"I drink to it, Dr Johnson!" I said grinning, feeling the sherry washing around inside me crazily. He laughed and we clinked our glasses. What a jolly sound they made!

"Well, that's good then, we're all sorted. I'm pleased. But now I'd better let you get yourself settled. Our Phoebe will show you your room, my lad." He moved to the door to call her. "We've set aside a nice little garret for you. That's what you writers like, ain't it? A little garret with your own wash-stand. It's tucked nicely out of the way up on the third floor."

Hearing Phoebe's name both stirred me up and settled me, though I think my smile may have looked a little crooked as I stood up. The door was opened to reveal Gertie, Ma Bucket and Phoebe all in a line and giggling in merriment. Bucket made his escape. After a moment, Ma Bucket dragged Gertie away whilst Phoebe began turning down the oil lamps in Bucket's parlour as the signal that the day was over. I felt awkward. Mr and Mrs Bucket were a very liberal couple, leaving a young lady alone with a stranger. I don't know what my mother would have said, but, well, I reasoned, I wasn't *really* a stranger was I? I was a member of the family now. Nevertheless, there was the matter of her hair. It was loose now and it fell over her shoulders. I could not resist gazing at her. I believed I caught a glimpse of her observing me, so much so that I had to look down quickly for fear she would think me a sort of Peeping Tom. I discovered a sudden interest in the buckles on my boots.

"Aren't you going to finish your sherry, then? Pa don't like stuff being wasted," she said, bringing it to me with a winning smile. She watched me drinking it, staring me straight in the eye. I felt every quiver of my swallow and the way my Adam's Apple slithered up and down in my throat making a noise like a frog.

"You're funny," she said at last.

"Am I?" I said, going red again.

"You're blushin' aren't you?"

"I ain't. I'm not. Well, what if I am?" I said, all on fire.

"You're always going red. Aren't you used to talking to young ladies then?"

"*Very* used," I lied.

"You don't *look* it, I don't think. You don't look it at all."

"I'm not used to talking to ones who are as bold as you," I ventured courageously.

"Do you think me forward then?" she smiled archly. "Do you think me a *minx*? Ma Bucket says I am. What do *you* think then?" she smiled again. "Ma's been telling me all about you. So you see it's not my fault is it, Mr William Aloysius Jakesbere?"

"Has she?" I said trying to look serious. "And what has she been saying, Miss Phoebe Bucket? Nothing that might embarrass me, I hope."

"That wouldn't take much would it? But I'm not telling you for fear you'll grow big-headed." She stopped then and looked me up and down without disguise. I came over prickly and hot. She gave me *such* a look, in fact, as was typical of a Bucket, as if I was being fitted for an outfit and she would soon be able to tell me all my measurements. When she held out her hand my pulse began beating *so* loudly I felt sure she would be able to hear it. "Come on then, silly," she said. "Don't you want to see your room?"

My hot hand in her cool one felt thick and throbbing. She first dragged and then danced me along - and I felt I was in a dream. Ma Bucket appeared at the bottom of the stair. Phoebe quickly dropped my hand and bit her lip, dropping her head as if in guilt.

"Don't let her tease you so, Will. She's a flirting young madam and will 'ave you dancin' to her tune, the way she does the rest of us. I can see you'll need some protection from Miss Madam here!" Phoebe continued to look down in mock remorse as Ma Bucket embraced her slender waist and kissed her. Whilst she continued with the pretend admonishment, wagging her finger at the delightful Miss Phoebe, she led us up the staircase. All the way up, Phoebe kept turning and laughing at me; I attempted to keep my eyes from looking at her, but it was hopeless!

# Chapter 9

I slept blissfully that night and it seemed too that Inspector Bucket was cheerful, for he had been summoned to a meeting at Scotland Yard and felt that fresh intelligence about the Beast might be coming his way.

"Detectives aren't supposed to have private secretaries, you know," he said with a wink, "so they'll not let the likes of you into the inner-sanctum. But I want you along side of me from now on, my boy, though you might have to twiddle your thumbs for a while! Well, get on, fetch your cap - and don't forget the notebook!"

By the time Whelks and his cab came up, there was a farewell party of the whole household at the doorway: Ma Bucket and Gertie and Hetty, the maid-of-all-work, and even Patch the dog and the house cat, Buttons. But I confess that I only had eyes for a certain Phoebe Bucket as the cab rattled off into the mist across New Bridge Street and into the morning lights by the quivering river.

Passing the tall buildings of Westminster and Whitehall, we arrived under the huge weathervane and clock that were the sentinels of Great Scotland Yard. A guard of shiny stove-hatted constables stared blankly ahead as we passed them and entered the cavernous corridors of the grey and airless building. Our feet echoed on the stony floor and unseen doors shut like cannon fire grumbling in the distance. Bucket had an office here, rarely used but shared with the rest of the detective contingent. Bucket passed this office with barely a glance and hurried on and up a bronze staircase lined with the portraits of civic worthies, past and present, to the office of Sir Richard Mayne. We were greeted here by an enormous, stony-faced constable with eyes like black beads. He wore immaculate blues with silver buttons and a leather belt that squeaked as he stood up. Bucket was ushered into Mayne's office and I was deposited on a hard bench where I was scrutinised continually, as if I might be planning to steal Scotland Yard's silver.

It seemed an age that Bucket was detained. When the door was first opened, I heard a hubbub of voices and when it was closed I strained to hear anything at all. Once or twice I felt I heard a voice raised that sounded like Bucket's itself, but my guard looked at me as a warning. I subsided into my wearisome study of the chequered floor tiling. I was in this dull reverie when the door burst open as if a stopper had been suddenly released from a shaken up bottle of fizzy wine. Bucket emerged in fury. He barely glanced at me as he left the office, such was his anger. He swept past as if he failed to recognise me at all, and I had to jump up and hurry behind his muttering figure as he stomped back down the staircase in his wrath, not stopping until we were out again in the windy yard. Here, he swung straight into the public house by Groves the fishmongers. He sat down disconsolately and abruptly ordered a hot gin and sugar. He swallowed this in one gulp and called immediately for another from the trembling landlord. I waited patiently. Finally, he seemed ready to notice me again, banging his tumbler down on the table-top with some disgust.

"The Exhibition! That's what! The Exhibition! What d'yer think of that, Will, eh?" I nodded sympathetically without understanding. "A murderer on the loose. A child killer. The Beast who mutilates his victims and leaves them for dead. And what do they want me to do? They want me to *guard* Hyde Park, that's what!" I had never seen Bucket so angry. "They've given it to Filcher. Toby Filcher, green behind the ears, who thinks if you've got a forehead like an ape you must be a villain. And they call *that* science! What do you think of that, boy? I'm to be in charge of the park and Filcher's to be in charge of the Beast!"

When Bucket had calmed down and returned to something more like himself, I got the tale out of him in the right order. Sir Richard Mayne, the Commissioner, was the man in charge of important criminal cases at Great Scotland Yard. He had been in his office, sure enough, but so was Sir Charles Grey. Grey was in charge of security for the Great Exhibition at Hyde Park, the Crystal Palace, as the press loved to mock it. The Home Secretary himself had written letters ordering that Bucket be taken off the child-murder cases. Complaints had come in against him, Mayne said, though he named no names. *Another* detective was to investigate the Beast, one who could bring a fresh eye to the case. And, anyway, Bucket's expertise was needed elsewhere. It was his knowledge of the pick-pocketing gangs of London that the country had more need of. The fact that he only had responsibility for deterring and capturing the petty pilferers who might be in the park itself, rather than any responsibility for the *actual* Crystal Palace, a role ceded to someone else, only added insult to injury.

Bucket had been famous in his early days partly because he had such an intimate understanding of the mind of the low-life criminal. He had developed a sort of intimacy with the petty pick-pocket gangs and the small-time thieves of South and East London. The ironic thing was that Bucket often got complaints about this too. His Lords and Masters did not like such 'fraternisation' as they called it. These were the days when, if a policeman knew the name of a robber or a fence and dared to visit one of his night-houses or drinking dens, it made the copper as guilty as the villain himself. Sir Charles was not troubled about this at that time; all he wanted was that Bucket should scare off the pick-pockets and the thieves in Hyde Park itself.

Although Bucket was fuming, I was excited. And I wasn't the only one. Ever since the January of the year before, when Prince Albert had announced the organisation of the 'World's Fair', *everyone* was getting excited. The Exhibition was Great Britain's way of announcing its confidence, of declaring itself the greatest nation on earth. Who could deny that? If you were a costermonger from Camberwell or a poor boy from Peckham, the Exhibition was designed to make you proud to be British. The entire world was going to come to London to see us in our pomp, and we all meant to be seen. I was looking forward to being Bucket's special agent and being privy to inside stories on the Exhibition for *Reynolds' News*. I tried to persuade Bucket of the Exhibition's importance. After all, this was no ordinary fun-fair. Britain's reputation was at stake. Truth be told, it was a position of great responsibility to be looking after the park on such a great day. There was, for example, the possibility of political intrigue. In the late forties and early fifties, all the Kings and Queens of Europe seemed about to be tipped off their thrones. Her Majesty's Government was shaking in its ermine stockings to think that revolutionaries might be hiding in the bushes of Hyde Park. Only two or three years previously, the Chartists' 'liberty' talk was stirring up the whole country and it looked like they might *really* turn out the government. Although the hoi polloi weren't to be allowed into the Palace itself on the opening day, and nor for some little while after, amongst the crowds in the park there was bound to be somebody wearing a red hat or hiding a pistol under his vest.

But Bucket was more cynical about his role than I was. He knew the prosaic truth. Revolution was not to be *his* brief. He was not engaged for hunting down Jacobites, as they were called in my grandfather's day. It was made quite plain to Bucket that his commission was merely to stop the dippers. Sir Charles had a wrinkled brow and a bad heart because he thought the open green of Hyde Park might become a honey-pot for all the pickpockets and rogues in London. England had to be wearing her best dress and ribbons, and was not to be seen in the foreign papers as a lady who could have her purse picked or her underdrawers rumpled.

Although Bucket reconciled himself to his new position, it did not stop him from thinking about the Beast. And so Inspector Filcher got little peace from him. Bucket visited the office in Scotland Yard much more than he used to and read all the papers and letters he could get his hands on. He followed Toby Filcher's investigations like a bloodhound that would not give up the scent. Nevertheless, news of the Beast had gone quiet and the scent had worn away. It seemed that our sighting of him at the Hell Club had sent him to ground.

For a time, Filcher had a veritable convoy of crooked types hauled into the police shops. Any poor rascal that had innocently helped a little duchess down from a carriage, any working man who spoke familiarly to the daughter of a gentleman, merchant or banker, or any vagrant who loitered outside a great house found himself hauled away to Millbank. If the poor chap had the misfortune to have a bump on his head or a nose with a wart on it, he might find himself shut away at the pleasure of the magistrate (especially one impressed by Filcher's command of the science of craniology) for far longer than was reasonable. None of these villains with bumps or fissures, lesions or eruptions to the skull turned out to be the Beast, but there were no more attacks on the daughters of the gentry, and their

Lordships were content to declare that Filcher was a success. The molestations of young girls that carried on in Cripplegate and Whitechapel in their dreary, horrible monotony were of no account anyway.

Despite Bucket's low spirits, he worked on doggedly and I saw then what a cunning and indefatigable worker he was. He carried out his duties in relation to the Exhibition with vigour, but it soon became clear that Bucket's true motives were his continued desire, nay obsession, to uncover more information about the Beast. Bucket was convinced that our killer was as likely to be a lord as a labouring man, a possibility their Lordships themselves were reluctant to entertain. He felt convinced that our man was paying some despicable villains or scurrilous servants to spy on the movements of aristocratic families so that their daughters might be kidnapped and subjected to the Beast's malevolent will. Bucket lost no time in starting a trawl through the sorts of dens and dives, penny gaffs and parlours that such as these might frequent in London. Of course this was just such an action that a man with responsibility for the protection of Hyde Park from petty villains might be expected to undertake. But Bucket was after other information. Once Bucket had made his presence known, all the villains in London would think twice about showing their faces in the environs of Hyde Park. What was of more importance to Bucket was that he would be able to uncover word from the underworld about the movements of his true target: the Beast. Two jobs for the price of one, as he put it.

We would often start and finish our day in a beer-house or gin palace, in the bear-pit or at the cock-fighting yard. However, we would take a turn at places of more superior entertainment too - in the gentlemen's clubs of Boodles and Blades, Whites and Bumbles, or in a box at Drury Lane. Some nights, the quality and the low-life would put in a joint appearance and Bucket had a cosy chat with many of them. This was his way, of course: to chat to the party of possible pick-pockets, fences, garrotters and shape-shifters as well as the bona-fide swells, as if he were their long lost pal. It was amazing how he just happened to have an uncle or a godson in the same profession as everyone he met.

Once or twice, Bucket sent me and Sparrow out by ourselves and we would enjoy a nostalgic trawl around the ale-houses of Woolwich. Archie Sparrow had already been singled out by Bucket as a likely-lad for this line of work. One of the destinations Archie had been despatched to was the night-house that we had already visited in Seven Dials. Sparrow's physog had a suitably crooked look if seen in the right light or under a billycock hat - fashionable wear then for ex-inmates of Millbank. His return visit was partly to sniff out any more news of the movements of the Beast. Sparrow pretended to have just escaped from a hulk and proceeded to ingratiate himself with a group of likely customers who had imbibed too much brown nappy. Their tongues were further loosened by his bobby's tanner – a coin which supplied them with extra doses of liquid encouragement. He heard nothing of anyone who might have been our man, but he did gather intelligence of some low sorts who had been in conference about a party of shoot-flyers, fogle hunters and dippers (thieves to you and me) that were to meet up at a certain lodging-house in Whitechapel on the morrow. It seemed that this merry band was planning to position child 'plants' amongst the innocent crowds of Hyde Park. These sweet-looking boys would hook a wallet or purse off you in a trice. We gave this rogues' conference a courtesy call the very next night.

Bucket appeared out of the shadows and shoved a sixpence in the paw of the pox-faced lookout in the alley before the alarm could be sounded. Once bribed, the spindle-shanked urchin ran off lively-fashion. What a picture it was when the comfortable household of hookers and shoot-flyers saw who had come calling! Over went their beer and pipes and out went their swag-bags and bodies. Our little party of policemen soon made them remember their manners. Bucket made a very pleasant speech in which he reminded all present of the charms of the cells at Millbank prison. He pointed out that although their day out at Crystal Palace might be profitable in the short-run, he would ensure that they spent the long-run on the treadmill at Millbank or at shot-drill in Pentonville. Bucket said he would be most obliged to them if they would advise any acquaintances in a similar line of business to their good selves, be they jerry sneaks or onion hunters, jilts or snow gatherers, all different types of petty thieves of course, that Bucket was about! In fact, one of the remarkable things about the Great Exhibition was that only twelve pickpockets needed to be arrested during the whole time of its opening.

# Chapter 10

During the first part of that year, Bucket did a good deal more than just catch pick-pockets, but not the thing he most wanted: to bag the Beast.

That spring, for me at least, was a time of continued relief and pleasure. When we retired to Vauxhall each evening, I wrote up my diary of the day's events under the bright blue eyes of Phoebe Bucket. My pleasure was spoilt only by Ma Bucket's determination that Phoebe and I were to be chaperoned at all times. Now that she knew I was sweet on Phoebe, her liberality, sadly, had faded. If it wasn't little Gertie's prattling or Patch chewing at my stockings, it was Hetty taking down the curtains or Ma Bucket herself coming in to supervise the tea things. Even so, my paradise was nigh complete. Bucket was pleased with my scribblings, Phoebe was pleased with my company and Reynolds was pleased with my reports. I sent off my stories on a daily basis and Reynolds stored them up for serialisation in the *Weekly News*.

Bucket, however, grew less and less content and he continued to paw restlessly at all his papers regarding the case of the Beast. In the winter months, the monster's doings had filled page after page of the newspapers but as spring approached there was no news of him. Detective Filcher was rumoured to have retired to a lodging house in Holywell Street, there to study his craniology diagrams. In fact, he was often seen drinking in the *Drover's Arms* nursing his own bumps. Bucket, meanwhile, was beginning to think our sighting of the Beast at the St James 'Hell' had indeed put an end to his escapades. But we were wrong. The Beast was to put in another appearance on the day of days itself, on the very day of the opening of the Great Exhibition May 1$^{st}$, 1851.

I remember the day well. Bucket and I had been awoken early by Hetty. We left the house in Vauxhall with nothing more inside us than a dish of tea, stealing out whilst the rest of the house were sound asleep. There would be time for breakfast later, or so Bucket promised through a sleepy yawn. According to my father's fob-watch it was just a half hour past four when we rattled across Vauxhall Bridge. The river was shining silver and already filling up with jaunty boats and barges. When we lurched into Westminster, I smiled to see the jolly, fluttering flag of a Chinese junk and started to rub my hands in glee at thoughts of the pleasures to come: the balloons and the bazaars, the coloured pavilions, the promenading and the trips to be bought on the Serpentine or Thames.

Bucket had business to do first. We drew up near Whitehall Stairs where the Inspector climbed down, rubbing the morning aches out of his back and the sleep out of his eyes. I watched him disappear into a police river-boat, where he was to have a last conference with Sir Charles Grey and all the big-wigs of the Metropolitan Force in charge of the safety of us all on this great day. The small wigs, Constable Whelks and I, waited in the cab.

Whelks was soon snoring. I sat listening to London waking up. When Bucket reappeared, materialising as always like some magician's trick, I was so wrapped up in these sights and sounds that I jumped. He shook Whelks awake and with his usual merry cry of "Away, my lad!" we jerked forward towards Hyde Park itself. We clattered past Whitehall Place as if we were royalty ourselves, escorted by police outriders on chestnut mares. Later on that morning the crush of cabs, broughams, clarences and post-carriages would stretch all the way back to the Strand.

Once we reached the famous old gate, Bucket was met by a gaggle of sergeants, all buffed-up in their shiniest uniforms, buttons gleaming and the naps of their toppers freshly wiped. Here, Bucket reminded his troops to keep an eagle-eye out for pitch and toss pie-men, card-sharps, thimble riggers, and the like. Confidence tricksters, the lot of them. With a finger on a shoulder here and a pat on the arm there, these police officers were sent away, joining up with their minions stationed all over the park and in amongst the slowly gathering crowds. At six o'clock on the dot, the gates opened and the first carriages, with their cheering, leering passengers, poured into the body of the bright green, airy park.

By noon, thousands streamed in from all parts of the smoky city, and from beyond, all to worship at the Crystal Palace. This name, given as a joke at first, never seemed as fitting as now. The great gleaming building in the middle of the park was indeed just like a giant palace. Of course, I was aching to explore the *inside* of the palace or, if not, to sail on the Serpentine on that splendid Chinese Junk. I imagined myself with Phoebe enjoying a romantic cruise out to Long Water, being served pekoe tea and being waited on by a pig-tailed servant.

Bucket had arranged an office for himself in a little pavilion he'd handily requisitioned just behind a refreshment tent, and it was to the latter that we headed off at first. When we had breakfasted, we made a leisurely inspection of the park, checking that constables were stationed as required and, more importantly, that our plain clothes men were circulating, watching over the tents and stalls. At a little after eleven, Bucket was forced to return to his office, for at noon the royal party was due to arrive. Although he had no responsibility for Her Majesty's security, and nor indeed for the security inside the

Crystal Palace itself, he was expected for a last parley with a police commissioner or two, who did.

I had some minutes to myself then, so I made my way to a raised viewing post from which I could see the sweeping panorama of trees and walkways, fluttering flags and stalls and sideshows in the park. This was when I first became aware of a Chinaman, wandering about amongst the crinolines and the coronets. He was gathering quite a crowd of excited little girls around him, many of them clearly the daughters of the aristocracy, dressed in their best frocks and crinolines in imitation of their mothers. I smiled as he led them off, pied-piper like as in Mr Browning's poem. It was only a moment or two later, when I had been watching a man on stilts walk by, that I noticed the children returning to their nurses and to other frolics and games and that the Chinaman was not with them. I thought nothing of it at the time, and made my way back to Bucket's 'office'. Finding this deserted, I walked next door and found him in the crowded refreshment pavilion, quite relaxed.

"There she is, my boy!" he said when I joined him. I stood to attention thinking it was the Queen herself come to take a crumb of cake with us. I looked around only to be disappointed, saying "I see no Queen."

"See no Queen, my lad? Then you've no eyes. For there she is. And there they are!"

My face split in a smile, for, of course, he meant the Bucket brood. There they all were dressed up in their finery: Ma Bucket, Gertie, Hetty and Phoebe too.

"No *Queen*, my lad?" laughed Bucket, all smiles. "It's royalty itself!" When the kisses were completed, we sat down again and ordered pots of tea and cakes galore. Soon enough, Gertie was fretting to be up to run around the park and see the sideshows. It

114

was just then that there was a sudden flare of trumpets and up went the balloon. Charles Spencer, the famous daredevil aerial balloonist, had taken off in a spurt of flame and he was soon soaring gaily high above us. I turned to smile down at little Gertie but she was gone. She was dashing out of the pavilion into the crowd crying, "Look, a Chinaman! I want to see the Chinaman!" Hetty, Ma Bucket and Phoebe gave chase but with the extraordinary numbers in the park it was no surprise when we lost her.

It became almost impossible to chase after her when the whole park was jolted to attention by an enormous boom of cannon fire. This was the announcement that the Queen was in the park - the first of twenty one guns making its salute. The crowd took this as their cue to rush to the open front of the refreshment pavilion and I was nearly toppled over. Along the road came the horse-guards to keep back the populace. We were stuck then until all of the royal carriages went past, and of these there were a great many, moving at a slow and stately pace. Prince Albert and Queen Victoria were in the first carriage, of course, waving at the happy, cheering crowds. After them came young Prince Eddie in his Highland dress and his sister looking like a little doll. It was at this moment that an aristocratic gentleman came hurrying in to the pavilion, followed by his retinue, calling out for Inspector Bucket at the top of his voice. This black-bearded gentleman and his sobbing lady burst upon him.

"I demand you take action, Inspector!" the gentleman shouted, taking Bucket vigorously by the shoulder.

"Ah, Lord Fox!" said Bucket, briefly turning to him before giving his attention again to the passing carriages. "What is it, my Lord? Is something wrong? Aren't you with the reception committee, my Lord? They'll be putting you in the stocks! The

Queen's nearly at the gates, you know. You'll need an escort to get you over there in time." This was what Bucket was like. He would converse in the same tone to a dustman or a duke with as likely as much respect for one as contempt for the other.

"This is no time for frivolity, man! Our daughter is lost! My wife thinks she has been abducted!" The rotund woman with him, Lady Fox, I supposed, began weeping anew at this. She had to be sat at a table and given some salts by one of her attendants.

"I believe I may be in good company then, your Lordship," replied Bucket, "for I think my own little minx may also have got herself lost. My wife is hunting for her as we speak. Upsetting as it is, I take heart, my Lord, from the fact that there are a multitude of policemen in and around the park and many stations where a lost child might be taken for safety. The organising committee have put up several signs, I think you'll find."

Just then, three or four of the multitude just mentioned bustled in with a little girl in a froth of petticoats and floods of tears. It was his Lordship's daughter, of course. Soon she was swallowed up by her mother and a nurse, both sobbing and swiping out at the little thing by turns. His Lordship soon forgot us, in relief, I supposed, at his child's return. He left hastily, leaving the women to chastise the girl, and to keep his appointment with the Queen. I wondered if his sudden exit might not be partly due to *my* presence. I had been hidden behind one of the pillars of the refreshment pavilion, the very base of which I had been using as a viewing point, and he had not noticed me at first. Nor had I got a good look at him. But I had seen him before, I realised. It was a face from the Hell Club where I had seen him naked and in the stocks, being flagellated by an undressed prostitute. Well, that explained Bucket's joke about the 'stocks' perhaps, for Bucket may have noticed him there too. However, I was distracted again as another 'lost' child came tumbling into the pavilion. This time it was little Gertie herself, followed by a scolding Phoebe and an out-of-breath Ma Bucket hanging on to her. But bold-faced Gertie wriggled free and ran straight up to Bucket shouting:

"It was him! The Chinaman ... I seen him!"

"What do you mean, Gertie?" said Bucket, looking down at her, hardly hearing her in the noise of the crowd and the passing carriages.

"You gotta listen! It's 'im! 'Im 'at hurt me on that night in the alley. Top-hat man and the dragony stick and the ring. It's 'im! I runned after 'im and I saw 'im with another lil' girl. I screamed when I saw it was 'im. I screamed really loud, ma, I did!" Gertie exclaimed earnestly, looking up at a wild-eyed Ma Bucket. "He 'ad a lil' girl with him. But she runned off when he saw me. He looked me right in the eye, he did. I knew I was right. It was 'im! He's turned into a Chinaman now!"

Bucket stuttered for a second but then turned quickly to the police officers around him with urgent orders for them to hurry to the Serpentine and the Thames to tie up the junks and to hold all the sailors for questioning.

"Where did you last see him, Gertie? Did you see where he was going?" he said urgently, holding on to her heaving shoulders.

"To the Palace," came her reply.

Two horses were called for at once and Bucket and I pushed through the crowds making a bee-line for the Crystal Palace itself. Perhaps I was going to get a look inside after all, I thought, if I didn't fall off the horse before then, for I was no rider. But our plan to enter the Palace was thwarted, for at the iron gates of the transept there was a great crushing crowd. Hundreds were just hovering and straining to look in, but the nobility were

117

already inside, filling the galleries and seats all around the main exhibition area so that there was no room to get by. A giant organ was playing and its booming voice drowned out all other sounds.

Bucket had dismounted but his shouts from the gates and his arguments with the doormen were not heard or were ignored. He had no authority here. His brief was only to ensure that the petty criminals of London did not manage to steal too many wallets amongst the bustling crowds in the park as a whole. The Chinaman, we could just about see, was, of all things, at that moment merging with the royal parade making its way towards the throne. Later, we realised the organisers must have assumed he was the Chinese delegate that they had been waiting for all along. The Indian display inside the Exhibition was full and so were the French, the Italian and the American ones, as well as all the other exhibits from all the nations of the Earth. But something had been promised from China and nothing had arrived. But now a Chinese ambassador had come instead!

Bucket looked on with horror when he saw his man. He signalled frantically to the policemen, the guardsmen and army officers supposed to be protecting the Queen. But all his waving and shouting was to no avail. In fact, the crowd inside seemed enchanted with the Chinese visitor. Apparently, the Queen and Prince Albert passed a word with a Brigadier with a pointed hat and the man we thought was the Beast, in his Chinese disguise, was actually put between the Duke of Wellington and the Archbishop of Canterbury. Everybody stood for the National Anthem and several long speeches followed. Bucket could do nothing until all this was over. By the time the royal party had moved off, the Beast had vanished into the crowd. Only when the royals made their procession out via the rear entrance was

Bucket able get a foot inside the front. But his man was gone.

We spent the rest of the day sending scouting parties out around the park in search of an oriental in silken robes. Nothing. When we got to the junks on the Serpentine and the Thames, their owners, who had had their vessels roped off, swore at us loudly, in ripe Anglo-Saxon accents indeed. Of course, they turned out to be some lads from Leytonstone who had seen a chance to pocket a penny or two from the holidaying crowds. They had got their women-folk to sew them up a bit of dirty dyed silk and had stuck some horses' tails to the backs of their heads to complete the oriental costumes. The 'junks' were nothing but painted trawler boats. They complained bitterly at their loss of trade. But more bitterness was to come.

That evening, when the park was closed, two bodies were found in the deep bushes by the Serpentine. The park keepers thought they were sleeping vagrants at first. But they were girls. Little girls. Daughters of Lords and Ladies. Their bodies had been mutilated and tossed into the undergrowth. The Beast had struck under the nose of the Queen. When the attention of the crowds and the police and press in Hyde Park had been on Her entrance and Her safety and Her presence, the Beast had struck. He had enticed two little girls away from the Crystal Palace and the stalls and the side-shows, into the quiet and dark spots of the park; into the shadows where he had raped, murdered and mutilated them. None of this came out until much later for fear of scaring off the public and upsetting Her Majesty. But Bucket was beaten and the Beast had vanished.

# Chapter 11

The bodies were taken to Christ Church, Belgravia. It was the early hours of the morning when we were told and Bucket was commanded to be in attendance. A sombre gathering of the police commissioners and government ministers responsible for the security at the Exhibition met in the pouring rain in the old cloisters. Black umbrellas dripped. Sir Charles Grey was trying to comfort and placate the parents. Their faces were as much touched by fury as they were by grief as they made their protestations to the high ranking policemen and dignitaries.

After they had identified the bodies of their children they left, continuing to vent their ire and threatening nameless repercussions that were to fall upon the officials responsible for failing to stop the murders. We replaced them in the stony chamber. When I saw the bodies on the cold, grey slab and saw the autopsy surgeon with his saws and buckets, the horror of it all overcame me. A police commissioner gave Bucket permission to examine the bodies and as he stepped forward the surgeon handed him a pair of rubber gloves. Bucket pulled the gloves up to his elbows and walked into the light from the gas jets to inspect the bodies, watched by the shadowy line of senior policemen and politicians. I glanced down at the poor, ruined bodies but averted my eyes quickly, for I had seen enough. The girls had been attacked in a frenzy.

"Stiletto?" Bucket finally asked. And the surgeon nodded. Sir Charles, who had returned from his doleful farewell to the parents of the dead, came up out of the shadows.

"Well?" he asked.

"The Beast," said Bucket into the darkness.

There were others who should have been blamed of course. The safety of the public in the park was not Bucket's direct responsibility and the case of the Beast had been given over to Inspector Toby Filcher, conspicuous by his absence. But Bucket's name was associated with the Beast and he was therefore suspended from all duties.

Several weeks had passed but Bucket was still in a black mood as we sat one night in his room.

"First he gets away from me dressed as a lord and now as an oriental!" Bucket said, tipping back more sherry than was good for him. It was the audacity of it all that made him so bitterly angry, as well as the panicky reactions of the politicians and the police. The order went out to pull suspicious characters or vagrants or the deranged off the streets. Any inspector or police sergeant looking for glory, or any ordinary policeman looking for fame, might do it. And many a simple-minded soul who behaved strangely on the streets of London found himself coshed in a dark cell in many a police station. The treatment of all thieves and low, poor, criminal types in London's police stations got worse. Sergeant Blown in Little Vine Street, and all his ilk, cheerfully stuffed ten and more so-called villains into the holes made for two or three that Bucket had already demanded reform of for holding five. Of course, some of these rogues and savages might have deserved their fates - but none of them were the Beast.

The atrocities of this fiend were always on Bucket's mind and it rankled with him that the monster had escaped his clutches twice. Bucket had one of the Beast's intended victims living in his own home after all, and one other he knew of, Nancy Naiskins, had had a near escape from his clutches. Bucket's own daughter had died of smallpox years before. He was still wearing his mourning ring. Perhaps that was at the bottom of it all. In the secret recesses of his heart, Bucket had vowed to himself that no more little innocents should be allowed to perish.

Bucket had his eye on the newspapers and police reports ever more alertly now. There had been no more sightings of the Beast nor any atrocities specifically accredited to him. He reasoned correctly that his quarry would vanish again after this latest manifestation, not that this brought him any consolation. He travelled across the Channel to confer with a famous private detective of his acquaintance about a French villain with similar traits to the Beast. When he returned, he shut himself up secretly with a loyal friend, Sergeant Meehan, and went over the names in my black book again and again. Meehan, meanwhile, fed Bucket with the latest intelligence to be had.

Ma Bucket was growing increasingly worried about him.

"Speak to him, Will," she said anxiously. "He won't listen to me, you know. See if you can get him to think of new things. Get new cases. Get his mind off the old one. Get him to start planning for the retirement he keeps talking of. Get him to talk about his new Investigative Bureau. He'll listen to you if you talk of it. He'll just think I'm nagging."

So it was that on a warm day, late in May, I was sitting with Bucket in his snug parlour. He seemed more cheerful after hearing the news that he was to be reinstated to carry out his former duties. Wiser counsels had prevailed, it seemed, and Bucket's suspension had been deemed too harsh; London still required a policeman with his talents and Hyde Park was safer from pick pockets with him in charge. Bucket, however, saw it as very much a temporary reprieve. Notwithstanding this, Bucket's mood had been improved by the arrival of another letter from his French correspondent, clearly related to the case of the Beast. He was re-reading this with some excitement when I decided I would do my duty by Ma Bucket.

"Now then, Mr Jakesbere," he said. I knew he meant business because this was my Sunday best name. "You've done well in writing up our doings over the last months. You make me sound quite like Monsieur Vidocq here, the way you apostrophise me," he said waving the letter at me, "but now that we're in the lull after the storm, it's time I set you to work on the greater chore."

So saying, he got up and heaved down a great box-file from a high dusty shelf. A snow-storm of other papers followed after it.

"W-what are these?" I stuttered as he plumped the file and the stray papers in my lap.

"Why, my boy, my *papers* for you to get in order, that's all! I'm wanting you to write my *complete* history you know. A happier ending for the story of the Beast, of course, when it comes," he said with a frown. "Not just all this piffling Exhibition stuff! There are other notable things I have achieved, as some might still admit. I think you have an eye for writing, and I can trust you with some of the, shall I say, more delicate cases I've dealt with over the years. What's more, my boy, I intend to retire soon." He became morose again for a moment and slumped down in his armchair. "Perhaps their Lordships were right. I'm not fit to be a detective policeman any more. I've let our man slip through my fingers twice, haven't I, eh? Well perhaps it's time to start my own long-promised, eh? My very own Investigation Bureau at last!" He smiled wanly. "But before I do, I should like to get my papers in order. And that's to be *your* job."

I was looking at him like a goldfish. He stood up again, all animation.

"Now, you'll find official reports from all the cases I've been on since my time with the Force. You'll find newspaper clippings too. You'll be able to piece together the stories from those, won't you, my boy? I expect you'll want to interview me about them all, eh? That's what you scribblers do, ain't it?" He blew the dust from the top of a large box and opened the lid. "Now start off with these letters, if you will. Since I've put it about that I'm starting my own bureau, I've had a mountain of letters sent me from people wanting me to do things for them. They need sorting and filing, my boy." He was all action and I was all confusion. I felt I was back in *Reynolds'* office, drowning under a sea of paper and ink.

"You can start on them now, my lad," he said, suddenly making for the door and leaving me under a clutter of paper.

"Now?" I asked. "But ..." But it was too late. He was gone. I confess I felt somewhat disenchanted with my new role. Up until then I had been an assistant to Bucket in his search for criminals, low and high; now I was to be nothing but a filing-clerk. Nevertheless, I had not forgotten my training back in Chatham with Uncle Silas and, as I got to grips with the muddle of papers and began to create order out of chaos, I started to enjoy my peep into Bucket's past, in a dusty clerkish sort of way.

Amongst the papers dealing with these past cases, there were dockets and memos and lists and cuttings from newspapers and periodicals, as well as letters and notes from his various clients. In one box there was a whole bundle of Bucket's black books, just like the one I now did my scribbling in. These were where Bucket kept notes about his previous cases. Sorting out his spidery hand was going to be a detective case in its own right.

When I began to make headway amongst the bundles of news cuttings, I found a page from *The News* about the infamous murder of Lawyer Tulkinghorn. And then I found the one from

124

*The Times* about the Charles Gill business and all the cases, in fact, that had made Bucket famous. Gill had threatened violence to the old Prime Minister, Lord John Russell, and there was a long report about Bucket's involvement in this affair, according him high praise. Alongside it, bundled in carelessly, was a letter from Lord Russell himself. But the one that really made my eyes pop out was the one thanking Bucket for saving the Queen in the Robert Pale affair, written in the hand of Prince Albert himself. I marvelled at that one for quite a time, laying it out on the table as if I was already planning its position in the memoir I would be writing of Bucket's life. When I turned back to the box-file, lying on top was a letter from Chesney Wold, in Lincolnshire, from one Sir Leicester Dedlock, Baronet.

"It is with sad but solicitous thanks," it began, "that I have instructed my secretary to write to thank you belatedly for your most delicate and considerate handling of my affairs." And so on. There were many more like this too. Some were just scrawls from customers who could hardly write, from working folk saying a thank you or begging for help in something or other. But the most were from the nobility or from the new merchant classes, all eager to engage Bucket's assistance despite, or perhaps because of, the latest horrors.

Most dated back from before the spring, it has to be said - but there were many of them. There was one from a Lady Mercer of Pall Mall 'importuning' Bucket's help in a 'delicate family affair'. It mentioned Sir Leicester Dedlock by name as having given a 'particular recommendation of Bucket's services'. I noticed that many of the letters referred to Sir Leicester Dedlock's case. It was apparent that Bucket had received a strong testimonial from this gentleman. Some of the letters were signed with names that I half recognised. There was one, for instance, from Lord Montague

Dreadnaught, 'residing at Oblique House, Mayfair', asking Bucket to help locate his lost son. This Dreadnaught character had a reputation in the past as a philanthropist, as well as for his famous house in Belgravia, near to the even more famous Lord Chesterton's grand semi-palace. The son had absconded after a family misunderstanding, so the letter said. This made use of Sir Leicester Dedlock's name too. I confess I laughed, however, when I saw the one from Sir Michael Pilgrim, MP for Richmond, talking about his 'difficult problems' with a 'young lady'. This Pilgrim was a bit late with his cry for sanctuary because his story was already emblazoned all over the *News of the World*, and rare stuff it seemed too. There were about a dozen more like this. When I realised what a feature these letters from the nobility might be, I began to make up a list of 'New Cases' for Bucket's later consideration. I ordered them alphabetically, just as Uncle Silas had trained me to, and I was beginning to get on expeditiously.

Phoebe looked after me by bringing tea and sandwiches. She kept dancing in just as my eyes were going double with all the spidery handwriting I was reading. Then my eyes would go out on stalks looking at her. But who could blame me? She was a beauty, and I did not mind confessing it.

"Pa Bucket is a horrible nasty beast!" she said on one of her visits. "Keeping you locked up in here like a prisoner with all these horrid dusty boxes and papers!"

If I could have had my way, I would have put them all away in a moment and thrown myself on her mercy but, just as I was about to, in would bounce a giggling Gertie or a dusting Hetty or a bustling Ma Bucket. And, of course, they would always time their entry for just the moment that I was daring to steal a kiss. Then Ma Bucket would scold everyone away, Phoebe too, and I would be left with my papers again. Dust instead of kisses.

As the afternoon wore into the evening, Bucket himself came in to see how I was progressing.

"You've done well, my boy. Why, these are in good order already!" he said with approval. "You've not disappointed me in your attentions to your work, nor in the quality of your scribing, my lad!" I felt quite blown up with praise. Remembering Ma Bucket's commission that I should keep Bucket away from gloomy thoughts of the Beast, I took the chance to ask a question.

"What will we do now then, Inspector? For a new case, I mean? There's a lot of interesting ones here that you could take on."

"You mean forget the old one?" Bucket raised a rueful eyebrow and started turning his mourning ring.

"If you mean the Beast," I continued tentatively, "and I suppose you do, well, the Beast has gone away again now, surely, and anyway he's not our business anymore, is he?" I stuttered to a close.

Bucket's face wrinkled up and he seemed to be chafing his ring-finger as if he would pull it off. I cursed myself for naming the taboo topic. Bucket leaned back and gave a sigh.

"No, lad, not gone away. Gone to ground, perhaps, but not gone away. After all, he seemed to go quiet for a long time after we first made his acquaintance, didn't he? We made him fair scuttle away then, eh?" he said ruefully. "Off into his darkness. But it didn't stop him crawling out of his lair again, did it? Killing more children."

He became rapt and distant for a moment as if reconciling something in his own thoughts.

"The crowds," Bucket murmured. "P'raps he saw them as a

127

cover rather than a danger." Then he turned his eyes full on me again. "No, evil might pause but it don't go away. I've learnt that, my boy. I've learnt that." Bucket stood up, smiling weakly. "But we *have* given him *pause*, ain't we lad? So not all is failed if we take proper stock, eh?"

He was talking to me but seemed to be thinking aloud, part justifying his actions, part planning ahead. "I've got all my constables out watching for the wanderings of little ones and making sure they return to their homes, those bodies I can spare from Prince Albert's folly that is! I've had all their Lordships alerted to a Beast with a taste for the children of the aristocracy or those that look like them - as if there are any of them who're not talking of the Beast anyway!"

Bucket wandered mournfully over to the window, looking out at nothing. "Of course, they all seem to think our man is bound to be a low-life creature or a bedlam case, don't they? Well perhaps he is, but they don't think he might be one of their *own*, do they?" He turned to me, to emphasise his train of thought. "Either way, the Beast *knows* we've seen him. Twice. The trouble is, Will, he may even now be taking care to disguise himself again." Bucket sat down and leaned towards me intently. "He's been a gentleman and a Chinaman in our sight, hasn't he? Some say he's appeared as a red-haired dervish on horseback, like Spring-heeled Jack I suppose they mean." He pondered again. "Or even as an old woman, wasn't it?" He leaned back in his chair once more. "Well, maybe. But that don't seem to fit him, if you ask me. What will he be next time, eh? A soldier d'y' think? A sailor?"

"I expect he could complete the nursery rhyme if he'd a mind to," I ventured, risking a joke. "He likes a costume, doesn't he? Perhaps he's just the tailor who makes all the clothes!"

"Well," Bucket smiled. "We can't arrest everyone we see in fancy dress, can we? Though some would seem to like us to." For a moment, I thought his morose mood had lifted, but then he was on his feet again, pacing restlessly.

"I've had all the gentlemen's clubs in the City watched since January," Bucket said. "But if our fellow *is* a gentleman, at least by rank, he seems to have changed his habits for the time being." He smiled a sour smile then and, in the midst of his pained reverie, patted me on the back a little sharply. "But we've not been idle, have we, my boy? That piece of the Devil's flotsam might be my last investigation for the Detective, but I *shall* have him!" he shouted, banging the table, violently. Ma Bucket came in to see what was amiss.

After she left, soothing him with whispers, and half-scolding, half-encouraging me to move Bucket on from his obsession, the Inspector poured himself another sherry and leaned back in his chair.

"Now, my lad," he said at last, a little more calmly. "Perhaps we should move on, eh? What have you got for me? What shall be the case to launch our new Bureau, eh?"

Gladly, I showed him my newly created file of possible new cases. At the top was the letter from Lord Dreadnaught.

"Ah, my boy, a very detective-like choice."

I looked at him blankly.

"The *black book*, my boy. Look at it. I'll play hazard with you that you'll find that name recorded there."

Bucket was back in the old line of thinking again, but I confess that name had been irritating me. I felt sure that I had seen it before. The book was in my inner pocket as always and I turned to it with excitement. I looked to the door for fear that Ma Bucket would come in and scold me for leading Bucket back towards thoughts of the Beast. Leafing through the dense pages, I found the entry that I had made from the list of clients at the Hell Club. There it was: *Dreadnaught. R.*

"I thought it rang a bell, sir, when I saw that letter from Lord Dreadnaught."

"The letter is in the hand of his Lordship *himself*. See?" said Bucket, interrupting me and leaning over to pick up the letter again. " '*Lord Montague Dreadnaught, Oblique House, Mayfair*'. In his *own* hand you see, my lad. The old gentleman *must* be a worried man. The aristocracy don't often dirty their own fingers with such stuff, young Will. But, look, the name you've recorded in the black book is an R, not an M, as you can see. Even so, perhaps there's a fortunate link between the old and the new here, eh, my boy? Mayfair it is!" he said, rising and gathering up his familiar things.

"Mayfair, Inspector!" I smiled. "Perhaps we'll meet the old Duke of Wellington?"

"Perhaps we might, for Dreadnaught was quite a personage in his younger days, you know. He entertained many of the great and noble of his time. He's left his country seat now and resides always in London. The question is, who will *inherit*, eh? Not the lost son, I'll wager."

"Will we just call, Inspector? Don't you want me to write to arrange an appointment?"

"Bless you, my lad, I've already sent word by a boy. Lord Dreadnaught is expecting us at twelve sharp," said Bucket, smiling, standing up to go. I was astonished, but Bucket continued to bustle about for his things, speaking to himself more than to me. "I've had Sergeant Meehan out having a quiet word with the other gentlemen that enjoyed the entertainments of that particular Hell Club we visited. None of them match what we know about the Beast." He turned to me with excitement. "And this name is the last on our list."

Ma Bucket or no, there was no keeping Bucket from this particular track.

# Chapter 12

Lord Dreadnaught's Mayfair home looked like a mansion to me, as Constable Whelks drove us up to the gates. A surly-looking porter opened them for us and glared unpleasantly as we rode past. Past the porter's lodge and bisected by a finely white-gravelled drive, there was a courtyard paved with shiny stones and surrounded by rather overgrown greenery, neglected bushes and topiary that had lost its shape. The place was named Oblique House and oblique it *was*. The house was built at a strange angle, set back to catch the rays of the sun, I supposed. Land in Belgravia was beginning to be scarce but this house still boasted a large garden, if ill-tended in places. As we drove up to the courtyard I caught sight of its lawns and flower beds stretching back beyond the house and, beyond those, its miniature 'wilderness'. We rattled to a stop outside a grand and ornamental door decorated with an enormous knocker in the shape of a gargoyle and with panels of Regency feathers from the days of the old Prince of Wales. Looking up, I could see that the house was four storeys high and so well appointed with windows that one would never have thought there had ever been such a thing as a window tax.

Suddenly, a thin figure appeared out of nowhere to hold the bridle of our horse, and stood staring open-mouthed at us. This was Mad Joe, as we discovered later. And mad he looked too, dressed in a crazy mixture of coloured flannels and wild looking furs - like a hunter from the Americas ready to flay us alive perhaps. He held his head at an angle much like the house and kept tossing his barnet of red hair whilst playing with a brutal looking broad-handled knife. His long red hair fell down onto his face like a mask, but the black slashes of his eyes squinted at us from beneath the swirls of hair as if he were pondering what manner of beasts we were.

We alighted from the cab and dusted ourselves down. Constable Whelks got down too and, looking quizzically at the strange boy, began to look about for where he might stable the horse. As he did, a hefty boy came hurrying up, belatedly, to furnish this information, yelling at Mad Joe as he did so.

"Be off! It ain't your job, bedlam boy!" he shouted. I wondered for a moment if we were going to have some fisticuffs to entertain us, but Mad Joe simply dropped the bridle and walked off with a hard look. The big lad said not a word to us but wheeled round his great girth and led Whelks, cab and horse, to the back of the building where I supposed the stables were.

Bucket and I were met by a big-wigged footman. His name was Alfred, I discovered later. His face was made-up with white paste or powder and his hair dusted over as if he were a footman from a bygone era. What a contemptuous look he welcomed us with! His movements were sharp and impulsive which made study of his face difficult but his thin figure was clearly enough delineated, costumed in the dress of a servant that might have appeared in some grand opera from the last century - or at least my fancy of what such an outfit might be - all wide cuffs and shiny buckles. His hands were sheathed in pale kid gloves over which he shook his wide-frilled cuffs. Most impractical for a footman's uniform, but perhaps the whim of a master from a bygone generation. He scowled as he ushered us into the grand entrance porch of the house, perhaps thinking us beneath him in his fine costume. He gave a short, pugnacious bow and commanded us to wait.

This was not at all what I had expected by way of an introduction to the manners of the swollen and titled.

Nevertheless, Bucket seemed to be beginning his detecting even as we stood. He was measuring the character of the members of the household thus far, and examining the dimensions of the buildings as if with some inner surveying instrument. I resolved to do like-wise, opening my reporter's eye. I already had a mind to pen a little descriptive scene for *Reynolds'* on the habitats of the rich - and I began inwardly composing. As I pondered my treatise, out through the ornamental front door there came a shuffling old man. This was Mr Merit, Lord Dreadnaught's personal man-servant or butler. This old chap was pale-skinned with a limp, a stoop and a face lined by worries. Alfred, who had bestowed on us his reluctant salutations, was a relatively young man in comparison. And yet *his* face was covered with layers of paste as if to cover the sufferings of a lifetime and was closed to enquiry, whereas Merit, undisguised in his age, wore his features open and, apart from his hair, unpasted and undusted with powder. He bowed in a deep, slow, old-fashioned way, quite the opposite of Alfred, and asked us in a tremulous voice if we would follow him. Just then, I noticed two ugly-looking characters in billycock hats appear around the distant corner of the house. They might have been villains from Whitechapel (polishing their jemmies and sizing up the house for a burglary as they leant against the very walls they intended to scale) rather than the gentlemen you would expect to see in a Mayfair mansion. But when I turned to look again, they were gone, as if called to heel by a third party who was out of sight. I noticed Merit glancing uneasily in the same direction.

As we walked through the entrance doors, I saw several footmen standing like wax-works around the room. Merit called to the nearest of these to step forward and take our coats. As the footman did so, like some mechanical soldier, the fellow's glassy expression curled into something of a sneer, though whether aimed at us or at Merit for ordering him from his waxy sleep, I knew not. Bucket, however, had clearly fastened on to the personage who seemed best fitted to be questioned and he wasted no time in engaging the old butler in a friendly chat, quietly depositing a large coin in his hand.

The vastness of the hall into which we stepped took my attention away from their conversation. It had a floor that swept away like an enormous chessboard, making me feel quite dizzy. It was of such a size that it was like being back at London Bridge Station, only without the steam trains. The hall was studded with numerous alcoves housing marble statues or bronze heads or footmen, like the one who had just vanished into an ante-room with our coats. But we did not get far in before our way was barred by yet another man-servant dressed flamboyantly. This was Monsieur De Blarde and he was Lady Dreadnaught's man. We had from him an icy welcome. The old fellow, Merit, came over completely mute as soon as his peer began to speak. De Blarde was costumed in the style of older days, powdered and pasted, but somewhat more foppish than the head footman, Alfred, and with a cruel red mouth - handsome, perhaps, but in a sharp, effeminate way. He was of middling height but thin and, like Alfred, seemed to think himself far too good for the likes of me, or anyone else for that matter. He looked foreign enough to match his name, too. He was quite *un*-servant-like in his manner. Underneath his coat he wore leggings with silver buckles. He too wore pale kid gloves and his shirt cuffs were heavily worked. Merit wore a more simple costume with narrow cuffs, as if he were from a different branch of the serving classes. I liked his branch better. It took no detective skills to realise that neither De Blarde nor Merit had much regard for each other.

"Welcome to Oblique 'ouse," said De Blarde with his quaint French accent. "Per'aps you will wait while I tell my Mistress you are 'ere." He gave an intimidating glance at Merit as he walked past us. The direction he walked in struck me as odd, for surely his mistress did not live in the stables. Bucket seemed untroubled enough, nonetheless. He continued his conversation with Merit as soon as De Blarde was gone. Whilst they talked, I was curious to see what De Blarde was doing. I turned to peer through the huge windows, or at what I could make out through the small gaps in the heavy, brown velvet drapes. I saw De Blarde talking urgently with Alfred. There were bobbing billycock hats to be seen too, but the exchange was brief, for soon they had vanished from my eye line. When I turned back, Bucket was asking Merit about the comings and goings of the household.

"And how many horses are stabled here, Mr Merit? A good few I'm guessing. And plenty of carriages, no doubt? A cabriolet or two, eh?" The old fellow's manner seemed to lighten, as if only the evil eye of De Blarde had been worrying him. "Now, my old Uncle Toby," Bucket continued, "did I tell you he was in the service line too? There's a coincidence for you! Twelve horses they kept where he was man-servant. Carriages a-plenty! A cabriolet and a brougham at least. Lord Grimshaft's estate it was. By the end of his time, old Toby'd been promoted to be Lord Grimshaft's personal secretary. Personal secretary, no less! Do you happen to know his Lordship?" smiled Bucket. "And the devil if you haven't just the look of him, sir - my Uncle Toby I mean, not Lord Grimshaft!" Bucket laughed. "Just the look, indeed. In fact," he said, in a confidential tone, "I shouldn't be surprised if Lord Montague Dreadnaught didn't have the same thing in mind for you, Mr Merit, sir. Oh yes! I shall certainly mention your solicitous manner to his Lordship when I see him.

Cab goes out often, you were saying?"

"Quieter just recently, sir," the old fellow said in a near whisper. "If you'll come this way, Inspector Bucket, Lord Montague will see you in the Library."

"Quieter, eh?" Bucket never gave up once he got his teeth into a bone. "Just the spit of him, you are, Mr Merit. The spit of old Toby." Bucket was incorrigible. He always seemed to have a relative in just the same job as *whoever* it was he was questioning!

"Why," Bucket went on, getting into full stride, "my Uncle Toby was left quite a nice little endowment in Lord Grimshaft's will too. He liked to chat about old Lord Grimshaft's doings. Quite proud of him he was. How is Lord Dreadnaught, by the way? Poorly, I hear?"

I lost track of the conversation here, because I had to mind my step around the grand furniture that we were passing on our way across the giant chessboard floor of the reception hall. This was my first visit to a Mayfair mansion and I felt a little overcome. I could imagine my story in *Reynolds' Weekly* now: *"The Opulence of Oblique House"*. Once upon a time, perhaps in happier days, I told myself, this room might have been awash with light. I could just imagine how the way that the house was set back would have enabled it to catch every angle of the sun as it progressed through the day. Some splinters of light still sliced in here and there, in spite of the great dark curtains hung deliberately to keep them out. Little Catherine wheels of light still jumped up and down over the silk walls. They danced around in the halo of a heavy silver chandelier that was hanging down over us like the crown of an eastern potentate. However, it was the magnificence of the marble staircase curling up to the right and left that took my breath away. I had never seen such a thing in Woolwich,

Deptford, nor Chatham neither, you will not be surprised to hear. I nearly cricked my neck looking up at its sweeping height. When the decorated clock started chiming, I almost fell over. Then I came up face-to-face with a tiger's head looking down at me as if it would once have happily enjoyed me for its breakfast. Or perhaps it was taking more of a fancy to the antelope's head mounted on the opposite wall.

As Merit led us upwards, I paused under the very guns that might have bagged these beasts. I had never seen such blunderbusses. On either side of the gun case were full length portraits of two handsome women. They were of two almost identical beauties, but one seemed more natural, if such a distinction can be made. The other was harder in the face. In fact, I would say that the woman in this painting, or the painter himself, was attempting an imitation of the other lovely creature. Apart from the difference in the softness of their faces, they were almost doubles of each other - sisters perhaps. There was one other difference: the harder-faced sister was wearing a rather manly signet ring. I was just investigating this, when Merit called.

"If you'd come this way, sir!" he said nervously, as if he were worried about leaving either of us alone. For Bucket had already scaled the first flight and was investigating some other paintings that reached as high as the ceiling. Merit was looking anxiously over the baroquely gilded stair rails and then returned to escort me to where Bucket was waiting. Bucket gave me a conspiratorial grin and then smiled broadly at the line of portraits on the walls above us - portraits of Dreadnaughts past. Their gimlet eyes seemed to be saying, "What are you doing here, Jakesbere? Get back to Chatham!" Bucket stood beneath these contentedly, however, and as we grew level with him he knelt down nonchalantly and picked up a half-covered canvas frame that lay against the wall. He lifted the edge of the covering before Merit could stop him. A portrait of a young man appeared.

"Ah, the disgraced son, eh, Mr Merit?"

Merit looked as if he would have liked to snatch the picture back but Bucket was holding it out of his way for at least long enough for me to consider its features. It was a portrait of a gentleman who might have been in the thespian line. The hair was dark and lustrous, making the gentleman look like one of our romantic poets - Mr Coleridge in his portrait as a young man, perhaps, or Lord Byron in the picture where he is dressed up as a Greek Prince. The gentleman's hands were elegant and expressive, rather like the ones in the picture of the soft-eyed beauty in the hall.

"Please, sir, I wish you wouldn't," Merit said, taking the picture back at last.

"What is it, Mr Merit?" Bucket asked. "Will someone be displeased that I've seen the displaced son? Who'll be angry, eh? Not Lord Montague, surely?" Merit gave no answer but looked wildly around him. "Don't worry, Mr Merit," Bucket continued. "I think your friend is still in conference with his mistress." Merit covered the portrait again, leaning it carefully back in its place against the wall. "A sad business, eh?" Bucket sighed. "Who would have thought that Lord Dreadnaught would have such a thankless child?"

"Not thankless," said Merit in a whisper.

"No?" Bucket replied, already moving across to another picture, a dull landscape of trees and fields. "Not partial to landscapes much myself, Mr Merit. What about you? Rather hastily hung too. Very hasty." He looked Merit directly in the eyes. "I don't believe it was you that had the hanging of that picture, Mr Merit," Bucket said seriously. "No, I don't believe that at all. Am I right? You'd be a man of care, now, I'm sure of that! You'd do the job as it should be done, as would befit the house of a Lord of the Realm. Well, just like my Uncle Toby would." Bucket spoke almost conspiratorially here. "Not long since the other was taken down, was it? The picture of the son, I mean?"

Merit made no reply, but we seemed to be at our terminus anyway. He knocked on the mahogany doors facing us. They opened onto shadows and in the shades stood Alfred, the footman who had met our cab with his contemptuous countenance. I recognised his long nose and his paste-like complexion. When he stepped out into the light for a second, I caught his look. It was a look I had once been given by a drunken labourer when I had bumped into him in Woolwich High Street – as if a mere clearing of your throat would give him enough offence to feel he was entitled to throttle you. But perhaps it was Merit that Alfred's evil eye was focused on. It was not a look becoming of a servant or a gentleman.

# Chapter 13

The doors to Lord Dreadnaught's library were opened and Merit announced us in a quavery voice: "Inspector Bucket and his assistant Mr Jakesbere, my Lord." He closed the doors on us, creating a world of darkness. I thought that Alfred had retired with Merit at first and I felt somewhat concerned for the old fellow. Alfred looked as if he could be unpleasant. But then I felt a tingling of my spine as if someone had stolen in behind us and was hiding in the shadows to eavesdrop.

When my eyes adjusted to the gloom, I could see the old Lord tucked away at the end of the long, grey room. He'd shut himself into a little hole at the end of the huge library like a blind old spider in its web. It might have been a handsome room once. There was a grey mountain of ancient volumes covering the walls from top to bottom - but it was more the musty smell of decaying paper and dust than the sight of them that I had noticed. Dreadnaught sat like a dark crab covered by a shell of gloom.

"Don't stir yourself, sir," said Bucket, speaking out of the gloom like a ghost. "These occasions are always difficult for a gentleman such as yourself. For you are sensitive to a hurt, sir. *That* I can perceive. Gentlemen such as yourself have a feeling way of conceiving such hurts that speaks of honourable distinction - of a delicacy, sir, much to be admired. And I do admire and honour it, sir. Indeed I do. Yet, humble as I must be in stating it," he continued, "I have been privy to the sensitivities of noble families before, sir. You must think of me as an organ of hearing close to your own thoughts. I speak boldly I know, sir, but you needs must unburden to me your deepest grievances in the knowledge that I, Inspector Bucket of the Detective, am but an agent in the employ of yourself, Montague Dreadnaught, Honourable Lord of the Realm. May we sit, sir?"

His Lordship seemed stunned. Nonetheless, one could tell he liked this sort of talk. He waved his hand in a lordly gesture. At least I think he did. I took my lead from Bucket, found a chair in the dark and sat.

"I am most reassured, Inspector Bucket," began his Lordship in a straining, breathless voice, taking great gasping mouthfuls of air between every few words. Nevertheless this was a voice that might once have commanded with authority. "Your manner is most gracious, Inspector Bucket. My friend, Sir Leicester, said you would be thus."

"How is Sir Leicester, sir? Well, I hope? In spite of his still too recent sufferings, I mean?"

"No. Not well, Bucket. Indeed barely out of mourning since the demise of his fair lady."

"I'm very sorry for that, sir," Bucket said graciously.

"Yet he is well enough, Inspector, to send word to me via his secretary of your good reputation. He led me to believe that, that you are a man of, of ..."

"Discretion, sir? Yes, sir. I think my actions over many years may verify that."

"And?" The old Lord seemed to nod in *my* direction.

"You wish references for my assistant, Mr Jakesbere, sir? Of course you do. A half-wit sir. He understands very little of what is said to him, but Mrs Bucket and I have taken pity on him and hope to put him to good use. We've taught him to write, sir, and that is of some agency to me in my work - though his scribing is often just a nasty scrawl. You must see him, sir, as merely a shadow of me. An engine of my brain. Pay him no regard at all, sir."

142

"See? We can hardly expect anyone to see at all in here, my Lord." A musical female voice pierced through the gloom and shook me out of my goldfish pose, and my alarm at being called a half-wit. A little false light came in with her. This was Lady Dreadnaught, of course. Her stony-faced man-servant, De Blarde, came behind her and stood in the shadows – unless he'd been there all along. When my eyes adjusted again, I could see that she was the living image of one of the paintings from the lower gallery. She spoke in a rich, round voice but there was something else in the mix of her voice that might have suggested she had also spent some time in a foreign country.

"Why did you not inform me that the Inspector was here, Montague?" the lady asked, abruptly.

The old Lord straightened up like a soldier caught slouching. She was a beauty, I must say, if a slightly faded one now that she had passed into her middle years. All the light in the room seemed to cluster around the glitter she gave out, a glimmery glow from all the jewellery hanging from ear and neck and finger.

"You know I don't want to trouble you over my problems with Richard, my dear," said the lord, wearily.

"Nonsense," she replied sharply. Then she nodded in our direction. "- Inspector Bucket, I believe?"

Bucket had stood up when her ladyship came in and I did likewise. Bucket bowed, as did I - half-wit as I was.

"Pray be seated." As she spoke, De Blarde crept out and pushed a chair under his mistress and then crawled back into the shadows. The silver buckles of his costume and the powder in his hair caught the light a little for a moment before he became invisible again. Her Ladyship sat herself down where a splinter of daylight hit her. The dust motes did a dance in the haze. The ring on her finger gave out a rosy shine.

"You must forgive my husband, Inspector. He has not been well. He suffers much from a migraine and from a stomach pain, and he is nearly blind. His eyes are pained by much light. We must keep everything shadowy for him."

"My dear ..."

"Don't worry so, my Lord," she interrupted. "You know that if we must keep you in the dark for your sight's sake, we will willingly do so."

"I have grown accustomed to the darkness, it is true, Inspector," Lord Dreadnaught wheezed breathlessly. "My last wife loved to sit in the light. But since she passed away I have grown blinder and blinder and the light of day pains me. Now it is Lady Dreadnaught who is my sole balm and my only illumination."

"You are too gallant, my Lord. You tire yourself with your courtesy," she said, bowing at his compliment. They had a very formal manner with each other, I thought, but perhaps that was just the way with the nobility. Lord Montague carried on in his whispery, strained voice.

"I am often ill. Sometimes with stomach cramps and then with dryness, raging thirsts, vomiting. But you will think me an old hypochondriac. You have not come to hear about my illnesses, my domestic arrangements."

"Indeed not, Montague," his wife agreed. "But tell me, Inspector Bucket, do you not think my dear Montague's friends must have once mocked him mightily for allowing his furnishings to be spoiled by such a profusion of natural light? You must wonder that Lord Montague's first wife could have been so profligate, Inspector. She was too wasteful with your goodness, my Lord," she said, turning to her husband. "At any

144

rate, *I* can tolerate a little shadow to please you. But as you say, Montague, the Inspector will not want to hear our household tittle-tattle. Let us, if we must, proceed to business, Inspector, for you see my husband is exhausted already."

I fished in my inner pocket for the notebook and, finding a finger of light, licked my pencil to start my note-taking.

"My son…" said the wheezy old Lord, but he didn't get much further.

"He has absconded, Inspector," her Ladyship interrupted." He has left in disgrace. Lord Montague will not communicate this to you but his son has grieved him to the heart. My husband is too proud a man to give you anything but the bare facts of the case, Inspector. But I am his wife and I feel how deep the cuts are."

"My dear -" his Lordship gasped.

"Well, I have said it. I shall not speak another word." She reached in her sleeve for a handkerchief to dab her eyes but, upon not finding one, was furnished with one by De Blarde, who jumped out with a handful of blue silks. She gave him a sidelong glance as he dipped back into his shadowy corner.

"Pray, ignore me, Inspector," she said dabbing at her eyes, "but I cannot contain my emotions when I see such a fine and worthy gentleman as my husband scorned by such a thankless son. Ignore me." There was more dabbing, and the old man tried again - his speech becoming more hesitant and fragmented as he struggled.

"My son has disappointed me, Inspector. Following pursuits that a man of my generation objects to. The path he has chosen is not in keeping with the Dreadnaughts. He ignored my wishes for a good marriage." Lord Dreadnaught hesitated for a moment before gathering  breath for his next words. "Challenged my authority as a father.  Has now eloped, with a common servant girl! Ran after her most dishonourably." He looked towards his wife, obviously struggling with his speech. "Her Ladyship is correct. He was so good once. A loving boy but, wilful. Now he is nothing but im, im…"

"Immoral, sir?" Bucket asked bluntly.

The old man nodded, sadly. "I am not prudish, Inspector. No. But I talk of wild disorder and, de, degenerate habits. It pains me to describe my son thus." Her Ladyship dabbed at her eyes again, looking down into her kerchief the while. "Drinking. Uncontrolled. Gambling debts. Bath houses. Opium and opium dens," Lord Montague continued haltingly.

Her Ladyship made a noise as if she might sneeze with the stench of this reported degeneracy.

"I am sorry, my dear," the old fellow wheezed, noticing her distress.

"And have you some evidence of this behaviour, Lord Montague?" asked Bucket briskly.

Dreadnaught nodded. "Bills. Invoices. Demands. Letters. Reports…" His voice was sounding more and more like a strangled bird. "A torment to me. Lewd acts. Sexual licence."

"And you've reports of this too, have you, my Lord?"

His Lordship gave a nod.

"Yes," Bucket continued. "Doubtless you have, or it would be a calumny of your own son, wouldn't it now, my Lord?"

Bucket's voice had an ironic edge to it, I felt. Her Ladyship seemed to agree with my interpretation because she looked uncomfortably away into the corner of the room.

"This is quite a list of heinous crimes, Lord Montague," Bucket said. "A long list for just one man to have committed. Can he *really* have been such a, such a beast? And yet he was once such a loving son, you say? To what cause do you attribute this change in your son, sir?" Lady Dreadnaught seemed about to speak but Bucket hurried on. "You seem to be suggesting it might have been the servant girl who was to blame. But, my Lord, do you really believe that such a weakness in your son *could* have been present, raised as he was to fulfil his obligations to a family of such antiquity as your own, Lord Montague? I've seen the portraits that grace your walls, Lord Dreadnaught. On those walls lie the images and the traditions and the examples of Dreadnaughts past. Could one little servant girl have turned over the values of all those generations?" Bucket drove on. "Strange indeed if the progeny of such an illustrious family as yours, disciplined from birth and by blood to raise his head above the common, was affected by such a weak cause."

"The girl was a hussy, Inspector," Lady Dreadnaught said sharply. "I will not mince my words, Montague." She turned to Bucket, fiercely. "I will be frank even if my husband will not be, mere woman as I am. You are a man of the world, Inspector. There is nothing we can say that would shock you."

Bucket looked but was silent. Lady Dreadnaught went on.

"This girl, this gardener's daughter, was a very devil. I cannot but think it is her wild Irish blood that made her so bold. She would do all she could do to deliberately entice gentlemen of noble birth, Inspector. Everything. *Of course*, she was encouraged by her father. He saw some profit in it no doubt, some advantage by playing on the soft heart of his master, my husband."

"My dear ..." the old man tried but little came out.

"I stand corrected, my Lord," she answered him, "but it is important that Inspector Bucket should know how you have been abused." She turned to Bucket again." And I speak not just of a gardener, Inspector. There have been - and there still *are*, Inspector – *other* servants who think that length of employment

147

gives them privileges that excuse indiscretions, who think that their deranged and dangerous behaviour will be tolerated by His Lordship because of a sense of duty and honour that goes back generations. A gentleman of less kindness and liberality than Lord Dreadnaught would never have tolerated such: a man-servant who has not followed the rules of duty and obedience and a so-called stable boy whose mental state is a danger to us all."

"My dear," the old man wheezed. "We discussed these differences before. Inspector Bucket does not need to hear such stuff."

"Perhaps not, my Lord," she started again, "but I *do* tell him so that he knows the conditions that we have lived under - as if *we* are the servants and *they* the masters!"

"Indeed, ma'am," said Bucket, "though perhaps we could stay for a moment with the misdemeanours of the gardener. You were saying, my Lord?" Bucket's casual manner of dealing with Lady Dreadnaught took my breath away. But she would not be halted.

"I'll say not another word. Gavelstone was a drunkard and a thief and his daughter a red-haired witch. There, I have finished."

There was a tense silence. I carried on scratching in my book whilst everyone remembered to breathe. The old Lord seemed in a great deal of discomfort, as a matter of fact. His lady poured him a glassful of water from a decanter by his side. He gulped at it, coughing in pain and distress. She wiped his mouth for him as if he were a child.

"I'm sorry this interview is distressing you, my Lord, my Lady," Bucket said, "but if I am to find your son I must ask you these questions. Forgive me, madam, but might the strong feelings you've just been describing have been caused, perhaps, by some animosity betwixt you and Sir Montague Dreadnaught's son?"

Her Ladyship gave a gulp. She dabbed her eyes again.

"Perhaps," continued Bucket, "he harboured feelings of some jealousy towards you on behalf of his own dear departed mother when you first married Lord Montague? That might be so, might it not?" asked the Inspector quizzically. "Mr Richard Dreadnaught is not *your* son after all, is he ma'am?"

The lady was a pale shape in the semi-darkness but it seemed to me that her complexion became even more ghostlike as Bucket spoke.

"Forgive me, sir," said Bucket, giving the Lord a hint of a bow. "But it is not a secret, is it sir, that there was another, an earlier, Lady Dreadnaught? Your first wife, I mean. More than fifteen or sixteen years ago, it must have been. I remember it well, sir. *The Times* carried an obituary. Your first wife was but a young girl herself when she died, I believe. Forgive me for recounting these painful facts, but she died, I believe, whilst giving birth to your daughter. Your second child I heard it was, my Lord. Is that correct?"

A dewy light seemed caught in the old man's eyes. "Enough!" he said, managing a tone of authority at last. "Such questioning is intolerable, impertinent!"

"Forgive me, my Lord," replied Bucket in a calm voice, "but, I repeat, you have asked me to find your son. He may not wish to be found. He may not wish to return. I must ask such questions, for the answers may be material to the case. They may explain his state of mind and indicate what he might be doing and where he might be."

"Spare me now, I beg you!" the old man cried, fully coherent now, but with a pain in his voice altogether beyond simple

149

discomfort. "I *do* wish my son returned. My wife didn't want ... me to call you. Perhaps she was right. She said it would open old wounds. And yet. And yet. He is still my son. The child of a happier time. He will be a prodigal son on his return."

Lady Dreadnaught looked away into the shadows as if she wanted to run off there. She thought better of it and got up to sit at the old gentleman's feet instead.

"You overtax yourself, Montague," she said. "You are not well. You must not make yourself sick again." She looked up at Bucket. "Inspector, you can see how my husband is struggling to find breath."

"I must at least say this - " The old lord seemed determined to continue, a determination which gave rise to a movement in the shadows behind us. "It is true that my son and I have argued almost since the day my first wife died. She died in childbirth. A daughter, as you said." His voice faded.

"A weak child. Weak in the body, weak in the mind," Lady Dreadnaught continued, impatiently. She turned to her husband and he gave an almost imperceptible nod. "By the time I knew her she was prone to hysteria and fits of madness."

The old man struggled to speak again. "Her birth was not worth the death of her mother." But the effort was too much for him and he subsided into silence. Lady Dreadnaught laid her hand on his arm.

"Lord Montague was forced to have recourse to the alienist," her Ladyship continued for him. "We had no choice but to have her committed to a sanatorium for the mentally unfit."

"I see," Bucket said in a cold voice. "And what did your son have to say about this, Lord Montague?"

"Lord Montague's son had been away at Oxford, Inspector," Lady Dreadnaught replied. "But he had given up his studies to continue his scandalous behaviour, as an actor in the common theatre."

"Shameful," muttered the old man.

"My husband and his son quarrelled. Lord Montague refused to acknowledge Richard as his son whist he continued to disregard his father's wishes for his future." She turned to the old man who seemed to be trying to speak again. "Do not speak, Montague. Just nod to confirm that I speak your words truthfully. That will suffice, will it not, Inspector?" Her Ladyship looked icily at Bucket. Lord Dreadnaught clasped her hand and nodded. "It was during Richard's absence," she continued, "that these unfortunate incidents of insanity occurred with his sister. He learnt of his sister's incapacity through..." she hesitated, " through another source. Then Richard wrote to say that he would return. Lord Montague forbade this. Richard challenged my husband's judgement on this, as on many things. He has rejected all the obligations that he owed his father, as a son." The old lord's head had sunk deeply into his chest. Her Ladyship gripped his hand and continued. "He gave up his place at Oxford University and we believe he is now intending to pursue a scandalous engagement with the daughter of the gardener - the girl that I have already mentioned, Inspector."

"I see," Bucket said quietly.

Her Ladyship kissed the old man's hand and straightened out her silks as she stood to address Bucket again.

"You are correct, Inspector, when you say that Mr Richard Dreadnaught is not my son. I fear I am not worthy to be a replacement for such a mother as he once had, nor for such a paragon of a wife as Montague now misses so grievously."

"My dear -" the old man struggled to interrupt her.

"Though, God help me," she said passionately, "I have done all

I can to take her place."

"My dear, you have and are …"

"I have tried to be a mother to him, Montague."

"My dear, my dear, you mustn't -" but the old lord gasped to a close.

Lady Dreadnaught seemed to be actually weeping. There was an embarrassing silence - though Bucket sat through it like a statue.

"And, yes, Inspector," she said after dabbing her eyes with her handkerchief, "Richard *did* take against me. No, don't stop me, Montague. You *know* it is true! From the first moment of our acquaintance he took against me and tried to drive a wedge between us. But I shall be silent if you wish it." She walked away and sat meekly on a chair under the window.

"Well, Lord Montague, Lady Dreadnaught," said Bucket at last. "I thank you for your frankness." Bucket stood, and I did too. "In normal circumstances to track an absconding person would be a matter of some difficulty. They might have gone abroad. They might have disappeared into the country or into the depths of the city. But the information you have afforded me tells me otherwise. Your son clearly has a powerful tie of attachment to this young daughter of the gardener. So, if we find the girl, we find the son. Or so it might seem, eh? Now, do you know where the girl has gone, Lord Montague?"

"No, Inspector." The lady answered for him. "Both gardener and daughter were dismissed."

"I understand. Well. A little more difficult then," said Bucket, taking a few paces up and down the room. "I shall need details of your son's movements and habits if I am to trace him, my Lord. I shall need access to his rooms and his things, and the names of his friends and acquaintances. I shall need a likeness too. He is a modern gentleman, no doubt? Perhaps he has had a daguerreotype taken? If, as you say, he is of the theatrical persuasion he may have gone in for such a thing. I hear such contraptions are very fashionable. Mrs Bucket was after persuading me to sit myself, as it happens." Bucket ceased pacing and turned to the old man. "But if not, perhaps you have a portrait? A miniature, possibly?" He looked across the room at the figure of Lady Dreadnaught, now a silhouette in the corner's gloom. "Perhaps a smaller version of the portrait that has been removed from your walls, my Lord?"

Things were tense before, but now the rigidity in the air seemed palpable. The old man's head turned towards his wife, trying hard to see her in the darkness, I thought.

"I only removed it so that it would not grieve you, Montague," she said softly, standing and walking towards him. "Please don't be angry with me. As in all things, I removed it only in concern for your feelings."

There was a shuffling noise behind us. Something in the corner, in the shadows - a flash of something silvery. Bucket did not appear to heed it. His concentration was on everything in front of him.

"Forgive me, Lord Montague," he said. "I had no idea that you hadn't given the order for the removal of the portrait yourself."

Dreadnaught shook himself. "Yes Inspector," he said, obviously in answer to an earlier question. His voice was fading now. "A picture of my son and what you will, to find Richard."

"I'm grateful, my Lord," Bucket bowed. "I shall need to talk to all the members of your household, of course, for they may know something of your son's disappearance and whereabouts. I will also need to look into some rooms."

"*Rooms,* Inspector Bucket?" Lady Dreadnaught said sharply. "Why the rooms? Surely there is no need for such intrusion?"

"He may have left a clue somewhere, Lady Dreadnaught. A clue to his whereabouts, I mean, madam. A note. A letter from the girl. Perhaps something she has left herself that might be found in the servants' quarters that might disclose his whereabouts."

"You are aware, Inspector," her Ladyship said in her steeliest tone, "that the associates of Gavelstone will be prejudiced against my husband?" Bucket ignored her comment and took up his stick from the side table.

"I am beholden to you, your Ladyship, your Lordship," he said, bowing. "Rest assured in my judgement as well as my discretion. I shall do all I can to please. I am not, in this, acting as Inspector Bucket of the Detective, am I? I am not investigating a crime now, am I?" He paused. "I am merely tracing a lost son and returning him, if I can, to the bosom of his family home." He looked at Lady Dreadnaught. "Am I correct in stating the limits of my commission, my Lady?"

Her Ladyship failed to answer. The wheezing voice of Sir Montague spoke up again.

"Your fee?" he asked.

"Don't stir yourself, Lord Dreadnaught. These indelicate things, though necessary, will be dealt with by Mr Jakesbere here. Once I've instructed him he acts like a machine, sir, a veritable piece of mechanics, sir. Half-witted as he is." He indicated in my direction. "But in that fog that he sits in sir, indeed *because* of that mist, we may trust to his discretion, sir, as you may trust in mine. No, nothing will pierce Mr Jakesbere's fog. Nothing will come out that I have not put in, will it my boy?" Bucket said, turning to me. I gawped as per usual. "Forgive his dullness, my

154

Lord and Lady." Bucket gave a last bow and turned to the door. "I bid you good day, for now."

De Blarde appeared, as if from nowhere, to open the door. In the sudden light, I saw another's legs. Already her Ladyship was engaged in anxious whispers. Mr Merit did not appear again.

The light of day on the stairs, faint as it was, was a blessed relief. De Blarde followed us out after a word or two with his mistress. He looked irritated. Bucket started chatting to him just as he had done earlier with Merit, but De Blarde did not seem very inclined to be sociable.

"Thank you, Monsieur De Blarde," Bucket said. "I hope we haven't inconvenienced you and your masters too much. It must be a great trouble to you - this business, eh? What with the riding out in your master's carriage and the returning it for your Lady's use. It must make rather too much of a horsy odour in the dining room on the return of the driver, I should think." I had not a clue as to what Bucket was insinuating, but De Blarde seemed to know, for his powdered face became even whiter.

Whelks was waiting for us, ready mounted on top of the cab, when we emerged. As we were about to ride off there was a wild yell and a scurry of activity from the corner of the house. It was the hefty stable-boy hurtling along in a panic. He seemed to have been rolling in the earth by the looks of him.

"Get him away from me!" he was yelling. "He's gone cracked again! He ought to be locked up!" And Mad Joe appeared, lurching after him. Joe's red hair was sticking up, and he too was covered in filth. His head was shaking in a fury. He held his ugly knife aloft and was waving it as if he meant to do mischief. The yelling boy was broad in girth and had arms like a wrestler's but he was shaking in fright, nonetheless. Whelks was about to get down to intervene, but, before he could, Mad Joe started twitching more violently and grinding his teeth like a bedlam case. He seemed to be foaming at the mouth. The next minute, the poor fellow was flat on his back with his eyes rolling and his tongue flicking around in his mouth like a snake. What shocked me was not so much the violence of the fit but the cruel way that the other lad just laughed as Joe wriggled around in the dirt of the roadway.

"Look at him! Just look at him!" he was laughing. Three or four men appeared from the stable area then - gardeners or other workers on the land perhaps. One grizzled man, whom I was later to know as Ebenezer, knelt down and shoved a stick under Joe's tongue.

"Go and tell old Merit," Ebenezer spat out. A man sauntered back to the house without hurry. When the mad boy became still, two others swept him up like a puppet and carried him off, head lolling between them, into the nether-reaches of the mansion.

"Been a-teasing that Joe all the time I been in that stable!" Whelks said, with a sigh, but to no one in particular. We settled ourselves in the cab, quite glad to get away by now. As I climbed up I noticed that we were being watched: by Alfred with his look of contempt and De Blarde with his stony eye. And then there were the ugly coves in the billycock hats that had kept well out of our way - but had clearly been looking on all along.

The cab jerked forward and left me on the floor, as usual. It was whilst I was on the floor, with Bucket looking down at me shaking his head, that I felt sure I heard a new or, perhaps, just a different voice. It was somebody shouting across the courtyard, calling out commands or threats in an angry voice. I half-wittedly wondered where I had heard such a voice before.

# Chapter 14

Returning to Vauxhall, I was able to forget our uncomfortable engagement at Mayfair in the pleasant company of a certain young lady. I'd managed to steal a half hour alone with Phoebe in the parlour. Bucket, meanwhile, was closeted away with Sergeant Meehan. He was clearly intrigued by Lady Dreadnaught and wanted Meehan to make enquiries about her Ladyship's history before she had married Lord Dreadnaught. Meehan was also bringing Bucket up to date with the movements of various members of the Hell Club's clientele that we had listed in the black book. They were engaged for some while. Sparrow had left a note with Hetty, reminding me to meet up with him at *The White Lion* and, as Sparrow's note made our meeting sound important and Phoebe was called upon to help out with the daily chores of the house, I dragged myself away, albeit with reluctance.

Once I was on my way back to St Giles, there was a certain pleasure to be had in thinking about how far I had come since I had left Chatham. There were my stories for Mr Reynolds and my work with Bucket – not to mention being in the bosom of the Bucket family. But most of all, there was Phoebe. I know Sparrow was keen to brag to me about Alice but now I had some bragging of my own to do.

Just before five, I hopped off a crowded omnibus at the Alms Houses, full of the joys of spring. *The White Lion* was smoky and noisy already, what with early finishers from the markets and late starters for the evening factory shifts. I could not help noticing an old drunk making an exhibition of himself in the corner, supping more heavy porter than he could cope with. But there was no sign of Sparrow. I hoped he wasn't going to let me down after I'd sacrificed time with Phoebe to come and meet him. I asked the landlady – a rolling fat woman with a cheery smile – and she pointed me towards the back parlour. This was a room she kept for her workers: a tidy place with flowers scattered around in little blue and white jugs. Here it was that I found Sparrow. His sweetheart, Alice, was with him and they looked as if they had eyes for no one else, spooning over their tea cups. I felt it wrong to spoil their tete-a-tete and nearly did a turnabout, but Sparrow caught sight of me and was all jolliness. He pushed back a chair for me and started making formal introductions. This brought out the roses in Alice's cheeks. It made a change to see someone else colouring up other than myself!

"Now then, Alice," said Sparrow, "ain't we goin' to have these 'ere teas. I 'spect Jakes is parched, ain't you old man, bussing it here all the way from Vauxhall?"

"We will in a mo, Archibald," said Alice, "but I'm still waiting on my little helper to bring us in a jug of milk, so we shall have to wait. But meanwhile we can tell Mr Jakesbere why we've asked him to come, can't we, Archibald?"

"You must call me Will," I said, all smiles, "that is, if I might call you Alice. Or you can call me Jakes if you like. Though, I don't suppose it's a polite name for ladies to use." Alice smiled in return but Sparrow blustered on.

"Oh, blow me down if I ain't got a memory like a colander, ain't I Alice? O' course, he don't know yet, do he?"

"Not if you hasn't told him, Archibald, how could he?" said Alice, sensibly enough.

"Well," I said, "come on Sparrow, old bird, do put a pal out of his misery, you're keeping me on tenterhooks here! What's your news?"

"Well, Jakesy, I shan't beat about the bush no furtherer, shall I

Alice? What do you think, Jakes? Me and Alice, eh? Me and Alice!"

"You and Alice what?" I grinned.

"Why, me and Alice is engaged to be married, that's what!"

I jumped up and gave him a good thump on the backbone.

"Why, Sparrow, you're a dark horse and nothing but! My heartiest congrats to you, Archie!" This brought us all to our feet. I shook his hand with extra gusto whilst we all laughed. "And congratulations to you too, of course, Miss Alice!" I said, and then there was more shaking of daintier hands and more laughing. "Why, Sparrow," I said, "I shall order us a drink to toast your engagement!"

"Thank you, Will," said Alice, "but that's what the tea's for, ain't it, Archibald? We mean to celebrate like a respectable couple - with *tea* - don't we?"

Sparrow looked a bit glum for a moment but he soon perked up at the sight of Alice's loving looks.

"And now tell Will the other, Archibald, dear."

"What oth'? Why, o' *course*, Alice, sweetest. The other! Jakes, you don't mind, do you? About your *room* I mean? That room of yours at Mrs Peckers, Jakey?" As usual, once Sparrow had started on a speech, his words were coming out in one gush. "You see, what with me 'aving to travel back to King's Cross every night, to the Station House, I mean, it's a bit inconvenient now that I'm docked at St Giles all the time. I mean, well, it's quite a way, old chum! Quite a pretty way, as you know, Jakesy - especially as me and Alice shall be seeing each other a lot more, in the engagement line I mean, you know, Jakes." Here he gave her a mischievous look and she gave another charming blush. "And what with her being here in Mrs Beddows' employ with a room to herself an' all, well, it would be more convenient for us both if,

159

well, if *I* could have *your* room on a permanent basis." I was about to answer but Sparrow's flood of words continued. "Putting not too bold a point upon it. I mean, you know I took your room, temporary like, when you went out to Bucket's and you being out of favour with Mrs Peckers and me being *in*, by virtue of my being a *respecrable* police constable and all that," he laughed. "*And* engaged to be married to boot and it being quite nearby an' all, your room I mean, quite nearby, old Jakes. And Inspector Bucket himself wanted me near at hand see, so he let me off my bachelor accommodation. Well that's why it's all working out so proper, ain't it? Well, what do you think, old man?"

"I've not a clue what you're asking me, old bird but if it's that you want to stay at Mrs P's you're welcome. And if Mrs Peckers will have you, Sparrow, she's *welcome* to you!" *I* laughed now. "I should think she's given up on me months ago. She won't expect me back. As it happens, Bucket has paid off my bills for me, so that I can live with him permanently. What do you think of that, eh? Old Ma Peckers probably thinks I'm rotting away in a gaol in Newgate like some terrible felon!"

"Well, to tell you the truth, Jakes, that's just what she *does* think," grinned Sparrow, "and, well, to be honest with you, she's already taken me on as a proper lodger. But I wanted your … your … What's the word, Jakesy, you know! Always good with words is Jakes, Alice …"

"Approval is what he means, Will," said Alice.

"Well, you have it even if you don't need it!" I said with glee.

"But that wasn't what I meant, Archibald, was it?" said Alice, giving him a nudge.

"Eh? Oh!" he spluttered, and then he stood up, straightening his suit.

"And I wants to ask you, –William, if you would do me the honour of standing up for me? As my Best Man. At my wedding, I mean. When we have it, that is."

I said I would and that I could not think of a finer man I would rather stand up for on such a great day. And that started us all off on another round of standing up in the present and shaking hands and laughing as if the very day had come already.

When we'd recovered and sat down again, flushed, Alice said:

"And you must come to tea at my aunt's in Camden, by way of a proper engagement party. Will you come? Will you? We would be very obliged, wouldn't we, Archibald? You can bring a friend if you want," she said looking me in the eyes. "Are you courting? I expect you've got a young lady you might want to bring?"

"Alice!" Sparrow spluttered, "Don't say such things! Don't you know that old Jakes here is a confirmed and most particular old bachelor, ain't you Jakes? We may as well swop places all round and let him have my dorm with the single chaps at Hunter Place, eh? 'cept he's not in it for the copperin' - he means to make a proper go of it scribblin'. He writes for *Reynolds' News*, Alice, as I told you." Turning back to me he began to splutter anew. "Jakes, with a young *lady*? Why, he'd never no sooner go out with a girl than be shot from a cannon, would you Jakes? It'd make him blush like a bunch of beetroot!"

"If you must know, Sparrow," I said with a good deal of justified irritation, "I *do* have a young lady that I'm courting, and I'm courting her right now!"

Sparrow laughed again. "It's not one of your childhood sweethearts, is it Jakesy? Not little Polly from the shoe shop in Francis Street is it? Or is it Lizzie Edgar with the runny nose?"

"No, Sparrow, as you well know, it isn't! And for your information, you're not the only one who's getting engaged!"Although I felt justified in my rebuttal of Sparrow, and despite the fact that Phoebe and I *were* getting on well, on reflection I was aware that I should by rights have mentioned our engagement to *Phoebe* first. But he had goaded me, you see.

"Well, who *is* it then?" Archie grinned at Alice, who grinned and blushed in her turn. Luckily, I was saved from further embarrassment by a timely knock at the back parlour door. Alice called to come in and a little girl appeared. She danced up to Alice and plumped a can of milk on the table. When I saw who it was I could not believe my eyes: it was none other than Nancy Naiskins, who I had last seen by the fever houses at Seven Dials.

"Mr Ja'esbere!" she called out laughing when she recognised me. "Mr Ja'esbere! You said you'd come to see me again, you and 'spector Bucket. He promised to tell me stories about Patch and 'is little girl that's dead. Where is he?" she danced in excitement, "Do your ears thing! Do your ears!"

"Is this your secret sweetheart then, Jakesy?" Sparrow laughed.

"Don't tease so, Archibald," said Alice. "You know perfectly well she's not, though how Mr Jakesbere knows Nancy Naiskins is a mystery to me!"

Nancy perched herself on a stool by my side and stared at me as if she was wondering why I hadn't begun my show of ear-jigging already. I felt my ears glowing red as if in acknowledgement.

"Nancy and me have met before," I said, smiling. "When I was out with Bucket that first night, Sparrow. You were there too, you know! That's right isn't it, Nancy?" She nodded happily. "But more to the nub, what are *you* doing here, eh? Is your ma well? And how's the baby and your old dad? And your brother, of course. Has he got over the fever?"

At a nudge from Alice I stopped. "The boy's passed away," she whispered. "The poor mite got hisself over the fever all right but then he went and copped it with the 'fluenza." More loudly, she said, "Me and your ma are friends, ain't we, Nancy? Your ma and mine knew each other, didn't they, darling? Long since - and now Nancy's out and about again, doing errands for her ma, *we* sometimes gives her little jobs, don't we?" Nancy nodded in agreement. "Especially now I'm earning regular in *The White Lion*, serving and that." Alice stopped and reached for her purse. "Oh, and that reminds me, here's your h'penny for fetching the milk, Nancy. Now you go back and tell your ma who you've seen." Nancy danced to the door. "And mind you run all the way and talk to no one at all! Do you hear?"

What a change! She was a bony little thing when I last saw her. Now at least she looked like she wasn't going to fade away!"

Turning at the door the little girl stared at me again.

"Do the ears, Mr Ja'sbere!" she said.

As all eyes were on me I had no choice, I supposed. I levered up the muscles, as of old, and set-to with a twitching, for the life of me. As soon as the jerking took hold, Nancy screamed with delight. Alice gave out little trills of laughter and even Sparrow squawked - though he'd seen the ear-trick many a time. Nancy danced off, beaming.

"How *did* you do that, Will?" Alice gushed. "It's quite a trick!"

"Oh he's a master at it, is Jakes," said Sparrow. "Now show her that one where you ..." but fortunately she was interrupted by the arrival of Mrs Beddows, the landlady.

"Archie!" she called urgently, "we need your help out front, if you please. Albert's not in and that old Irishman is making a shine again - I can't get him to leave. Make haste, if you will Archie!"

"But I ain't on duty, Mrs B!" Sparrow whined.

"Never mind *duty!* Get yourself out here and help me sort out this palaver!" Poor Mrs Beddows, she looked as though she might faint. Alice began wafting at her with a lace handkerchief. Sparrow stood up abruptly and, despite being out of uniform, immediately put on his policeman face and marched out into the public bar, treading as stridently as he could in his off-duty boots.

The old Irish gentleman was making a spectacle of himself indeed, tripping and falling, ranting and swearing as if taken by a drunken form of St Vitus Dance. The other customers were standing well away from him, for fear of getting sprayed or caught by his wildly swinging arms. He had clearly been slopping beer and knocking stools over, for he was standing in a pig-sty of his own making.

"Tries to throw me out, does yer?" he was saying, peppering his discourse with ripe adjectives from the Irish bogs. "Well I won't be thrown out. They's done it afore, a-throwing me out, for I won't be quiet. No, I won't be quiet." He swore again. "I knows what you're up to here. You're all the same! A-drinkin' and a-letchin' and then you say I's the one who's a drunkard." He cursed once more and the very air seemed to recoil.

"What's this? What's this?" Sparrow said sternly. "Lets 'ave less of your gum, old feller!"

"Come on then, if you can! Tink you're a toff do you? Tink you can have your own way!" The swearing did not abate. "Do what you like! Come on then, show me your paws!"

The old drunkard had his fists up now and punctuated each punch into the air with another curse. The poor fellow was clearly out of his wits. The public house had gone silent and all were watching him, half-amused and half-shocked. Although the clientele of *The White Lion* were hardly from the upper reaches

164

of the mannered middle-classes, it certainly was *not* a low beer-house, nor a shabby gin-den like the ones in Seven Dials or Whitechapel. In such hostelries as those one might *expect* to find fighting and swearing in the common rooms. But in *The White Lion*, even the public bar was clean and fresh, its sawdust and spittoons changed and washed out daily.

It was in this silence that the main doors swung open and a young woman entered *The White Lion*. One might have noticed her even without the sudden quiet, for she was indeed a beauty - very lady-like in her carriage, petite and with an elfin, child-like, complexion.

"Father, father!" she called plaintively, "I have been looking for you this past hour." She had a soft Irish lilt to her voice - not the harsh brogue of her father. "Please, sir," she said, turning to Sparrow, "he cannot help himself when he becomes drunk but he means no harm by it. Please would you kindly help me to calm him and see him to a seat?" The old fellow lost his fighting look for a second, tamed by his daughter's soothing tones - but this was merely a hiatus in his cursing, for he now turned his drunken venom fully upon *her* instead.

"You! You, is it?" he spat out. "You're the one who started all this! Oh yes, you and your toff!" He swore violently again. Sparrow stepped between father and daughter, fearing the words might translate into physical violence. He received only a round-house blow for reward. He stumbled back against the fire-hearth before losing his balance completely and crashing down amongst the ashes, sending the brass tools flying like splinters. In his haste to reinstate himself, he managed to snag his trousers against the fire shovel and tore his trousers as well as his pride. Alice came rushing over with a cry whilst the daughter ran to her father, only to be knocked to the ground in her turn. The drunken

Irishman saw Sparrow right himself and clearly fancied he could send him reeling once again. However, the old bird was not to be caught twice. Sparrow ducked back from the blow like a seasoned pugilist, grabbing the old man under the arms as he spun around him. Next, Sparrow heaved the old chap in the air as if he were a little boy that had been caught fogle-hunting. This seemed to take the wind out of the old fellow straight away, and he slumped like a doll in Sparrow's arms, slithering to the floor as if his bones had just been filleted in Woolwich fish-market.

To everybody's horror the old man now started weeping and vomiting into the sawdust. There were groans of disgust all around - and curses too. Some of these were not exactly complimentary to the Irish. The customers made for the doors to avoid the stench. Alice ran off straight away to fetch a mop and bucket. Despite her pretty dress, she set to, mopping up the worst and sprinkling fresh sawdust when she'd done. Mrs Beddows drew new draughts and the disgruntled customers who had remained took to their seats and the consolation of a fresh pint of ale. Sparrow and the daughter half-dragged, half-carried the old man back to a corner seat. A change had come over him by now. Sparrow had drawn his sting and the old fellow was sobbing like a baby.

"I'm sorry, my dear. I'm sorry my love," he spluttered through his tears. "Can you forgive me? I'm a foul old man. An eejet. A disgusting old man."

"No, my dear, no, father," she hushed him, kissing the top of his head where the hair had bristled up. Sparrow and Alice and I sat down beside her. "I am so sorry, ladies and gentleman," the young woman cried, more to the room than just to us. "He has been so dejected since he lost his position and has taken badly to the drink. Forgive him. Forgive us both. I've tried to stop him

166

wandering off but he's strong in body and strong-willed too. I beg your pardon," she said, and then, standing up, "I'll be taking him home straight away."

"A good idea, miss, but I doubt you've strength enough to carry him by yourself, if you get my drift. He'd be a bit of an 'andful, I'd say," said Sparrow, "a right walloper!"

"I am not as young or as weak as I seem," the young woman said with sudden fire.

"Wrap him up and shove him in your lock up, Sparrer!" said a rowdy voice from the bar, a customer not to be placated merely with a fresh jug of ale.

"*Constable* Sparrow to you, Dobsy – and keep yer nose out!" was Sparrow's stout reply. The young woman's face showed deeper anxiety now, once she had realised Sparrow was a police officer. "You see, Miss," said Sparrow, sensing her distress, "there's some here who'll think I should carry him over to St Giles's Police station for 'im to sleep it off in one of our cells – but, if you'll let me, we'll help you 'ome with him instead, won't we, Jakes?" I nodded and Sparrow continued to reassure the young woman. "Your old dad's got himself corned, true enough, but I'm the only one that harm's been done to, ain't I? Apart from a bit of bad language and high spirits, there's no damage done, is there?" He appealed now to Mrs Beddows, who scowled. "I'll see it's all right with the landlady, miss," Sparrow continued, "and then, well, apart from the insult to yourself there's nothing to complain of. I'm off duty today as it happens, so *I* won't be laying charges and I'm sure we can settle with the landlady for the breakages and the inconvenience, can't we? Well, if *you* don't demand I arrest 'im," he smiled at the young woman, "then we can let him off, can't we, Miss?"

"That's right, Miss," Alice joined in as she threaded the needle from her pocket-housewife, already saving Sparrow's trousers and his blushes against when he would need to stand up again. "We don't want the poor old feller shoved in a cell, do we, Archibald? Why, he'll be up against the magistrate in the morning and then, Miss…"

"Gavelstone."

"Miss Gavelstone'd be shamed and have no end of trouble. The poor old dear couldn't hardly help himself anyway, could he, Miss? Could he, Archibald? Could he, Mr Jakesbere?"

We all shook our heads in confirmation of this humanitarian view - although mine was already shaking in surprise at the name I had just heard the young woman call herself.

"No, Archibald," Alice continued, putting the final stitch into the side of Sparrow's trousers. "If you make it all right with Mrs Beddows, I think we could let Mr Gavelstone sleep it off upstairs in my room, instead of draggin' him in that state through the streets. What do you think?"

"Oh no! I can't put you to any trouble," said Miss Gavelstone anxiously.

"I won't hear another word about it, Miss Gavelstone," Alice persisted. "But we must get him upstairs sharpish in case a customer wants to start making an example of him, and presses charges against him." Alice looked around at one or two customers near the bar who seemed to be discussing just this. "That wouldn't do, would it, Miss?" Miss Gavelstone was shaking her head but Alice wouldn't be interrupted. "Now, I've got a little cot he can lie down on, and I've got some water he can clean himself up with and, after a little sleep, I dare say he'll be right as rain and ready to sup with the queen. What do you say, Miss?"

"You're very kind but, but, I couldn't."

"Now, now, I won't take no for an answer, will I, Archie?" said

Alice. "No I won't, Miss Gavelstone."

"Well, you are kind, and I am worried about father," Miss Gavelstone began to relent, looking nervously around. "Please, call me Sarah, at least."

"Well, there you are then, Miss Sarah, it'll be for the best, honest it will." And, so saying, Alice bit off the end of the thread from her needle and hurried Sparrow away, safely repaired, to soothe Mrs Beddows with a coin for the cost of the broken pots. Finally, Miss Gavelstone assented with reluctance but also with many more gracious expressions of thanks. I managed to half-carry the old fellow up the stairs whilst he wept on his daughter's shoulder.

Once inside Alice's room it was with some difficulty that we bent the old man's bones to get him to fit the little truckle-bed that Alice had pulled out from under the stair-head. His daughter washed him from a bowl of warm water. Then she made him sip sweet tea from a little cup that Alice handed over for the purpose. This domestic scene seemed to me then as if a picture from an illustrated Bible or a religious lithograph, where an old preacher is nursed by a pretty maiden. Sparrow came up, after soothing Mrs Beddows, and stood by the door regarding the intimate splendours of his sweetheart's boudoir like a man in bliss. He no doubt felt it was money well spent if it led to him being allowed to enter this holy of holies. The old Irishman looked around at us like a child whilst he was nursed and then, taking one long confused look at his daughter, dropped his head back into a sudden deep sleep.

Whilst he slept, we sat cosily together on a long settle that Alice used for a low table. We were people suddenly made familiar by shared experience and nothing was said in the contented silence. After a few moments, Alice rose to make tea for us all and

169

Sparrow rose too, taking the opportunity to act his part in this play of a wedded couple entertaining their friends.

The interlude allowed me to give voice to the enquiry that had been in my mind since I had first heard the young woman speak her name downstairs. "Miss Gavelstone," I began, but stumbled to a stop, blushing at my own precocity. I had become suddenly aware of myself almost squeezed-up against this fine young woman on the little settle, thrown into an intimacy brought on by the aftermath of the hot fighting and the sickness downstairs and now the domestic quietude of Alice's private room. Her smile, however, encouraged me. "Miss Gavelstone," I continued. "When I heard your name downstairs just now, it rang a bell with me. Your father, he's not the Gavelstone who was recently a gardener to Lord Montague Dreadnaught, is he?" A shadow crossed her face and she looked into the corner where Alice kept her work basket, as if something had been lost there. "Lord Dreadnaught of Mayfair, I mean," I added.

"Dreadnaught?" she said, still looking away. "No, no, Mr Jakesbere, no, I have not heard of a Lord, of a Lord Dreadnaught."

"No, Miss?" I continued hesitantly. "Are you quite sure? You see I'm an assistant - an associate more like really - to Inspector Bucket of the Detective. I expect you've heard of him? He's quite famous, you know." She flinched a little, I thought, but otherwise had become quite impassive. "We're looking for the whereabouts of Lord Dreadnaught's son, as it happens. His name is Mr Richard Dreadnaught." She could not disguise her reaction to the name and she faced me, unblinking.

"Mr Jakesbere, we are in your debt, both my father and I. And we are indebted to Miss Alice and Mr Sparrow, too. I am very grateful to you all and I owe you an explanation, I know. And I

170

will give it, to be sure I will. Only I ask you to believe me that I know nothing of the whereabouts of the Mr Dreadnaught you mention - nor do I wish to know of him and neither do I wish him to know of me."

Her voice was trembling. She looked away. But after a pause she had composed herself and faced me again with an irresistible pleading in her green eyes.

"I beg of you to keep my secret and to allow me to keep silent about my history for a time yet."

We were interrupted then by Alice and Sparrow, bringing the tea, and our conversation was at an end. Although the young woman continued to be all charm and gratitude for the rest of our time together, she had indeed become a stranger once again.

# Chapter 15

Despite Miss Gavelstone's pleading, I had planned to talk to Inspector Bucket about her at the first opportunity. My intentions were sound and determined, I can assure you. But one thing pushed out another, as they say. I blame it on Sparrow to begin with, for he insisted on taking a meal with me after the incident. And we talked over our news in the public bar till quite late. I also blame it on the weather. You see, there was a violent wind blowing up as I left *The White Lion* and I was forced to button my coat up fast. And then it started to rain. A real squall.

Then, of course, crowds begin to gather wheresoever an omnibus is spied, and when one finally deigned to stop to allow a few more passengers to squeeze into an already wet and uncomfortable space, there commenced a wild struggle for the seats. I was forced to give way to a matronly lady. I would like to pretend I did so out of good manners, but I fear the truth is that her swinging skirts knocked me sideways and I was undone by her hoops. I had no choice then but to make a reluctant climb up the perilous iron ladder to the top of the bus. Normally, on a fine night, such a station would have suited, as by choosing such an option one might escape the stinking straw within, as well as the additional disincentives of fleas and cigar smoke.

However, riding on this most open part of the conveyance on such a night as this exposed me to the torrent that the rain had now become. If circumstances had not resolved themselves into such a picture, I am convinced that my determination to inform Bucket of my intelligence regarding Miss Sarah Gavelstone would have been fulfilled. But by the time I had returned to Bucket's house I was like a drowned cat. And so you see, I blame my failure on a Sparrow, a hoop and the rain.

The Vauxhall house was dark and, although I had not thought it too late, all seemed asleep at first. What a surprise it was, and what a pleasure it was then, to find that when I had softly opened the door and made a quiet entrance for fear of waking the guiltless sleepers, I met the soft embrace of Phoebe, who had been waiting up for me. Thus, I suppose, I should blame my failure to speak to Bucket on her – but that I cannot do. And so I shall blame it on myself. Indeed, Bucket was still awake, for I heard the shuffling of papers in his little parlour or study, where he was no doubt sipping at a sweet sherry and pondering late into the night as he was wont to do. But here was Phoebe taking off my wet things in the half dark. She led me up to my own garret and made me sit in front of the grate, whilst she built up the coals. And so the fire must take some of the blame. She did not even call Hetty. As I warmed myself, she began to dry my hair with a hot white towel. And thus it was that in that warm dampness, what with the steam from my wet clothes and the glow from the fire, I lost all ability to maintain my decorum. She leaned down and I looked up and our lips met in the warmest of kisses.

We were all snuggled-up like a married couple, squeezed up and wrapped round each other on the fireside chair. All thoughts of police business, of Sarah Gavelstone and Richard Dreadnaught were forgotten. How, indeed, could such trivial things be remembered? Whilst we kissed and embraced, I told her about Sparrow and Alice and about how I was to be Sparrow's best man, all in a whispered half-entranced voice. The Gavelstone business did come into my mind then, I admit, but was expelled again when I recalled what I had said to Archie and Alice: that Phoebe and I were courting and were going to get engaged in our turn. I felt myself blushing, and paused in our

173

intimacy. The former would not have been seen in the low candle light but Phoebe felt my hesitation.

"What is it, Will? Do I shock you?" I turned away for a moment but Phoebe would show no mercy until I had given my confession.

"I told Sparrow we were ..." I hesitated and then tried again, "that we were courting and that we might get engaged." Phoebe had been teasing me by putting her face in front of mine when I tried to look away, but my words stopped her in her tracks. She looked at me seriously and took my face in her hands.

"Oh Will! *Did* you?" Her voice was so soft and sweet it melted me away. She kissed me full on the lips, deep and long. Clearly the house was more awake than I had thought; Gertie had been listening at the door and not asleep at all. And just at this moment she burst in.

"Will and Phoebe are gettin' married! Will and Phoebe are gettin' married!" she shouted. "Ma! Ma!" she shouted from the top of the stairs. "Will and Phoebe are gettin' married!" The whole house came to life. Ma Bucket came in, clutching her night dress to herself with both arms but then, taking one look at us, let go of her grip and hastened Phoebe away, calling her a minx.

I did not venture from my room for the rest of the night for fear that I would be evicted from the house for entertaining an unchaperoned Phoebe Bucket in my room. When I finally submitted to sleep I dreamt of being showered in hot rose petals, and each one turned into a kiss. One, at the end of my dream, was unaccountably rough. I woke to find it was the cat, Buttons, licking my face.

Ma Bucket was pouring some water in my wash basin. I became immediately anxious, for it was Hetty's job to prepare the water for the household's morning toilet. I suspected this was a sign of my imminent eviction. I reflected that Ma Bucket had smiled at me and I hoped it meant I was forgiven. I was left alone to complete my ablutions until Hetty knocked with the command that I was wanted in Bucket's study. Now I was truly convinced that I was undone and was to be summarily dismissed from the house. Ma Bucket's crooked smile had just been the grin on the face of the executioner's assistant, I thought to myself. I began to regret that I had abandoned my lodgings with Mrs Peckers and feared I might become a homeless vagrant like the poor souls in St Giles High Street, sleeping in the cold in Cripplegate churchyard. But, of course, Mrs Peckers would hardly let me back now, not once she had found out how 'unrespecrable' I had become.

Feeling weak and pale, I knocked on Bucket's door in dread. He was all buttoned up in his greatcoat and was at his most blankly business like. I feared he might have been awakened by the disturbance in the night and still be angry at the infringement to his sleep or his night-time reflections, as well, of course, as angry at the injury to his daughter's morality and the reputation of his household. I felt the shame profoundly. It was a vivid physical sensation, like a freezing shower of cold water being poured all over me. He faced me with a stern look as I stood in the doorway.

"I wanted to warn you, Jakesbere."

"Yes, sir," I said, looking down, shame-faced.

"Before you sat down to breakfast, I mean."

"*Before* breakfast?" I gulped. "I see. I'll get my things. If that's your wish."

"No lad. I don't mean you to have *no* breakfast. Quite the opposite, in fact. I thought I ought to say a word of warning about you satisfying your appetite."

The shame was too much. I dreaded a stinging lecture about my lack of self-control and about my abuse of his kindness and Phoebe's innocence. And yet I hung on like a condemned man to the hope in that word 'warning'. Perhaps I was to be reprieved and the block was to be spared me.

"We're off back to Lord Dreadnaught's house in Mayfair and I want to get there early. There'll be some rich food where we're goin', my lad, and I don't want you to make yourself sick. These big houses are famous for giving visitors a good feed, and in this particular case they may have other reasons for plying us with food and drink, and attempting to make us groggy. We need to stay fresh and alert. So, have a sizeable breakfast this morning so that you're not too tempted by the fare in the house. Beware of the rich stuff in particular."

"*Food?*" I gasped. "You wanted to talk to me about food?"

"That's all, lad, yes. But mind you watch out!"

Ah, now it was coming, I thought.

"Watch out, and be careful. Keep your wits about you. I don't like this De Blarde fellow, nor some others of the servants that Lady Dreadnaught keeps around her. She's got a thing or two to hide, methinks. The whole household seems like it's hiding something to me." I stood dumbfounded. "All right, my lad? Well, don't stand there with your mouth open! Get about your business. Whelks'll be calling soon. I shall be wanting a word with him while you get yourself ready." I continued to hover like an idiot. "Well, off you go then!" Closing the door behind me, I felt a fool.

In the breakfast room Phoebe, Gertie and Ma Bucket all met me with smiles. Gertie was giggling actually. Ma Bucket kept giving her little slaps. Bucket started to carve thick cuts of the breakfast ham, but I was too churned up to eat and declined the food when offered. Love and relief had filled me up. All I could do was stare longingly at Phoebe Bucket and nibble at the end of a piece of toast. Bucket shook his head at me as he helped himself to two slices of ham, a wing of cold chicken and two eggs. When he had finished eating and we climbed into the cab, all I could think about was Phoebe Bucket.

# Chapter 16

The rain had persisted all through the night and for most of the morning. This time the gates to the porter's lodge were shut and we had to wait for the surly porter to come out and open them. I noticed that there was a little side door for pedestrian callers to enter by. I couldn't help noting that its lock seemed one that might be easily broached. Despite the obvious reluctance of the porter, we were clearly expected and the gate was opened to us without a word being spoken. The porter kept his face well hidden from us under his billycock hat, or perhaps it was just from the rain. It occurred to me that he did not look, and was not dressed, as you might expect a porter to be, looking more like one of the men lounging against the walls of Oblique House whom I had seen on our first visit. He also looked as if he might be drunk.

Whelks cried out, "Whoa boy!" as we reached the house, and the little horse that was pulling us juddered to a stop. When I had picked myself up from the floor of the cab, I noticed a shadowy figure peering out at us through the long windows of the reception hall. Whoever it was soon moved back out of sight with a twitch of the long drapes. We took a minute or two to collect ourselves and for Bucket to give some instructions to Whelks, and, as we were about to step out from the cab, out came the footman who had greeted us before: Alfred. One could tell he was not fitted for this job. He was awkward in getting the steps down. He held the door open for Bucket with his left hand but let it go swinging back at me so that it caught my shin quite a bark. I saw Mad Joe again, too. The thick-set stable lad from before was shouting at him as they led Whelks and our steaming horse away to the stables.

Bucket and I splashed our way through the puddles to the door, where we removed our over-shoes and shook the rain off. De Blarde met us at the door, and I asked innocently where Mr Merit was and received the cold answer that he was ill. Thus, my enquiry contemptuously brushed aside, we were shepherded up the stairs and into the library where we had had our previous meeting.

It was better lit this time and I was able to take in the splendour of the room, its books, its busts and cabinets. De Blarde left us, to alert his mistress, I supposed, and as we waited we were served tea by a little bustling maid with a very girlish sort of face and figure. She kept looking around at Alfred as he stood with his face in the shadows by the door, almost hidden as he was by the curtain drapes that covered that side of the wall. Ada was the maid's name, as I found out later. She had a look of Phoebe about her, I thought - although not such a beauty, of course. Nevertheless, in a crinoline and a bustle I could see she might have done for a lady herself or, more accurately, she might have passed muster as the younger daughter of a titled gentleman.

De Blarde's sharp voice brought me out of my contemplation. "Her Ladyship will permit an audience. You must wait 'ere." As he turned away, he added, as if the information were of no consequence, that the master had a migraine and that he would be unable to see us. It seemed to me that it was strange that the aristocracy should always have migraines, whereas the common classes had to get by with a headache. Nevertheless, the poor fellow apparently suffered a great deal from these pains and so perhaps I was being unkind. We had been told that his migraine was associated with the blindness that was apparently creeping up on him. Bucket helped himself to more tea and a thin biscuit from a silver tray. When I was offered one I declined, as my stomach still seemed full of a sort of churning love for Phoebe.

We stood when her Ladyship came in, De Blarde in tow.

"Most delightful, these biscuits, my lady," said Bucket, in lieu of a greeting, "quite melt in one's mouth."

The lady was not charmed.

"My husband has granted you free access to our house, Inspector," she said icily. "His command I may not override although I trust my *own* apartments and those of Lord Montague *at least* are sacrosanct?"

"If I'm to find a way of tracing Mr Richard, then, I'm afraid, needs must, ma'am. But I am, of course, most obliged to you, my Lady, and I don't wish to disturb Lord Montague Dreadnaught or yourself."

"At least there is comfort in that," Lady Dreadnaught interrupted.

"I don't wish to disturb your Ladyship or Lord Dreadnaught more than is *necessary*, I mean," Inspector Bucket added with a smile, holding his cup and her gaze steadily.

"I must remind you again, then, Inspector," she said coldly, "that this house has suffered much at the hands of my step-son. His actions have caused an upheaval here. They have inflicted such a wound on the household that even *you*, Inspector, may be surprised." She stopped - waiting for Bucket to say something, I supposed. He just bowed his head. She turned angrily as if ready to go.

"Please give my condolences to Lord Dreadnaught on his incapacity, my Lady," Bucket said, when she was almost at the door. Alfred opened it from the shadows. "No doubt you've made the arrangements for my assistant, Mr Jakesbere here, to be shown the house as I asked in my message? Perhaps you might ask your man to arrange for me to use the library as a place where I can interview members of the household. If that is convenient?"

De Blarde looked daggers, at being called 'her man', I supposed. Alfred followed her Ladyship as she left, whispering into her ear. Turning to De Blarde, her Ladyship gave him the slightest nod and granted Bucket a contemptuous curl of her lip before departing in a flurry and a swish of silken skirts. De Blarde paused for a moment, perhaps to assert his authority or to reclaim his dignity, and then followed on.

Bucket sat at a desk upon which were arranged files of papers and began investigating the properties of the room from his seated station, quite oblivious to the papers or me, for the time being. De Blarde was back in a few minutes with a written list of the household members and servants. Bucket ignored him and De Blarde left without a word. The Inspector continued his contemplation and I knew him too well to disturb him when he was in one of these mystical reveries. All this reading of signs and surfaces was a mystery to me. Instead, I listened to the voices from outside to see if I could hear something in them. Thus it was again that I heard the voice that had disturbed me before, a voice I could not quite place. Bucket, meanwhile, had finally decided to open a folder of papers, fanning them nonchalantly on the desk.

"Don't be alarmed, my boy," he said without looking up. "What you're hearing is the rehearsal for the play we are about to star in. Our role is to read these papers that have been so carelessly abandoned here. You see? We must just read our script and act out our roles as faithfully as they. This, for instance," he said, picking up a bill, "is a gambling debt to the tune of 75 guineas from 'Whites'. Ah, here's another one from 'Boodles'. Another fine gentlemen's dining club. And, here, debts settled by

181

Lord Montague Dreadnaught, but debited against the name of 'R. Dreadnaught'. D'you see that, eh?" he said, showing me the signature. "A little blurred in the writing. You see. Interesting. What d'yer make of that?"

I made nothing of it as it happened, but it seemed to mean something to Bucket, as such things always did.

"Ah," he said, picking up a batch of paper, "bills in payment to an apothecary in Chelsea and," he flicked over another, "Hampstead - an account for opium tincture and laudanum. Quite a mighty amount too! Look at that!" He passed it to me. "And, here, a bill for morphine - a German version of opium that can be taken in through a needle, my boy. Very modern. And, yes, here's an invoice for injecting equipment. Mr R. Dreadnaught seems to have quite a habit!" Bucket flicked carelessly through another pile of papers. "And, what have we here? Ah, bills from costumiers and outfitters for theatrical garments. Quite a range of fancy dress. And these? Well, blow me down, invoices for rustic wear and bills for *women's* garments, Jakesbere, my boy. And they're all down to the same account and signed with the same smeared signature: 'Mr R. Dreadnaught, Mayfair'." The mention of these dressing up items made my pulse beat with excitement. The Beast, of course, was known to wear disguises and indeed we had seen him ourselves dressed up in an oriental costume.

Just as I was about to exclaim about this to Inspector Bucket, the door behind us opened. Bucket made no movement to return the papers to the desk. De Blarde was about to usher in one of the stable boys, the first of Bucket's interviewees. But before the stable boy could enter, De Blarde gasped audibly and, shutting the door, rushed over to us to snatch up the letters and bills from Bucket's hand.

"Monsieur!" he screeched, "you are looking at Lord Montague's private papers! I shall 'ave to…"

But Bucket cut him off.

"That accent, Monsieur De Blarde," Bucket said, apropos of nothing. "I can't quite place all its components." Turning suddenly to face Lady Dreadnaught's man-servant, he said, "La Belle France, eh? What a country, n'est-ce pas? Revolution and violence and wonderful culture too. But I have a feeling there's also a whisper of something else in your accent. Sicilia perhaps. The land of Garibaldi, eh?"

De Blarde was silent.

"No? Well, p'raps it's just France after all then, eh?" Bucket turned back to the pile of documents. "I have a French friend, as it happens, and we discuss such things in our line of work. Accents, disguises and the like. We write often." Bucket looked up again. "We like to share stories of the villains we come across. Unsolved crimes and the like. A sort of professional hobby, I suppose. Oh, p'raps you know him? Monsieur Francoise Vidocq. Have you heard of him, by any chance?"

De Blarde maintained his silence but his lips tightened.

"Very famous in France, I believe," said Bucket, watching De Blarde intently. "He's a bit of a celebrity amongst those in the know in this country too. No? You don't know him? Oh well, he's in the detecting line, same as me. Private investigator though. Private Inquiry Bureau. You know the sort of thing, I expect. I'm making him my model you see. You've never heard of him, then?"

De Blarde's eyes narrowed. He looked as if he wanted to burst.

"I shall speak to my mistress about zis, zis discourtesy, Inspector Bucket," he said, turning away from Bucket. Gathering himself, he addressed me coldly. "Meester Jakesbere, I 'ave instructions to show you the 'ouse and its chambers. If you will?" De Blarde turned dramatically on his heel.

As he did so, Bucket whispered in my ear: "Don't forget to count the windows, Jakesbere and see if you can find me something else with Richard Dreadnaught's signature on it. Not on a bill, though. See if you can find a *personal* letter. Look for a signature that's *not* smeared, a nice clear one. And," he added, "keep your wits about you. We don't want you forgetting anything, do we?"

I followed after De Blarde, pushing past the line of servants to be interviewed, in some confusion at Bucket's last remarks. Looking back through the open doorway, I saw the Inspector settling himself more snugly behind the desk. The stable boy was hovering nervously.

"Come in, come in," Bucket called to him cheerfully. "Make yourself comfortable. I've got a nephew in the horsey lark, you know, my lad. A stable boy for Lord Todmore." Just then the double-doors closed and the sound was cut off.

'Forgetting anything?' I pondered Bucket's last admonishment inwardly. And then it dawned on me. With all my excitement about Phoebe, I had forgotten again to tell him about my meeting with Sarah Gavelstone. But I could do nothing about that now, for De Blarde was waiting with candles at the bottom of the staircase.

"Zis way, s'il vous plait," said De Blarde with evident irritation, handing a candle to me, and we began the ascent of the stairs. We had reached the higher floor, passing two closed and dark doors, before I remembered my task and found my voice.

"Er, what about these rooms, Mr De Blarde?"

"They are Madame's personal rooms. You have no permission to inspect those."

I hesitated, wondering whether I should insist but he marched on before I could. Around the corner the candle's flame revealed a hallway with heavy drapes pulled across several doors. "Furniture in storage," he muttered as explanation, and then abruptly, "Meester Richard's chambers. You may inspect. I shall wait."

I felt as if I was being marched around by a bluff Sergeant Major, but I walked in as instructed and he closed the door behind me. This behaviour seemed most strange, but nonetheless, I continued to do as Bucket had asked.

It was dark in the room, as was the rest of this strange house. The curtains were drawn against the teeming rain and the gloomy daylight outside. There was but one small gas-jet lit, obviously in preparation for me, and it was fizzing fitfully in a baroque holder by the door. The shadows swooped up the walls. Even so, as my eyes adjusted, I could see it was a large suite and clearly the apartments of a wealthy gentleman. My experience of the inner chambers of the houses of the aristocracy was slight at this time, but I realised I was in a sort of reception room, where the young gentleman of the house might greet his private guests. The floor was covered with a handsome Turkish rug and its spaces filled with expensive furnishings, all of oriental design like something out of the Arabian Nights. There was, for instance, one of the smoking contraptions I had seen in the Hell Club, a hookah, its long pipe decorated with the markings and the mouth of a giant snake. There was an Adams fireplace, fine but somewhat spoilt by a veneer of grey dust which had blown up from the ashes of a pile of burnt papers which lay in the hearth. I reached for a brass hearth-tool, the tongs fashioned in the shape of a harem lady, her legs acting as the opening parts of the apparatus.

185

At first my investigation amongst the ashes was as merely idle as it was futile, the residue being the result of charred paper which crumbled further into incense-like ash as I stirred. However, I noticed that there was still a remnant intact amongst the cinders like the tail-end of a letter that had been only half destroyed. I picked it out carefully with the tongs, carrying it beneath the flickering gas light to investigate. It was indeed a letter, as I had thought. I could just make out the signature: 'R. Dreadnaught'. It was slightly charred but clear enough to read, and I could see that it wasn't smeared. I folded it carefully and placed it in my trouser pocket.

The bed chamber was lit by another fitful but brighter jet. This was another room that might have been deposited in response to a wish granted by some Arabian genie: exotic paintings, carved and polished wood and purple drapes. The wall seemed full of eyes, peacock fans and portraits of Indian ladies. However, it was the pile of clothes on the floor that took my attention next. One had no need to be a detective to see that whoever had been here had left in a hurry. The writing desk was similarly chaotic – covered in papers and spilt ink. There were more bills, like the ones downstairs: receipts from money lenders; unpaid bills from expensive eating houses; letters from exclusive Gentlemen's Clubs. Amongst these was a letter from Crockfords, an exclusive gambling house frequented by the aristocracy. There was silky notepaper printed with the name: 'Richard Dreadnaught'. Next to this was a stack of embossed cards, the top one reading, 'Whites and Brookes', another Gentlemen's Club. The bed curtains were pulled back and hanging off as if they had been jerked suddenly.

I ignored the piles of clothes on the bed for a moment, remembering that Bucket had wanted me to count the windows for some reason of his own. I drew back the drapes. The light was weak outside and the rain still teeming down. The catch was stiff but, once released, the large panes fell back like wings over the gardens, allowing me to see the sweep of the house. A little maid was carrying slops wearily through the rain. I could just make out the glint of light on a set of windows along the outer wall. To my left, I spied the same, from the window of Mr Richard Dreadnaught's reception room and beyond, another. I closed the window. On the bed many of the garments were nothing but greasy rags, smeared with what seemed to be theatrical make-up or ointment. However, there were under-clothes and stockings and other women's clothes. I was bemused.

At the far end sat a dressing closet. On entering this, I jumped in alarm because the first thing I saw was a Chinaman, or rather a doll, a mannequin, dressed up in a Chinese costume. I did not know if it was the one I had seen at Hyde Park or not, but the coincidence seemed too obvious for me not to conclude that it was. I nearly did run off to Bucket then.

There were two other mannequins, one dressed in the flannel breeches of a navvy and another child-sized one which was dressed in the clothes of a daughter of the aristocracy, crinoline, hoops and all. There were hat-stands piled up with many hats and wigs. There was a billycock hat and a big feathery bonnet too. There was loose silver and jewellery, constructed from varied gems, everywhere I looked. Against a wall there was a pile of shiny walking sticks of all shapes and sizes and cunning designs. It did not take me long to find one with a dragon's head handle. I nearly *did* run off to Bucket then, for that was surely it! My haul of evidence was complete. But there were more threads to follow.

On the dressing table there were sticks of thick make-up, jars of creams and brushes and false noses and ears, and in fact everything imaginable for the purposes of changing one's identity. In the very centre of the table was a jewellery box, encrusted with a dusting of gems. Inside, wrapped in a black velvet cloth, was a ring. By now my heart was beating fast. I picked it up and, turning it around, I saw that it was set with rubies which formed the single letter: R. With a dry mouth and a racing pulse, I slipped this into my pocket along with the remains of the letter. Now my investigations were truly complete and the identity of the Beast, who had been mistaken for a Chinese dignitary and disguised himself as a woman, and possibly as a labouring man, was revealed. Here too was the make-up that he had used in disguise and, most incriminating, the signet ring which Nancy Naiskins had described in her exacting, childish way. We had been brought to this Mayfair palace to find clues to the whereabouts of an errant son but had discovered instead the identity of the Beast himself: Richard Dreadnaught, no less, son of Lord Montague Dreadnaught, peer of the realm. I steadied myself and, taking up my light, made my way back to the door, acting as if I had found nothing. I began to think that I would make a good detective after all.

# Chapter 17

De Blarde was standing outside Richard Dreadnaught's room as I left it. He had removed the glove from his left hand and was filing away at his long fingernails. The thought occurred that his nails were a little overlong and these actions a little effete for a mere man-servant, be he ever-so-smart or ever-so-well appointed. I said nothing, though, and so, wordlessly, he took up his candle and led me on past more darkly-curtained hallways and up on to another floor, this greyer, narrower and more shadowy still.

"The servants' chambers, Meester Jakesbere," he announced contemptuously.

There were a number of dark doors along a long corridor to my left, disappearing into the gloom. On my right, a huge ottoman chest stood in front of a heavy curtain. "Mr Merit's room. Mrs Daniel's, the cook. The premiere footman's room. Some others for the higher servants," said De Blarde, pointing vaguely along the corridor. "You may look." It seemed to me now that further investigation was futile but, employing what I felt was a new detective cunning, I decided to maintain the pretence of interest.

"Where do the under-servants sleep, Mr De Blarde?" I asked, feigning a detective-like zeal.

"There are some more rooms above," he sneered, "but the servants sleep where they work – in the scullery for the scullery maids, in the stable for the stable boys."

"In the garden for the gardener, I see, Mr De Blarde, thank you."

De Blarde led me to the first door on my left. I opened it to reveal a room in a cluttered state. Whoever had lived here had just moved in or out. Empty picture frames lay on a side chair. There were old strips of rugs from downstairs, still beautiful and exotic but rolled-up, ready to be re-used. A naked iron bedstead was pushed up next to a tiny fire-grate. There was a small trunk. Stumps of yellowing candles were lined up on the mantle-shelf. A small table by the bed held a few personal things: a pitcher and jug, brushes and combs, a yellowing towel. I mentally counted the little semi-barred window into my audit, as demanded by Bucket. This seemed to be the pattern for all the rooms. They all looked the same, as if the residents were new, temporary or had just left.

"Was Lord Dreadnaught's son friendly with the servants, Mr De Blarde?"

"I do not gossip, Mr Jakesbere. But, I am told, yes."

As we closed the door on this room, Alfred, the head footman, appeared like a ghost at the end of the long dark corridor - the light of his candle sending shadows running towards me. His grey-powdered head was lit up by the excrescence from the yellow flame, and his hair was flopping, or so it seemed, as if ill-adhered to his head. De Blarde went to him and their shadows coalesced grotesquely in the light, Alfred's angular head leaning over De Blarde's ear urgently. I felt that De Blarde looked suddenly anxious or angry or both. It occurred to me that Alfred had come to tell De Blarde it was *his* turn to be interrogated by Bucket, an interview that De Blarde would perhaps not relish much. I took the opportunity to strike out alone, seeing that my warden was now otherwise engaged. This was more a matter of pride than any real desire to continue my enquiries into the rooms of the house, for I already felt that its chief secrets had been revealed. However, I was surprised by Alfred's indifferent behaviour. There was clearly some command communicated in the household that I should continue to be chaperoned, yet Alfred was content to shadow me at a distance and in silence. His movements were indeed crepuscular, creeping always in the shadows or the half-light, guarding his candle-light jealously, as if contact with me might contaminate him. The feeling was mutual.

I had a sudden thought about Dreadnaught's aged manservant, Merit, who seemed conspicuously absent from the house, and asked Alfred to show me to his room. My voice seemed dry and somewhat thin on the dark landing and he did not seem to hear me at first. I repeated my request more loudly. Alfred shook his head mutely but turned up towards the uppermost landing, clearly expecting me to follow. This was a meaner place still - meant for the lowest servants, I supposed.

The rooms were mostly bare, empty of all furniture or objects of any kind. But *one* seemed inhabited. A light flickered under the door and cruel laughter was echoing from it. Two pairs of steel-shod boots stood outside, caught in the light spilling from under the door, one pair upright and one fallen. I walked past this door rather quickly, I confess. I thought I heard a swallowed but sneering sort of laugh from Alfred when he saw me scurry by. I fancied there might be men wearing billycock hats inside that room with the boots outside, probably having a meeting with a jug of ale - or something stronger. I walked on past two or three other rooms, empty and all with their doors open. Peering in one, I stopped to inspect a small and cheap print left on the wall. It was of Ireland. I wondered if Sarah Gavelstone, the gardener's daughter, might once have slept here and perhaps not so long ago. I scoured the room for any sign that she might have left about her lover's whereabouts, but there was none. Despite Alfred's demeanour, I decided to show him that I was not to be intimidated.

"I shall need to see Mr De Blarde's room. And yours too, of course," I said boldly. I could hardly make out his face in the gloom but his head moved as if surprised, or at least further amused by this request. "You never know," I continued, "Mr Dreadnaught might have been in there at some point and left some such thing as might help Inspector Bucket track him down." Alfred's figure barely moved for a second but then suddenly jerked into motion, leading me back around the other side of the landing and taking me down to two rooms next to the big ottoman chest. I was surprised he did not make it more difficult for me. He pointed at the rooms and then stationed himself some distance off, as usual, as if all this was beneath him.

The first of these rooms was larger than the other servants' quarters and so I imagined it to be De Blarde's. It had an intact piece of Turkish carpet, to make it more like a room for someone who might like to put on airs – like our Monsieur De Blarde. There were silver wigs and pots of powder and make-up on the Regency dressing table. That and the rug must have been gifts from downstairs. On the wall there was a series of daguerreotypes. They were either half-dressed or naked, moustachioed men in gymnastic poses or smiling rakishly at the viewer, Corinthian in manner, as my Uncle Silas might have said. Next to them were a number of studies of small boys in swimming attire or naked. Much to my surprise, when I turned, I saw Alfred's figure in the doorway. Perhaps he had come to move me on, thinking I was lingering over-much, but his face was turned away from me, looking in the direction of a giggling sound that was emerging from the adjacent room.

"Alfred?" a female voice called. "Is it you? It's Ada." The voice sounded flirtatious. It belonged to the pretty little serving wench who had laid out tea for us. "Oh," she said, on seeing me as I stood out in the corridor. "I didn't know *you* was here." Alfred was angry but said nothing. Even from behind I could see his body was visibly shaking. "I was waiting for you, Mr Alfred. Mr De Blarde wants you, so I was told … to do with that policeman feller." For a minute, Alfred seemed non-plussed but then he took her by the right arm with his left, squeezing the soft flesh just above her white wrist. He whispered something in her ear. She winced and said aloud, "All right! I will, I'll tell 'em I promise!" He gave *me* a look of murder - in case I felt left out, I supposed - but lingered no longer than was necessary, though enough for me to see the packed make-up on his face sweating a little and his eyes black-red. Then he hurried off.

"Well," Ada said, rubbing her arm. "He's a right 'un, ain't he?"

"You've struck him dumb," I said, trying to comfort her with a joke.

"D'you *think* so? I don't know where I am with him. He can be so nice but then he comes over all horrible! He hurt my arm then! Did you see? It'll come up in a bruise, that will."

"Nasty," I agreed. "What did he say to you?"

"He said he 'ad to go and see your detective feller. Your boss wanted to ask the two o' them questions together. I wasn't to leave you. Not to let you nosey around. Says I have to get De Blarde's big men to come out and check on you."

"Did he now? I didn't know he could talk!"

"Oh blimey!" she said, pale-faced suddenly. "Me and my mouth. It'll be the death of me, it will! Don't let on I told you that, will you? You're a good gentleman, ain't yer? I'm a bit sweet on 'im, if you must know. I don't want to fall out with him. He might come back and twist my other arm. He can be a bit rough sometimes."

"I won't tell!" I said. "You can trust me, all right. My name's Will, by the way. Ada, isn't it?" I held out my hand but she looked at it suspiciously, thinking perhaps she should be more wary of me.

"D'you know," I said, trying a Bucket trick on her, "you remind me of someone."

"I don't, do I?"

"Yes, you do. My own sweetheart, as it happens."

"You're a cheeky one, ain't yer?" she smiled. "This is a lark though, ain't it?" she said cheerfully. "I'm hoping that Alfred might want *me* as a sweetheart one day, if I plays my cards right - so it's no use you trying your copper tricks on me!"

"Oh I'm not a Peeler!"

"You're not?"

"Oh, nothing like."

"Well, what are you then? Nebby-could-never from the Bible?"

"No. I'm sort of a, a personal assistant to Inspector Bucket. But, listen," I said looking around. "Can you keep a secret?"

"Depends what it is, don't it?"

I leaned toward her. "I tell you what."

"What?" she said leaning into me.

"I think Alfred likes you."

"Get off! He don't!" But she was hooked. "Do yer? Do yer really think so? Really?"

"Oh yes! He doesn't say much, does he? But I saw him looking at you when you brought us the tea in the library."

"Did yer?" she grinned. "I thought he did too, as a matter of fact!"

We laughed.

"Oh but he did say *something* about you. He told me," I paused for effect, "he told me he'd like to talk to you, only he's too shy."

"Shy? Him?" she guffawed. "I doubt it!"

"Well, why don't you find out? Why don't you wait for him when he comes out from seeing the Inspector? He might want someone to talk to. The Inspector can get a bit rough when he gets his teeth dug in."

"No. He told me to stay with you and to get them bludgers out to check on yer."

"Bludgers?" I asked.

"De Blarde's thugs. Ain't you seen 'em? Right rough types." She stopped, looking around nervously. "So, I'd best go and get 'em before I gets in more bovver. You just stand there. And don't you go nowhere or he'll have my guts for garters, or they will!" She began to back away from me.

"No, wait. Don't do that. Look, I'm not going anywhere, am I? I'm only the assistant. It all means nothing to me. I've looked in all the rooms up here anyway. Nothing in them, is there? Everyone seems to have vanished. The only people that seem to be here are your friends the bludgers!"

"Ain't my friends," she frowned.

"No? Then why get them? I'm doing no harm, am I? In fact I was thinking of having a nap. No one'll know, will they? That's what *they* were doing, if you want the truth."

She looked quizzically at me.

"Your bludgers," I explained. "I went past their room. All I heard was snoring. I don't suppose they'll be very pleased to be woken up, will they?"

"No," she said, flustered, "I s'pose not but ..."

"That's what put me in mind of it," I interrupted, "having a bit of a lie down, I mean. I could just nip into one of these rooms and shut my eyes for ten minutes. Now what harm could there be in that? No one would know, would they?" I gave her my most

195

winning smile. "Not if we don't tell them, I mean." I could sense that she was wavering. "Go on, I'm not half tired! I've been up since five! Look, you go and wait for your Alfred and let me get forty winks."

She laughed. "Do you think I should? He *told* me to wait with you and take you up with me to the bludgers."

"Oh you don't have to do that. I don't even know what I'm s'posed to be looking for, as a matter of fact!" We laughed together. "I won't get up to no mischief, promise. How can I? I'll be fast asleep. Land of nod - if you'll let me that is."

"Well, if you're sure?" I gave her a weary look. "All right then, I will!" And having suddenly decided, Ada held up her apron and hurried down the stairs at once.

I wasted no time. That ottoman had seemed odd to me - the one placed so carefully in front of the curtain. I was convinced it was there to disguise what was behind it. Re-tracing my steps quickly, I found it, scrambled over the top of it and pulled the curtain aside. I was right. There were three fine steps going up to a decorated door, just like the ones that led into the master bedrooms. I looked around. All was quiet. The door was locked, but for a boy used to breaking into the warehouses around the dockyard by the Woolwich Arsenal, this lock was easy meat indeed. The keyhole was only a one-ward lock after all. My father's pen-knife blade would slide in easily and a turn or two would do the trick. Indeed, the lock gave almost immediately and I was in.

This was no servant's room. Who on earth could it belong to? It backed on to the servants' landing clearly enough, but that was about the sum of the link. The first thing I noticed was the extravagantly ornamented ceiling decorated with nymphs and men with hoofs for feet. The centre of the room was taken up by

196

an enormous four-poster bed, shielded by a Japanese screen. The whole room was enveloped with purple drapes and adorned with both heavy and light furniture that looked like it had come out of a French boudoir or had been shipped in from the Indies. Lacquered cabinets nestled in every corner or alcove.

The walls themselves were covered with peacocks' eyes, just like the ones I had seen in Richard Dreadnaught's room. Where there was no peacock there was silky golden paper covered in daguerreotypes of little girls. Some were dressed like ladies or princesses, wearing tiaras or coronets, and some were semi-naked. There were more of the mannequins I had seen in Dreadnaught's room too. Was this yet another chamber belonging to this disgraced young man? In my innocence, I found myself wondering what sorts of strange pastimes these aristocrats enjoyed, and my mind returned to the scenes I had witnessed at the Hell Club.

On the dressing table there was an assortment of unguents, powders and creams. There were also brushes, false noses and padding and straps of all shapes and sizes. An oddly designed pair of scissors lay next to these objects, one handle shaped as a naked woman and the other a naked man. They left little to the imagination in their design but would be of little use for the actual purpose of cutting anything, for the cutting edges were the wrong way round. There were two ornate cases, lying open, but what objects they might have held was beyond my knowledge or experience. One was a hinged sheath and the other a velvet lined box with oddly shaped compartments. Looking up, I noticed the mirror above the dressing table and felt suddenly shocked at seeing my own reflection in this bizarre room. I looked like a thief and I was afraid that my image might be fixed in the mirror always - just as a murderer's image is said always to be fixed in the eyes of his victim.

I was feeling a sort of panic by now and badly in need of some air. I noted that the windows stretched all along one wall. I counted them, remembering Bucket's edict, and realised that one was not a window at all but a glass-panelled door. It opened easily enough. The rain had stopped but the air was cool and I took several deep breaths to steady myself. I was standing on the top step of a narrow stairway. It threaded its way under the servants' rooms to the west and then spiralled downwards. It was made of stone and ornamented with dragon-like gargoyles. Their ugly mouths were dripping with the rain.

Peering down, I could see that the steps seemed to join with one of the rooms below until they trailed off, I supposed, out into the gardens. It was as I was considering this that I became aware of the sound of something crashing from somewhere far behind me. It must be Alfred or De Blarde returning, I thought in a desperate panic or, perhaps worse, the bludgers with their iron-shod boots. I jumped back into the room and leapt across it, nearly knocking over tables and chairs and the precious Japanese vases. However, I was able to be back at the door by the servants' landing by the time the sounds from below had become material. I felt considerable relief when I realised it was only Ada who had returned. My relief turned into concern when I saw that she was crying and then into alarm when my sudden appearance caused her to scream out in surprise.

"Shush, Ada. It's only me, Will. If you scream again you'll get us all in lumber!" I said gripping her arms.

"Oh, you!" she cried shaking herself free. "It's all your fault an' all! You *promised* me. You're just like him! You never know where you are with men and that's the truth. You, you're just a big liar! See what you're doin' now sneakin' into places you're not wanted to sneak into. You'll get me dismissed you will - or worse. 'Go down and comfort him', you says. I had to wait for ages till Alfred came out - your Inspector must have been with him a long time. They were in there together an' all, him and Frenchie, Mr De Blarde, and Alfred, I mean. He nearly bit me poor head off when he saw me. He was so *mad* with me - I thought I was goin' to get knocked on the head, I did! I ran up here and then to make it worse I dropped my tray, I was so nervous! I don't know what I shall do, I really don't." She began wiping her face with the edge of her apron and sobbing still louder.

"Shush, Ada, shush!" I begged. "You shall have 'em upon us! If we think quickly, we'll be all right! Now come on Ada, bear up, do as I say and go along with me *whatever!* All right? It'll be a lark won't it? Eh? Now, listen, all you've got to do is let me get along into Alfred's room where you were before. And you must stand by the door! I'll make it right, honest I will!" She was confused but she did as I said and just in time.

"Thank you Ada," I said as De Blarde and Alfred appeared on the landing. I was standing in the doorway to Alfred's room as if I was just leaving. I held a cup in my hand which I had snatched up from a little table just inside the door. It was the cup of tea that Ada had left for Alfred when she had hoped to surprise him before.

"Thank you for the tea, Ada," I said, as if we were alone. "I was most unreasonable parched looking through those dusty rooms. And it was a very kind suggestion of yours that I might have a nap in Mr Alfred's room." I looked up then as if I had seen them for the first time. De Blarde regarded me suspiciously through his beads of eyes. He was tense but he seemed to half-believe me. Alfred, standing further back, seemed to believe me too - either

199

that or he had seen that I had perhaps saved *him* from reprimand. De Blarde had expected the bludgers to be guarding me, I supposed. "Quite a comfortable bed that, Alfred," I said calmly, "but you should get some more of your private things put in there. It'd be a good deal cosier with a few knick-knacks."

They all looked relieved in their different ways. Ada curtsied to De Blarde and smiled sweetly at Alfred. De Blarde gave a contented nod. Alfred was silent but I took that for contentment too. Ada seemed content anyway and hurried away, dabbing her eyes.

"Ah, Monsieur De Blarde," I said feigning to notice him for the first time. "Now I'm refreshed after my beauty sleep perhaps we could get on with the tour. I'd like to see Mr Merit's room now, if you please. Lord Dreadnaught's son might have visited his father's butler, mightn't he? So we can't leave that one out. He might have left a note there or something to tell us where he's gone to, eh, don't you think?" I felt pleased at over-mastering them with my counterfeiting and moved down to Merit's room before either could answer. Though, in truth, I was anxious to move away from Alfred and De Blarde, for both of them made my flesh creep.

"And is this his room?" I asked, standing outside the one room on the landing I had yet to visit.

"Oui, of course, Monsieur Jakesbere," De Blarde said catching up with me. "We shall make the call, n'est-ce pas?" And so saying, De Blarde knocked hard on the door. There was a silence and then a frail voice called out in response, quivery with age, or fear.

"Who is it?"

"C'est moi, Monsieur De Blarde, mon ami," he answered. "Meester Jakesbere wishes to see your room." De Blarde did not wait for permission but swung the door open immediately. De Blarde paused in the doorway and Alfred brushed past me to join him, his back to me. I stood behind them, almost blocked from Merit's sight, but I could see that the poor fellow was sitting white-faced on his bed, clutching a scarf to his throat and shaking as he looked up at them. Mad Joe was with him. That seemed strange to me. Almost at once the latter jumped up and jerked out his knife, the vicious, broad-bladed skinner's knife. He had it in his fist as if he meant to do serious mischief to one or both of them. For a moment, Merit seemed to exercise some control over Joe, for he put his hand on the boy's arm and the hand holding the knife went limp. However, this was merely the preliminary to some sort of wild fit.

"It's all right, it's all right, Joe!" the old man cried. But Joe was well beyond hearing. He had provoked himself into such a climax of contortions. Whether indeed he would dislocate his own neck, or saw a head off some other, I did not wish to wait to witness. He had provoked himself into such a climax of contortions, such a seizure of spasms, that he fell to the floor, writhing and kicking involuntarily, grinding his teeth and spitting out flecks of foam. Merit held him till he was quite still and, when he was, looked up at them with terror in his eyes before saying an odd thing: "I'll cooperate. I promise."

"Of course, Meester Merit," De Blarde replied, opening the door wider. "It's only Meester Jakesbere, he wait to see you. You must tell Joseph be more careful with his knife. He 'as no need to be afraid of our visitor." De Blarde stepped to one side so that I could be seen. Alfred was standing over Merit and the fallen Joe like a stone sentinel. "I am sorry, Meester Jakesbere," De Blarde continued. "Poor Joseph, as you see, he sometimes 'as, how you say, the fits. That is what you call them in England, yes? And poor Meester Merit is a little unwell too. Non? Under the weather, I think you say. Do you wish to explore the room, Meester Jakesbere?"

"No, no, thank you," I said. "I think I've seen enough."

# Chapter 18

By now, as you may imagine, I only wanted to see Bucket's comforting face and tell him of all the things I had seen so that I might be relieved of all this weight of evidence. To my dismay, De Blarde seemed determined on executing his mistress's decree to the full. I was to be taken on a tour of the *whole* house. Alfred turned away and disappeared into the dark doorway of Lady Dreadnaught's rooms and I followed on after De Blarde.

I was taken on a trawl through the basement, the cellars, the kitchens and every pantry or storeroom it was felt fit to waste my time in. Just when some relief seemed at hand, and the nooks and cubby holes of the house had been exhausted, De Blarde passed me on to my next tormentor. This was the grisly-faced gardener called Ebenezer, whom I had seen before. De Blarde whispered instructions into this fellow's be-whiskered ear. As the only words I was able to decipher were 'garden', I began to comprehend that I was to be taken on a futile tour of the lawns, the outhouses and miscellaneous potting sheds. It was clear to me that my new guardian no more wanted a stroll in the wet than I did, but a disc of silver was dropped in his gunny bag, by De Blarde, and Ebenezer was contracted.

Thus I began a miserable tour of the overgrown and neglected grounds. I was led up the garden path, in and out of the damp and dripping out-houses and through water-logged garden plots till my boots were sodden and my feet frozen. Behind me I kept hearing the bark of iron-heeled boots. I did not much relish the sound of them at all. I dreaded to look behind me but, when I did, my anxiety overcoming my fear, I saw only shadows. I had no choice but to follow my grizzled guard with the gunny sack, fearing all the more that behind the next ghostly tree or tormented piece of topiary I might meet my end and be stuffed into his filthy bag.

We trudged across a water-logged field to an ornate summer house. This building afforded me a sense of relief at first but then I saw that it was positioned precariously, leaning over a small wilderness of jagged boulders and tumbled stones. In kinder circumstances one might have perceived such a sight as a romantic chasm, but my dread was such that I felt I must have been led here merely to be hurled over the edge, to be pierced by the sharp rocks. When I became aware that my guardian seemed merely to be drawing breath and that no steel-booted echoes could be heard, I recovered from my terror for a moment and began to review what I had seen.

Beyond the summer house and the miniature wilderness were streets and fine Mayfair houses and I began to yearn to be out of the tangled chaos that Oblique House had become. After a while, we double backed to the seeding shed. Whatever instructions had been given him, my jailor meant to earn his shilling, rain or no. And then it was the potting shed. And the tool shed. This was a bigger building and looked as if, in happier times, it might have been where the gardeners would have gathered for a brew and could watch over the work of others as they did so. I looked around at its sad state now and wondered hopelessly why on earth I had been brought here. Ah, I thought in a fit of irony, perhaps Richard Dreadnaught had been out here once and left his forwarding address under the pruning shears. Apart from my own feelings of exhaustion, and my nervousness about the bludgers, it was clear to me how neglected the garden and grounds were, from the overgrown and dense bushes at the front to the weed-strewn lawns and flower beds at the back.

After all this, even the horsey smell from the stables was a relief

- that is, until I saw Mad Joe again. His seizure was over, it was clear. There seemed no threat of violence. Even so, I was relieved to see that he was sitting well away from the little brazier where I had stationed myself in order to get some warmth back into my frozen limbs.

Whilst I rubbed the life back into them I watched him sitting precariously under the horses' legs in a bedlam of his own. He was squatting on piles of bloodied furs or skins, torn, perhaps, from fox, ferret or stoat. He was engrossed in a vile form of employment with his knife - hacking at a piece of dead animal as its head lolled. After a moment or two he became aware of me. He regarded me with such malevolence that I was glad I was not one of the creatures caught in his cruel snare. His intense regard felt like a steel trap closing in on me. His eyes, red and piercing, were not the eyes of a 'boy' at all. I realised I had been duped by all this talk of him being a stable lad. This was obviously just the way certain types of employees were described at aristocratic mansion houses. A boy in such a place might in fact be an old man, I realised. Joe was not old but he was certainly, I began to see, a man sure enough.

As he returned to his grizzly task of splaying the dead creature on his lap, digging in his flat blade and spraying up flesh and fur as he worked, I imagined what it might feel like if he had substituted *me* for the kill in his lap. I shuddered. He was not averse to showing off his pretty blade to all who might watch. However, I did not object when he waved it at the two bludgers in billycock hats, who had just now come in. I felt that I should not have minded him skinning *them*. I realised they had indeed been following me on my vain travels. It was *their* heavy steel-shod boots I had heard splashing in the rain behind me. My only comfort was that they looked about as drowned as me. They paid little attention to me at first. However, they were soon drawn to the warmth of the smoking brazier and I did not relish their company around the fire.

What a relief it was when the comfortable figure of Constable Whelks materialised, from a cosy corner where he had clearly been napping, and came over to greet me by the brazier. He had been making himself friendly with the horses and the horse-boys all afternoon, as instructed by Bucket. He was happy as a horse himself, supping on soup and veal pie as if it were nothing other than a full bag of oats he was snuffling at. Whelks paid no attention to my two spymasters but they eyed *him* nervously and thought better of lingering at the brazier. Whelks gave me a wink but said not a word. At any rate, the sight of such victuals seemed to act as a hint to my grizzled gardener friend, and we were soon up and making our way to the main house - via the straight route this time instead of the scenic one.

It seemed like hours ago since we had set off on our travels and I was aching all over and felt that I was fading away - just like the day. The sights of the afternoon were still all a jangle in my head. I was struggling to piece together the meaning of it all. I was sure much of what I had seen I had been meant to see. But what was meant and what was not? I was less sure about that.

Back in the house at last, through one of the back scullery doors, I was pleased to meet up with a friendly face. It was Ada.

"Mr Will, you devil! You nearly got me in right lumber, you did! But I s'pose you got me out of it an' all. I reckon Alfred were quite pleased with me in the finish. But look at you, all wet. Well, come on, don't drip all over master's floor. Come in and get yourself a dry. *And* you, Ebenezer. You can come in too, if yer comin'!"

Until that moment I had not had a formal introduction to my

guide up the paths and round and round the garden, but I supposed it was better late than never. Ebenezer, as was, slithered in like a snail.

"Go on with you! Here! Sit down in that corner and take a bottle o' beer," Ada scolded him.

"Master said…" he grunted incomprehensibly. I was amazed when I heard his voice. I was amazed that he spoke *at all* after an afternoon of tortuous silence and incessant rain. First, there had been a nearly silent Alfred and then this grimly dumb Ebenezer; I had begun to think that I was in a house of mutes. It was the first time I had heard a squeak from my warden. However, at its sound (like rusty wheels) I began to feel nostalgia for the silence.

"Never mind what Master says," interrupted Ada, "he'll be all right with me. Master said we was to feed and water the poor beggar, didn't he?"

"Well," the rusty wheels groaned.

"Oh, go on, you don't 'ave to watch over us like you do your prize petunias! I'll see he does no snooping - where snooping ain't wanted that is. Sit down. Drink yer beer, can't yer!"

Ebenezer hovered, but he seemed pleased with his invitation to a bottle of ale and squatted down on the corner settle to make better acquaintance with his new friend. Indeed, in no time he had attacked several more bottles kindly supplied by Ada and he seemed in a half-doze.

"Who's the 'Master', Ada?" said I at last, deeming it might now be safe to make more enquiries if my guard was slumbering. "You don't mean Lord Dreadnaught I suppose?"

"No! Course not," she replied laughing. "We 'ardly never sees him. No. I mean old Frenchy. *He's* the master 'ere.

"De Blarde, you mean?" I said.

"Yes. He's the feller. Stinker, ain't he?"

And we both laughed, for he surely was.

"Well, I'd *like* to talk, Ada, but I should be getting back to *my* Master, Inspector Bucket, I mean."

"Oh, well before you does, Frenchy says I was to give you yer vittles down here with me, see? Your Bucket'll be eating off a silver tray in the library! Don't you worry about 'im! Us 'assistants' and servants shall have to stay in the scullery and make do!"

I really was anxious to see Bucket, but the thought of food was presenting quite an inducement to stay. I hadn't touched a thing but for a bite or two of toasted bread since breakfast, but now my tour of the house and gardens had made me ravenous. I supposed sharing a morsel of bread and cheese with Ada could do no harm. To tell the truth, I was pleased to have a sit down after my marching up and down like the Duke of York. And soon we started to have quite a merry chat. She put me in mind of Phoebe, as I had said earlier. Although Phoebe was prettier, Ada came a close second. She gave me some warm towels but didn't offer to dry my hair, as I affectionately remembered Phoebe had.

Ada gathered various eatables and displayed them on the table. And quite a collection it was - a feast in fact! Bucket might keep his silver tray. After all, I considered, he had not been traipsing around the gardens for hours. For a start, there was fish, a little green and still full of rather dull eyes but with plenty of oily flesh on it. Then there was a plate of pork. This was cold but Ada considerately warmed it up for me for a minute or so on a plate which was hanging over a kettle. And there were pies: veal, beef and several of pork, all with their jelly-stuffing quite running, as well as a big plate of sweetmeats.

"I don't know as I feel right about giving you this lot, but

Alfred told me to specially."

"Alfred, eh? Very kind of the old chap," I grinned, choosing an oozing pie and beginning to tuck in with great pleasure. "Well he is your beau, isn't he? If he says you should lay out a feast for me I say it's very gentlemanly of him and I say why shouldn't you?"

"It's not that," she began. "It's just that it's all a bit, well … and *I* shouldn't want to be eatin' stuff that's been …"

I took another bite into the pie before she could finish. To tell you the truth, I was famished and was hardly listening.

"Well," she said, "I suppose I *should* do as he says. I don't want him to get all mad with me again, do I? Gets cross sometimes, he does. I *like* him," she hesitated, "but, well, he can be scary. Sometimes I think he's not …"

"Not what?" a rusty voice said, like a saw biting into a log. Ebenezer, the gardener, looked up. Ada gave him a tut and poured more beer from a foaming jug. He slumped back in contentment and began to snore.

"Only, just don't eat too …" she was saying, but I was pouring myself a satisfying dram of beer from the same ale jug after she had put it down and didn't quite hear above the musical sound of the beer glugging into a tankard.

"Aren't *you* eating, then, Ada? There's too much for me!" I said, as I tried a piece of pork.

"I don't like the look of it much," she said. "Been warmed over too many times from the Master's suppers from the week before, if you ask me." At least, I think that was what she said. I was watching her lips as they moved and thinking how she was quite the double of Phoebe. Quite the double. I was taking a spoonful of cook's sweet trifle as I watched her. And a big spoonful of clotted cream.

"All right then, might as well be goose as gander," she said and reaching behind her, grasped a fat green bottle of sweet sherry. "Cook's special, this is, but don't take too much of it or it'll make you sick."

I knew that Inspector Bucket was partial to a sweet sherry, although this one *was* a little tangy. I wondered if he was supping from the same store, in spite of him warning me not to take any rich food or drink. Well, I thought, as I contemplated the gleaming green bottle, if *he* could, I could! As I tipped back another glass, I thought, there could be no real harm in it.

"So what's your Inspector fella after then?" Ada suddenly asked, changing the subject.

"Ah," I replied, tapping my nose. "Confidential that is!"

"Is it about '*im*?"

"Who?" I said, taking another swig of sherry.

"'*Im*. Mister Frog. *Creepy* he is, ain't he? Don't you think so?" When I put my empty glass down and began to look at her seriously, she stood up in alarm. "Oh sir, you ain't been triflin' with a poor girl again, 'ave you? You ain't gonna tell him what I said, are you? I was forgetting myself. I didn't mean nothin' by it!"

"Ada, Ada," I said, taking her hand and guiding her back into her chair. "You've no need to fear me. We've already said what a stinker he is, ain't we, eh? We tripped him up earlier, didn't we? He won't catch *us* out. What larks, eh? And anyway, you can tell me what you like. I'm just the assistant, aren't I? I was always known as 'Confidential Will', when I was back in Chatham! Will, that's my first name. Did I tell yer? What you tell me stays in here." I tapped my head.

"Well, I wish I knew what was going on. No one knows nothin' and that Mr De Blarde!" she scowled. "He gets us all out into the stables, don't he, and he tells us we get paid extra if we're loyal to 'im, and do as we're asked and whatnot and say what we're *told* to say, and all that, but he 'as his big bullies behind him, don't he? His *nasty men*. His bludgers, swinging their big clubs just to make sure we get the message. Mind you, Alfred seems to be Mr Frog's special favourite. I could see Alfred looking at me from that first day I got here. 'Andsome he is, in a pasty sort of way. I don't know as I 'old with men wearing make-up like he does but I suppose it's with him coming over from France with old Froggie. That's what they're like over there, ain't it? Fashionable for a man to get all powdered up, I expect. Some o' the other girls say he's nasty. But I think he's got lovely eyes. He makes me feel safe, Alfred does, see. He's got a way with him. He can make a girl feel special. He told me I looked like a *lady*." She struck a pose to show that she was. "What d'yer think of that?"

"Well, he's right there!" I thumped the table in agreement. Ebenezer stirred but did not wake up.

"But old Froggy - *creepy* he is!" Smiling, she added, "Your Mr Bucket is nice though, ain't he?"

"Has he inter.. inter... has he talked to you then, Ada?" My words seemed to be slipping away from me somehow.

"That he did. I was trembling too when I was called! But he only wanted to know how long I've been here. 'One month come Tuesday,' I says. 'That'll do then,' he says. 'What, is that *it* then? The inquingsition is over, is it? Over before it's begun?' I says. 'Yes,' he says. 'Well,' I says, if that's all there is to bein' a detective, I think I'll be one *myself*, begging your pardon for rudeness'. Then he says, 'Well, if you're going to be a detective, I'm going to be a scullery maid!' Then we 'ad a right larf! He started telling me about his niece who's a maid up in Carlisle - where's that then?"

"It's up north somewhere," I said, tipping the sherry back. We began to giggle quite merrily together for no reason at all. Ada re-filled my glass.

"You're squiffy you are!" she giggled.

"Tostificated!" I said. We laughed again then till a voice like sandpaper interrupted us.

"You want to be careful what you're a-saying and who you're saying it to, Ada!"

"Oh, Ebenezer! You gave me a turn, speaking up suddenly like that! Be off with you! I'm only saying what we all think!"

"Maybe, but the masters don't like these Bow Street Runners crawling around the place."

"What you talkin' about? Mr Will here is just an assistant. Go on with you, you old misery, put your feet up and stop worritin'. Here, 'ave another bottle o' beer. Mr Froggy has given us permission to drink it, Alfred says. So put your feet up and have another lush."

"What's all this offal doin'?" Ebenezer asked, picking up a sweetmeat from the table as if seeing it for the first time. "Should have been chucked out for the pigs days ago."

"Yes, well. That's what I said. But Alfred says I can give it to Mr Jakesbere here."

"Alfred, Alfred, Alfred! That's all you can blinkin' talk about! Well, who's Alfred when he's at home, eh? Well, your Peeler friend's welcome to the lot of it. Him *and* the pigs. Bring me one of those fresh-baked muffins, and I'll say nothing."

"Oh, you ..." she began, but she got up anyway.

I began to notice an uncomfortable churning in my stomach. The things on the table seemed to be crawling about. Ebenezer *did* put his feet up as invited and he swallowed another jug of ale in almost one swig.

212

"They can stick their secrets anyway!" he said, wiping his mouth with a dirty sleeve. His tongue was loosening, whatever his instructions from De Blarde had been. Ada gave him a shocked look. "There's no point in hidin' that!" he said. "These Peelers ain't stupid! Well perhaps one of 'em is," he added, looking at me, I thought, and then at the debris of fish heads and damp pie-crusts. "None of us shan't last long here anyway. We'll be away just like the last lot in case we start *knowing* too much."

"Ah! That's why all the rooms are like they are," I said suddenly. They seemed to have forgotten I was there.

"They had a big clear out you see," Ada said, feeling freer to talk, now that Ebenezer seemed more at ease. "All the old servants have gone, except for Mr Merit, o'course."

"Merit?" Ebenezer guffawed. "Why he'll not be pushed out, no not *'im*. Not till they carry 'im out in 'is coffin, that is!"

"Oh Ebenezer!" said Ada. "Who's doin' all the talkin *now*?

"I shall talk when I wants to!" he shouted again, to emphasise his rights. "And neither you nor your precious Alfred or De Blarde or none of his bludgers will stop me!"

Ada was quiet but gave Ebenezer a piercing look.

"Old Lord Monty won't let Merit go anyhow." Ebenezer said, ignoring her. "Lady Muck's always tryin' to get him to dismiss old man Merit, but he won't." It was Ada who looked around now. Ebenezer swigged back another glass and directed his next comment to me.

"Ain't you noticed 'ow the old feller is scared of them all?" I said I had noticed, although I don't think it came out as clearly as I had intended. "And Mad Joe," Ebenezer continued, "he's all set to murder anyone who so much as puts a finger on the old man. See that you don't get in knife-swiping range of that one or he'll cut your gizzard out of you for tuppence! *There's* one that wants

213

draggin' away and putting in a Bedlam 'ospital before there's a murder, I'll tell you that for free and liberty."

"Well, Joe's harmless enough really," said Ada. "I ain't saying he ain't scary, but as soon as he gets hisself worked up enough to hurt anything, he ends up having one of his fits. Ebenezer seemed unconvinced. "Mr Merit looks after Joe good and proper, though, don't he?" Ada continued. "Never misses giving him his medicine and everything?"

"Bah, that's just mugwort, that is," Ebenezer said scornfully. "Merit gives it to him in that green stuff. Absinthe, they call it. Never does no good anyway, just puts him to sleep. Don't stop his fits."

"Anyway," Ada persisted, "it's sweet the way they look after each other, I think. They ain't neither got a soul to care about 'em so they look after each other."

"Oh *yes,* they do *that* all right!" sneered Ebenezer. "There's some that say old Merit is Joe's father!"

"Never!" gasped Ada.

"Well, why not? Joe's always up in the old man's room, ain't he? He should be sleepin' in his rightful place in the stables amongst the beasts if he's a proper stable boy. That Merit was a bit of a rascal in his young days, they do say."

"Oh, Eb', it's all just gossip!"

"Well, maybe so, but there's *something* odd about them, ain't there? It ain't natural, I say!"

This was the last thing I heard them say, through my cloud of grogginess, for then I must have drifted off into a blank sleep.

When I opened my eyes again, Ebenezer was snoring and Ada had gone. I seemed to be in some sort of waking dream where I was walking in and out of endless garden sheds. I heard a voice then, right in my ear, and I jumped in case the bludgers had come for me. But it was Ada.

"Mr Will! Mr Will! Wake up! There's been a message. Cor, it's like waking the dead. I opened my eyes. "There's a message for you."

"Message?" I mumbled from a drunken sleep.

"Your master's wanting you. He's been calling for you. Wants you to meet him in the library. Now!"

I remember thinking how drunk Ada must be as she unaccountably kept splitting herself in two, against all natural laws. At last, I jerked awake as I realised what she had said. I supposed she meant Bucket when she said 'my Master.' I was angry that she had not told me long ago but, on the other hand, I did not want her to think I was at Bucket's beck and call. I was my own man.

I waited a few moments, longer than I meant to actually, for it took me a long time to get out of the chair. There was something wrong with it and it would not let me up! I made my farewells and staggered upstairs to the main hall. The chequered floor made me feel dizzy again, and I had to hold on to a statue of a lady with no arms. It took me a while to find the main staircase. The footmen just stood in their alcoves. They did not even watch me, let alone come to my aid. When I finally found the stairs they seemed to burst out like gigantic arms, winding to the west and east. I chose one side at random and gripped the gilded banisters with a fury, but they kept sliding out of my hand in a most peculiar way. I stumbled on up until I met the portraits of Dreadnaughts past, once more.

"You're drunk Jakesbere!" they said. I knew I had to get back to Bucket now for urgent reasons indeed. But I could not remember what they were for the life of me.

Bucket was alone in the library when I found it. His figure was

215

a blur. "Sit down, my boy. What have they done to you?" he said anxiously. "You look terrible!" The chair came up at me like a wall. I must have fallen into a dreamy sleep for the next thing I knew, my stomach seemed to be trying to change places with my mouth and I was walking around the library, propped up over Inspector Bucket's arm. His face was uncommonly close to mine and his voice kept changing as if it was coming up from a vault. What was wrong with the old man?

"We've some cunning enemies here, Will," he said. "They've led you a merry dance by the look of you! I thought you'd have been equal to it after our exploits together." His voice sounded disappointed, I thought. "But, never mind, my lad, it's time we took the air anyway. We'll have a turn around the building, shall we, rain or no? We'll see if that don't bring you back to your senses. We need to compare notes, my boy."

The floor seemed continually slipping away and it occurred to me that this diagonal floor under such an oblique ceiling might have been the cause of all the problems in the house. Then I remembered. I had found out who the Beast was! As soon as I remembered who he was, everything would be all right. We passed the footmen in the hall and they all seemed to look like Alfred. A coat was thrown round my shoulders. I stumbled out on Bucket's arm into a grey world of fitfully falling rain. Bucket marched me around the buildings. As we stomped through the puddles he made me recite after him the number of windows he counted. It was a peculiarly infantile game for a grown up detective to play, but I humoured him out of respect. When he had got to thirty, we seemed to have got back round to the porticoed front door again. Even though the cold rain was falling onto my face and we had walked all round the mansion, my head was still swimming.

216

"And how many did you count inside, Jakesbere?" Bucket asked, with rain running off the nap of his hat.

I tried to find the answer in my befuddled brain, but, looking up at the windows as I did, the sudden change in altitude, so to speak, made me feel even more queasy. There were so many things I wanted to tell Bucket, but they seemed to come lurching up in my mind just like the contents of my stomach were lurching into my mouth.

"Inspector," I began, "I forgot to tell you, I met the old gardener. Only that was the other day. There's something today too. Oh, will you forgive me? And his daughter, Sarah...and I said I was courting Phoebe. And Joe, the stable boy, he's the Beast and Mr Merit is his Pa, and he skins people alive. But the thing I have to tell you that's really important is - it's a ring!"

Whether or not Bucket really understood my drunken ramblings is hard to fathom for he looked at me pitifully, sideways on, and his face seemed to dissolve in streams of water. Just then, Whelks came out from the stables leading the horse and cab, plashing through puddles. When I looked up at him in the crazy light, I could not tell which was horse and which was constable. I began to feel my stomach lurch again, as if my guts had turned into some fox that had got stuck in my belly and was eating its way out. I suddenly thought, all right then, I'll let him. Thus it was that when I smelt the rich stench of jelly from the pink pork-pie that Whelks was eating, my stomach did a somersault and the hot fox was out. I had disgraced myself.

"Oh dear!" said Bucket, as I took to my knees and watched something grey fly from my mouth in horrible spasms into the stew of the rain.

"Is it Vauxhall then, Inspector? Or back to St Giles?" Whelks said, as the rain poured from the top of his hat in a stream and I

217

knelt in the dust.

"Take us back home, Whelks," Bucket replied, wearily. "I shall need you again early on the morrow, mind. You can tell me what you found out in the stables then. At least we might get something useful out of the day from what *you've* discovered. What a disappointment the lad's been, eh," he continued, thinking I was deaf to his words. "Let's get him home and give him a sharp dose of Mrs Bucket's cod liver oil."

Despite my disordered condition I felt a deep sense of shame. I had been made a fool of by the entire Dreadnaught household. And now I had let Inspector Bucket down and made a fool of myself.

# Chapter 19

"It's not decent, Phoebe," a voice was saying.

I came out of a black unconsciousness the next morning to the awareness that my head was on someone's lap. And then I heard Phoebe's voice above me.

"Oh Ma, stop going on so. He's asleep isn't he? He needs looking after, the poor soul."

"But you shouldn't be nursing that poor boy in such a way. It's not decent." The other voice belonged to Ma Bucket. I kept my eyes shut.

"Poor Will's been ill, hasn't he? And, anyway, this is the most comfortable way of nursing him."

Phoebe was dabbing my head with a soft towel. "D'you think he's handsome, Ma?" she said after a moment. "He's got such nice curls and funny fluffy eyebrows, hasn't he?"

"Stop fiddling with him, girl!"

"D'you think he'd make a good husband, though?"

"Get off with you, you forward little madam." said Ma Bucket, relenting, "I will say this for him, he's got the looks of his old pa, and Michael was a handsome chap, God bless his soul. And Will's a hard working lad true enough and bright too."

"Do you think he likes me, Ma? Just a bit I mean?" Phoebe was asking. My heart was beating fast.

"*Like* you, my girl? Why he's been in love with you from the minute he saw your smiling face!" said Ma Bucket in reply. "But you shouldn't tease him so. Now, come along, that's enough! We must get him awake so's we can give him something to settle his stomach. Your Pa's waiting to go out with him on urgent business, as you well know!" said Ma Bucket with determination.

"Well, I think Pa's quite the cruellest, meanest, grumpiest old pa that …" Phoebe was saying, but the mention of Inspector Bucket brought me fully awake.

"Inspector Bucket," I muttered. "I must speak to him!"

"You'd best swallow some of this first, young Will," said Ma Bucket, and, before I knew it, I was swallowing something foul on a spoon - designed to settle my still churning stomach, I supposed. When I had recovered I staggered to my feet.

"Sit down, boy, before you fall down!" a deep voice called. "I'm *here*, my lad. Can't you see?" And it *was* Bucket. He had been there all along. "Don't go disturbing yourself for me," he said. "I'm only the cruellest, meanest, grumpiest old man that ever lived." Phoebe gave him a sorry look.

"Y- you must think me a complete fool, Inspector," I managed to stutter out. "But I'm all right now, honest I am," I lied. "I've got to show you something. I've had it for an age. Here in my pocket all along. I found it in the son's room. Richard Dreadnaught. It's all solved … solved! Look!" And I felt in my pockets for the ring. But there was no ring to be found.

"Solved, is it?" said Bucket. "Well that's a blessing, then! That'll save us a deal of running around, that will, won't it, eh?" In my consternation I had risen shakily to my feet again, but Bucket began easing me down immediately. "Sit down, Will, you'll be sick again if you keep leaping about. I've never seen such a one for tumbling about. First it's cab seats you can't stay in and now you can't keep yourself steady on a chair! Don't excite yourself, Will. You've had a sticky turn and that's the truth!" Phoebe regarded me with affection all the while. "Here," Bucket said, holding up a chain from which swung a ring. "Is *this* the ring you mean?"

It was. I took it in my hand. The R in the circle of stones

flickered back at me. "Yes, well," Bucket continued dryly. "Your young Miss Phoebe here emptied your pockets when you were asleep. Though she'd no *business* to be going through a young man's trousers, had you, young lady?"

"He couldn't sleep properly with that jabbing into him," Phoebe said, all innocence.

Bucket's eyebrows rose an inch. "Still," he continued, "this being this and that being that, there's no harm done as yet. That is just a matter of a young man's trousers, but this is a more serious matter to deal with, and time ain't on our side, Will!" A note of disappointment came into his voice again. "This ring you hid in your pocket *may* mean something or it may not. Didn't you think that it was all just a bit *too* easy, eh?" he sighed. "Didn't you think that you might have been *meant* to find it? Just like we were *meant* to read all those bills and those debts and so on? Eh? As it happens, I think your best bit of detective work was getting that scrap of a burnt letter with Dreadnaught's signature on it." I began to reach into my pocket. "Yes, we took that out of your pockets too. Very interesting that is." He paused. "Still," he conceded. "We shan't really know anything till we're able to get on, shall we now? And we can't get on properly till *you're* fixed up and better. And when you *are*, we shall pay a swift visit to Miss Nancy Naiskins. *She's* the one to put us to rights about that ring. She saw it on his finger after all. She'll know it right enough." He stood up and made as if he was about to leave. But, pausing, he asked me a question that penetrated deeply.

"But have you anything *else* to tell me? Has anything *else* slipped your mind?"

"Charlie! Don't be so sharp with the boy!" Ma Bucket warned.

"No. I mean yes," I spluttered. Bucket waited. "I nearly forgot. I found out that Lord and Lady Dreadnaught have changed almost all their servants in the last few months."

"Well, yes Will, I think *I* could guess at that!" I felt desolate at his biting response.

"You mean it all means nothing?"

"No, my boy, I don't say that. Everything means something in our game." He made as if to leave me again but I was determined to repair my good name in his eyes despite Ma Bucket's efforts to protect me.

"And I found out something about the stable boy," I added urgently, "the one they call Mad Joe. He goes out. At night, I mean, and he comes back all bloody."

Bucket looked at me sorrowfully. "Oh, so that means *he's* the Beast now, does it? We've ruled out Richard Dreadnaught after all, have we?"

"Well ..." I began.

"Poor Joe likes to skin animals, doesn't he?" Bucket said. "A horrible habit that, unless you're a Red Indian on the American prairies of course. But it doesn't necessarily mean he rapes and kills little girls, does it?"

He saw me look hurt. Ma Bucket took his arm and took my part silently. Bucket relented.

"I don't mean to scold you, Will. What do *I* know, eh? An old fool of an Inspector?" He sighed. "All these things you've found out *are* important and we shall ponder them together, lad. But let's *measure* our evidence before we jump to naming our villain, shall we, eh?"

There was a knock. The fat face of Constable Whelks filled the doorway. "Righto, Whelks. You're a bit early for us. We'll be an hour or so yet I should think, whilst young Will here is nursed. Take the weight off and 'ave a sit down." Whelks gave me a wink and made himself comfortable on a parlour chair, quite like one of the family.

"I promised Nancy Naiskins some ribbons, my dear," Bucket said, turning to his wife. "I promised them long since and should have taken some by now." He turned back to me. "Well," said Bucket, regarding me more kindly. "Get yourself ready as soon as you can.

And so Bucket and Whelks began to talk. Whelks's comfortable voice started as just a warm hum but as time wore on - and Ma Bucket called Phoebe away so that I could rest - it began to shape into words. And I began to listen.

"Well, as I was saying, none o' the stable lads or the adult hands would talk to me at first," Whelks said. "They're all in terror of those bully boys hanging around the house. I don't suppose you missed an eyeful of them, did you, Inspector?" Whelks asked.

"No, Whelks. I've been wondering about those since we saw them on our first visit," Bucket said thoughtfully. "I've had Sergeant Meehan make a few enquiries about any escapees from the prison ships. You'll not be surprised to know that they were conveniently left out of the list of servants that was given to me. But, go on, you managed to get one or two of the stable hands to tell you something, I suppose," Bucket added.

"Well, once I'd shared a few horsey stories with them they let their guard slip a bit," Whelks admitted. "And, well, to cut a long story short, Inspector, I did find out one or two things about that Joe character and that Mr Merit. It seems that Mad Joe was actually *born* in the 'ouse and was brought up there. One of the stable lads told me that Joe had a terrible temper on him and could be dangerous. He'd struck out at a little wench once when her teasing of him was more than he could bear. But, apparently, he never does much damage because as soon as he gets worked up, his fits come over him and he drops into a dead faint!"

"And why wasn't he just dismissed along with all these others who've been moved on?" asked Bucket.

"Well, Inspector, the rumours are it's to do with the previous Lady Dreadnaught who 'ad a soft spot for the boy when she was alive," Whelks continued, "and I've 'eard that Lord Dreadnaught holds his first wife's wishes very dear. One lad said that Mr Merit always sorted out any of Joe's problems with his Lordship so that the boy didn't get dismissed."

"And why would Lord Dreadnaught listen to Merit? Did they have an answer for that?" Bucket asked.

"Same thing, I think," said Whelks. "Merit was a favourite with his first wife, even though the second Lady Dreadnaught is always trying to get rid of them both. It seems to be the only thing the old lord won't let Lady Dreadnaught 'ave her own way about."

I was beginning to feel sleepy again, in front of the fire and listening to these familiar voices, but I was awake enough to hear Bucket ask if there was anything else.

"Yes, Inspector," said Whelks. "The odd thing is that, though old Merit seems to be the only one who can tame Joe when he gets angry, the boy's been known to get violent with the old man 'imself at times."

I may have dozed off for a moment then, for next they seemed to be talking about the variety of vehicles kept in the stables. Something about how there was not a *mark* on any of them, as Whelks was saying. I remembered suddenly what Bucket must have been asking. Long ago, that night at the Hell Club, Bucket had scratched a mark on the Beast's cabriolet as it clattered past us, and he had nearly gone under the wheels.

"No, Inspector," Whelks was saying. "I 'ad a gander at all the vehicles they keep and though they 'ad a private 'ackney amongst them, it looked all spick and span as far as I could see. A bit *too* spick, to tell the truth, like it 'ad had a new lick o' paint quite recently."

The next thing I was aware of was the clattering of horse's hooves outside the window. I had dozed off completely. Bucket had completed his questioning and Whelks had been out to bring the horse and cab around, ready to take us away. Next, Bucket appeared with his greatcoat and hat already on.

"Come on then, my lad. You've rested long enough, surely. You've been mollycoddled by these women for *far* too long anyway! We've work to do! We need a word with Miss Nancy Naiskins."

"Oh *must* he go out, Pa?" begged Phoebe, who had brought water for me to wash with. "He's not *nearly* better, are you, my love?"

My heart leapt at her words but Bucket gave her a quizzical look before continuing. "He's better *enough* and, yes he *must*, Miss. But even if you do think me mean or grumpy or cruel, if he must suffer then so must you. I mean to make you come along with him to see that he's right and doesn't topple over on me!" Phoebe clapped her hands with delight and began kissing and embracing Bucket with glee. "Be off with you, girl!" he said. "What is a mean old man to do after all? I can tell that you won't be separated from him whether I will it or not! Though I know you'll be a deal o' trouble!" Phoebe began bustling for coats and gloves straight away, in case Bucket should change his mind, I suppose. "*Mind* though," Bucket said. "It'll be a squeeze in that cab and it's not much of an outing to be visiting people in such desperate straits amongst the miseries of Seven Dials!"

Suddenly Gertie, who'd been ear-wigging, as usual, piped up,

"Me, me too! Can I, Pa? Can I, Ma? I want to see Nancy Naiskins too! Can I, Pa, please, please!"

# Chapter 20

It seemed to take an age to travel to Seven Dials. The rain had eased off in the night but there had been a new downpour in the early morning and the roads were still slippery wet. The poor horse skidded continually, but it kept plodding on notwithstanding. During this journey, as instructed, I soberly informed Bucket of all I had seen whilst we were at Mayfair. He sighed and shook his head as my revelations continued. Phoebe listened admiringly and squeezed my hand in encouragement. It may be that her innocent attentions were again the cause of my omitting one important piece of information that had serious consequences later. But the blame of course is all my own.

At last we emerged into the crooked alleys and broken-backed houses of Seven Dials. There seemed to be more mire and offal flowing in the streets than ever. It made me feel nauseous to look upon it and to smell it, for it stank of soot and sewers and sickness. The closer we were to our destination the quieter we became. Little Gertie's face became paler and I could see that Bucket was beginning to regret allowing her to accompany us. Clearly her young mind was revisiting the memories of her sad and recent past.

I recalled that in the first days after she had been rescued, Bucket and I had endeavoured to trace any family that she might belong to, searching these same tumble-down alleys and miserable streets in vain. We had found only one person, the Mrs Baxter that used to give Gertie bread. Mrs Baxter was a kind but disturbed soul, scraping a living amongst the rats in a tumble-down building by Field Lane. I remember she had looked at Gertie with disbelief.

"Her, never seen 'er afore, Mister," she had croaked, perhaps thinking that we had come to do harm to her if she did recognize Gertie. "What did yer say yer called her? Gertie? That's a flowery name for a bit o' peg meg, ain't it? But look at yer, now, though!" she had relented. "A little princess ain'tcher? Look at yer," she had cackled, pawing at Gertie's dress whilst Gertie herself hid timorously against the greasy wall. For a second, the haunted expression that we had seen on Gertie's face when we had first seen her at St James had come over her again.

"Don't letta take me! Don't letta take me!" poor Gertie had sobbed. Bucket had to hold her tight. I remembered how this desperate job of trying to find Gertie's rightful mother had broken his heart. "We won't, girl," he had whispered to her. "We're only trying to see if we can find your proper mummy or daddy."

"Her mummy and daddy?" the old woman had croaked with her eyes rolling. "Well, her daddy's drunken in the gin 'ouse and her ma's in the workhouse – if she ain't on the trade. If they ain't both dead and buried in the bone-yard I mean. But look at yer. Look at yer, now, eh?" she had cackled again. She was not an unkind old soul. Bucket had rummaged in his deep pockets and produced a large handful of coins. The old woman had forgotten us in her excitement at such riches. We did not submit Gertie to such torment again.

As we passed the choked streets around the ancient rookeries and the haunts where Gertie would have spent her first years, Phoebe held her hand tightly like the sister she had become, for, of course, Phoebe too shared dark memories of the same shadowy streets. There were crowds of dripping creatures making breakfasts from the refuse of the streets and the drunken or near-dead twitching back into life after their nights in beer-houses or gin-palaces. The black and crumbling buildings loomed out of the rain like rancid cheeses riddled with maggots. As we turned into a stinking alley, the sun made a pale face through some inky clouds.

At last, Whelks drew the cab to a stop with a splash. Getting down, he looked about for a likely-lad who might be trusted to look after the horse for a minute, for the price of a penny. After a moment he lighted on a little sooty-faced urchin whom he clearly felt he might trust. The cabbage he seemed to have for an ear and the splinter for a tooth made him look most untrustworthy to me, but the sight of a couple of ha'pennies suddenly made him at least adopt a look of honesty. When Whelks promised him another penny if the horse was still in one piece when he returned, his dark eyes lit up.

After this interlude, Phoebe and I, and Bucket and Gertie, walked hand in hand along the alleys, stepping carefully over the floating offal. Whelks led the way, carrying a great bag of sea-coal on his broad shoulders, turning around to check that his cab had not already been chopped up for firewood or the horse minced for breakfast. One or two ugly faces leered out at us from the shadows of the alleys, but when they saw it was Bucket who was amongst them they managed a sort of grin. He spared them all a word and a touch on the arm or shoulder, sometimes pressing a coin into a grubby hand as we picked our way on. Bucket was carrying Gertie now and Phoebe was holding her skirts up above the mire. At last we reached the crumbling building where the Naiskins lived, and then dived down into the dark cellar where John Naiskins' door marked the opening to their subterranean home.

"Come, 'ave ya?" said a blunt voice as we threaded our way down. "Caught him yet, 'ave ya?" said the voice again, echoing up at us from the stony walls.

"Make way, John Naiskins," said Bucket. "I can see you're not a gentleman as is fit to be spoken with. I want a word with your missus and your daughter, so don't be holding me up." He pushed past the wiry, angry figure of John Naiskins, as the latter lurked in the shadows sucking on a piece of straw.

"Mrs Naiskins!" Bucket called out as he stood at the cellar entrance and looked into the ramshackle room. "It's Inspector Bucket and Mr Jakesbere. I've brought Constable Whelks with me and he's brought some sea-coal for you." There was no answer. Bucket nodded at Whelks who staggered in and plumped down the heavy jute bag by the makeshift grate. Naiskins followed on half-drunk, watched for a second with a look of contempt, and then blundered back up the crumbling steps, giving a bow-legged urchin a clout for his trouble of being in the way. Whelks followed him out as if he feared Naiskins might sniff out his horse and sell it to the knacker's yard for glue.

"Inspector Bucket!" said Mrs Naiskins, coming from behind a dirty curtain, straightening her clothes and wiping her hands on a rag. "Why! And you've brought a lady an' a child. Bless me! You must come in out o' that doorway and try and dry yourselves if you can." Although she stood amongst the creeping insects and the dripping water of the crumbling cellar, she moved with grace, brushing fallen debris from stools and picking dirty things up from the floor.

"Don't trouble yourself, Mrs Naiskins," said Phoebe.

"But, I've nothing to offer you and we've as many puddles in here as out there!" She looked around anxiously for a moment. "Where's John?"

"Slung his hook at the sight of me, I think!" said Bucket. "But, we can make ourselves cosy without him, I should think. Well,

don't just stand there, Mr Jakesbere, get us a fire cracking and…"
Phoebe stepped forward on cue and started unwrapping the
bundle she carried. "I hope you'll excuse the liberty but we've not
had time for breakfast, so Mrs Bucket has packed us up a bit of a
picnic. We hope you'll let us share it with you?"

Whilst the food was being laid out, Bucket had been looking
around for little Nancy. "I'd hoped for a word with your little
'un, is she not about?"

"She's been staying with Miss Alice at *The White Lion* over at
Cripplegate, sir. They're quite the best of friends. Miss Alice 'as
been teaching Nancy to read her letters. She should be back any
minute though." As she spoke, there was the clod of heavy boots
on the steps and a sudden squawk.

"I'm back, mother!" a child's voice called. She hopped inside,
not noticing us, it seemed. "And look who's brung me 'ome."

"Sparrow!" I shouted. So that was whom the heavy boots
belonged to.

"Jakes!" Sparrow exclaimed, and worked my hands like a water
pump. The minutes after that were filled up with greetings and
introductions and explanations, as if we were all guests at some
great house, and the two little girls danced around each other in
glee like life-long friends. Sparrow was on his best behaviour,
you will not be surprised to know. After all, he had just stumbled
into a hovel and found the great Bucket staring at him! But
Bucket seemed to have left the Inspector at the station for a little
while and joined in the jollity with the rest of us. Soon we were
all sitting around the broken table, sharing old wooden boxes for
stools, cutting into the bread and passing plates of ham as if we
were at a banquet.

When breakfast was over, Bucket brought out the red ribbons
he'd promised, much to the pleasure of the two little girls, and

Phoebe set-to plaiting their hair.

"I thought you'd just made her up, Jakes, s'truth I did!" Sparrow whispered to me, nodding at Phoebe. "But she's capital, ain't she?"

"Shut up, Sparrow, she'll hear!" I hissed.

"You've caught yourself a pretty little fish there, Jakes," said Sparrow, ignoring me, "and I'm blessed if she don't seem to like *you* too! Wait till I tell Alice, tonight! An' I'd like to see the look on Mrs Pecker's face when I gets back to my lodgings and tells her you're *not* in jail in Newgate, as she still thinks you are, but courting the ward of Inspector Bucket!"

"How is the old hypocrite?" I laughed. "Still respecrable, I hope!"

"Oh yes, ain't she? But she don't 'alf like 'avin' *me* there, Jakes. She feels 'pretected by the law', she says, what with me bein' a *particular* friend of Inspector Bucket his-self."

"A friend of the Inspector's, are you?" said Bucket, surprising us both by coming up behind. Sparrow scuttled to his feet, embarrassed. Bucket sat down, giving him one of his looks that seemed to be measuring you up for a sojourn in a lock-up. "As you are a *particular* friend of mine, Constable Sparrow, I've got a job for you. By the time I get back to the station," he said, scribbling some instructions on a piece of paper, "I want you to have summoned this Mr Gavelstone, the gardener that you and Mr Jakesbere have made the acquaintance of, and bring him back with you to Cripplegate, so I can ask him a few questions."

Sparrrow went white, fearing that he was in trouble with Bucket for not arresting old man Gavelstone for the breach of the peace in *The White Lion* the other day.

"I've written a note here," Bucket said, folding it in two, "that tells you what I want you to do with him when you get him back to the station. As a *particular* friend of mine, make sure you carry out my instructions to the letter. Well, go on then, *take* it," said Bucket, looking him in the eye and waggling the paper irritably. "Now 'op it!"

"Now my girls," Bucket said, calling Gertie and Nancy Naiskins to sit by him. "Nancy, my dear, have a look at this ring I have in my pocket." So saying, Bucket brought out the Dreadnaught signet ring that he had strung on to a chain. Suddenly, Nancy snatched at it as if it was an insect she was crushing. She held it tightly, and then after a second opened her hand. She held it close up to her eyes and turned it round and round as if she were a little doctor inspecting the grisly product of an operation.

"That's it," she said. "That's the ring the man had." Gertie bent down to look - equally intently.

"Are you sure now, Nancy?" said Bucket. "I need you to be quite sure, my dear. Look again for me, will you?" She looked *him* in the eye now, with the same professional expression. "That's the ring. But it ain't a picture. I know what it says now, cos Miss Alice taught me some letters. It says R." She handed it back to Bucket abstractedly, as if it was altogether forgotten. She held out her hand for Gertie and then they ran off to play together, as if there had never been a ring.

"That's it then, Inspector," I said with confidence. "Mr *Richard* Dreadnaught. The son of Lord Dreadnaught himself. I said he was the one, didn't I? And here's the proof!" Phoebe smiled at me proudly.

"So it seems, my lad," Bucket replied, "so it seems, but ..." Bucket's caveat was interrupted by the door above us being thrown back with a violent clatter and the spectacle of John Naiskins tumbling down to us, drunker than before.

"Where's the jemmy, Tilly?" he shouted, looking around

233

wildly. Nobody moved. "The jemmy!" he shouted viciously. "Where is it?" He started throwing tools and rags into the air. "Damn me, I'll…" but he failed to finish saying why he should be dammed. Instead he looked about him as if he had suddenly seen us all. "Still 'ere are you?" He turned to scowl at his wife. "Enjoyin' yourself wiv your swell pals, are you? Cosying up to the Law, an'all, eh? The *Law*? Ha! Still *'ere* is it, the Law? Mr Meddlin' Bucket? Why don't you hoof it, eh?" he spat out, waving his arms and fists at Bucket in implacable anger. "What use 'ave you been, whilst little girls 'ave been done-up by *swells*? What do you do, Bucket, but sit and drink at *my* table!" His voice was full of contempt and his eyes full of red rage. Nonetheless, Bucket held his gaze coolly and Naiskins was the first to look away. "Where's that jemmy?" he said at last, turning and shouting at his wife again. Mrs Naiskins began to weep. "Tell me quick," he continued, "or I won't answer for it and you shall have a dose for your trouble. A *dose*, d'yer hear me?"

To my horror, Phoebe stood forward and stepped boldly between husband and wife. Naiskins regarded her coldly for a moment as if he would enact his violence on her person, but he seemed unable to sustain concentration on any one thing for long and merely cursed again, continuing his wild search.

"Naiskins!" shouted Bucket sharply, stopping him in his tracks. "What's all this about? What d'yer want a jemmy for, eh?

"I ain't a-scared of you, Mr Interfering Bucket. Don't you *know*? He's been *seen*!" Bucket looked dumbfounded for a moment. "Yes, that's made yer stare, ain't it?" Naiskins said triumphantly. "He's been copped! The Beast! The Beast what you let slip through your fingers, Mr Precious Bucket! We've found him without your help."

"Who have you found?" Bucket said in astonishment.

"Haven't you been listening?" Naiskins sneered. "We've spotted a swell that's been seen visitin' Mrs Mason's by the work-'ouse."

Bucket turned pale.

"These last two days," Naiskins continued, "he's been seen lurkin' outside old Mason's and askin' questions o' poor folk passin' by. As brazen as you like, for 'e knows you lot won't 'arm him. But *I* mean to give 'im a good slatin'!" He pulled up his jemmy at last. "Ah, my beauty! We'll see 'ow this'll sting 'im!"

Bucket took a step closer. "I'll advise you now, John Naiskins, if you take the law into your own hands, you'll end up spending your days and nights in Millbank on shot drill!"

"Too late, Bucket! Too late! There's a band of us, see? We mean to use lynch-law on 'im, seein' as the real law won't do nothin'. Now, out of my way! We shan't let 'im escape this time!"

# Chapter 21

Bucket was out and up the stairs after Naiskins. He moved as fast as I had seen him move that night he had chased the cab at the Hell Club. I was left with a dilemma. Here were Phoebe and Gertie in a strange house all by themselves, but I needed to be with Bucket - chasing the Beast. Mrs Naiskins was crying. Phoebe was comforting her. Gertie and Nancy were staring wide-eyed with their thumbs in their mouths like babes again. In a second I heard Bucket's police rattle clattering and then a yelling from the stairs. Voices were echoing back and forth. I hovered in an agony of indecision.

At last Phoebe looked up from the sobbing woman. "Go after him then, Will," she said. "Go on! We shall be all right. Send for us when you can. We can't leave poor Mrs Naiskins." My heart beat proudly for Phoebe as I leapt up the crumbling steps two by two.

At last, emerging from the reeking alleys and courts, I was back on the greasy, wet road. Bucket was well ahead of me but ahead of *him* was a mob of angry men. The clatter of Bucket's rattle was drowned out under the thumps someone was giving on an old iron pot. The road was already awash with shadowy figures, but now they seemed to be all swimming together, swaying to the same tune. More and more grimy-faced and wiry men - with some small barefoot boys and girls - were creeping out of the hovels to this call. Some of them were carrying sticks, others shovels or just bits of ugly, broken wood. Bucket was shouting at them and his rattle was clattering insistently but they were taking no notice of him. It was with some relief that I saw Whelks splashing up, hollering at us from his seat on top of the cab and shuddering to a stop in a fizz of horse steam. Bucket bustled up and a second later I joined him whilst Whelks wheeled the horse around.

We could make no way though the narrow alleyway and so Whelks was forced to make for the wider thoroughfares. Putting my head out of the window and looking back, I could see an ugly crowd gathering by a beer-house. Swollen by the numbers of flushed and drunken men from within, the mob disappeared down a crooked and narrow alley. We were going the wrong way about it as far as I could see, but even so, in five minutes or thereabouts, we were back by St Giles and driving on madly for the almshouses and the house that Naiskins called a 'baby farm'.

However, we were not to reach our intended destination. Our quarry, it seemed, had circled back to *us*. As we skidded around Cripplegate, receiving the abuse of the stall holders and pedestrians along the high street as we did so, a running man burst out of an alley onto St Giles Green, pursued as if by wolves. I knew him straight away. I recognised him from the picture Bucket had uncovered at Oblique House. It was Richard Dreadnaught - the Beast!

He was followed by a roar that seemed to hover in the sky like a cloud - and then the cloud manifested itself as the mob appeared and hurtled after him as one - one creature with a monstrous red face, wet with running, and baying for blood like a wolf. The Beast skidded on the road and they were nearly on him - but, as quickly, he found his footing and was up and running, like a fox chased by the baying hounds. *We* skidded and screeched to a halt too, the horse nearly falling under the wheels as the cab reared up. I was on the floor again by now, of course, but Bucket was up and out. I scrambled after him, in time to see Dreadnaught leaping though the church doors of St Giles and the doors banging shut.

237

The mob was wild but they had tumbled now near enough into the maw of St Giles Police Station itself, out of which, in response to Bucket's rattle, there emerged a stream of policemen, winding their rattles in turn and waving their sticks. What a noise it was! Rattling and drumming and calls for blood and vengeance filled the air. Dreadnaught must have had some old fashioned notion that he could claim 'sanctuary'. If he had, the Beast was soon to be disabused - for the door was bundled down like so much matchwood and he was dragged out without mercy. I almost had a moment's pity for him. I had never heard such a blood-thirsty roar. Whether everybody in the mob knew who Dreadnaught was, or even why they were there, I was uncertain; nonetheless, their blood was up and I thought they would rip him apart in front of my eyes.

I confess that even I felt overwhelmed by the mob hysteria. I was possessed by a desire to attain a position at the front of the mob, to exercise my own repressed urge for revenge in fury at the monster's despicable acts. I am ashamed to admit to such an animal instinct for revenge but something in me *wanted* to see him ripped apart. He had ripped children apart, hadn't he? He was only receiving justice. Those who carried him from the church hurled him down like a dead carcass onto the mud and began to set about him with their sticks. Luckily for him, it was not those with shovels or jemmies who were at the front or he would have been dead within a minute. At this moment, Bucket jumped in - risking his own life, there is no doubt. The mob was ugly and it had blood in its eye. It would turn on anyone who got in its way.

What Bucket did next was extraordinary. He began setting about the mob with the brass end of his staff. Those at the front clearly felt, at first, that this was a compatriot arriving with a particular vendetta against the Beast who was perhaps a little over-enthusiastic with his beatings. While they sucked their knuckles, seeming to leave the fallen man to the mercies of this new avenger, Bucket managed to drag the bleeding body of Richard Dreadnaught back against the church wall, where it had some protection. By then the police had got to the front, heaving themselves through with their truncheons whirling. They formed a semi-circle around Bucket and the Beast, protecting them both like Roman legionnaires guarding a fallen Emperor.

The mob was taken aback by this show of organised force from the policemen of St Giles Station. They lost their animal lust for a moment but, when they recovered, they started cursing and bellowing at Bucket and the police phalanx in an only too human sort of way. I had managed to squeeze closer by now, getting kicked and shoved for my trouble. I caught Bucket's eye and he nodded at a corpulent and sweating constable to let me through under the great ham-bone of his arm. Bucket was wiping the blood away from Dreadnaught's head with his own handkerchief under the protection made by this police cordon. As I joined him, he tossed the rag to me with a look. I supposed he meant *I* was to be the nurse-maid now. I had no inclination to doctor 'The Beast of London Town'; indeed, it brought a nauseous taste into my mouth.

The Beast had already received a vicious wound to the head. The blood was flowing freely and the rag Bucket had given me for the job was already sodden. As I dabbed at the wound, the fevered head recoiled in pain beneath me. I had my first look into the face of a murderer - my first close-up look at someone who could rape little girls, mutilate them with a knife, and leave them for dead. The truth is, he did not seem so much of a beast, lying there with his blood seeping slowly into the mud. Indeed, he seemed almost child-like himself: a little thin and care-worn, his dark hair clotted up with blood and his face a mess of bruises. He was moaning, so he was still alive – just. A wave of pity came over me and I found I had to force myself to remember what grievous and despicable acts he had visited on innocent children and what, indeed, he had tried to do to Nancy Naiskins and to our own little Gertie. This thought made me none too gentle with him. Mud covered him from head to foot, but one could still see that he wore the clothes of a gentleman. His eyes flickered half-open for a second or two and he gave out a louder, more plaintive groan. I remember thinking how he did not actually *look* much like one would think The Beast might look, not what one would *understand* to be the face of a cruel monster.

Small fights had broken out between some police and the mob as the crowd grew angry again and turned their attention to the custodians of the law themselves. Individual members of this angry mob were screaming hysterically at their fellows, egging them on. "Boot 'em! Boot 'em!" some cried, as if it were the police who were the villains now. Fortunately, reinforcements from St Giles Station arrived, the mob was matched and some decided to give up the fun and limp away.

Now that the crowd was pushed back, Bucket returned from marshalling his forces and bent down beside me to see the hurt the Beast had taken. Despite the increased presence of the police, I was still wary of the mob members at the front of the crowd who had had their knuckles rapped by Bucket. They were licking their bruises and eying him and me with as much hate as they had previously shown for the monster. There only needed to be a small chink in our defences and these leaders would resume the battle. John Naiskins' head was amongst those in the front rank, sneering and yelling insults. I could not tell if this abuse was aimed at Dreadnaught or Bucket, although Bucket took no account of it either way. In fact, he had Dreadnaught's hands in his own like one might cradle a baby's, turning them over as if looking for something in them. He was muttering to Dreadnaught - or to himself - I was unable to tell which. I remember thinking how strange it was that Dreadnaught's hands should have been so different from what one might expect from the hands of a killer. They were not clawed or hooked like an ogre's but, instead, were neat and almost elegant. Finally, Bucket decided he had found what he wanted and he stood up, observing the seething, baying crowd still swaying in opposition against the police phalanx. Indeed, his general observation became a particular one, staring with intensity into the eye of each individual. This look was one of undisguised rebuke and must have made even the ugliest-looking member of the mob uncomfortable in his boots. Bucket had a trick of just looking and making one feel guilty. It was as if he knew all the heinous deeds one had ever committed and was saying, 'I feel for you and I know you're only human, but I'm sorry, I shall just have to take you away and have you locked up in Newgate.'

Before long, under the siege of such regard, the mob at the front began to quieten. Of course, this species of silence was one that seemed to have its own inherent loudness, a degree of silent volume that transmitted itself through the whole crowd, like a sudden silence in a church service, and soon, it seemed, the whole mob had become still. There was something almost magical about Bucket in moments like this. How did this one, quite corpulent, not very tall and slightly ageing figure, have such an effect on so many who stood around him - rabble as they were?

"All right, gentlemen!" he called out in a stentorian voice when

241

he perceived the moment was ripe. Those who were still bawling out deeper in the melee became quiet and looked embarrassed, as if caught out talking at a funeral. "You've got him. He's caught. Here he is." The crowd watched Bucket warily. "Now I am going to take him into the station. And we shall sort him out. Have no fear of that!"

"Get on wiv yer!" a mocking voice called, breaking the spell.

"You've left him roaming round to do his mischief long enough!" called another. A voice I recognised only too well. "D'yer think you can keep him safe now then, Bucket?" The word Bucket was snarled like a swear word. Some other ugly voices called out in support of this sneer and the police at the front had to brace their arms to stop a fresh charge.

"Oh yes, John Naiskins," for that was who it was, of course. "That I can! We shall take this 'ere gentleman - if gentleman he is - and lock him up safe. *Safe* I say! And if it *is* him who's been committing the heinous crimes that you all know about, I'll be the first to be glad to see him swinging at the end of a rope. The first!" There was a low murmuring in the crowd at that. "You *know* me, don't yer? You *all* know me, but if you don't, I'll tell yer - I'm Inspector Bucket of the Detective, and I've been on this patch for half my life. I've served you and your families for this generation past, as many of you know!" There were one or two complaining murmurs in the crowd at this. "Yes, it's true - I've had harsh words with some of you. And you've needed them an' all. And some of you have spent a night or two, or more, in my cells. But if there's one thing you know about me, you know I've been fair by you, and I've always been honest with you and told you what's what and been straight with you." The muttering stopped. "And do you know what? I'm not sure that this 'ere beaten-up bloke is really the one you're lookin' for. If he was, I'd have put a boot in myself!"

"O' course he is!" someone yelled from the back.

"He might be and he might not be," Bucket replied, "but I ain't going to allow you to take the law into your own hands! I don't want to be having to fill our lock-up with the likes of you when there's a *real* villain to be caught." He looked around fiercely. "Now, I'm telling you, and I'm warnin' you, and I'm orderin' you, to put away your cudgels, your jemmies and your shovels - and go home! And I mean do that now! Now, then." He looked around. "On your way!"

The low muttering broke out again but, to my amazement, they did listen - drifting off despite themselves. Even Naiskins followed on, once he realised that the flames had been burnt out of his comrades and that the heat had cooled. The diversion was over and the entertainment was done. The mob had dissolved into individuals and these individuals began to want their victuals or only just then noticed it was raining or that they were muddy. There were still a few who could not resist a jeer and there were some small children who had tagged along for the fun of it, tossing a few stones at us before running away.

Bucket commanded two hefty constables to fetch a pallet. They came back after a minute or two and the unconscious Dreadnaught was deposited with not much gentleness. Nevertheless, a guard was formed around his body and it was marched off across the chewed-up green of St Giles, to the station. As they moved off, there was a last flare-up from the departing crowd. I heard a policeman call angrily, "Get back!" and as Bucket looked up, I heard a familiar female voice:

"Richard!" it called. "Oh, what have they done to you?"

It was Sarah Gavelstone.

# Chapter 22

A tremor of guilt and shock went through me. I had hardly thought of Sarah Gavelstone since our meeting in Alice's room at *The White Lion*. She had asked me to keep her secret and now my guilt was twofold: firstly, for not telling Bucket that I had found her straight away and, secondly, for finally giving her away. The shock was in seeing her child-like and distraught figure coming through the dispersing crowds and realising fully that she had some kind of link to the Beast.

Dreadnaught was her lover, although how a pretty thing like her could have been in love with such a creature, I could not guess. And she *was* in love with him, clearly enough, as she stood feverishly sobbing over his bloodied body. The two policemen who had charge of him were great hulking fellows, one with fists like hams and the other, if a little thinner, no less beefy and with a vivid purple birthmark splashed across his face that made him look like he was permanently angry and ready to charge into battle. Nonetheless, even these two specimens of Her Majesty's Constabulary were charmed by Sarah Gavelstone's guileless affection for the strange man sprawled on the wooden pallet.

Bucket must have realised who she was but he stood back and observed her quietly as she pawed at his unconscious body like a bereft animal, clutching at his unmoving hand. Surely Bucket would wish to interview her, but for the moment he maintained his silence. The two broad-shouldered constables carried him inside the station and Miss Gavelstone followed. I was trying to keep my face hidden all the while, but she found me out soon enough and began begging and pleading – as if *I* had power over what might happen to him. The policemen tolerated her walking along with him and holding his hand tightly, even as they carried him inside the station and deposited him unceremoniously in a lock-up. However, she would not release her hold even then, but knelt by his side, kissing his hand and weeping by turns. They had to drag her from him in the end. The station was all confusion with it - except for Bucket who maintained his sphinx-like demeanour, ignoring her hysteria. It seemed that he was more concerned for the health of his new prisoner than for his prisoner's romantic life with Sarah Gavelstone. Whilst she sobbed and chafed at his hands, Bucket hurried out to call for the doctor. In Bucket's absence the two policemen pulled Miss Gavelstone away from the Beast at last, and the door to the lock-up was bolted on the unconscious prisoner whilst she commenced to pound on it, sobbing and shouting his name as if in a delirium.

"Richard! Richard! Richard!" she called, in such a fit of anxiety that my heart went out to her. I felt duty-bound to intercede on her behalf.

"For pity's sake, let her sit in with him, can't you? It can do no harm!" I said.

"Oh, very likely!" said the one with the purple birthmark. "As if we would, eh, Blakey!"

"Oi, Oi! Who's this a-givin' us orders, then, Cokey?" said Constable Blakey to his friend. "Don't you start gettin' ideas above your station, young feller," he said, as he stood with his broad back against the door. "You might be Inspector Bucket's assistant but you *ain't* a copper now, are you? You heard what the Inspector said to the mob. He *promised* the monster'd be locked up, and locked up he'll be, won't he Cokey? Whatever this little miss does."

"Oh, very likely!" said the other.

Whether it was Constable Blakey's determined words or my

intervention that caused it, Sarah Gavelstone became suddenly quiet. She had been bruising her tiny fist against the cell door fruitlessly but now she appealed to me directly, and in a voice quite calmly rational.

"Why are you locking him up, sir? What do you think he's done, please?"

I was taken aback by this change in her from steam to ice and it took me a moment to open my mouth to answer. To my amazement, before I could, she began with her cries again - starting another desperate plea.

"My father! My father, where've you put him? Where is he?" And with that she began running round the room looking for *this* gentleman now and calling out *his* name in a panic. Of course, she must have known or been left word that her father had been taken to the station and that he would be here by now, but Constables Coke and Blakey knew nothing of that, perhaps, and stood gaping, surprised, no doubt, by her spirit. Both stood scratching their heads, half smiling, one stroking his square chin and the other pulling his purple ear - as if the answer to her question might be there.

"Miss, Miss!" I called. "Your old dad's well. He'll come to no harm. Constable Sparrow's with him. You remember Sparrow, don't you? The chap your dad took a swing at in *The White Lion?* He's not hurt, so you mustn't harm yourself with fretting." Again my intervention seemed to stop her in her tracks, but only to return her to her first complaint, banging on *Dreadnaught's* cell as if her life depended on it and calling *his* name again in cries of agony. By now, Blakey and Coke had decided that she had best be restrained.

"Now that's enough, Miss, or you'll be breaking yer precious knuckles on the door in a minute," said Blakey.

"Very likely!" said Coke, and each of them took an arm and pulled her away with gentle force. At that moment, Bucket appeared with Sparrow and someone who ended at least one half of her anxiety: her father, looking frail, if relieved, to see his daughter. The policemen released her and she all but fainted in his arms. He in turn nearly fell into Sparrow's, who had to hold the old fellow up.

"Now then, now then...shush, shush, what is it?" the old man said, holding her tightly like a baby and stroking her red hair. "Shush now. Your old daddy's all right. He's all right, surely now, shush. These fine fellers ain't goin' to chain yer old dad up now, nor put him in Bridewell yet awhiles, are you Mr Sparrow? Shush now, me darling."

"Certainly not! We ain't, Sir. Certainly not! We ain't, Miss," said Sparrow.

After these explanations, and more of a similar kind, and more shushing and more stroking, she did indeed *shush* - until she suddenly remembered her *other* complaint and started off again with fresh vim, leaving her father almost tumbling back into the arms of Sparrow. She slipped under the arms of Blakey, like a matador avoiding the bull, and began to bruise her knuckles on the bolted door anew.

Suddenly Bucket appeared. "Open that lock-up quick, Coke," he commanded, "before she does herself a mischief!" When Miss Gavelstone saw Dreadnaught was still out like a light, spread-eagled across the flat pallet, she began sobbing and kissing his hands again. Bucket sent in water and towels and smelling salts and he let her get busy with these, nursing Dreadnaught until the doctor arrived.

Doctor Simpkins shuffled in eventually, gasping for breath and clutching his leather bag. He knelt down and began rummaging in it, bringing out scalpels and saws, hammers and blades, glass tubes and suction pumps, and, finally, surgical dressing. "You've cleaned the wound, I see," he gasped. "A good job done too." And so saying, he extracted a pair of steel scissors from the side pocket of the bag and began cutting Dreadnaught's hair away from his crown, grunting with each snap of the blades. Miss Gavelstone watched tearfully as this scourging went on. Next, a glass jar was brought out along with a thin, flat blade and Simpkins began spreading a viscous yellow ointment above Dreadnaught's brow as if he were spreading butter on bread. This operation done, a thin needle was found and threaded with shiny catgut amidst sharp gasps for air. I had to look away whilst the needle penetrated Dreadnaught's yellowing flesh. It was a blessing that the prisoner was unconscious, for the doctor was hardly gentle. When these incisions were finished, and the thread cut and tied close to the swelling wound, a bandage was wrapped around his crown. Now the Beast looked like a Turk, surely the last exotic costume he would wear until he tried on his gallows clothes. When all this was done, Miss Gavelstone cried out again:

"Will he be all right, Doctor?"

"Oh he'll be all right. Oh yes. I won't say it's not a nasty gash, young lady," said the doctor, "and the blow that caused that was what had knocked him out, I've no doubt." He stood up unsteadily. "Don't you worry, he'll be fit to face the hangman soon enough." Miss Gavelstone looked more confused than upset by this. Doctor Simpkins took two small flasks from his bag: drinking from one and unstopping the other to put underneath the nose of the prisoner. Whether it was the efficacy of these salts or the sharp stinging he had suffered from the needle, the Beast seemed to regain consciousness. His first waking noise was a moan of pain, as might be expected. His eyes flickered and began to open. His first sight was Miss Sarah Gavelstone leaning over him, still clutching and kissing his hand. Seeing her made him agitated. He tried to speak and looked as if he might try to get up. The doctor pushed him down again and Dreadnaught collapsed as if the air had been pushed out of him.

"Keep him still or the stitches will fall out," Simpkins grunted, turning carelessly from his patient to replace his equipment in the leather bag. Dreadnaught's eyes had shut but Miss Gavelstone called his name and he seemed to flicker awake again, his lips moving in another effort to form words. He was certainly made of strong stuff, monster or no. Bucket took Dreadnaught's free hand as he tried to speak, turning it over as I had seen him do outside.

"You must sleep now, sir," he said with a tone of gentleness and courtesy that I found somewhat shocking. "There'll be time enough for talk and asking of questions when you've recovered yourself from the bashing you took from those sticks." Bucket looked across at Miss Sarah then, as if they were parents leaning over an ailing child. "He's got a solid constitution, Miss. He's 'ad a rum old clattering but here he is nearly right as rain!"

It is true to say that, by now, I had become familiar with Bucket's mode of address when he was speaking to innocent women or children, but I could not comprehend why he was talking in such convivial terms of a child killer. By all that was just, he should have been giving the Beast a clout with a shovel and put paid to him – anyway, that was my belief. His style of talk seemed to suit Miss Gavelstone though and she looked at Bucket gratefully.

"I think you should just let him sleep it off now, Miss," he said. "I can see you and the gentleman have a strong attachment which I should like to hear you tell me more about. But that can

249

wait till you both feel better, eh? It's waited long enough till now." He looked up at me rather too meaningfully, I thought. Of course, I wanted the floor to open and swallow me up.

"May I stay with him, Inspector?" the girl said with such yearning that I could not see how Bucket could refuse such a winning request. He glanced at the doctor, whose face seemed to say, 'Let the *Beast* have his *mistress* stay with him? You *must* be mad if you allow that!"

But Bucket interpreted his face altogether differently. "Well, our Doctor Simpkins says you can, Miss, if you've a liking to. Nurse him all you like is the doctor's prescription, ain't it, Simpkins? But you *must* let him sleep now!"

Whatever the doctor's prescription, he was done, and made his exit from the room. Sarah Gavelstone acquiesced to Bucket's request and let go of Dreadnaught's hand. "Mr Jakesbere and I will just need a bit of a chinwag with your old dad while you sit," said Bucket. For a moment she became distressed again but Bucket put a comforting hand on her arm. "Don't worry yourself, Miss. We shall just be wanting a cosy chat with Mr Gavelstone, that's all. I gave my constable clear instructions to treat your father gently and to make him a cup of tea. Sparrow'll be serving him up another just as we speak, I should think. We'll send in one for you too, and when you're content that Mr Dreadnaught's on the mend, you can come and join us, eh? We need to hear *your* tale too - though I've a feeling Mr Jakesbere here has already heard some of it."

With this barb at me, Bucket guided us out as if he were protecting the cot of a sleeping baby rather than the bed of a Beast that would *devour* a sleeping baby if he might have his own way!

I could not help but wonder what Bucket was doing.

# Chapter 23

Over on the other side of the station, in a private office set aside for the interrogation of villains, sat Constable Archie Sparrow and Mr Gavelstone. The scene at the table was out of keeping with the room's penal purpose, for on one side was Sparrow, daintily pouring tea into two china cups, whilst opposite him was old Mr Gavelstone poised with a milk jug. The latter looked a far more respectable gentleman than the inebriated Irishman I had last seen squaring up to Sparrow in the bar of *The White Lion*. His accent was still rich but there was a deficiency of those choice words I had heard him employ earlier, such words as I had not heard since I had departed the naval dockyard in Chatham. The old gardener and Sparrow seemed the best of friends, once Sparrow had assured him that his daughter was calmer now and that he, Gavelstone, was not to be arrested after all.

"I'm obligated to you, young feller," Mr Gavelstone was saying, whilst pouring milk. "You gave me a scare when you turned up at my lodgings. I know that I owe you an apology for taking a swing at you. I'm obliged to you for not arrestin' me *then* and I'm obliged you'll not be arrestin' me *now!*" He let out a rich laugh and punched Sparrow on the arm so hard that Sparrow spilt tea into his saucer.

"It *was* a capital uppercut what you gave me, Mr Gavelstone, I'll make no bones about it," Sparrow declared. "I said to my Alice, *that* Mr Gavelstone, he let loose such a roundhouse blow as I wouldn't have expected from a man half his age!"

"Gave you a good stingin' didn't it? What a wallop eh? Why you went right over on your ar…"

"Mr Gavelstone," Bucket said coming in behind me, "it's good of you to come to the station to help us with our enquiries. Most gracious of you."

"I don't mind at all, at all," said Gavelstone, all conviviality.

"Pour Mr Gavelstone some more tea, Sparrow," said Bucket. "Been a gardener all your life, I expect, Mr Gavelstone," Bucket continued, "man and boy, I shouldn't wonder. A noble calling that, Mr Gavelstone. I'd often thought of being a gardener myself as a youngster. I had an uncle that was an under-gardener in Cork when he was a young man. He used to bring us a pineapple at Christmas."

"Pineapples!" exclaimed Gavelstone.

"Lovely that pineapple was!" Bucket enthused. "Why, I think I kept its head by my window for many a month as a souvenir. I often used to think of that big house and garden that it would have come from."

"I know it! Dashed if I don't know it!" said Gavelstone, bouncing around in his chair with delight. "Why, I was brung up in Cork. Used to go thievin' there in the squire's orchards when I was a young seed. An *under*-gardener, you say? I'll wager I knew him!"

"I gather from Mr Jakesbere here that you had a falling-out with Lord Dreadnaught a while back?" said Bucket.

"Falling-out is right! It was all the doings of that so-called son. He was the cause of it *all!* The gallows is what he needs!"

"Well, Mr Gavelstone, if he's done what we think he has, the gallows is what he'll get. But these *doings* you mentioned. What do you mean exactly?" asked Bucket.

"Nothing but a rake!" the old fellow exclaimed. "No young girl was safe with him. The poor young lasses in service were just there to serve *him* - in his wicked ways, I mean. There's many a house where the master or his sons will take liberties with a young lass, but usually there's someone there who'll keep an eye out, keep a rein on it, if you take my meanin'," Gavelstone added. "But this one was *particular* in his habits. Liked the serving-girls to dress up for him. Wanted them looking like ladies. But he liked the *young* lasses best. The little girls just out o' their wet drawers. But his mother wouldn't hear of nothin' said against her son."

"Just a moment, Mr Gavelstone." Inspector Bucket held up his hand. "Lady Dreadnaught, you say? Now, Mr Gavelstone, think very carefully for me, would you? *Which* Lady Dreadnaught did you have in mind?"

"Why, the latest one o' course. You don't think I meant the *first* Lady Dreadnaught, did you? A *proper* lady she was. No, by Gad, I don't mean *her*. Why, she was but a young woman when she died, God bless her soul. It all went to rack and ruin when the new one became the mistress at Mayfair." He stopped to take a glug of tea.

"You're talking about the *current* Lady Dreadnaught then – and *her* son?"

"That's the one," the old fellow confirmed.

Bucket seemed stunned and I had dropped my pencil. The old man seemed oblivious to our surprise. Bucket leaned forward urgently. "You mentioned *her* son?" said Bucket. "We're not talking about Lord Montague's son then? We don't mean *Richard* Dreadnaught?"

"What? Well, bless me, of course not! Young Richard was the best o' the lot o' them – in spite of what happened betwixt him and my Sarah."

Bucket was agitated. "And so, the *latest* Lady Dreadnaught has a son too, has she?"

"Oh yes! Frederick, his name is. Devil I called him." Bucket glanced across at me. In that moment I felt a sudden shock that I had perhaps been blaming the wrong person all along. "Kept 'im quiet from us at first, didn't she?" the old man continued, whilst I wrestled with my own thoughts. "Even kept 'im quiet from Lord Monty when she first married him. He'd been in trouble see. Some trouble in France or such like."

Bucket pondered this for some moments and began writing a note on a piece of paper whilst Gavelstone and I watched him and each other.

After a minute, Bucket called Sparrow over. "Sparrow, see if you can find Sergeant Meehan and give him this note. Tell him to get on with it straight away."

"So," Bucket continued, as much to himself as to anybody else, "Lady Dreadnaught has been keeping the existence of her own son secret from us, has she?" Then, turning to the old gardener, Bucket continued, "What did Lord Dreadnaught say when he found out that his new wife had a grown up son that she had kept from him? Shocked I imagine?"

"He was surprised right enough," Gavelstone replied. "We all were. But, she soft-talked his Lordship round, didn't she? Said her son had been away and had only just told her he was coming back to England.  She spent her time making her own boy sound like the loving son and makin' poor young Richard Dreadnaught sound like a villain instead."

"And where will this Frederick be now, do you think?" said Bucket. "We saw no sign of him at the house in Mayfair."

"Did you not?" said the old man. "Well, he might have gone away again, I suppose. He was always in and out o' the house at odd times when I was there." The old man leaned forward confidentially. "But I'll tell you what, Inspector, you might have

254

seen him without knowin' it were him!" Bucket's eyes widened, as did mine. "He always liked to dress up, you see. One time as one of his own bully boys. Another time, as a doctor come to wait on old Dreadnaught. He did it all the time. He liked to fool everyone. Loved it. Peculiar, I called it."

Bucket's eyes flicked across to me as if to share his amazement at the revelations we were hearing.

"Peculiar, indeed, Mr Gavelstone," Bucket said.

"He weren't the only one who liked to pretend he was something he wasn't either," the old gardener continued. "When his Lordship was first introduced to the woman who later became his new wife, she had tricked him with her looks, hadn't she? She does herself up to look just like his long lost beloved. Mind, she had a bit of the *look* of the first Lady D anyway, right enough. Only much harder in the face, I would say. O' course, he couldn't see that she was tricking him. She swallowed him right up. Seemed like his first wife reborn to him, I suppose."

"And what was the talk about her when the new Lady arrived? Did you know what her previous name was?" Bucket asked.

"Oh, she had several. That's what the rumours were anyway. I think she was Bouchard. Something like that. They say she came from foreign lands, I don't know where." Bucket began another note whilst Gavelstone continued his tale. "When she met him, she said she was a friend of the first Lady D from when they were both children. She said she'd only just read of her passing-away in the papers. Well, that was the story we heard. Took us *all* in at first, but it was the old man she fooled more than anybody. As soon as she had him under her sway she started to take over, see. He let her, too. Well, the old man was almost half-dead with grief by then and getting deader by the minute. That's when she started her nasty ways. Started to be more of a tyrant than a mistress. And things got worser and worser." He was silent for a moment, apparently considering these things.

"Go on, Mr Gavelstone. How was it worse?" said Bucket, looking up from his notes. "You were saying that Lady Dreadnaught tried to make Richard Dreadnaught, his Lordship's own son, sound like a villain?"

"Oh, yes." The old man nodded. "Young Richard and his father'd already had a falling out, so it was ready seeded ground, so to speak. The old man can't read anything anymore, so it was easy for Lady Dreadnaught to keep him in the dark if it suited her. She acted as wife *and* sec'a'tary for him, you see? Any letters," he paused, "well, she opened and read 'em to him. That's what Mr Merit said, anyways. There might have been stuff she didn't want him to see about herself and her devil of a son, that's what I think. She *controlled* Lord Monty. And then the wicked business started."

"And what wicked business was that, Mr Gavelstone?" Bucket asked, leaning forward.

"Wanted to change all the servants. Take on new ones. All of a sudden everyone you knew was sent packing, or threatened with bad references - or just plain threatened. Even those like Mr Merit and me, that'd been toilin' there for most of our workin' lives. There was some there as had had *their* fathers working there too!"

"Mr Merit? Lord Montague's man?"

"That's 'im, that's the one."

"You were saying that Lady Dreadnaught dismissed all the servants. When was that?"

"Well that was after. After all the scandals, I'm meaning." Gavelstone paused looking quite confused all of a sudden.

"Jakesbere, more tea for Mr Gavelstone," Bucket said, seeing the old man dry up. Gavelstone looked up slyly from under his lids.

"Have you nothin' stronger, Inspector? The years o' diggin' and plantin' has given me a thirst that hot water and a tea leaf won't shift. I can feel what I'm sayin' is comin out all Irish, as you English would say. All topsy-turvy. It all gets mixed up in my head, so it does. If I have just a little wet o' the whistle it might help me get things in the right order."

There was a knock on the door and a familiar head leaned in. "Just a moment, Mr Gavelstone. If you don't mind, Mr Jakesbere and I need to have a word with our colleague outside."

Gavelstone looked up at us plaintively.

"We'll have a sherry by way of a medicinal break in a moment, sir, never fear, and perhaps something to eat as well," said Bucket, smiling at Gavelstone and gesturing me into the hallway.

"Did you find Sergeant Meehan?" Bucket said urgently to Sparrow.

"Oh yes, Inspector, he's on the case already: sending out for a search of all papers and documents for references to Mr Frederick Dreadnaught."

"I've another name for him too," said the Inspector. "His mother's name was Bouchard. Tell him to find out what he can about her too and tell him I want all information sent to me post-haste wherever I am, for I feel we shall soon be moving fast." Sparrow began to go, but Bucket held him back by the shoulder. "When that's done, I need you to carry out something a bit dangerous for me, Constable Sparrow. Do you think you can do that?"

"I'm your man," said Sparrow proudly.

Bucket began writing out an authorisation docket for Sparrow as he was speaking. "I need somebody back at Oblique House.

Not inside the house, but watching from the outside. I want you keeping an eye on all the comings and goings. Let me know if anybody leaves the house. Follow them and send word back to me if they do. I might need Whelks here with me, so take a cab and Constable Cobb to support you in case of emergencies. Mind you skulk about in the bushes and don't let yourselves be seen. Jakesbere'll go with you in the first instance to show you the lay of the land. He's had a bit of a tour and he knows it pretty well, I should say." He grinned at me ironically, adding, "Once Sparrow and Cobb are settled somewhere snug, get back to me as quick as you can, Jakesbere. Right, get yourselves something to eat and off you go."

With that, Sparrow went off to find Constable Cobb whilst I found my greatcoat and cap. As we were leaving, I saw Inspector Bucket returning to the interview room clutching a bottle of his favourite sweet sherry under his arm with two glasses in his hand.

My mind was reeling, having heard the revelations about the Dreadnaught family and especially about the existence of Lady Dreadnaught's son. Nothing seemed to fit anymore. It had all seemed so simple. I had convinced myself that Richard Dreadnaught was the villain, that he was the Beast. I had been wrong.

The daylight was drooping as we drove into Mayfair. Sparrow and Constable Cobb donned greatcoats to cover their uniform and heaved their packs of provisions onto their shoulders, and the three of us left the cab in a street a walk away from Oblique House and continued on foot. I led them to the porter's lodge, fearing all the time that we might meet one of the bludgers, Frederick Dreadnaught's bully boys, as Gavelstone called them. The gates, of course, were locked and a chain had been passed around to secure them still further. I peered through the front window of the lodge just where the bell-pull hung. Spread out comfortably in an armchair was, indeed, one of Dreadnaught's bludgers, or so I thought, asleep with an empty bottle in front of him. I pointed out the little side gate to Sparrow. Grinning at me, and remembering our old Woolwich days, he brought out his knife and began working at the lock. In no time it had given, and Cobb, Sparrow and I were through.

I led them along the line of overgrown bushes and topiary that led up to the front of the house. Skulking here under cover of the bushes, we peered together up at the house. Fitful shadows moved across the windows, but otherwise the house seemed still. We had not spoken above a whisper since we had left the horse and cab in the streets and we continued in silence now, as I gestured Sparrow and Cobb to follow me round the house and past the stables. Here there was more life. I could hear the jeers of the stable lads, perhaps teasing Mad Joe as usual, but we moved on quickly, keeping low and in the shadows as we walked.

The lawn leading up to the summer house was still water-logged. We heard the whinny of a horse that was tethered to a rail and threw ourselves into the wet grass. Once it became clear that there was no rider we stood up again. We all looked warily at the small wilderness, its boulders and rocks looking sinister in the gloom of the fading afternoon. We heard a raucous noise then, as coming across the lawn were two of Frederick Dreadnaught's men, who had women with them, or girls, and they were heading for the summer house. I wondered for a moment if I might get a glimpse of the mysterious Frederick himself, perhaps appearing out of the shadows holding the hand of a little girl dressed up like a duchess. I shivered and gestured towards the others to follow me quickly back around the edges of the garden and into the sanctuary of the tool shed.

"You can get a good view of the back of the house and the summer house from here, Sparrow," I said in a low voice as we squatted down for a rest.

"It's a bit snugger than the bushes too, ain't it, Cobb," Sparrow whispered. "We can leave our stuff here and take it in turns to nap."

"I'd be careful you don't have too many of those, old Beak," I said. "You might find Bucket would be angry if he knew. Now," I added, "I'll lead you back round to the front where you can hide in the overgrown foliage to watch any comings and goings."

Leaving their equipment in the tool shed, covered up by an old piece of sacking, we made our way carefully back to the front of Oblique House. Here I left them both as they struggled to get comfortable under the cover of the bushes, watching the front of the house under the gloomy sky.

When I returned to St Giles, Bucket was looking worse for wear, and old Mr Gavelstone was almost asleep, an empty sherry bottle on the table next to them. The Inspector was interviewing Sarah Gavelstone. I don't suppose she would have been too pleased with Bucket for allowing her father to start drinking again.

Bucket looked up at me and said, "Oh, you're back, are you? Good thing too! Sit down, my lad, and get your notebook out, so as I can give my hand a rest." He turned back to Miss Gavelstone. "And now, as I think you've told me all we need to know about yourself and your father, perhaps you can shine some light on this ring?"

I looked up at this, for it was the finding of the signet ring in Richard Dreadnaught's room in Oblique House, the same ring that had been identified by Nancy Naiskins, that had led me to

260

the conviction that Richard Dreadnaught was indeed the Beast.

Bucket placed the ring on the table and looked hard at Sarah Gavelstone. "Does this ring belong to Richard Dreadnaught, Miss?" he asked, in a serious voice.

She picked up the ring with surprise, looked at it closely and returned it to the table in disgust. "How did you come by this, Inspector?" she asked sharply. Old Mr Gavelstone stirred and came back into bemused wakefulness at his daughter's raised voice.

"Could you answer my question please, Miss?" Bucket said firmly. "Is this Richard Dreadnaught's ring?"

"No, it is not, Inspector," Miss Gavelstone answered calmly. "Richard wears no such ring, and has never done so."

"Then why were you so surprised when you saw it, Miss?"

"Lady Dreadnaught tried to give Richard such a ring," Miss Gavelstone explained. "She pressed it on him again and again many times, even in my hearing. She seemed determined to make him wear it. She had a *pair* made, you see - one for her own son, Frederick, and one for Richard. They are like the one she wears herself. You may have seen the portrait of her wearing her ring at Oblique House. I think the gift may have been her way of befriending Richard when she first married his father. It angered her very much, but Richard refused to accept it and has never worn it."

"I know, Miss Gavelstone," Bucket said. "I noticed he has no mark of ring-wearing on his finger." The Inspector turned to me. "I think Monsieur De Blarde may have been misleading us about that ring, Jakesbere," he said, "placing it for you to find in Richard's room. It seems that he and Lady Dreadnaught, or whoever else is in league with them, may have been misleading us about many things all along."

My memory of how I had been tricked and led a trail that only exposed my own foolishness came to me again, in all its shameful clarity. But something was still nagging at me.

"Then why did the ring have R for Richard?" I burst out suddenly. They all turned to look at me.

"Lady Dreadnaught's son was known to her as *Rico,* Inspector," said Sarah Gavelstone, "and he *does* have a ring."

I felt the blood drain away from my face.

"But who the devil is this De Blarde feller you mentioned?" asked the old man suddenly. He clearly had been worrying away at this thought for some time. "That's a name I've not heard afore …"

"Well, you said you'd been dismissed for the best part of a year, Mr Gavelstone. Who knows what changes there would have been, eh? All the servants were changed over time, as you said yourself."

"That I did. He'll be one of her Ladyship's new servants, or another one of her nasty-men, I'll be bound."

"Who *is* De Blarde, then, Inspector?" I asked.

"Yes, Mr Jakesbere, who *is* he?"

# Chapter 24

The Inspector promptly sent a young constable back to collect his correspondence with his French friend, Vidocq. Bucket clearly felt that there might be something about Monsieur De Blarde in these letters.

Meanwhile, Sarah Gavelstone had returned to her vigil, sitting with Richard Dreadnaught, and her father was made comfortable in an armchair. Bucket wanted to talk me through his own scribbled notes on Gavelstone, and what I had missed of his daughter's interview. I turned to my notebook again and resumed my shorthand.

Gavelstone had told Inspector Bucket how Frederick Dreadnaught had returned from France after the marriage of his mother to Lord Dreadnaught, hiring his own servants (or thugs as he had put it) as soon as he had come to London. Since his arrival, Frederick had been manoeuvred into such a position by his mother that it was probable that he would one day inherit the Dreadnaught fortune. Richard, the legitimate son, had been discredited. Although it was Frederick Dreadnaught who had abused young serving-maids in the house, it was made to seem as if it were Richard Dreadnaught's fault. Because the old Lord and his son had fallen out, and Lady Dreadnaught had control of who her husband might see and what he might hear, his Lordship had believed the stories fed to him.

"I think we may have our man, Jakesbere," Bucket said to me. "For it seems this Frederick had an inclination for dressing young girls who were in service in the house as aristocratic ladies and then, well, you know, my boy - taking advantage of them. It seems that old Gavelstone caught Frederick Dreadnaught actually in the act. And what's worse, he said there was knife-play involved, and blood." He paused so that I could take in the significance of this. "The girls were paid small sums of money or threatened with further violence if they didn't keep silent," he continued. "That and darker threats of the loss of their position, and ruin."

"So Frederick Dreadnaught is the Beast. What a fool I've been, Inspector," I exclaimed, looking up from my notebook.

"We mustn't jump to conclusions yet," said Bucket patting me on the shoulder. "Mind you, it all may be coincidental, but this Frederick seems to like dressing up too, doesn't he? Do you recall that Gavelstone said he'd seen him in costume both as a working man and as a doctor administering drugs to his Lordship? It seems he would live these parts for weeks at a time and enjoyed fooling everyone."

"And is he still at Oblique House, Inspector?"

"Well," Bucket answered, "he may have already evaded us, or he may be there in one of his disguises."

A shiver ran through me at the thought that I might have spoken to the Beast or been alone with him. "Are we to go back to Mayfair now then, Inspector?" I asked. "He may slip past us again."

"Not if Sparrow's keeping his eyes open, he won't," said Bucket. "If he's there, and in hiding, he'll think it's the safest place to be. I don't think he'll make a move yet and we have further evidence to collect and other matters to attend to."

Bucket went on to tell me how Sarah Gavelstone had told him of their dismissal from Mayfair and how she had tried to keep away from Richard Dreadnaught.

"A wise woman that!" Bucket said. "She knew that Lady Dreadnaught and Frederick were just waiting for Richard and her to elope together, so that they could prove that Lord

Dreadnaught's son wasn't worthy of his inheritance. She said it broke her heart to keep herself away from Richard and, the trouble was, he thought that she was *really* separating herself from him and because of that they became estranged. But Sarah Gavelstone knew it was the only way to protect him from ruin. So then, of course, she had to find a way to support herself and her Pa, and she found work at Mrs Mason's house."

"You mean the baby farm that John Naiskins had spoken of?" I asked incredulously.

"Don't remind me, lad," said Bucket with a frown. "The description she gave me of Mrs Mason matched what the nursemaid told us at Cheyne Walk and what Polly Meakin told us at Vine Street. But it's even worse than we think, my boy," Bucket said. "It seems that this Frederick had attacked Lord Dreadnaught's daughter, Caroline, and got her with child."

I could not repress a gasp. "Wh-what!" I stammered, horrified. "A brother and his sister?"

"Well, step-brother, step-sister," Bucket said, correcting me, "but I know, my lad. A dreadful business." He sighed deeply. "But it's worse still. It didn't take much for her Ladyship to persuade the old Lord that this was just another example of Caroline's hysteria that he would remember from her childhood, and so that poor girl was committed to a madhouse, like many innocent young women in the same sort of trouble."

"Why would he believe such a thing about his own daughter?" I asked, amazed.

"A sad tale, my lad," Bucket sighed. "He blamed his daughter for his first wife's death in childbirth. It doesn't take much for wealthy relatives to get a troubled woman committed for madness, if they've a will to," Bucket pondered. "There's many a doctor who will look to his purse and testify to the insanity of a rich man's daughter to save the family's shame."

"But the child? Did it die?" I asked.

"Sarah Gavelstone didn't know," said Bucket, "but she believed that, if it was alive, it would be to a place such as Mrs Mason's that the baby might be taken, to struggle or die there out of sight."

Bucket seemed weary as he thought of this dire possibility, and slumped into silence. "But now, my lad, I must sleep off this sherry that Mr Gavelstone encouraged me to drink." I raised my eyebrows at this but Bucket seemed not to notice. "And then, when I've had my forty winks, we must wake Richard Dreadnaught and see what he has to tell us. Meanwhile, Jakesbere, I want you to escort Mr Gavelstone and his daughter back to *The White Lion*." He paused a moment. "But tell her I shall need her back here soon, I don't think I could keep her away from Mr Richard Dreadnaught even if I wanted to.

I walked with the old gardener and his daughter back to *The White Lion*. I cannot pretend, however, that it was a pleasant walk. The streets around the High Road were filling up with the late evening trade: street urchins looking out for an easy dip, and gin-bibbers already red in the face from a session in a nearby gin-palace. The weather was inclement too, and the rain that had hardly abated all day had mixed with the animal ordure in the road and mingled with the effluent from Meux's brewery.

Once I saw them safe and sound with Alice and Mrs Beddows, I took the return route to St Giles Station. I was not altogether content to be greeted in familiar terms by the street urchins and the old vagrants who crawled about the streets of Cripplegate. A legless beggar sitting on a wooden trolley seemed to think me one of his special intimates, for he grinned at me in sympathy out of his black gums as I passed by - implying perhaps that I needed to divest myself of at least an arm or a leg if I was to make a living at the trade. The police were familiar with me too, but their attentions were even less welcome than the beggars, as they seemed to think me an interloper in their station. It was only the protection of Bucket in the past that had persuaded them to accommodate me.

In the inner office, purple-faced Coke was on duty. It was clear from his agitated manner, and the way he beat his truncheon on the wall, that he was in an irritable humour. The cries and bangings from the lock-up where Richard Dreadnaught had been confined were evidently the cause of his annoyance.

"Your feller's woken up. Very woken up, should you be particular," Coke sneered at me," and just when all good Christians should be thinking about going to bed!"

"Dreadnaught, you mean?" I said.

"I thought he had *another* name? Beginning with a B? And I won't argue with you which B neither! Stop that clattering, you monster," he shouted in the direction of the lock-up, "or I'll clatter *you!*"

"Let me out! Damn it! I demand to be released!" Dreadnaught was yelling. Of course the police were still thinking he must be 'The Beast', or why else would he be in custody?

"Stuff up your 'ole!" Coke yelled back. "Stuff it up, I say, or I'll stuff you so very tight you'll wish you *had* stuffed it!" And so saying, he beat his truncheon on the wall again.

"I demand to speak to your superior! Do you hear? I demand it!" Dreadnaught yelled again. He had discovered the metal grille on his door and, like any thief incarcerated in a cell, had found something to rattle up and down against it.

"I'll rattle *you* in a minute!" Coke called, beating his stick in reply. I really did think he might open up the cell and carry out

267

his threat. It seemed to me that it was only his suspicion that Bucket might be displeased that made Coke hold his arm.

"I'll wake up the Inspector," I said.

"Oh wake him, will you? He must be sleeping very sound not to hear this B's banging. Stuff your 'ole!" he called again, with another tattoo on the wall.

Bucket *was* in a deep sleep when I tried to wake him. Only when I had called his name three times and shaken him twice did one eye slide open. He regarded me with this eye for a second or two until its brother flickered open and together they turned in the direction of the commotion from down the passage.

"What's that racket, Jakesbere?" he said. I began an answer but Bucket cut me off. "Fetch me a cup of tea and take one to Mr Dreadnaught, if that's him givin' me a migraine. With my compliments." The Inspector half sat up, scratched his neck and gave a grunt. "Tell Coke that our guest is to be taken into Simpkin's snuffy and given some fresh clothes - and when we're both more civilised I'll come and take a proper statement."

"He's ... I think he's a bit angry, Inspector," I said. "He might make a bit of a fuss."

"Got a sore head 'as he? Well so 'ave I, as a matter of fact. Give me a pencil and a bit of paper." I did so and Bucket scribbled a few words using the arm rest of his chair as a desk. "Give him that," he said. "That'll make him docile. Now get someone to bring me that tea."

Constable Coke was decidedly unhappy with the instructions when I gave them to him. "Take 'im tea? Take 'im to the doc's room? Take 'im a very big clout round the ear'ole, more like!" He was even less happy to be instructed by *me*.

Nevertheless, the teas were sent for and I stood outside the cell door holding one of them whilst Coke rehearsed a blow with his

268

truncheon. "Shut your cake 'ole!" he called in an effort to compose Richard Dreadnaught, who was still rattling against his cage.

I pushed the note that Bucket had written under the door for fear my hand would be bitten off if I did otherwise. This brought on a silence. Such a silence that Coke and I regarded each other for a moment, both wondering if the prisoner had fainted. After this, Coke tried the key and, pushing the door inwards, stood ready with his cosh. Dreadnaught was sitting meekly on his pallet, reading and re-reading Bucket's mysterious message.

"I've brought you some tea," I said stepping forward somewhat nervously.

"What? Yes, thank you," he said, taking it up politely. After a sip he said, "Where do you want me to go?"

To everyone's amazement he followed us like a lamb to the little sick room which the police doctor kept as an office. Here there was a neat bed with some sheets and a pillow, a jug, fresh water and all the paraphernalia of the doctor's trade. The last time I had been free to observe Richard Dreadnaught I had been convinced that he was indeed the Beast, but by now I knew better, to my shame. In this fresher room, where the light was better, I saw an innocent-looking man, his head wrapped in ugly bandages. He sat down on the bed calmly.

"You see," he said, as if we would know what he was talking about, "I have done as asked. Now, when will you bring her to me?" He clutched the piece of paper I had slipped under the door and thrust it towards me. "This note declares that Miss Sarah Gavelstone will be allowed in to see me if I am calm and go where I am bid. It is signed with the name Inspector Bucket. So, as you see," he said, gesturing towards himself, "I am calm. So where is Sarah? And who is this Inspector Bucket?"

"It's me, sir," said Bucket, walking into the room holding his cup and taking another deep draught. "Can I refill your cup? You must be parched."

"I have been sorely abused, Inspector!" he began, jumping to his feet.

"Not by my constables I hope, sir," Bucket said.

Dreadnaught ignored this. "Where is Miss Gavelstone? You promised you would find her and bring her to me if I was calm. I have kept my half of the bargain, but I will not be calm if I have been duped."

"Not duped sir," said Bucket, shaking his head at Coke who stood in the doorway with his truncheon ready drawn. "Thank you, Constable Coke. That will be all." Coke looked unhappily at the Inspector, not quite believing that he was being asked to forego the deployment of his truncheon. "Coke!" said Bucket sharply.

"Very well, very well," said Coke disconsolately as he turned and shut the door after him - a little louder than necessary.

"Miss Gavelstone has already been here, Mr Dreadnaught, so she won't need much finding," Bucket said, sitting down on a bedside chair. Dreadnaught sat on the bed.

"I thought I was dreaming!" he said, putting his head in his hands. "I saw her face but I thought it couldn't be true. But she was real. Where is she?" he said, becoming agitated again.

"I've sent for her, sir. She's not far away. I'd like a little talk with you alone though, before she arrives. Mr Jakesbere here will take some notes, if you don't mind." I sat at Simpkins' desk and cleared a space.

"Those men! Why did those men set upon me?" said Dreadnaught, suddenly remembering what had happened to him. "They wanted to rip me to shreds!"

270

"That's true enough, sir," said Bucket.

"Why? What do they think I have done?"

"They think you've been molesting their children, sir. Molesting and a-murderin' their own poor little girls and several other little girls that belong to your own class, sir. That might explain their anger."

"What? Good God!" gasped Richard Dreadnaught. "They think that *I* have been molesting and murdering their children? That I'm the *Beast*?"

# Chapter 25

"Calm yourself, sir," said Inspector Bucket, "nothing'll be gained by hasty action and much might be lost. You'd do better to sit." There was a pause and then Richard Dreadnaught did sit. Bucket took out his little ornamental snuff box. "Would you care for a pinch, sir? Might help you to calm your nerves a touch." Dreadnaught fidgeted disconsolately in his chair. "No? I suppose you're more a cigarette man, ain't you?" Bucket sniffed up his snuff and continued as if in the middle of a Sunday afternoon conversation. "I noticed the case in your coat, as a matter of fact. Go ahead."

Dreadnaught did so, reaching into his pocket with his right hand to pull out a silver box engraved with the initials R. D. He watched Bucket warily all the while.

"You mentioned that you thought you had been duped a while ago," said Bucket, "and I fear you have been, though not by me, sir. You see, sir, I knew a gentleman in Woolwich once," continued Bucket, "when I was a sergeant there, and he had a fancy for cigarettes. He was duped once as well. Chap by the name of Barker." Bucket leaned forward. "He was tricked by a sort of a family connection - as in your case I mean. He had a step-brother, just like you. His half-relative had been signing dockets for tradesmen with Barker's address and by impersonating Barker's signature, you see."

Despite the look of consternation on Richard Dreadnaught's face, Bucket carried on with his strange tale. "Well, the step-brother built up quite a debt using Barker's name: hatters bills, tailors bills, cobblers bills. That's when it all came out: payment for a pair of shoes." Dreadnaught looked as bemused as I felt. "The thing was, my friend from Woolwich, Barker, he only had the *one* foot. Lost it at the very end of the Greek war fighting against the Ottomans, see," explained Bucket. "I think *your* step-brother has been doing the same to you, sir, though the case of the foot itself is different, of course."

"You talk in riddles, Inspector, while my life is near ruined," said Dreadnaught, with irritation.

"I talk about *debts*, sir. That's how *you* were duped. That and other nasty complaints made against you. Caused a bit of a fall-out with your father, I do believe." Dreadnaught looked hard at Bucket and shook his head. Nevertheless, he saw that Bucket was encouraging him to talk and so he obliged. The one cigarette was hardly out when he reached for another, lighting it from the stub of the last.

"I see you know a great deal about me already, Inspector," said Dreadnaught, pointing with his cigarette, "and I see I must defend myself. Debts, yes, they were my undoing. But my debts were ones bred from boyish enthusiasm rather than," he paused, "rather than from vice. At Oxford I became an enthusiast for theatricals, you see, Inspector. I confess I spent rashly on establishing grand productions and promoting grandiose foreign tours."

Dreadnaught drew deeply on his cigarette and continued his tale. "I upset my father by wanting to *do* something with myself other than just oversee his foreign estates, Inspector. But I only had eyes for literature and the arts. I admit I began to be enraptured, perhaps obsessed, by the world of the theatre. My father saw this, frankly, as dissolute. I was supposed to be an idle gentleman of the *old* kind you see - not the new."

"Well, sir," Bucket said consolingly, "I've been known to take part in a few amateur theatricals myself at one time, though my old dad used to think me a little bit, well, Corinthian."

"Exactly what my father would call it, Inspector! Exactly!" exclaimed Dreadnaught. "But I am ahead of myself." He sighed before continuing. "I had worked myself out of the favour of my father long before, since the death of my mother, in fact. I would not stand by and accept the way he treated my sister, you see, my sister Caroline."

"I am told that your father blamed the birth of your sister for your mother's death on the birth of your sister, sir," said Bucket.

"You have been informed correctly then," Dreadnaught replied. "Perhaps you can see why I began to treat my father with contempt?"

Dreadnaught stood up and began to pace about the small room. "As soon as I was old enough, I was anxious to get away from the family home. Only my affection for my sister held me there. My father had already planned a match for me, in the old way of arranging such things. A marriage to the daughter of a wealthy second cousin of his in Northampton. I am afraid I was contemptuous of such a match, for the opposite reasons for which he approved of it. The young lady was indeed rich but had no good qualities as far as I could see, unless you call *wealth* a good quality," he added, looking across at Bucket.

"I think the *poor* might see it that way, sir," Bucket suggested. "But do go on, sir."

"Well, Inspector, be that as it may, it was only my affection for my sister that helped me keep my patience. That, and the friendship we both developed with Miss Gavelstone."

He paused and looked at Bucket as if this might be the cue for Miss Gavelstone's entrance. When it was clear she would not come yet, he continued, pacing as before. "Sarah had been brought up beside us, you see - almost as a friend rather than a servant. She learnt her lessons from Caroline as Caroline learnt

274

them from her governess. The three of us shared a childish interest in books and in art and music. My father felt I was demeaning myself by liaising with a *common servant* - a mere child, as he saw her - he was unable to see Miss Sarah's qualities for what they were, blinded as he was by her class."

Bucket made a noise of agreement but Dreadnaught misunderstood it. "You must not laugh at me, Inspector," he said angrily.

"I assure you I am not laughing, sir," said Bucket calmly.

Dreadnaught was appeased and went on. "I had become quite democratised, radicalised perhaps, by literature, by poetry - Shelley, Byron ..."

"Ah, now, that's a name I'm familiar with, sir," said Bucket with enthusiasm. "I like a bit of old Lord Byron myself, as it happens. I'm all for the democratic spirit. Nothing wrong with that, sir."

"Well," said Dreadnaught, looking at Bucket with interest before continuing. "My father threatened to dispense with Mr Gavelstone's duties as a gardener on many occasions. But at heart, I think he wanted to keep my affection and so, for a long time, he did not act on his impulse to have the Gavelstones dismissed."

He sat down heavily with a sigh, saying, "But then this new woman, Mrs Bouchard, came into our life and took over *his*. Such regard as he had for me was worn away by the lies she told."

"Oh, but that just sounds like a touch of natural distaste, sir," said Bucket. "It'd be no wonder, would it? I mean, your old dad forgetting the memory of your Ma for the new Lady Dreadnaught and spurning his son who, as you say, didn't always do as his father wished."

275

"Of course, Inspector. Perhaps you are correct. Nonetheless, I believe I was astute enough to understand what was happening in my father's house. He was a man of sorrow and he felt his lonely state with great pain, but this woman's deceits were transparent. She preyed on my father's deep love for my mother by making herself almost into my mother's image. You must understand, Inspector, that my father was old and infirm already when he met Mrs Bouchard and fell under her spell. Indeed, I might say that my poor father has made this something of a habit, falling under the spell of women, I mean."

"I think we're all guilty of *that*, sir," Bucket said pointedly. "My own Mrs Bucket has quite an assortment of enchantments, if you don't mind my saying. Even Mr Jakesbere here is not impervious to the charms of the fair sex, are you Mr Jakesbere?" I did not answer, apart from in a blush. "And perhaps you're not quite so impervious yourself, sir."

"You speak truly, of course, Inspector," Dreadnaught said, flattening the charred remains of his cigarette. "But the argument I put to you is that my father had given up all responsibility for himself, as well as the government of his house and his estates to a woman who...well, you know my feelings. He has allowed this woman to take *all* the decisions affecting his livelihood and all such decisions are, of course, in favour of her own son."

"I gather that Mr Frederick wasn't with your step-mother when she first met Lord Montague?"

"No, indeed. At first, in fact, we knew nothing of his existence. It was only after the marriage had already taken place that he appeared in our midst." Dreadnaught was becoming increasingly agitated now and began to pace again for a moment, before turning to face Bucket. "May I ask if you are conversant with the concept of the doppelganger, Inspector?" asked Richard

Dreadnaught.

"Oh, now then," Bucket scratched his head. "You're taxing me with that one, sir. You really are. Let me see. You'll be talking about Mr Goethe there, won't you, sir? I believe *he* was a gentleman in the theatrical line himself. Now let me think. I shall 'ave to dig deep. Does it mean a sort of *shadow* of yourself?" He looked up at Dreadnaught. "I think that's it, sir, your own ghost, so to speak. Am I right?"

Bucket took another pinch of snuff while Dreadnaught stood regarding him with the same open amazement that I often showed myself.

"You are a *remarkably* well-informed man, Inspector. My step brother, Mr Frederick Bouchard, as he was first introduced to us, *he* was such a shadow, such a doppelganger to me. I felt he had come to swallow up my life and *replace* me. Just as his mother attempted to imitate my mother, he tried to imitate me! Of course, he is forever using creams and unguents on himself, covering his foul complexion with actors' makeup. You see, even there, in the way of theatrical pursuits, he follows me!"

"His complexion, you say?" said Bucket, his eyes alight with interest.

"Well - I should pity him, should I not? He had suffered from smallpox as a child. Riven by it. He is horribly marked, you see, and he keeps himself always covered with make-up."

Dreadnaught sat again, reaching for another cigarette. "Well, I *did* take pity on him. We talked at first, you see. I tried, at least, to be civil to him. Once, he even confided in me. He was very drunk, I recall. He told me how he had contracted the disease from the daughter of an Earl when he himself was but a child. He talked of it as if the girl had contaminated him on purpose. He was exceedingly bitter about it. He almost died you see. It almost

277

blinded him and he suffered agonies. He has an in-built vanity, it seems to me, and he cannot bear to be seen as he really is."

"I see," said Bucket. "And did he manage it? To cover up the scars and what not?"

"Oh yes," said Dreadnaught. "I bow to his supreme skill as a cosmetic artist. He has developed a most expert way of covering his blemishes." Dreadnaught drew deeply on his cigarette. "As I say, these things excepted, there is a likeness in our outward appearances. His mother replaced mine and Frederick replaced me! What virtues I had in my father's eyes were taken by him and all his vices began to be subscribed to me."

"What vices were these then, sir?" asked Bucket.

"Drinking. Gambling. Debts. Opium use. Whoring. Women. Perhaps men and boys. Molly houses and bath houses. But his taste in truth was for girls, young girls. And all such young creatures that he came into contact with he left ruined. He was a devil but he played the innocent in the eyes of my father, blinded as they were by his wife."

"And he managed to pass the blame on to you, sir?" said Bucket.

"Yes. The scurrilous and abusive affairs he had with servant girls and young ladies of our acquaintance were all laid at *my* door," Richard Dreadnaught said with disgust. "Of course, my father became easily persuaded of my guilt when my relationship with Miss Gavelstone became warmer. He would not be persuaded of my honourable intentions towards Sarah, but saw it as a stain on our family name."

"But surely you talked to your father about all this - defended yourself at least?"

"He would not grant me an audience, neither to see nor listen to me - and she, my step-mother, was always the sentinel at his door." Dreadnaught put his head in his hands. "I vowed to give up my place at Oxford to stay with Sarah. I would take what little money I had and go into commerce, anything. Anything to be independent of my father and to start a new life with Sarah. But, well," he sighed, "Sarah and I argued. Frederick gloated. I confess a sort of wild, irrational jealousy overtook me - I felt there was something secretive between him and Sarah that she had not spoken to me about." Richard Dreadnaught looked off into the distance as if re-living a scene from his past. "One night, I came upon him with Sarah in the summer house."

Bucket blew his nose. "Yes, Mr Gavelstone told me that Mr Frederick had made advances to his daughter. You were *worried* she might actually *like* him then, eh?"

"No!" Dreadnaught shouted, raising his fists as if he wanted to strike something. "Only my mad jealousy thought that. I saw that Frederick had his usual brutes with him - casual working men or ex-convicts that he had hired and who sprang to his aid whenever he was challenged. They often slept in the summer house and would carouse into the early hours. They manhandled me that night, as soon as they saw me approach - threatening to hurl me over the rocky precipice into the miniature wilderness on my father's land. But I escaped from them and came upon Frederick, cursing him and ready to strike him. For once, he did not call for their aid but instead drew a knife on me."

Bucket jolted. "A knife?"

"Yes," answered Dreadnaught, "and no ordinary one. He pulled it out from nowhere, or so it seemed. I pushed him to the ground before he could strike. I do not believe Sarah saw him spring the blade for we were wrestling on the earth by now."

Dreadnaught stood up and was all but acting out the scene now as we watched him. "It was me she called on to end the fray: 'Stop it Richard! Stop it!' she called. I remember it vividly. In my madness I felt she was favouring *him*. My shadow. My double." He sat again, miserably. "I dreaded that now my doppelganger had truly taken over everything. I ran off in a childish pique."

"And what was Miss Gavelstone's reaction to this?" asked Bucket.

"She was most honourable, Inspector," Dreadnaught said earnestly, "not wanting me to give up my life for her. She had insisted that I should leave her all along, that I should give up my relationship with her." Dreadnaught seemed tearful, putting his head in his hands momentarily. "I interpreted this not as the love of me, that it was," he said after a pause, "but as a rejection. I went up to Oxford without baggage or books that very night. I left her only to punish myself, you see. But within days, I had received a letter from Sarah, explaining what had happened - how that man, Frederick, had tried to impose himself upon her - and by then I was ready to return - to duel with my step-brother if needs be."

"Perhaps not so wise, sir," said Bucket.

"That's what Sarah would have thought," he replied. "She told me that my father had been persuaded to *disown* me if my relationship with her continued. A formal letter from my father's solicitor was to be forwarded to me with this information. It had gone that far, you see, Inspector."

"And how did Miss Gavelstone learn about this, exactly?" Bucket asked.

"Through the kind agency of Mr Merit, my father's butler, who continued to be attached to me despite his steadfast loyalty to my father. As you might imagine, Inspector, this development inflamed me further and I was ready to *fly* back to London, but

Sarah is wise as well as honourable. She saw that this missive from my father could not be anything other than a stratagem by my step-mother on behalf of her son to *impel* me to do *exactly* that: to make me return to London and to Sarah in order that the threat of disinheritance could be carried out. Soon, indeed, I received this promised letter from my father's solicitor." Dreadnaught regarded Bucket directly. "You see how wise my Sarah is, Inspector?"

"Indeed, I do, Mr Dreadnaught. You'd do well to continue to follow the advice of that bright young woman. But what was it then, after all, that made you come back to London?"

Dreadnaught lowered himself still deeper into the chair with a sigh of heavy weariness. Just at that moment I heard a voice from outside the room, but his sudden subsidence into the seat had hidden the sound from him and he continued, oblivious to it.

"The letters from Sarah that had come so frequently suddenly ceased," Dreadnaught went on. "They stopped without warning and what exacerbated my anxiety was that the letters ceased just at that moment when I felt that Sarah was hinting at some dreadful fate that had overtaken my sister. I fretted but I waited."

I felt I heard another noise from outside but Dreadnaught seemed to be in some reverie and did not hear. "Then I received word from Mr Merit," he was saying, "telling me that Sarah's letters had been obstructed, that she and her father had been dismissed and that he feared that Caroline, my sister, was abused and defiled by that beast of a step-brother! All that Merit knew was that Caroline had been committed to a sanatorium for the mentally deficient!"

He looked up. "I was in a fury, Inspector. I did not know which of these calamities to deal with first. But, inspired by rage, I returned to Mayfair, determined to expose Frederick and his mother to my father. But I was turned away by Frederick's brutes."

"You were not able to see your father?" said Bucket.

"My father was told that I had returned in a drunken state to threaten *him* - and that I had absconded with Sarah. I only wished that I *had*, for by then I had lost track of Sarah's whereabouts completely." Dreadnaught looked towards Bucket earnestly. "Fortune smiled upon me in just one regard, Inspector, for I had been given a hint about where my sister Caroline might have been sent to. I had been trying to find Sarah so that we could rescue Caroline together, but a devilish time I had of it, searching for her in this God-forsaken city."

"Oh, it's not as bad as all that, is it, sir?" Bucket said, turning round and calling towards the door. "You can let her come in now, Coke!"

The door opened and the beetroot face of Constable Coke appeared - followed swiftly by the bright face of Sarah Gavelstone. Of course it was some while before Bucket was able to get Richard Dreadnaught's attention again, so passionate were their embraces.

"We think you're innocent, Mr Dreadnaught," Bucket said at last. "There's nothing to be gained from keeping you here, so I'm going to let you go back with this young lady to *The White Lion*, where I've asked Mrs Beddows to find an out of the way room for you and to keep an eye on you before I send somebody else to relieve her." The couple beamed but Bucket warned them earnestly. "I advise you to take extreme care, though," he said. "Your head might still be a bother to you - and I don't just mean from that clonk you had. It's the *face* on you that'll be your problem! There's some people out in the world who still think you're a murderer and might want to give it another wallop. So take care!"

Richard Dreadnaught nodded but could hardly take his eyes from Sarah Gavelstone's face. "I think I know where Caroline might be, Sarah. I am told that she has not been badly harmed, but she is in a mad-house. We must try to rescue her at once!"

"Now sir!" said Bucket sternly. "You haven't been listening to what I just said. You need to show a bit o' patience. You don't want to be seen out and about for a day or two until we've cleared up a few bits and pieces of business. If, as you say, Miss Caroline isn't being too badly treated, she'll be all right for a bit longer, won't she? She won't have much longer to wait for help. I'll send my men out to track her down for you. It'll be safer that way," he added.

"The Inspector's right, Richard," Sarah said. "You mustn't put yourself in further danger."

"That's right, Miss," agreed Bucket. "And if Mr Frederick don't already know you're about, sir, we don't want to frighten him off, do we? I know him of old you see. If he *is* the so-called Beast, if it *is* him I'm after, I don't want him scared off. I've lost him once or twice before, you see."

Bucket sat down again pensively. "If Frederick *is* the Beast," he continued, "it seems to me that he likes to hang around and taunt his foes whenever he can. He seems to take a pleasure in it or he'd have been gone long since. Perhaps he's one of those that thinks it's safest to stay in the place he'd be least expected to. If he is still at Oblique House, I don't want him thinking I'm onto him just yet. He has a habit of disappearing, when things get a bit too hot for him."

Bucket began to gather his things together, and was speaking as he busied himself. "I'm going to ask my own daughter, Phoebe, to keep an eye on the both of you to see that you don't get into any more scrapes! She wants to be of service in the detecting line, you see, and apart from that, it'll keep her from mooning about a certain gentleman friend she has lately been seen with."

I became embarrassed at this reference to myself and showed it in my face by blushing bright red. Sarah Gavelstone smiled, thinking, I suppose, that that there were other foiled lovers in the world besides herself and Richard.

"We must do as the Inspector thinks best, Richard. I feel I can trust him." She smiled at him and it was clear that Bucket was pleased by her confidence in him.

"As for the poor babies at Mrs Mason's, they certainly *can't* wait!" exclaimed Bucket. "We shall deal with them *straight* off. But I'll need a bit of a conference with my advisor first, of course."

For a moment, I believed that I had at last vindicated myself in Bucket's eyes and that it was indeed me that he was wanting to take council with; however, I was soon to be disillusioned, for he had another in mind.

"Stop scribbling in that blessed book, Jakesbere, and let's get back to Vauxhall, my lad. We must have a parley with Mrs Bucket."

# Chapter 26

When I woke up the next morning, I was anxious to see Phoebe Bucket, whom I had not seen since we had abandoned her and Mrs Naiskins in Seven Dials the previous day. Of course, Whelks had seen that she and Gertie were safe, bringing them home soon after we had rescued Richard Dreadnaught, but she had been at the back of my mind throughout that long day. At breakfast, we were all speaking at once, telling each other our news, while Phoebe and I secretly held hands under the table.

"Jakesy, Jakesy!" Gertie was spluttering with her mouth full of food. "You should 'ave seen how good Phoebe was yesterday, lookin' after Mrs Naiskins when she was all upset and then, well, you should 'ave seen 'er when that nasty mister came back - he was like a madman. He started Nancy cryin' and then we thought he was goin' to clout her one but Phoebe stared him out, didn't you Phoebe?"

Phoebe laughed.

"He got all angry then, Jakesy," and Gertie's face became contorted into a monster's with eyes bulging out and cheeks blown up like footballs. "Started threatnin' us an' all, didn't 'e Phoebe? Then Mrs Naiskins told him not to 'ave such a sore ar..."

"That's enough Gertie! I'm sure she said no such thing!" Ma Bucket interrupted.

"It is! It was, weren't it, Phoebe? That's what she said, weren't it Phoebe? Or it might have been a sore 'ead she said. Anyway, she did! And then he started swearin' at Mrs Naiskins."

"Don't you dare say any of *those* words, Gertie!" said Phoebe.

"Bless me, I should 'ope not, or I shall have to get some soap and water ready to wash your mouth out!" scolded Mrs Bucket.

"I thought he was goin' to hit her then, Pa!" Gertie said, appealing now to Bucket who sat in rapt distraction, oblivious to the hilarity. "But Phoebe stood up to him, didn't you Phoebe?" Gertie continued, untroubled by Bucket's lack of response. "Ooh, you should 'ave seen 'er, Jakesy, you would have wanted to *kiss* her!" Here the child broke out into uncontrollable giggles and childish imitations of the noises that she clearly felt a kiss might make. Despite Gertie's innocent expostulations, and the way they drew attention to my increasing intimacy with Phoebe, my thoughts were at that moment on the dangers Phoebe may have exposed herself to - and these were the concerns that I expressed to her under the cover of Gertie Bucket's giggles.

"No, of course not, Will. I didn't do anything silly," she smiled. "I just let that bullyin' John Naiskins know that I was there and that he was dealing with a member of the Bucket family! Oh, *do* stop your giddiness, Gertie! I only told him, my love, that if he should shout at me he would have to make his apologies in front of Mr William Aloysius Jakesbere. And that stopped him in his tracks!"

Gertie nodded in glee, "He started lookin' round to see if you was hidin' in the room, Jakesy! Then *she* said you was her fiancé and you'd beat him till his black was blue if he laid a hand on anybody!" Gertie laughed.

"I did *not* say Mr Jakesbere was my fiancé, Gertie! Take that back!"

"You did! You did!"

"Don't take no notice of her mischievin', Phoebe," smiled Ma Bucket.

"She did! She did! You should 'ave heard 'er, Jakesy!"

"You might have got yourself hurt, my love!" I said.

Should there have been any doubts before regarding our

mutual affections, our intimacy was now exposed for all to see. We had both called each other 'my love'. I grew so overcome at this thought that I felt impelled to excuse myself from the company.

Later, when I had cooled myself, I found Phoebe was alone in the parlour. Bucket had taken his wife aside for the 'parley' he had promised, and Hetty was dragging a complaining Gertie off to help with the chores. Phoebe and I were left alone and that is all I shall say on the matter.

That evening, I was alone in my room, thinking about the vicissitudes of the last few days, when Hetty knocked on my door with a message. "Mr Bucket says you're to be ready to go out in five minutes, Mr Jakesbere!" I was a little surprised by this sudden command. I had been keeping fewer vampire-like hours since I had been living my happily domesticated life at the Buckets' and the truth was that I would have liked an early night.

However, I recalled what Bucket had said about wanting to visit Mrs Mason and the 'baby farm', and attempted to compose myself for duty. Apparently, Phoebe already knew about this arrangement, as Bucket had told her that he wanted her to act as a chaperone for Sarah Gavelstone and Richard Dreadnaught. One of Inspector Bucket's trusted men was to escort her in a cab to *The White Lion* so that she could do her duty, just as I left to do mine.

Much to my surprise, I saw that Whelks's cab was already furnished with a passenger. I was perplexed to see a strange young woman ensconced on the bench, and, I may add, she looked equally discomforted at seeing me. I noted the urgent manner in which she pulled down a ragged headscarf so that it should cover her features. In this movement I was able to observe that her hand was missing a portion of its index finger.

This was all the evidence I required to realise that I was in the company of Miss Polly Meakin again, that is, the young woman whom we had taken into custody that fateful night when the Beast had attempted to abduct our very own Gertie outside the Hell Club. I remembered Polly Meakin's account of how she had sold her hair in an attempt to alleviate her desperate poverty and reasoned that it was the luxurious growth of dark curls that adorned her once shorn head that had momentarily confused me as to her identity. Indeed, although still ill-dressed, she looked quite clean and well-fed. However, as to the purpose for which she was to journey with us that evening, I had no idea.

"Away, my lad!" Bucket called out after he had settled in beside us. We were off, rattling across Vauxhall Bridge towards Cripplegate just as the evening was turning into night and the gas lamps turned into stars along the river.

Bucket was quiet on the journey. To tell the truth, he had communicated little with anybody since we had returned to Vauxhall, apart from what had occurred in his *parley* with Mrs Bucket. It was Polly Meakin who finally broke the silence in the cab. She was keeping herself at a distance from me but it was impossible not to notice her sense of discomfort. Whilst she attempted to persuade herself of my non-existence, she was determined to force Bucket to acknowledge hers.

"You won't leave me alone with her, will yer sir? Promise you won't! She'll scratch me eyes out if she's half a chance, she will!"

But Bucket's eyes were not to be caught. "A baby farmer!" He was talking to himself. "And on my patch too!"

The great hulk of the old almshouse loomed darkly as we rounded the corner past St Giles Church, its four black chimneys exhaling sooty smoke into the leaden sky. A little way further on, the horse pulled up. Whelks came around like a shadow to lower the step and we all climbed out - Polly Meakin the last of all and taking her time about it. All was silent in the street. We were greeted by a line of terraced houses that stood like cloisters at the back of the almshouses, under a dull moon.

"You'll stay with me, won't yer, sir?" Polly Meakin demanded for the third or fourth time. Still, she received no answer. Bucket strode on towards a door with a rusty grille at the darkest end of the alley. Two shapes materialised out of the dark. One was Constable Coke. His face was lit up by the swinging bulls-eye, making his birthmark rash look like a splash of blood. The other was Constable Blakey, looming over us enormously, nearly as wide as he was tall and with fists like ham-bones. There were others I did not recognise in the dark, but the silver buttons on their collars and tunics caught the swinging lights and their shadows flitted and flared up the walls of the crumbling buildings.

We stood under a high barred window, from where we could hear a grim noise: the low and hopeless sobs of neglected babies. With a signal from Bucket, Coke knocked sharply on the door. However, the effect was merely a dull thud. There was a look of enquiry between Constables Coke and Blakey, interpreted by the latter to mean that something heavier was needed in order to arouse those within. Taking a truncheon from his belt, he banged with force on the metal grille. The clang rang out loudly in the gloom. I feared the very building might crumble and crash into dust, but, once the echo had died, there was silence. Even the horrible moaning sounds stopped for a moment.

Then we could hear voices from above. Next, a patter of feet as the inhabitants shuffled and tumbled their way down the staircase. And, finally, curses:

"Damn dat doise! Don't chu doh we're dosed up for the day,

damn yer! We want dho more. Take yer childer somewhere else! We're full!"

I had heard the muffled tones of this stuffed-up nose somewhere before. Bucket touched one of the men on his shoulder and he and his fellow constable stole off along the dark lane that ran by the back of the house. Meanwhile, Bucket called through the grille:

"Open up! This is Inspector Bucket of the Detective!"

Bucket's stentorian tones caused another moment's silence but then the shuffling began again more urgently, if with a considerably more secretive tone. Something was being moved. Bucket was indifferent to these attempts at subterfuge, for he had all the possible exits secured.

"Open up, I say!" he called again.

The door did ease open then, but only enough to reveal a milky, sickly eye, underlined by a sagging bag of flesh, illuminated by a spluttering candle.

"Good edening, Inspector," the voice began, in recognition of its visitor. "Dis is a late call. I didn't doh you knew where my crib was."

"Stop your piffle, Ralph. I've always known where you slept but now I know what you've been up to."

And indeed I too now knew who our host was: the wall-eyed drinker Bucket had spoken to in the beer-house we had visited on that long ago evening in the Dials. Constable Blakey burst the chain as if it were a piece of string and went bounding up the rickety steps. Bucket followed, brushing the gaping Ralph to one side.

"Dis ain't right, Dister Bucket!"

"You're correct there, Ralph! It's not right at all," Bucket said and then called out, "Mrs Mason, Mrs Mason. I want a word

290

with you!" Ralph gave Bucket a swift look out of his one good eye and took to his heels in an attempt to exit via the broken door. Constable Coke collared him and slipped a pair of handcuffs on his wrists.

We rounded the corner of the narrow wooden stairs and pushed open a grey door. It was the smell that assaulted my senses first: illness; urine; human decay. After a moment, my eyes adjusted to the yellowy darkness. Constable Blakey was already standing against a pock-marked wall where he was lit up by the swinging light of his bulls-eye. He was holding his nose with his other hand, pinching his nostrils with two sausage-like fingers. In a rocking chair - feigning indifference - sat a large woman muffled up in shawls. What took the eye was her elaborate wig of stiff hair, pompadour-like, as worn by French ladies in salon engravings. Its bizarre elaboration was out of place in this squalor. At first I thought it was a bag of woollens that she cradled in her arms, but the bag was in fact a muffled baby, wheezing and moaning and poorly covered in rags.

"This is a late visit, Inspector. Can't respectable people be at peace in their own 'ouses now?"

She had a rough and unpleasantly croaky voice, almost like a man's, it seemed to me. Bucket ignored her comment and took Blakey's bulls-eye on a tour around the room. The light played over a tarpaulin sheet that had been hastily thrown over bare and creaking floorboards. There were bumps in this sheet as if it was covering up stumps or balls - except that the bumps were moaning. And some were crawling. Bucket waved Blakey forward to lift off the sheet. I confess I felt impelled to look away.

The yellowy light picked out tiny faces. Children were spread on the floor like corpses - some near dead or perhaps just asleep in their own squalor. Some others just had the strength to moan.

Some seemed to be only able to squirm like insects. On the table, a tincture of watered-down gin-slop was illuminated by the flare of the bulls-eye as it passed. There were indeed children here, but some were no more than infants - some as young as a week or two and some perhaps of a year or more. Most seemed to have been more or less squeezed into wooden crates covered with a smattering of straw. Some had their legs tied so that they could not move. Others could not have moved should they have been able, as their cots so tightly encased them that they might have been coffins.

Mrs Mason threw her burden down on the floor where it gave a feeble moan and she stood up with her thick arms on her hips, defiant. "There's no law agin' it, Inspector. If young girls gits 'emselves into troubles and can't afford to look after their own childer, 'oo else do you think'll take care of 'em but the likes of me, eh?"

Bucket was ablaze.

"No law about taking them in, Mrs Mason, you're right there!" he said. "But I should think that the magistrate might want to know about how you look after them! Somebody's got to stop the likes of you from turning babies into bones, haven't they?"

At this moment I feared he was about to strike her, for he was pointing his hand at her in such a way that it looked like it might turn into a fist at any minute. She must have thought so too, because she turned suddenly and ran for the back stairs - only to bump into the bodies of Doyle and Clove, the other officers in wait - and one other body too that caused her more serious anxiety. Mrs Mason's eyes seemed to pop out of their sockets as if she had been stuck on a spike, but not because Doyle and Clove had gripped her arms - it was the unexpected reunion with Miss Polly Meakin, escorted in via the back-entrance, that seemed to cause this phenomenon. It was clear that the two of them were acquainted, albeit also true to say that after this wordless introduction Mrs Mason became somewhat shy. You will recall that they had been companions on that night when Mrs Mason had given Polly Meakin and her friend a sixpence to sell Gertie to the Beast.

"Bring her forward, Doyle!" Bucket commanded. Mrs Mason struggled, but her ungainly body was soon dragged into the light of a lantern.

"Now, Miss Meakin, if you'll also be so kind as to step forward please … that's it," said Bucket. "Will you take a good look? Don't be afraid now. - Clove, play your lantern over the suspect, will you?" And he did. "Is this the woman?" asked Bucket. "Is this the woman that paid you to help her to abduct the child you took to Duke Street?"

Polly Meakin looked.

"I think so, sir, but I ain't sure, I mean I *ain't* sure, honest," she said with a pained look at Bucket's severe countenance. "I know the wig - I mean *she* had a wig like that on right enough, the woman I told you of, I mean, only it's what were *underneath* that I remember. If you were to …"

Bucket elongated an arm and, with his finger, flicked the wig from Mrs Mason's head. The old woman - for old and hag-like she was with the false barnet whipped off - emitted a shriek like a stuck pig which promptly became a scream as she thrashed around in Doyle's arms in her efforts to retrieve it. She was like a wild cat. Bucket held her off disdainfully at arm's length whilst Doyle gripped her more tightly still and Clove shone the light of the lantern all around her skull as if he were a barber showing a head to his customer. And what a yellow and pock-marked thing it was. And there - yes - there, just under a tuft of spiky black hair and a crooked ear was a livid red mark, a nevus as large and round as a sovereign.

"That's the woman," said Polly Meakin.

Blakey all but carried out the spitting, snarling woman - screaming for her wig the more loudly, the more closely she was brought to the street. Of course, by now, despite the lateness of the hour, word had spread and a small crowd of onlookers had gathered, including hunched-up old women on crutches and sickly-looking children from the alms house. When Mrs Mason appeared with her naked head exposed, a derisive cheer went up and one or two hard objects were thrown. Indeed, the very smallest of the onlookers struck her with a gnarled stick picked up from the street for the purpose.

Whether those in the crowd had a particular bone to pick with the old hag or were just there to mock, I did not know. If mockery was their objective, however, they had little time for it, for in a few seconds Mrs Mason was bundled into a police vehicle behind two snorting horses and was hurried away, still screaming, into the night.

Turning from this scene, to look back at the house, I was surprised to see a group of stalwart women of the neighbourhood, who were marching into the crumbling dwelling, carrying a variety of medicines, blankets and flasks of milk. These women were all ready to be mothers to those babies and infants who might be rescued from upstairs. As I looked back at the street, I realised that I had lost Bucket amongst the crowd of onlookers. When I spied him out again in the shadows of the alleys, I saw he was in conference with Sergeant Meehan, standing under a lantern and studying a batch of papers. Bucket was deep in thought when a constable handed him a scribbled note he had been handed in turn by, of all people, the stable-boy from the Mayfair house. The Inspector took it and read silently, the whole group of them bathed by the flakes of light from the lamp.

"It's from Sparrow, Mr Jakesbere," he said, as I came up to him, his face a mask of shadow. "We're wanted at Lord Dreadnaught's mansion in Mayfair. There's been a murder. Mr Merit is dead."

# Chapter 27

The bells were tolling out all over London as we rattled through the dark streets. But Mr Merit would not hear them.

When we came to Hyde Park and drove up through Mayfair, the moon seemed to hover palely over Oblique House, swollen and yellow. Our convoy of vehicles slid to a halt in front of the house in a spray of shingle. There was an eerie silence in the outer air but a medley of voices issuing from the house itself floated nightmare-like from its doors like a dark cloud. After a moment, a party of constables stepped down from their vehicles and out on to the grey path, their lanterns swinging, casting shadows across the weed infested lawns. When Bucket and I climbed down from our cab, not a soul came to greet us. No stable boys came out to sneer at us as on our earlier visits and no footman or manservant came to supervise our entry. Instead, the grand entrance doors gaped open in dismay.

In lieu of a butler, a ragged stable boy sat on the marble steps picking idly at the paint on a shoe-scraper. Small groups of servants were milling around the chequered reception hall. An under-gardener sat on the plinth of a marble statue smoking his clay pipe; a kitchen skivvy was swinging her legs from an alabaster table-top, lazily peeling the rind from a piece of bacon; old Ebenezer was playing dice in the alcoves with a footman who had removed his wig - all the better to store his coins for betting in. Not a soul stepped forward to announce us. It was as if we had stumbled across a group of motley schoolchildren released for a surprise half-holiday. The Headmaster and Matron were occupied elsewhere, so it seemed, and thus the children could indulge in their play. Most of the assembled people seemed to be hovering in anticipation of something, like passengers awaiting the 6.15 from London Bridge. Or as if someone had been promised a good whipping and they did not want to miss the public spectacle.

A few policemen began making attempts to restore order. Meanwhile, I strained to see if I could identify Sparrow or Constable Cobb amongst the groups in the hall. Of course, it had been Sparrow who had sent the message that had been delivered to Bucket. I discovered later that Sparrow had enlisted the carthorse-sized stable-lad, he who was partial to bullying Mad Joe, into riding over to St Giles. Sparrow, however, was nowhere to be seen.

After this brief hiatus there was a sudden uproar. At first, I was vain enough to believe it was a belated response to our entrance - or rather the entrance of Inspector Bucket. However, the cause of this sudden re-focusing of attention was to be found at the bottom of the sweeping staircase. A fracas had erupted involving two police officers and a brute of a man dressed in a muffler and wearing heavy steel boots. It seemed one of the constables had recognised him as an escapee from the prison ships and had attempted an arrest. The servants heaved towards them, as onlookers do when a fight is declared. A few pieces of furniture had been thrown onto their sides and a marble bust had smashed in a puddle of stone onto the chessboard tiles.

Bucket gave a terse command to Constable Blakey, who promptly weighed in amongst the spectators until he came to the epicentre of the fracas. Needless to say, Blakey had command of the situation. The struggling figure, soon brought under the persuasive force of Blakey's ham-fists, was one of the brawny men we had seen loitering around the house on our earlier visits - the ones in the billycock hats. This was one of the bludgers, as Ada, the scullery maid, had called them. This gentleman had now been brought to order, yelping from a blow that Blakey had delivered. I recalled, however, that there had been more than one of Frederick Dreadnaught's bullies and the others, it seemed, had made themselves scarce. The onlookers now looked towards Bucket, who had positioned himself a few steps up the staircase. But Bucket seemed more interested in the bludgers for the moment. With more terse orders, he sent policemen off to search the grounds and to make sure that any wanderers should be corralled in to the reception hall until further notice, especially any suspicious-looking characters. Again, a thought of the secret room I had discovered on my last visit came involuntarily into my mind, and I wondered if a guard ought to be set on the stairs that I had observed leading down from that hidden room to the back of the house. These thoughts were soon curtailed, however, by the late arrival of Constable Sparrow, standing above Inspector Bucket on the uppermost steps of the stairway.

"Not to worry, Inspector!" his voice called out. "Panic over! I've arrested the murderer already," he said complacently. "He's all tucked up safe and sound in the cook's room." Bucket had craned his neck around in surprise when Sparrow spoke and so I was unable to gauge the effect that Sparrow's words might have been having on the Inspector. "I've inquisitioned the keys," Sparrow blithely rattled on, "and I've put Constable Cobb on guard outside the door."

Sparrow was full of pomp, and I wanted to feel proud of him as he took command like this, but I feared he was simply making a fool of himself, jumping to conclusions as I had done before him. Bucket seemed uncharacteristically tongue-tied for the moment.

Sparrow ploughed on.

"I'm glad you've come, Inspector. The whole 'ouse is in a pickle, and the murderer hasn't stopped shoutin' and screamin' since I've had him locked up." There was no stopping him now. "Lord Montague's gone to bed with a migraine and Mr De Blarde's had to have a dose of her Ladyship's salts. As for 'er Ladyship 'erself, well ..."

But, by now, Bucket had heard enough. "Slow down, Sparrow! Who, exactly *who,* I say, *who* have you got locked up?"

Sparrow looked somewhat perplexed at this query. "Why, the 'einous villain 'imself, sir. The murderer what done it, sir. Him what plunged the knife into Mr Merit, to be particular, sir."

It seemed that Bucket must have raised an eyebrow - the one that could get a confession out of the thickest-skinned villain - for Sparrow became suddenly straight-forward and blurted out the facts: "Why, Mad Joe, the stable lad, of course!" he said at last.

There was at first a muted gasp from the onlookers in the hall at this information, and then a series of voices calling out in anger. "Mad Joe, I knew it was him," said one voice, and, "It's time he was locked away!" said another. "He's nothin' but a bedlam case..." a third opined. These and other contributions were offered, some utilising language of an altogether stronger sort than I have included here. These calls continued for a short time until Bucket's stentorian voice silenced them.

"And *who,* Mr Sparrow, is *guarding* the body of the *deceased*?"

I noticed that even Sparrow's face blanched at this implied criticism.

"Well," Sparrow said. "No one, to be exact, begging your pardon, Inspector Bucket. But my thinking is that, being dead, the deceased is unable to get up and move 'imself about." This response, although sound in logic, did not appear to satisfy Inspector Bucket.

"Get yourself to Merit's room!" Bucket bellowed so suddenly

that we all quivered. "See to it that nothing is removed or touched and that the body is unmolested - if it's not already too late!"

Sparrow seemed momentarily frozen. "Well, get a move on then, man!" Bucket commanded. Sparrow's long legs turned on the landing where he made the best of a slightly shame-faced retreat up the stairs.

This was the moment chosen by the cook to push her way to the front. "I want to make a statement, Inspector," she said grandly. She didn't wait for any response from Bucket, who waggled a finger in his ear and regarded her stoically. "I heard it all!" she continued. A rash of excitement lit up the faces of the listeners.

"Well then, madam," said Bucket. "You will tell us what it was that you heard, I have no doubt."

"Well," she began, "I'd just finished my work in the kitchen and had occasion to return to my rooms. That was when I saw Mr De Blarde with Mr Alfred. They were dragging Mad Joe into my room. My own room!" she said, looking around at her awed audience. "I had a shock, I can tell you!"

"I expect you did, ma'am. And it's no wonder. Anybody would have done in the circumstances. And did either of these gentlemen *speak?*" asked Bucket.

"Oh yes, Mr De Blarde shouted out, '*Murder!*' "

There came another gasp from the watchers.

"Now tell me, ma'am," said Bucket calmly. "Did Mr De Blarde shout out about the murder *before* or *after* he saw you?"

But either she didn't hear Bucket's question or she preferred to run on in her own way, for her next words were a declaration and not an answer: "It was that Mad Joe that did it. Mad Joe killed poor Mr Merit, that's who did it, Mad Joe, who should

300

have been locked up long ago!"

"That's right, Mrs!" a voice called.

"A devil he is, him with his devil's knife!" called another.

Bucket waited for the hubbub to subside. "And was Joe conscious when you saw him being taken to your room, ma'am?"

"Knocked out!" came the terse reply.

"And did Mr De Blarde tell you what had happened?"

"Afterwards, yes. Mr De Blarde came to speak to me personally - and that's not somethin' that he'll often do, I can tell you!"

"And?" asked Bucket.

"He'd heard screaming coming from Mr Merit's room, God bless his soul!" the cook answered. "He got there just in time to see that monster Joe killing Mr Merit in cold blood!" Murmuring began again in the hall. "Mr De Blarde told me that Mad Joe would've killed him too if he could've!"

The cook paused for effect and was rewarded by another collective gasp from the onlookers. "He had to get Mr Alfred to help him carry the murderer to my room for safety's sake," the cook said proudly.

Bucket seemed to be considering all this quietly but then suddenly thanked the cook and, turning away, began to climb the staircase - only to be stopped this time by a hand on his arm. It was Ada, the scullery maid, who had entertained me the last time I was at Oblique House.

"Excuse me, Inspector Bucket, but I thought you might like to know that I always take Mr Merit's hot water up to him before he puts out his light."

"Ada, isn't it?" said Bucket turning and smiling. "Ah yes. I thank you for that information. Will you walk with us up these stairs?" Ada said she would and Bucket questioned her as they climbed.

301

"And how was Mr Merit when you last saw him?"

"Well, he was still breathin', if that's what you mean! Joe was in Mr Merit's room. I sometimes take up Joe's medicine for him. Mr Merit sometimes has to calm him down, see."

"Go on. What had Joe been up to?" said Bucket.

"Joe had been going more mad than usual, if you want the truth." She looked around warily as if afraid that someone might be listening and disapprove of her talking. "He was waving that 'orrible knife around as if he wanted to do a mischief with it." She paused thoughtfully. "I didn't think he'd use it on the old man though. What a shocker that is!" she said. "But Mr Merit was all right when I saw him. He wasn't dead yet at any rate!"

We had come as far as Lady Dreadnaught's drawing room and here Bucket stopped.

"Do you want me to announce you, Inspector? As there's no one else, I mean?"

"No. Thank you, Ada. I should like to see Mr Merit's room first. But perhaps you'd be so good as to acquaint the master and his lady of our arrival. Perhaps that'll give them a chance to sort their faces out, eh?"

"I will, Inspector." And so saying she made herself ready to knock on the drawing room door as Bucket and I turned up towards the servants' staircase. The sight of the ottoman chest that disguised the entrance to the hidden room reminded me that there were still some things I needed to tell Inspector Bucket, but a loud commotion from above us made Bucket go on ahead before I could speak. The disturbance was in fact the voice of Joe himself, letting loose a volley of inarticulate shouts and screams. We hastened our steps and were met by Sparrow striding towards us.

"It's Joe, Inspector Bucket," he squawked breathlessly. "He's

302

still makin' a right old palaver. I told 'im to settle but, oh no, not he, he won't *be* settled nor locked up by the sound of it, Inspector."

"But I thought he was knocked out," said Bucket.

"Not now he ain't!" Sparrow answered. "He's chucking everything he can get his hands on at the door!"

"Well, we'll let him burn himself out, shall we, eh, Sparrow? No doubt the locks are easily broken here as I think you and Mr Jakesbere might know, but I expect they'll still hold against him throwing things at the door," Bucket said mysteriously. "Now, where's the body, Sparrow? Lead on, Constable."

As we made our way along the dark corridor, I wondered how Bucket knew about the locks, but then he always seemed to have a way of knowing things that were a mystery to me. We stopped outside the open door to Mr Merit's room and I recalled the look of terror on his face the last time I had seen him. For a moment my nerves failed me, for even in the darkness of the threshold of the room I had a dread of the body inside and a sense of the unmistakable aura of death.

# Chapter 28

Sparrow brought out a candle and a lucifer, which, once lit, shot flames into the corners of the room. The stark reality of Merit's dead body flickered into view. The hairs on the back of my neck seemed to stand up when I saw the corpse lying so still, but the feature that caused me to shiver was the sight of a huge hunting knife next to the old man's body, catching the light from the candle.

Bucket, however, seemed more interested in the contents of the room itself. He sent Sparrow for more light and when he returned with it the whirlwind that had struck the room was plain to see. The floor was a mess. Candles, candle-holders and clothes were tipped wildly over the frayed carpet. Pictures hung precariously on the walls, and what looked like torn-up letters were scattered confetti-like over the body and the floor. Mr Merit's writing table had been thrown over and jars of ink had spilled all over the carpet, the brown ink staining like blood. Bucket was particularly interested in the marble wash-stand with its plain white bowl. He dipped his fingers in it and swirled the water around contemplatively.

"A mess," he said at last. "Very messy." He looked at me. "Wouldn't you say so, my boy?"

"Looks like there was a violent struggle, don't it, Inspector?" I answered.

Bucket looked down at the body. "Yes. But a bit *too* messy, don't you think? Except for the body itself, that is. Very neat and tidy *that* is. Look at it." I did. "All laid out in a nice straight line, isn't it? It looks like Mr Merit called out for some hot water to make his toilet and then just decided to have a lie down and die, don't it? Without causing no bother to no one. See. Apart from all this stuff that's been chucked about, of course. He must have been fighting with the energy of a man half his age, eh?"

"His eyes ..." I said, really looking at the old gentleman's dead face for the first time.

"Yes. They don't look too much at ease do they, Will, eh?"

"And his mouth."

"*That* don't look like he was in the middle of a friendly chat neither does it? But the *way* he's lying, does that look *natural* to you, boy?" Bucket asked.

"He looks like…well, if it's not disrespectful to the dead, sir, he looks like one o' the wax works from a Chamber of Horrors, doesn't he?" I said.

"You might be right. But I'd have expected less mess and more gore, wouldn't you? A lot of ink everywhere, ain't there? Can't see no water though, can you? Funny that. Don't you think that in the great big struggle that caused this mess, the wash-bowl might have got knocked over? I mean, when everything else that could be chucked about *has* been chucked about - looks like someone missed that. It's still full, you see."

He looked around the floor. "Not any blood, neither. Can you see any, Will?"

To tell the truth, I could not. And nor did I want to. Bucket rose and, stooping over the body, reached beyond it to where the hunting blade lay. He took it up by the handle with his finger tips.

"Seen this before have you, Will?" he said.

Of course, I had known all along where I had seen it. It was Mad Joe's knife - the one he always had dangling from his belt, the one he used for slaughtering animals and skinning them. There was blood rusted on its tip and dry, dark splotches on the bone handle. All this I knew and saw - but a nod was my only answer to Bucket's enquiry.

"Don't seem right, Will, eh?"

"It's a blinkin' wicked thing!" I said with a shudder, shaking myself out of my silence. I began to feel somewhat unwell. I had seen for myself the way Joe had ripped the skin from a weasel with this very implement. In my mind's eye I imagined it being used on Merit, ripping him up cruelly in just the same way. Then, to my surprise, Bucket knelt down and, taking hold of the side of Merit's body, proceeded to roll it from side to side as if were indeed a wax-work. When he had achieved sufficient momentum, he held the body up with half its side raised off the floor. "Anything there, Will?" he asked with a grunt. I was afraid to look.

"No," I said, with some relief.

"*Nothing*? Nothing at all, I mean?" Bucket said again. "Have a *good* look. Any bits of that torn-up paper? Any ink? Anything at all of this other stuff that's been chucked about?"

I was ignorant of what Bucket expected to find, but indeed there was nothing there, and I reassured him of this fact again. It was actually the neatest and tidiest section of the room.

"Hmm, I thought not." Gently, he returned the body to its recumbent position. "Strange, don't you think?" he said, standing up and wiping his face. "I mean, if Merit was struggling with whoever it was who killed him - don't you think some of the stuff knocked about - knocked about like a whirlwind - would be *under* the body? Not just on top of it, eh?"

I began to ponder this new slant on the situation but my meditations were interrupted when Bucket knelt again and began to unfasten Merit's waistcoat and shirt. To my consternation, I realised that he was searching for the place where the hunting knife had entered the body. I was aware that many had been the reports in the London press of Bucket's investigations into the moribund bodies dredged up from the river. I had read of many myself before I began on my new London adventures back at the beginning of the year. I recalled the lurid accounts of bodies washed up on Chelsea Reach, at Waterloo or at Hungerford Stairs - and you must think me a lily-livered thing, but I submit in my defence that *you* were not there in the room when Bucket began his probings.

By now, he had pulled back Merit's shirt and, after wrapping his little finger up in a handkerchief, was inserting it into the poor fellow's wound. This interrogation was carried out as calmly as if Bucket were unplugging tobacco from a pipe. I watched in mounting horror. The wound he had uncovered was only a small incision, and it did not actually *start* leaking blood, and then only slowly, when Bucket insinuated his finger. I supposed, with simple reasoning, that given that Merit was dead he would not have minded the probing so very much. Nevertheless, my sensibilities were shocked. The hole was there right enough. I had never seen such a thing: the knife seemed to have pierced him like a needle, the wound commencing just under and almost on his side, and as thin as a quill - thinner indeed. Whatever had struck through him had killed him soundly enough but - and here I accorded with Bucket's observation - it had not left as bloody a stain as it might have done, not given the size of the knife that lay dull and inert by his side. The wound was more like a surgeon's incision than a murderer's blow. Perhaps, I considered, it had been the shock of it that had put paid to him as much as the sting of it.

"I've seen this before," Bucket said at last. "And on the same side of the body too. I think the French would call this 'sinister', don't you agree, eh?"

My Chatham French was of no help to me here and so, at that time, I did not know what Bucket meant at all. Nor did I have time to dwell on the matter, for the next thing was that he was asking for a loan of my handkerchief. To be candid, I was embarrassed by such a request, for it was grey and unwashed. Nevertheless, I gave it to him with good grace and a bad shudder, thinking he was going to continue by using it for an even deeper excavation into the old man's flesh. But no, instead he took to wrapping up Mad Joe's knife. I looked in consternation at the use that my own precious nose-rag was being put to.

"Keep that safe, Will," he said, leaving me in possession of the shameful thing. Meanwhile, he took two strides to the open door and called out for Sparrow. "Send a message to Dr Simpkins, Sparrow. Say that he's to drop everything and get up here quick as he can." Sparrow nodded and made as if to exit but Bucket was not finished. "Tell him I want a careful written and *witnessed* record of the angle of entry of the murder weapon *and* the size of the incision made. Have you got that, Sparrow? Exact I mean?"

Sparrow nodded to say that he had, but Bucket was still unconvinced and I was made to write it down so that the instructions were clear for Simpkins. Sparrow made to go yet again when I passed him the instructions - but was called back once more: "When the doc says it's all right, send someone out for the undertaker - but make sure you get the poor old fellow up on the bed and covered up in a dignified way before you do." Sparrow nodded sagely and hovered in anticipation of further instructions. "All right then - what are you waiting for? Off you go, man!" Sparrow vanished at last. The Inspector folded up his own handkerchief very carefully so that the blood would not smear and then tucked it into his pocket.

# Chapter 29

There was now no noise coming from the cook's room, where Joe had been imprisoned. I thought, for a moment, that he might have done himself some terminal mischief. However, on reaching the door itself, I realised that there *was* a noise, a low, mournful weeping.

"Sounds like he's stopped throwing things now, Inspector." It was Constable Cobb who spoke. All three of us cocked an ear to the door. When somebody suddenly spoke behind us, we all jumped.

"Begging your pardon, sir." It was Ada. "Her Ladyship 'as asked if you'd be so good 'as to tell her how long you might be talking to the murderer as," she paused, "let me get this right - as poor Mr De Blarde is most upset, what with what he's been through, and on top of that 'is Lordship 'as got one of his migraines and 'as retired to his bed. That's the message in a nut shell, though they took a bit longer sayin' it than that."

Bucket shook his head. "Well, well, Mr De Blarde is upset is he, Ada? And Lady Dreadnaught is anxious, you tell me. And, what was it? Lord Montague's *tired* and got a headache, eh? Well, we're all very sorry for them, aren't we? Very well, Ada, it's not your fault, but would you mind going back to tell her Ladyship and Mr De Blarde that, though it's a rum do that Mr Merit has been so inconsiderate as to go and get himself murdered and taken it upon himself to be dead, they might just have to be patient! Tell them that the trouble with being dead is that you can't *get* headaches or get upset or go to bed *ever* again! Tell 'em it's unfortunate and inconvenient, but true." Ada was about to go but Bucket called after her. "Oh, and you tell 'em, Ada, if you would, that though we may *all* be tired, I'm not Bucket of the

Private Bureau, as they might still think I am, and I'm no longer here to search for a lost son. Oh no, I'm Inspector Bucket of Her Majesty's Detective and I'm investigating a *murder!*"

"Right, sir," said Ada. "I will!"

As I watched Ada disappear down below, Bucket began speaking through the key-hole to the killer.

"Joe!" he called. "Can you hear me? This is Inspector Bucket here, Joe." There was silence from behind the door. "I'll wager Whelks told you about me, eh? You remember Whelks, don't you? The bobby who looks after the horses?" There was still no answer. Bucket persisted. "Well, he *knows* you, anyway. He told me he'd enjoyed a chat or two with you. That's right, ain't it, Joe?" There was still silence. "I'd like a little chat with you myself. I like the nags too as it happens." Bucket stood up and gestured for the key from Sparrow. "So I shall just be opening this door," he was saying. "I'm putting the key in," and he did so. "And I'm turning it now," and he did that too. There seemed to be some obstacle in his way at first but he was able to push it to one side with the weight of the door.

When it was open it showed a sorry sight. Joe, the so-called stable boy, was slumped in silence, like a broken doll, at the foot of the cook's bedstead. His thatch of red hair was all that could be seen of his head as it lay lolling on his chest. His out-sized face was buried in his hands. His knuckles were red and bleeding. Anything that could have been thrown about *had* been thrown about, just as in Merit's room. The inside of the door was pock-marked and dented from what must have been a continued avalanche from Joe's fists and whatever objects he had found to throw.

Joe *must* have been mad. It would have been in such a state of madness as this that he would have killed the old man: stabbed him with that hideous hunting blade. I had felt a moment's pity for Joe when I had seen him in his misery on the floor, but now I felt almost sick with anger. Perhaps Bucket shared my emotions, for he said nothing. After a few moments' observation he began to pick up some of the objects in the room until he found a candle and lit it. Joe looked up in a childish sort of way at the sudden flaring light. His face was ugly when it looked up, smeared with tears, but there was a sorrowful look about him.

"My nephew likes to do a bit of hunting and skinning like you, Joe," Bucket said, as if he was already in mid-conversation with him. Mad Joe's blinking eyes looked up at Bucket. "Had some lovely pelts, he did. Used to hang them on the parlour wall," Bucket went on, "weasels, foxes, even a wild dog's once." Bucket suddenly pointed at Joe's unmarked head. "You haven't been knocked out by anyone today, have you? No, it don't look it. You'd have liked to have given someone *else* a smack though, wouldn't you, eh? You'd have liked to have dug your knife in and given someone a bit of a slicing, I expect."

Bucket sat on the floor in front of Joe just like we had sat with Nancy Naiskins in the cellar at Seven Dials. "I once saw my nephew catch a weasel, as it happens. He cut its gizzard out in two ticks and had its skin off in a mo'. All in one piece. Lovely job it was. Quite an expert, see. Nearly as good as you, Joe, I should think. You'd 'ave liked to have done that to someone today, wouldn't you Joe? I'll wager that's true. Now, who might that have been? Was it Mr Merit who got your mad up?"

"D-d-d-" stuttered Mad Joe and began weeping quietly.

"What's that, Joseph?" said Bucket, nodding at me to make a note.

Mad Joe allowed Bucket to assist him calmly enough, and they sat together on the bed. His weeping was unabated yet he found time to feel around at his belt, where erstwhile his knife had had a place. He felt in vain, of course, for the vile thing was at that moment poking upwards at my ribs under my coat.

"Now, Joseph," Bucket continued soothingly. "Now that we're comfortable, you can tell us what's been going off, can't you?"

"M-m-m!" I supposed he was trying to say 'Merit' and Bucket's surmise was the same, for he placed a hand on Joe's shoulder saying, "Listen to me, Joe. Mr Merit is dead. Killed by a knife."

Joe rocked a little at this but Bucket held him firmly and made Joe look him in the face. Mad Joe continued to gasp and jerk but Bucket held on and he seemed to settle.

"Was it yourn, Joseph? *Your* knife that was used to kill him?" he was saying. "Eh? Was it?"

Mad Joe looked wildly at the door as if considering his chances of climbing over Inspector Bucket and running out, but the gasps and stutters resolved themselves into something worse - a kind of wild retching. Bucket held on more firmly still, nodding me away when I tried to aid him.

"We need you to tell us all about it, Joe. Just tell us the truth and you won't be in any trouble. All right? You'll be all right now."

Once more, I was shocked by the calm and considerate tone that Bucket was using to talk to this murderer, though I realised by now that this was one of Bucket's interrogative techniques, to lull his suspects into giving away information.

He waited until Joe's breathing settled down. It seemed to take a long time. He stroked his shoulder and arm in the meantime as if Joe was a dog that needed calming. And when he *was* calmer, Bucket began again.

"You *were* in Mr Merit's room, though, weren't you? Ain't that so, Joseph?" Mad Joe twitched again. Or perhaps it was what he used for a nod. "And had Mr Merit sent for you? Was that why you were there, eh? Was that why, Joe?"

Joe's head started to shake and nod and jerk again.

"Made me take ... my medicine."

"For your fits, Joe? But your medicine didn't always work did it, Joe?" Bucket asked.

"Sleepy. Makes me sleepy."

"I expect that's about all it does, eh?" Mad Joe was silent again. "Was Mr Merit worried you might be violent, Joe? That you might do something bad?" Bucket probed again.

"U-u-upset...a-a-angry!" he stuttered amongst the shakes, but at least the words were forming coherent shapes now.

"Who was upset, Joe? Who was angry? You or Mr Merit?" Mad Joe had twitched again. "Did he get angry with you sometimes, Joe? Hmm? Did he? I think he did get angry with you, Joseph, didn't he, eh? He sometimes got *very* angry with you, I expect - didn't he Joe? Very angry, eh?  Sometimes when you did bad things, eh? Was that what happened? You *did* do bad things, didn't you, Joseph ... chasing the scullery girls, waving your knife at the other stable lads, killing animals..."

"T-t-teased Joe."

"But did you kill *tonight*, Joseph, eh? Did you get angry *tonight*? Did Mr Merit give you a ticking off? And did you get angry, Joe? Is that what happened? The medicine didn't work and Mr Merit got angry with you and you got angry with him and you struck out at him, eh? You struck out at him, and then you felt the knife in your belt and you took it out and you used it on Mr Merit. Is that what happened, Joe? Eh? Did it? Did you kill Mr Merit, Joseph? Did you?"

Joe was jerking about through all of this and I became alarmed, thinking he might do himself, and Bucket, violence. But then he surprised me by speaking almost clearly:

"M-Mr Merit f-f- frightened. Frightened of him!" His voice was a little steadier, but his eyes continually flicked to the door as if he still contemplated making an escape. "Pr- protect him. Joe. Pro-protect him," he said determinedly. "But, the medicine. Gave me two lots. Made me sleepy. Felt dozy."

"I see, Joe. I understand," said Bucket, stroking Joe's back now as if he were a sick child. "You were too dosed up to do anything, weren't you, Joe? But who were you trying to protect Mr Merit *from?* Who was Mr Merit frightened of, Joe?" Joe looked down and ran his hand along his belt two or three times. "You weren't alone in the room, were you, Joe? You were almost asleep but you saw someone else had come in, didn't you? Tell me, Joe. Did someone else come in the room, Joseph?" Bucket demanded.

"D - d - d," stuttered Joe.

"Was it De Blarde, Joseph? Did Mr De Blarde come in the room?"

"D -Dreadnaught!" Joe blurted out.

"*Dreadnaught*, Joe? You can't mean Lord Dreadnaught …"

"F- Frederick. Mr Frederick! F-frightened my father!"

My eyes, I thought, it was true then. Merit *was* Mad Joe's father - as Ebenezer had insinuated. But where had Frederick sprung from? Was De Blarde indeed Dreadnaught? Were they one and the same? Bucket was trying to get at the same thing, of course.

"And who *is* Frederick, Joe?"

"M--Mistress's son."

"And Mr Merit was your father, was he, Joseph?" said Bucket. "Is that why he looked after you so well? He gave you your medicine and he wouldn't let them get rid of you, eh, Joe?" Joe's head was nodding in affirmation. "He wouldn't let the Master throw you out, would he, Joe? Even though Lady Dreadnaught

314

wanted you both gone, eh? Is that it? And the Master let you stay when everyone else was sacked because your old dad, Mr Merit, begged him. Is that so, Joe?" Mad Joe's head lurched forward once again in a wild nod. "It's all right, Joe, it's all right," said Bucket soothingly, stroking him again.

The Inspector allowed Mad Joe to rest for a while and then began again.

"Now, can you tell me about Frederick, Joe, can you, eh? - Can you do that?"

"K-killed..." stuttered Mad Joe.

"Who did he kill, Joe, eh?"

"Saw... saw..."

"What did you see, Joe, hmm? Tell me what you saw."

Mad Joe looked up at Bucket intently and began to speak quite lucidly.

"I - I-followed F-Frederick. Quiet. Like a mouse. S-sometimes on f-foot, sometimes...horse. S-saw him with ch-children. Children of ri-rich p-people. Or, p-poor ones from the s-streets. He made them d-dress up as l-ladies. I saw 'im...I saw him... c-climbing up on children... Hur-hurting children. M-making them b-bleed. Joe saw 'im w-wearin' funny c-c-clothes." Joe looked even more upset. "I seen 'im dressed up before. I seen 'im!"

"All right, Joe," said Bucket, "we believe you, don't we, Mr Jakesbere?"

I nodded. And I supposed I did believe him. Bucket went on gently.

"What sort of clothes did you see Frederick wearing, Joe?"

"Like in a p-pantomime ... a Ch-Chinaman's. I saw him wear that. And even a lady's ... stockings ... and a b-bonnet. And as a w-workman s-sometimes. Like those men he keeps that b-beat

315

you if you s-say anything, or just beat you because ... because they like to b-beat you...and D-d..." He fizzled out at last, nearly spent.

"All right, Joe. Just have a breath, eh. We all need a breath," said Bucket.

And breathe we all did.

Mad Joe was leaning right back now, with his head against the wall. Bucket was sitting with his head in one hand and the thumb of the other worrying away at his mourning ring. I was standing against a chest with the notebook open in front of me, but the pencil was still for a moment. I was thinking what a marvel Bucket was. It was as if he had been gently squeezing information out of Mad Joe, little by little, just putting enough pressure on to squeeze the next bit out, but soothing him as he did so like a horse-whisperer. I doubted that Mad Joe had ever communicated as much before in his entire life as he had in those few minutes.

"But why?" said Bucket, this time almost talking to himself. "Why was Frederick Dreadnaught frightening your father, Joseph? Can you tell me that? What had he done that Mr Frederick was angry about?"

"You!" said Joe, looking up at Bucket. "T-talking to you. He'd been t-tellin' you things and -" Joe looked wildly at the door again while his hand danced over his belt where the knife should have been.

"What is it, Joseph? You can tell me. Your dad would want you to, wouldn't he, eh?" Joe seemed less mad for a little while then and the jerking stopped.

"So, what is it, Joseph? Why was Mr Frederick angry with your old dad?"

"F-for s-saying he was going to ... t-tell the m-master."

316

"About what, Joe? Telling Lord Dreadnaught about *what*?"

"About *him* ... about Frederick ... pr-pretending to be a s-servant ... about 'im a-atta-attacking Miss C-Caroline. I saw 'im. I saw 'im do that, an' all! M-making her scream. Mr Richard n-not there to help and M-Master didn't know, see? Didn't know about F-Frederick's c-costumes. How he dressed up ..."

"And was your dad going to tell Lord Dreadnaught this, eh?" Joe let his head drop sharply for an answer.

"And what did Frederick do, Joseph, when your old dad said he was going to tell all this?"

"L-laughed. J-just laughed. He had a knife in his hand. One minute, just a hand and nothing in it. Next minute - a knife in it. Thin it was ... a thin knife. Came from nowhere ... Pointing it at dad. M-m-my dad was scared. Breathing ... He couldn't breathe. I was dozy. Sleepy. But I got *my* knife out..." His hands went to his belt again. "Wanted to k-kill, D-D. But ... but ... I s-started to f-fit. D-dad came between us. 'S-stop it, Joe', he said to me, 'Stop it!' "

And Joe did stop at this. His twitching eyes looked up at Bucket.

For a second I thought Joe was going to begin jerking again, but Bucket put his hands on his shoulders and whispered to him.

"It's all right, Joe. It's all right. You didn't do it. We know you didn't do it. Rest now ... rest."

And at this gentle command, Joe obeyed. He settled back on the rumpled bed. Bucket nodded his head at me as a sign for me to leave them both. I shut the book and closed the door just as Bucket was pulling the covers over the poor man.

I stood on the landing for a moment to collect my thoughts. Once more, I felt ashamed. I had jumped to conclusions yet again, believing that Joe had murdered his own father. I

317

pondered about what I *did* know. Joe had confirmed that Frederick Dreadnaught had dressed up as a servant. *He* was the murderer, the same monster that had attacked Nancy Naiskins and our own Gertie. But where was he now? As I was contemplating all this, I stepped quietly down the stairs towards Lord and Lady Dreadnaught's rooms.

Mid-way along the corridor, a hum of voices drifted from her Ladyship's private chamber. I suddenly felt overcome with an overwhelming desire to listen. The doors seemed to stare at me, daring me.

Someone was shouting, it seemed. The sound was muffled but I was sure of it. On a marble table outside the door, a solitary wine glass stood on a silver tray, a lick of red at its bottom. In the days of order, such a thing would have been unheard of. A servant would have whisked it away, but now the house had slid into wrack and ruin and it stood alone, evidencing the moral decline perhaps. If a glass could have a voice I would have sworn that it was speaking to me. Remembering the old days in Woolwich when Sparrow and I would employ such an instrument to listen at doors and walls, I picked it up and held it to the keyhole. I confess to looking around once or twice to see that the coast was clear but, thus reassured, I bent down to listen.

# Chapter 30

"Be quiet, woman, damn you!"

I could hear the voice clearly. Whoever was speaking must have been near the doors. As I listened, my heart began to beat faster, for although it was not a voice I recognised at first, it was a voice I felt I had heard before: the one I had heard outside the Hell Club in St James on the night that Gertie was attacked, the same phantom voice I had heard calling across the courtyard of Oblique House. I listened.

"Damn you!" the voice was saying, slightly high pitched and oily. "I've told you a dozen times, I had no choice! I only meant to scare the old man with the knife. Let's not go over this again!" the voice said angrily. "We should plan what is to be said to this damnable policeman you allowed to enter this house."

Something else was said that I could not hear and then the first voice spoke again.

"*Behaving normally* may not be enough! We may need to take more drastic action," it said coldly. I shivered, but after another interruption the voice continued with more heat.

"He was threatening to talk to Montague, damn him. I told you! I only meant to scare the fool. It would have been enough. Either that or he would have had a heart seizure - he was near enough to bursting anyway. I thought the old fool would just drop dead without my intervention!"

There was another voice then, previously unheard in this conversation. Whatever this voice said angered the first speaker, although I couldn't hear what it actually said.

"Don't start that again and don't patronise me, damn you!" the first voice shouted. "I've told you, that mad creature took his knife out! You've seen the thing, he uses it to skin animals and that was what he had in mind for me!"

The other voice interjected here but the oily speaker became shriller still.

"I would have done if he had got closer. I'd have made a pretty enough hole in him! That was when the old man came at *me!*"

Lady Dreadnaught spoke then. Her voice was easily recognisable, although, again, I was unable to hear what she said. But then I *did* hear. She had evidently moved closer to the door.

"Rico... Rico..." she was saying soothingly, as if trying to calm the other.

'Rico'? That name sent shivers down my spine. I knew at last that the Frederick, the *Rico* that we had hunted for so long, was actually there, behind the door where I was standing. If I had had the courage I might have burst in immediately to expose him, but I feared for my safety, and, besides, I remembered how I had always acted too impulsively. Bucket would have wanted me to bide my time.

"Damn you, of course I had to!" This was obviously *Rico* that was speaking. "He was going to tell the old man!" Rico continued. "The visits of that confounded detective  had encouraged him. Gave him the confidence to talk! I should have finished your dear husband *before* all this," the voice said contemptuously, "instead of waiting for *your* nasty little poisons to work!"

Lady Dreadnaught had nothing to say to this, but I almost gasped aloud.

Rico's voice went on: "Just the sight of my stiletto knife might have made the old man succumb to apoplexy instead of your slow death by arsenic. The inheritance would be *mine* by now!"

There was the sudden movement of feet behind me. I jumped

as far away from the door as I could. Coming along the corridor was one of Frederick Dreadnaught's bludgers, one who had escaped the searching constables. We stared at each other in shock at first and then as if we had both caught the other one doing something reprehensible. Just then I heard Bucket coming down the servants stairs and turned towards him. When I turned back, the bludger had vanished into another room. I was about to call out to Bucket but we were both distracted by the sight of two familiar figures coming up from below.

"Perhaps we can help his Lordship with that migraine now," Bucket said, regarding me, "and perhaps one or two of his other disorders, eh, Jakesbere?"

One of the two coming up was Simpkins, the police doctor, whom I supposed Bucket was referring to in relation to Dreadnaught's complaints. The other was Sparrow. "Now then, gentlemen," Bucket began in muted tones, leading them away from Lady Dreadnaught's door. "Sparrow, you must take Simpkins up to Merit's room to do the necessary, and then," he paused, reaching into his pockets, "follow the instructions I've written out for you here. Mind you follow 'em to the letter, Sparrow, my lad, to the *letter!*"

He passed a slip of paper across to Sparrow, who read it and then looked up in amazement.

"*Mad Joe,* Inspector? Begging yer pardon, but ain't he…?" Sparrow got no further forward with this complaint.

"Don't worry, Sparrow," said Bucket, "I think you'll find he's quite calm now." Bucket turned to Simpkins who looked more gaunt than ever and hadn't quite recovered from the exertions of climbing the stairs. "When you're done with the body, Simpkins, I'd like you to see what you can do for old Lord Montague. I've written a few things down here that might help you with your diagnosis." Another slip of paper changed hands.

"Irregular, highly irregular, Inspector," Simpkins said, after reading what Bucket had written.

I could see that Simpkins was even less enamoured of Bucket now than he was the last time I had seen him. Nevertheless, he began to make his way up to the dead man's room, leaning on the stair-rail on one side and using Sparrow as a crutch on the other.

All along, I had been desperate to tell Bucket about what I had heard in Lady Dreadnaught's room and of my encounter with the bludger.

"Well done, Will!" Bucket said, when I had finished, his eyes alight. "Well done, indeed! We shall make a detective of you yet! We shall deal with that bludger in good time, too. But now, if you're ready and you've got your pencil sharpened, we shall make our entrance."

He strode purposefully to Lady Dreadnaught's drawing room doors, pushing against them with surprising urgency. He was to be disappointed, however, for they did not yield to him immediately, as if someone were holding them shut. There followed a shriek of wild hisses and the sounds of physical rearrangements before the doors finally gave way.

The room was gloomy, as rooms in Dreadnaught's mansion habitually were, to accommodate, I presumed, his Lordship's migraines and sensitive eyes, or perhaps the light had just been recently doused. However, after a moment or two my eyes became more adjusted to the gloaming. The only substantial illumination came from some candles positioned by the door where we stood. Those and a few silvery lamps secured to the walls emitted an eerie light. It was a lady's boudoir, clearly enough, or what in my innocence I assumed such a room might be like. There was a side door adjoining this, I noticed, half open as if someone had just entered or left, and a heavily curtained wall opposite us that was full of shadows.

The room was silent now, but for the humming of mechanical birds that hung in a baroque, gilded cage from the ceiling and which called out intermittently with the high shimmer of silvery bells. I looked around in fearful anticipation to identify the infamous Rico, but saw only De Blarde. He lay on a dark chaise-longue in the centre of the room, spread out like an invalid. A flask of brandy on a tray by his elbow reflected blood-like flashes from the flaming red embers in the low fire. A goblet nestled in his lap under the froth of his long, wide, lace cuffs. His jacket was off. And he was wigless. His black hair was speckled with grey dust. He was in the process of moving one bony hand to his head. He began to moan as if he were suffering from an ague.

The other figures in the room, I supposed, had hidden themselves in the shadows. However, a rustle of skirts soon revealed Lady Dreadnaught. She was in a distant corner, but her dress caught what light there was in the dim room. I comprehended all of this in a matter of seconds, of course, for the eye can see at a speed with which the pen cannot write. Whilst I did, Lady Dreadnaught floated towards us like a ghost, brushing down her golden skirt with her thin, white hands. Behind her, I heard the swishing of a heavy curtain. The movement seemed to allow a slit of moonlight through a half-opened door leading to the outer world. Everything and everybody seemed lit up as under a lamp for a second.

"Do you never knock before entering a lady's drawing room, Inspector?" her Ladyship said with a voice of frost. Bucket said nothing. I took out the black notebook. "Well, at least you *have* come," she continued, coming closer to us so that we could see her eyes flash. "We can deal with this whole sorry business once and for all. It has put my household in an uproar, Inspector." Bucket was still silent. Although I could make out little of his expression as I stood a step or two behind him, it was clear that his silence disturbed her.

"You find me here still trying to comfort poor De Blarde," she continued, turning and walking towards the invalid. "Alfred!" she called into the shadows. "More brandy for Monsieur De Blarde - I feel he needs it."

I had been unaware of the head footman's presence until she called him, although Ada had told us he would be here. His silhouette stepped out of the dark corners where, servant-like, he had stationed himself. However, it seemed to me that another was hidden there too. Alfred bent over De Blarde and poured from the brandy flask.

"You must drink, my dear De Blarde," Lady Dreadnaught encouraged him. "It will help revive you." He did drink and Alfred slid back into the shadows.

Lady Dreadnaught now turned to face Bucket again. But I could see by the glimmer in her eyes that she was observing the reactions of her servants, though whether for comfort or protection, or out of wariness, I could not say.

"You have kept us unaccountably long, Inspector. We are all in distress because of the tragedy that has occurred in our house. We all wish to see an end to the horror of it all, and that mad stable boy put away where he belongs at last. Poor De Blarde has been quite hysterical." She turned to look at him but his head was lowered. "Our house is overrun by your policemen so that we can have no quiet. My poor Montague, my poor, dear Montague, has taken quite ill because of it all." Perhaps this was her trying to behave 'naturally' but the hysteria seemed to be hers and not De Blarde's. "You *must* drink, my dear De Blarde," she implored once again.

I still could not see how Bucket was reacting to her outpourings, but, in fact, he hardly seemed interested in her voice at all. His attention, as far as I could discover, seemed directed towards people's hands, as best as he could see them in the half-light. I followed his gaze and noted the occasional flash of the familiar signet ring on her thin finger: the ring, the sister of that other that I had found all those days ago in Richard Dreadnaught's room.

De Blarde's hands were still intermittently holding his head or toying, distractedly, at the cuffs of his sleeves. That his hands, too, were thin, was plain to see, even in the half-light. His pale gloves lay limply on the table beside him, glowing in the dark, like fish skins. However, Bucket's eyes seemed directed beyond him, even, and into the shadows. I noticed it was eyes that seemed to catch the light the most and every time anyone looked up, it was like fire-flies flashing backwards and forwards.

"Merci, Madame," said De Blarde, sipping at the brandy. Bucket remained quiet. His silence was discomposing for me but even more so, it seemed, for the others in the room. Everything became unaccountably hot.

Bucket's usual method of interrogation was to *talk* his villains into a confession. Sometimes, he would talk *at* them so much that they would scream at him how guilty they were before he had actually asked them a question that was truly material to the case. He seemed to insinuate their guilt in the way he spoke, as if he saw into their souls. His ruminations usually carried a hidden meaning that was only too clear: 'I know *all* about you anyway, and I *always* have, so you might as well just confess,' they implied. This was his habitual manner or method. This *new* form of interrogation, however, through silence, was a novel one that I had not seen him utilise before. It seemed as if he were waiting for the little worm of guilt that he had sent digging and delving by his silence to waken up the sleeping dragon of conscience and to make it roar out a confession of its own volition.

"Rico, I need a drink," Lady Dreadnaught said suddenly, in a voice charged with anxiety. Under the pressure of Bucket's silence, she had admitted that Frederick, Rico, was in the room. But who did this name *belong* to? She promptly took up her fan and began an aimless circuit of the room. "You can see, at least, Inspector, that my nerves are fraught," she said quickly in an attempt to cover up for her error. "I hardly know what I am saying. Mixing up names." She gave an embarrassed, false laugh.

I had stepped forward myself then, aware of other movements in the room. It was Alfred who came out of the shadows, although there was a rustle from the furthest corner from which no one emerged. "No, Alfred. I am well, thank you. You may keep your station," she said. "I am just a little hot, that is all." She flapped out her folded paper fan suddenly. "I need a little air." And so saying, she walked to the farthest end of the room and drew the curtains a little to one side, so that I felt again a breath of the cold night air come stealing in alongside a slither of moonlight.

"We have *all* been fraught, Inspector," Lady Dreadnaught continued. "Monsieur De Blarde was so upset by the dreadful murder of Mr Merit that he became quite ill, didn't you? Didn't you, poor De Blarde?" De Blarde did not answer. Nor did Bucket. The only voices were from the mechanical birds in the golden cage above her. All eyes went to them momentarily, as if in relief.

"Well, Inspector," she started again, turning back to us after taking deep breaths of the night air. "Is that terrible stable-boy safely in confinement? I believe one of your young constables has him locked away. Is that not so?" She fluttered her fan again and the false birds sang false notes over her head. "I begged and begged Montague to dismiss the boy, but he would not be moved, even by me. There was some strange bond between that boy and Mr Merit, you see. Lord Dreadnaught was attached to Mr Merit, Inspector, and insisted that he should be waited on by him *every* day, despite my protestations. But, Montague allowed himself to be swayed by his manservant, Merit, even to the extent of keeping such a clearly dangerous person as that boy in his employ. And now, you can see what tragedy it has led to!"

She looked for some response from Bucket. Anything. But he remained silent. Her voice became a half-octave higher. "There was gossip amongst the other servants that Mr Merit had actually *fathered* the boy. What do you think of that?" Bucket continued to stand in silence, observing De Blarde, who still had his head bowed. "What do you think of that?" Lady Dreadnaught repeated. "A child of some depraved liaison with some slut of a servant girl, I suspect." She flapped her fan so that it caught the edge of a table with a thwack. "You see, *this* is how such a son repays his father. You see, Inspector, *another* father abused by *another* son - just as my Montague has been abused by that scoundrel, Richard."

Lady Dreadnaught walked over to the Inspector, looking closely at him. "I hear that he too is in custody at last," she continued. "Is that not so? Arrested at last for his gross deeds, I hear." Her voice became a low whisper. "Montague will be bereft. The shame, the scandal." She looked Bucket in the eye. "But your duty is done, is it not Inspector?" she continued briskly. "The son has been located. The scoundrel has been found. We can all carry on as normal now, can we not? Montague will be devastated, of course, but he will understand and realise that Richard is not worthy of the line of Dreadnaughts. Not worthy to inherit the virtues of an ancient family. Richard too is guilty of dalliance with a woman of low birth, is he not, Inspector? That gardener's daughter, I mean. A witch! But she has gone and he has his just deserts. So, your duty is done, Inspector. Is that not so? It is done!"

She was almost screeching now. She looked at the Inspector in desperation. "Say something, Inspector Bucket, damn you! For God's sake, speak!"

I felt almost sorry for her. And more so as Bucket took one step forward towards De Blarde, ignoring all the outpourings of her monologue. "I hear it was you who found Mr Merit's body, Monsieur De Blarde," said Bucket blandly.

Lady Dreadnaught slumped despondently onto her chair in a gush of silks.

De Blarde gave Bucket a supercilious sneer. "Mais oui, I 'eard the noises, Inspector. Very loud. I 'eard them from below, when I was attending 'er Ladyship. You see 'ow her nerves are bad?"

"And so?" Bucket replied, ignoring this last observation.

"And so, I investigate, like you, Inspector. Like a police."

"I see," said Bucket. "And you found Joe there too, is that the case?"

"Oui."

De Blarde waited for another question, but Bucket too seemed to be waiting. De Blarde broke the silence first.

"It is true what 'er Ladyship say," De Blarde said, with emphasis. "Joe, 'e is dangerouse. 'E 'ad attacked Mister Merit before. You 'ave seen 'ow nervous the old man was, n'est-ce pas? Joe is called 'mad' by all the servants 'ere. You know this, I guess.

328

I try to stop such words, but you know 'ow some of the servants are."

Bucket continued his silence and his unforgiving gaze.

"But *mad* 'e is," De Blarde hurried on uncomfortably. "It is true. He 'as attacked others before. Some girls. Even myself. You 'ave seen his knife, non? Well, he *kills* with that. Not people, perhaps, till now. We 'ope there are no others – but 'e is dangerouse. You will 'ave seen the animal skins 'e keeps, the terrible knife 'e uses, non?"

"So," said Bucket at last, unimpressed. "Let me get this clear, Monsieur. You went to Mr Merit's room, to do *what*, exactly?"

"To come to the rescue, as you say."

"And what did you find when you entered Merit's room?"

"Fighting ... shouting ... Mr Merit, 'e was 'olding Joe, trying to stop 'im from violence," said De Blarde, becoming more animated. "He 'ad the knife in his hand."

"And the room itself," asked Bucket. "what sort of state was that in?"

"It was, 'ow you say, chaos, Inspector. The floor, it was covered with…" De Blarde hesitated for a moment before completing his sentence. "With things," he said.

"A *big* struggle, then," Bucket said. "It certainly was by the looks of it - things knocked off the wall and stuff thrown about and Merit's jug and bowl turned upside down with water everywhere, eh?" He looked closely at De Blarde. "Am I right?"

"Mais oui," said De Blarde promptly. "Mr Merit was defending himself, but Joe he 'as the knife."

"And how did you rescue him?" Bucket's voice was cold. "What weapon did you use to defend yourself against that terrible knife?"

De Blarde stood now. He fixed his wig upon his head and put

on his jacket, buttoning up the fine, brocade buttons. As he did so, Alfred moved to stand behind his lady, like a shadow.

"I was too late, Inspector," De Blarde finally replied. "I 'ad no 'weapon, as you say, and so could not save Mr Merit. I am just a manservant to her Ladyship. I am not required to carry a 'baton', as yourself."

"A knife then, Monsieur De Blarde? What about a knife?" Bucket looked hard at De Blarde before continuing. "I don't know much about being in service in Paris, Monsieur, but I have a friend who lives there who I write to. He tells me you need to keep yourself safe in some of those Parisian backwaters." Bucket's gaze seemed to become even more intense. "They had a spate of knife murders there, you see. Perhaps when you feel yourself in danger, perhaps when wandering the Parisian streets, *you* might carry a knife *yourself*, Monsieur, for protection, shall we say?" Bucket and De Blarde's eyes seemed to crackle across the shadows.

"The only knife, it was Joe's, Inspector Bucket."

"And so you didn't try to stop Joe yourself?"

"Bien sur, I try," said De Blarde, "but Joe, 'e 'as the strength of the ten men when 'e goes mad. I could not stop him."

"Did he knock you over then?"

"Mais oui."

"And I expect more things went over with you, eh?" Bucket said with a smile.

"Yes, things ..."

"Oh yes," said Bucket, "quite a mess was made. Inkpots knocked over and paper everywhere. Hardly an inch of the room where something hadn't been knocked over and chucked about in the struggle, eh?"

"Mais oui, you 'ave it."

"Have you got all that, Mr Jakesbere?" Bucket said, turning to me.

I nodded.

"You're quite sure about what you've said, Monsieur? I don't want to misrepresent you," said Bucket, turning back to De Blarde.

"Of course. You do not believe me, Inspector, I can see! You insult my 'onour, Monsieur!"

"Not at all. Not at all. I just need to be sure I have it right." Bucket paused for a moment. "And how was Mr Merit actually killed? Could you take me through that, Monsieur?"

"Inspector, enough!" Lady Dreadnaught called from her corner. "Monsieur De Blarde has had a shock. Surely..."

Bucket interrupted, ignoring her. "Monsieur?"

"Joe, 'e push Merit away and then 'e take out 'is knife. He thrust with it through Mr Merit's 'eart. In front of my eyes, I saw this."

"That must have been very shocking for you, and very bloody too, Monsieur."

"It was. To see a man killed just like that, like 'e is a pig," said De Blarde with what seemed disgust.

"Cowardly, I should say," agreed Bucket. "And like a pig being slaughtered, indeed, Monsieur. All that blood, eh?"

"It was terrible!" said De Blarde, wiping his brow.

"So, let us just summarise, shall we?" said Bucket, firmly. "Just for the sake of Mr Jakesbere's notes. Now, there was all this peg-meg that had been thrown about in the struggle: chairs and paper and ink and water and what not, not to mention all that blood, and then Merit topples onto the lot of it. Am I getting this right, Monsieur De Blarde?"

"You 'ave it," De Blarde said emphatically.

331

"But, go on, surely Mad Joe didn't just leave you alone and run off? He must have attacked you as well, eh?"

"Oui, he came for me ... but, Mon Dieu, I push 'im to the ground and he must have knocked himself out, Inspector. I was saved!"

"Ah, I expect he'll have a bit of a lump in the morning, eh?" Bucket said, thoughtfully.

"I am shocked, Inspector. I do not remember exactly but I drag 'im out before 'e can recover and..." again he hesitated for a moment before continuing, "and I call for 'elp. The cook," he said loudly, "she 'eard me. You may ask 'er, Inspector, if you do not believe. I carry 'im myself to the cook's room and lock 'im in."

"And that was it, was it?" said Bucket, waiting.

"The cook, she is, what you say, in a panic and she tells others of the murder," said DeBlarde with confidence. "There was uproar in the 'ouse, Inspector. She sent a boy for the police, I believe, and there was a constable here within a few minutes. I don't know how so quick."

"And what did you do in those few minutes, Monsieur?" asked Bucket.

"I stay outside the door," answered De Blarde after a moment, "until the police he arrive. You may ask 'im. He was one of your officers, I believe."

"And then?" asked Bucket.

"And then I tell Lady Dreadnaught the terrible news. And then I am exhausted. As you found me, Inspector," said De Blarde.

"A bit heavy, I should think?" said Bucket after a moment. De Blarde looked at him quizzically. "Mad Joe's body, when you carried it along the corridor to the cook's room."

"Well, that is correct," De Blarde said after a pause. "I call out for someone to 'elp and…" he paused again, "and Alfred, 'e come running, and then the cook. I could not carry Joe alone, as you say."

In the shadows, Alfred had stood up from whatever whispered conversation he had been having with Lady Dreadnaught, perhaps expecting to be questioned in turn.

"Of course," said the Inspector. "Well, thank you, Monsieur De Blarde," he said in a breezy voice, "I am most indebted to you."

De Blarde's relief was plain.

"But you'll swear to all this, won't you, Monsieur? It's just routine, you know," said Bucket with a smile, "just to confirm your statement is true."

"Bien sur," De Blarde said. "I swear."

"Well, good. That seems to be it then," said Bucket, turning as if to leave and then turning back, nonchalantly. "If you would just  sign that what you've told us is a true account, then, Monsieur De Blarde, we can leave you all in peace. My assistant here, Mr Jakesbere, has been writing down your statement as you speak, as I expect you've noticed. Perhaps you'd be so good?"

"Of course, Inspector," said De Blarde.

"And you too, Alfred," said Bucket, calling calmly into the shadows, where Alfred stood leaning over Lady Dreadnaught. "As you were there too and witnessed Mr De Blarde's actions. If you'd just sign on the dotted as well …"

Alfred had had no chance to answer or move when Bucket spoke. "But before you do, we might as well get the whole family in, eh? *All* the parties to the affair, so to speak, hmm? As it happens, I've already taken the liberty of asking one of my constables to bring some more light in, to go against this darkness a bit. Why," he laughed, "we can hardly see each other's faces, can we?"

He walked suddenly to the door and called out: "Sparrow! Bring 'em in!"

And in they came. And what a sight it was!

# Chapter 31

Constables Blakey, Spry and Coke came first, carrying their lanterns so that soon the whole room was flooded with flashing light, and the mirrors reflected a kaleidoscope of faces. Next, his Lordship was wheeled in on a creaking bath chair, pushed with some difficulty by Simpkins, the police doctor. The pair of them breathed asthmatically together, as if in accord. Then, to the greatest astonishment of all, in came the jerking figure of Mad Joe himself - carefully held under the arms by Sparrow. De Blarde and her Ladyship gasped aloud, the latter standing up to remonstrate.

"What is the meaning of this, Inspector? Why do you bring this *murderer* into our very midst? And Montague, why have they woken you so cruelly from your sick bed and brought you here? This is too much! My husband is an invalid, Inspector. I shall hold you personally responsible for any ... he is not well ... not well!"

The old Lord rubbed his eyes against the darkness of his half-blindness and looked straight into hers.

"Nothing to fear, my dear," he began in his breathy voice, struggling between each phrase. "The Inspector sent a message with Doctor Simpkins here. There was something ... something that I needed to see. I demurred, of course." He struggled for breath again. "For I have been used to leaving such things to you, my dear. But apparently the Inspector insisted." Her ladyship made a sort of strangled sound. "Don't worry, my dear," he gasped, seeing her distress. "The good Doctor here has given me something for my migraine and a particularly good ointment for my eyes. Strange to say, the pain has gone down a little, and I am beginning to see a little better. And it seems, my dear, that my stomach pains," the old Lord said incredulously, "my stomach pains, they may be due to - to poisoning! Poisoning, my dear!"

"W-what nonsense!" her Ladyship shouted, giving her fan a wicked flick of anger.

Lord Dreadnaught was not to be put off, however, but continued in a more determined voice. "The doctor said Inspector Bucket wanted to know why I had said nothing of ... of Frederick, my dear."

Lady Dreadnaught gasped.

"I have always followed your wishes regarding your son, my dear," he struggled on. "You said there was no need to implicate Frederick in the Inspector's search for Richard. The Inspector would meddle enough ... you said. And I agreed. But I think, now, I was wrong to keep the knowledge of Frederick's existence from him."

"Perhaps," Bucket said, "perhaps, my Lord, we might leave that for now and begin with signing the witness statements. Simpkins would have told you about those, eh?" The old Lord nodded. "With your permission, then?" Dreadnaught nodded again. "Joseph," said the Inspector, turning to the crazy figure of the stable boy. "Step forward, my lad. You shall go first."

Joe looked up in confusion. Sparrow still had a firm grip on him and was clearly looking uncomfortable about letting it go. "It's all right Sparrow," Bucket said. "You can leave off. He's safe!"

"Safe?" her Ladyship spluttered, turning from contemplation of her husband's newly determined face to the jerking figure of Joe.

Bucket ignored her intervention. "Perhaps we can use this," Bucket said, taking the pen and ink brought in by Constable Spry, and the notebook from me, to a solid-looking table in the room. Next, the metal nib was freshly dipped and the notebook opened at the correct page.

From the way Joe regarded the pen, one might as well have handed him some strange surgical instrument. He looked at it askance, as a thing he knew not the purpose of. After a pause, he reached for it from underneath, as if stalking his prey. Once he had it in his sights, he adjusted his fist and took the pen, as it were, by the scruff of its neck. He regarded Bucket and then the whole room in consternation. At last, taking courage, he held his right hand high in the air and, adjusting his grip for a third time, brought the pen down onto the page as if he were wielding an axe. He made a heavy mark that nearly went through the page, much to my annoyance, then looked around as if he had decided that now was the time to make his escape.

"Thank you, Joseph," said Bucket soothingly, patting him on the shoulder, as I blotted the page and turned the leaves. "And now, Monsieur De Blarde," Bucket continued, turning back to the body of the room. "You said you were willing to sign the statement you gave?"

For a moment, De Blarde seemed to share the same longing for escape that I had seen on Joseph's face but, nevertheless, with a smile of disdain, he shook his right hand free from its cuff and accepted the proffered pen. His grip was more like what one would expect from someone used to holding a manicuring device. He dipped it once and signed with a flourish. Lord Montague was now leaning forward in his bath chair as these proceedings were underway, looking intently at all the participants and watching everybody in the room as if he had been unable to see them properly for some time.

"And now, Alfred," said Bucket, "if you will come forward to witness Monsieur De Blarde's statement, I will be obliged." Alfred was mute as always and did not move. "Come, come, my

337

man," said Bucket, "don't be shy. Come out of the shadows there." Bucket held out the pen. Alfred stepped forward into the light after what seemed like ages. There was the slightest of movements from behind him, but it was Lord Dreadnaught's voice that was more noticeable: a strangled noise in his throat as if he wished to intervene. Alfred's pasty complexion seemed almost to be melting before our eyes, but he took the pen, holding it in his left hand as if it were a scalpel and, signing hastily, he withdrew into the shadows.

"One moment, if you please, Lord Dreadnaught," Bucket said, seeing that his Lordship was straining to climb out of his chair. "We are in need of a signet ring to seal the document, aren't we? Now, there is *yours* of course, your Ladyship," he said, glancing at her increasingly distressed figure, "but I couldn't ask a Lady to remove a ring, could I? Don't seem polite somehow." She put her hand up to her throat then, as if something was about to choke her.

"A ring for a son, my lady, eh? Just like your own," continued Bucket. Her Ladyship gasped and clasped her throat still tighter. Bucket turned to the old Lord. "And a ring for a *step*-son, Lord Montague?" The old man moved forward in his chair again, as if he would fling himself out if he could.

"One moment more, Lord Dreadnaught, please," Bucket said firmly. "If no one will come forward with a signet ring as yet, we can wait, can't we? Now, Mr Jakesbere, Joe's knife if you will?"

I had no hesitation in extracting the awful blade from where it had been digging a hole in my rib-cage all along. I placed it on the table. Bucket removed my grey handkerchief.

"This is the knife that supposedly killed Mr Merit, your faithful old retainer, Lord Dreadnaught." The old man's eyes seemed ever wider and clearer. "Look at its blade," Bucket said, regarding the assembly. "This is a *hunting* knife. A *skinning* blade, in fact. It's been used, by Joe here, for many unpleasant purposes, hasn't it, Joe? Given a bit of a shock to many a stoat and rabbit, I shouldn't wonder. Horrible, of course, but that *is* its proper purpose." Bucket looked a little harshly at Joe. "Scared the living daylights out of a few people when you've waved it about though, hasn't it, Joe? All those teasing servant girls, those mocking footmen and sarcastic stable-lads? They got you mad, didn't they, Joe? Of course, you *should* have kept your knife tucked in your belt and only brought it out for its *proper* purposes, shouldn't you?" Joe looked sheepish. Bucket turned back to the others. "But look at it, gentlemen and my Lady."

We did.

"Look at *how* it'd kill. See this long, flat blade?" he said, running a careful finger along its edge. "Now, that'd rip skin off nicely, wouldn't it? Gut a nice piece of cod for dinner that would, no bother. Anything that was ripped by that would bleed something horrible, wouldn't it? Prodigiously, you might say. Bleed something bloody, eh? Wouldn't it, Monsieur De Blarde?"

Bucket surveyed the room calmly. "Now, tell me this: how was it, then, that there was so *little* blood on the body of Mr Merit, eh? Dr. Simpkins here tells me that such a blade as this would make a gash in a man that might be as wide as a church door and it'd make a glut o' blood that'd fill a bucket besides, ain't that so, Simpkins?"

Simpkins nodded. Bucket's voice became louder. "And yet there was *no* blood in Mr Merit's room. Not a speck. Not a splotch. Not a slither. Funny that. Everything *else* was in a proper mess, mind you. But, *no* blood. Not even a bit of water spilled from the washing bowl. None at all. Someone must have missed that, eh? When they were making it *look* like there'd been a big struggle, I mean?" He looked towards De Blarde and Alfred. "All those bits and pieces that got knocked down should've been *under* his body if he fell down *after* the struggle, shouldn't they? Not *on top of it*! D'you see?" He paused. "Merit's body was left much too neat looking as well. No, *this* knife did *not* kill Mr Merit, did it?"

Bucket touched the knife for a second and then pushed it away disdainfully as a sign that he was done with it. Joe watched it as it described a slow circle on the shiny table top. Bucket stopped for a second. He calmly regarded the picture he had created: the lanterns swaying and flooding the faces one second with shadows and the next with light.

"Well, I'm amazed gentlemen," said Bucket, at last. "All that *blood* you swore you saw, when of course there was *no* blood. No blood, Monsieur De Blarde." De Blarde lowered his head. "Didn't you know?" Bucket persisted. "But you *weren't* to know, were you, Monsieur De Blarde? For, of course, you are *innocent*, are you not? Innocent of *this* crime, at least, eh?" Bucket's voice became more and more emphatic. "You didn't *touch* Joe did you, De Blarde? You weren't even *there* when Merit was murdered, were you? For then you would've *known* that not a *drop* of blood was spilt, the incision was so *very* neat. Of course, you *could* have done that, couldn't you, De Blarde? I know that well enough. For I know who you are, sir. Oh yes. You're no servant, sir, are you?" De Blarde looked up. "And nor are you, Alfred," he said suddenly, turning to the shadowy figure still lurking in the darkest part of the room.

All the eyes in the room followed his direction.

"Now, what should we call you really?" He was fixing Alfred with his eye and pointing at him with his finger. "What is it to be?" he continued. "Alfred? Frederick? *Rico*? Which name

340

would you like? Your names are many, just as your costumes are."

And at this, Alfred, or Frederick, or Rico, seemed to have had enough of the whole charade. He threw his grey wig to the floor and, moving into the full glare of the candle-light and the lamps, stood defiantly. The silent footman, Alfred, had disappeared. A bolder figure filled his place. He gave himself a shake, as if he were glad to be free of his old disguise, or as if he had decided that it had outlived its purpose.

Lord Montague could hold back no longer. He staggered to his feet. "Rico! It *is* you!" he said. "At first, I felt my eyes had deceived me...but it *is* you! And...all...all this while you have been masquerading in servant's clothes...parading as my Lady's footman."

The old man was breathing heavily. Frederick Dreadnaught looked at him with distain.

The old Lord fastened his eyes on her Ladyship as if the shutters had fallen away at last. "Rachel!" he called out. "Why? Why?" But this was all he could say. His strength gave way and he had to allow himself to be eased back into his chair. Simpkins attempted to calm him quietly, but the old man brushed him away.

"I see ... I see ..." Lord Dreadnaught whispered, once he'd recovered enough to speak.

Bucket had been staring at Frederick Dreadnaught, as I should call him now, all along. It was a look that would have shrivelled me.

"So, you have come out into the light at last, have you, Frederick Dreadnaught? It was *you* who killed Mr Merit and you killed him with your *own* knife, didn't you, Frederick? You killed him with a knife that makes a *fine* incision, like a scalpel."

341

The intensity of Bucket's gaze did not falter. A tremor of silent shock passed through the room.

"I have seen such a mark before, Frederick Dreadnaught," Bucket said, with fierce severity. "I have seen it in the bodies of the victims of the so-called 'Beast of London Town'."

There were gasps now from every part of the room.

"And I have seen it in the bodies of those little girls you killed at Hyde Park."

Lord Dreadnaught gave out a sort of strangled cry at this, but Bucket went on remorselessly. "I have seen it in the flesh of children punctured by the 'Beast of Belgravia'. Seen it in the skin of innocent girls pierced by the 'Beast of Seven Dials'."

Bucket's voice had reached a crescendo. But as he continued, his tone became more calmly business-like. "It's *you*, isn't it, Alfred? Frederick? Rico? What *shall* we call you? No matter. You see, the width of the blade you used matches the wounds made on the bodies of children washed up on the banks of the Thames and the wounds in the bodies of those little girls at the Exhibition. I've had that checked. It's the *same* blade you used to mutilate the bodies of young girls in Paris, isn't it?"

Frederick Dreadnaught looked Bucket in the eye for the first time and almost smiled.

Bucket went on. "We have a sort of *guild*, us Detectives, you see. I'm not much of a one for the writing lark but I've penned a few little notes to my friend Vidocq over in Paris, you see. I think you might've heard of him. You and *your* friend Monsieur De Blarde, eh? You're *both* well known to Monsieur Vidocq, oh yes. Monsieur De Blarde here made himself famous for being good with a blade eh? In fact, I've heard that you might have *taught* Mr Frederico all he knows." Bucket turned to face De Blarde again. "Till he out-did even you at the last," he continued. "I'd be surprised if even *you* weren't a little put out by your protégé's behaviour. But of course, you'd fallen under Mr Frederick's spell yourself by then, hadn't you? Got a little *too* fond of him." De Blarde blanched at this. "That's the information I have from Vidocq, anyway," the Inspector continued. "He writes a very good letter does my French friend, very informative."

De Blarde seemed about to speak but Bucket turned back to the Beast. "You've a number of different family names actually, haven't you, Frederick?" The Beast looked back at him, stony-faced, but for the sneer his upper lip made. "You *and* your mother," Bucket said, turning to her Ladyship. She stood transfixed.

"Mrs *Steel*, I think you were first, ma'am, weren't you? The wife of a Mr Thomas Steel. And Frederick here is your son by that poor gentleman. An industrialist, I believe, who fell on hard times. He died a touch suddenly, didn't he, eh? A strange 'internal hemorrhaging', as my memory of the papers recalls." Bucket's voice was cold. "You could've made a bit of a fortune from his death, couldn't you, ma'am? Terrible stomach pains he had before he died - so the coroner's report had it." Lady Dreadnaught made another involuntary sound. "Yes, I've read that too. Might almost have been *arsenic* poisoning, wouldn't you agree?" Her eyes looked into the corner as if looking for an escape route there, but Bucket persisted. "Would've been all right for you and young Freddy, wouldn't it? Once you'd got over your grief, I mean. But then Thomas Steele's debtors came out of the cupboard, didn't they? And, well, the poor fellow weren't worth half so much after all, was he?"

Bucket paused, as if consulting his mental records. "You took up with a Monsieur Bouchard, next. Only a month after, I believe. Got over your grief quick, I suppose. A banker from

343

Paris, weren't he? Half Italian, my friend Vidocq tells me." Bucket paused again to consult his internal record. "You returned with him to Montmartre, as I recall. Perhaps that's when you became Frederico, eh?" said Bucket turning to the Beast. "Or Rico, as your mother called you earlier. Now then, Montmartre. That's where you developed your personal *tastes,* shall we call them?" Bucket looked at Rico with contempt. "You met up with your friend De Blarde who showed you how to use a stiletto blade, didn't he?"

De Blarde fell into a chair, putting his head in his hands. Frederick Dreadnaught turned to look behind him where the curtain swayed.

"But Mr De Blarde had *other* tastes though, didn't he?" Bucket continued, looking at the prone figure in the chair. "Didn't you, Monsieur De Blarde? You liked *men,* I believe, *and* boys, so I'm told. Isn't that true, Monsieur?" De Blarde sighed in despair.

"I expect you grew a bit too fond of your Rico here, though, didn't you?" Bucket continued, remorselessly. "You didn't mind helping him with his own little fancies as long as he came back to you in the end, eh? But ..." said Bucket, "it was definitely *girls* that *you* had a taste for, wasn't it, Mr Frederick?" turning to the Beast again. "My friend Vidocq told me all about the attacks on young girls in Paris. He was a bit confused at first. You see, the man who'd been killing in the streets of Paris seemed to like *boys.* What *was* happening? It was young *girls* who were being assaulted now. Daughters of well-to-do parents too, Vidocq tells me. Always *young* ones though, or older girls who looked younger than their years. Sometimes it was poor girls who'd wash up nicely to look like little rich ones. Killed in the same way by the attacker of the boys in the Paris streets, that is, with a stiletto blade. And killed by someone who knew how to handle

344

such a thing - or had been taught."

The Inspector began to circle the room, as if he were drawing a rope more and more tightly around the motionless figure of the Beast. Once again, I was astonished at the breadth and depth of Inspector Bucket's knowledge.

"But," Bucket continued, "the fatal wounds started to appear on the *opposite* side of the wretched victims' bodies. Our *right*-handed killer was killing with his *left* hand now. Right to left, boys to girls. There you have it!" Bucket announced to the room. "The same attacks, the same deaths. But the girls always suffered something worse: mutilation by a steel blade, faces and bodies pricked all over so that they came up in small scars like smallpox." The Beast was still motionless but a contemptuous smile, of sorts, had started to creep across his face.

Bucket turned back to her Ladyship. "It's strange, isn't it, ma'am, that your second husband, Monsieur Bouchard, died in such mysterious circumstances? 'Arsenic overdose', as the Parisian Coroners' Office put it. Wasn't that so?" There was an agonised groan from Lord Dreadnaught, and Lady Dreadnaught looked away again in shock and shame.

"Vidocq felt that he'd tracked down a *couple* of suspects for the monster who might have been carrying out the attacks, but then they seemed to vanish into thin air. Just about the time *you and your son* arrived in England, ma'am, as a matter of fact. Strange that. And then, lo and behold, there was a spate of attacks on young girls in *London* too. Same thing: daughters of the aristocracy, or those that looked like them. Or even those that the killer could *make* look like 'em. Assaults. Rapes. Mutilations. All done by a very thin blade. Italian styled, apparently. A stiletto." Bucket paused, looking back at De Blarde. "Of course, it was Monsieur De Blarde who helped us out in the end."

345

De Blarde looked up in horror. "You followed when Frederick came to England, didn't you? Grown fond of him, hadn't you? A *strong* attachment, I should say. I expect when Rico looked as if he might get caught, you wanted to protect him - so much so that you even agreed to act as a servant, didn't you? Rico's idea of course, but you went along with it." Bucket addressed the whole room now. "You controlled the servants of the house here so that Rico, disguised as Alfred, could disappear into corners when danger threatened. But you've been *used* yourself, haven't you, De Blarde?"

De Blarde looked as if he was about to speak, but Bucket held up his hand. "Rico here," Bucket continued, "would have let you swing on a rope for him without a backward glance. After all, he's willing enough to let you appear to be the one last seen with Mr Merit. Hmm?"

Bucket looked in turn at Lady Dreadnaught, De Blarde and Frederick. "But, here you all are - exposed at last. And it was the murder of Mr Merit that gave you away, Frederick Dreadnaught. You stabbed Mr Merit under his *right* arm and the wound had gone in an *upward* direction. As Simpkins, my Police Doctor here, will swear to. Only a *left-handed* man would strike in such a way. Just as a *left-handed* man might smear a signature that he was forging."

This last was a revelation to me. So this was why Bucket was constantly looking at people's hands and why I had to find a copy of Richard Dreadnaught's signature that wasn't smeared, proving *his* innocence and the *forger's* guilt.

But Bucket was continuing to speak. "The death wounds on Merit's body and on all the other poor young girls were made by *you*, Alfred, *you*, Frederico Steel, *you*, Rico Bouchard, *you*, Frederick Dreadnaught. What *shall* we call you? The Beast, I

346

think. A Beast who killed with a vicious stiletto in his *left* hand!"

"Like this, Inspector?" said the cold, high voice of Frederick Dreadnaught.

And in his hand there appeared the very one: a thin, silver blade, with a point like a needle, conjured up out of his sleeve. I remembered then the long thin sheath that I had seen in Frederick's hidden room, for the instrument that he wielded was the one it must have housed. His voice was chilling and there was madness in his eyes; not bedlam-madness like Joe's, born of fits and teasings, but a madness that was demonic.

# Chapter 32

"No, Rico!" his mother called out suddenly, running to him.

Frederick Dreadnaught stood still for a second and the point of the stiletto gleamed in his hand. But then, with a sudden movement, he leaned forward and, lengthening his arm almost carelessly, executed a single lunge to her neck, just as if he were flicking away a fly. I could not believe what had happened at first. Neither could she. For a moment she seemed unsure what he had *done*. She regarded him as if she were about to enquire something of him. Lost for words, or unable to speak, she touched a finger to her neck. A single smear of blood leaked between her fingers like a tear. She sat down as calmly as if she were about to wrap a napkin around her neck for dinner, except for the way in which her pupils rolled in her eyes. It seemed that once the Beast was out in the open, there was nothing to restrain his shameless violence and contempt for all.

"Rico!" De Blarde shouted.

"Be quiet!" Rico replied, in a voice of steel.

"Rico, it's no use. They 'ave you," cried De Blarde moving towards the Beast.

"*Be quiet,* damn you!" the voice struck out again, aided this time by the same carelessly executed flick of the arm that had been made at his mother. There was the same reaction: disbelief from all. The Beast had perpetrated two seemingly mindless acts of violence towards his own mother and his best friend, as carelessly as other men might squash an insect. A shudder of terror went through the room that seemed to paralyse all who watched.

After a moment's hiatus, De Blarde fell to his knees as if in prayer, clutching his neck. The first to shake himself out of shock was Bucket, who made a sudden movement towards Frederick Dreadnaught but was too far away to reach him, I am glad to say. The Beast flicked the stiletto. "No, Inspector. I would not advise it. The blade is swift."

"Not so swift that it could keep off five policemen, I fancy," said Bucket, recovering his calm.

"Ah, well, perhaps you are right, Inspector." He regarded us one by one, as if measuring our necks and the distance and speed that would need to be negotiated in order to use the blade on us all. Despite the Inspector's defiant words, no one dared move. "But you do not want more killing, do you, Inspector? I *could* kill more, if you wish. It is nothing to me. I am quick, you see, quicker still than De Blarde, who first taught me the trick. But, perhaps you are right. To keep you at bay I shall need another tool and some help, perhaps."

As he spoke, he flicked the stiletto into his right hand and, with a shake of his sleeve, a pistol fell into his left. As if this was a prearranged signal, there was another sudden appearance; a figure emerged from the curtains by the covered door. It was the man in the billycock hat and the iron boots that had stared at me on the landing - and he held a blunderbuss in his hands, one of the two that had been mounted in the glass cabinet in the entrance hall.

"I am sure you are familiar with my friend's blunderbuss, Inspector," said the Beast. "It has been responsible for the despatch of many a wild beast, I believe. But perhaps my little weapon is one you are less familiar with: a pepperbox revolver, Inspector."

I had never seen such a weapon before, but then I remembered that perhaps I had seen the velvet-lined box that contained it. The one with the odd-shaped compartments in the hidden room.

"Your friend, Vidocq, didn't tell you about *this*, I'll wager, Inspector," the Beast continued. "I used it on one or two of my expeditions into the Paris night when there was greater danger of ruffians. I kept it up my sleeve. Do you remember, my dear De Blarde?"

De Blarde gargled blood, still on his knees. "Pourquoi, Rico? Pourquoi?" The blood pulsed between the fingers of his hand that held his neck. "You know I 'ave done everything for you … everything. Rico … I *loved* you!"

"You imbecile," the Beast sneered. "*Loved* me? Why, you are *depraved*, do you not know that?" De Blarde crumbled to the floor. A policeman moved to catch him, but Dreadnaught pointed his gun and the dark-faced thug raised his blunderbuss higher. "No, Constable, let us just leave the deranged fool to sleep, shall we? You see, our fingers itch, and the slightest movement from foolish policemen would entice us to exert such pressure on the triggers of our weapons that perhaps a blood-bath would commence."

A half-word, half-groan came from his mother. He turned on her with venom, still pointing his pistol at the rest of us. "You stupid, stupid woman! You *would* have me wait, wouldn't you? 'Wait', you said '*this* time a *rich* inheritance would be ours!' That was *always* your story wasn't it? Wasn't it, mother? In Paris you said the fool, Bouchard, was rich. You lied to me then. And you used to punish me when I wanted girls. Oh yes, I remember. Even when I was a child in England, you denied me. You bred me to think that I should inherit all the wealth that I might want. That I should have a*nything* I wanted! But then when I wanted a *young girl* I was punished for it. That stinking little child. Look what she did to me. Look!"

He began to rub at his cheek where he had been perspiring,

and as the cakes of paste seemed to fall away, he slowly uncovered a face terribly lined and pocked with smallpox scars. "Look at me! Look at me!" he shouted.

Everyone in the whole room looked at him with fresh distaste. "Oh, you loved to imagine us little children married when we grew up, didn't you?" the Beast continued. "You fancied me with little Lady Margaret, didn't you? You fancied us as little Lords and Ladies too. But look what she gave me instead: smallpox! The girls didn't want ugly Rico then, did they? Well, then I would *punish* them. You *women* - you're *all* in league against us men, aren't you? Black spiders, you are."

His mother cried out then but it was a pain not of the flesh.

"Yes, mother. Your poison did for my first father. Your poison did for my second, but neither had anything to give us! *Dreadnaught* would be different, you said. You would make the old fool fall in love with you and he would be at our mercy and his money would pay for all the mistakes of the past."

Lord Dreadnaught, forgotten almost in the horror of it all, was struggling once again to get out of his chair, his breath coming in such short gasps that it seemed he might collapse.

The Beast ignored him. "Fortune would be mine, you said. Your poison would rot him from within and my poison would rot his mind away from his dear, dear Richard. *Dear* Richard, who *all* the girls loved - while they ran away from *me*, unless I tickled them with my blade. What trouble we have had with *dear* Richard! And if Richard were near now, how *he* would feel the point of my blade! You should have let my stiletto do its work on this old fool too!" he said, suddenly regarding Lord Dreadnaught with loathing.

The old Lord, who had been groaning all along in his chair, suddenly found such strength in his anger and in his shame that

351

he lunged like a dart towards his step-son with a terrible cry, knocking the gun out of his hand. Then everything became a blur. There was the horrible stench of gun powder, and a sudden thundery shock of an explosion pushed out of the barrel of the blunderbuss. There were screams and gasps of horror. I fell to the floor. I did not know I had, but I found myself prone. Mercifully, the reactions of my body had taken precedence over my numb mind and my legs had collapsed under me. It was as if a huge hammer had struck all the air out of the room with one colossal heft.

When I *could* think again, and the grey and acrid smoke had cleared, I became aware that I was not alone in falling to my knees. Bucket and Simpkins, Sparrow and Joe, Coke and Spry and even Blakey were curled up like snails. At first, apart from this, it seemed that nothing had changed: Lady Dreadnaught was still clutching her neck, with blood slowly colouring her fingers a deep red; De Blarde lay still.

But what *had* changed was the figure of Lord Dreadnaught, who lay face down on the carpet in a deep red pool of his own blood; and the fact that the curtain I had seen covering the door to the outside world was pulled back. The door that had been slightly ajar all along was now closed, and the noise of a metal bar being brought down outside could be heard as it was locked in place by Frederick's henchman. Steel, Bouchard, Rico, Frederick Dreadnaught, The Beast - was gone.

# Chapter 33

Before any of us had climbed to our feet, more officers were at the door, drawn there by the gun shot.

"Out!" yelled Bucket suddenly. "After him! He'll be away across the gardens!"

Sparrow was the first to move. He jumped up and, pushing the gaping constables to one side, hurled himself down the stairs. He soon disappeared, followed by the other policemen, only to be jammed up below with the throng of house-servants coming up to see what was afoot. Bucket stood over the body of poor Lord Dreadnaught for a moment, and then went in turn to Lady Dreadnaught and De Blarde who, despite their wounds, might have still been breathing.

The forgotten Mad Joe now whispered to me. "I know a way!"

I looked him in the eye. "And so do I!" I said. Joe retrieved his hunting knife and he and I, partners now, ran out of the door and *up* the stairway to the hidden room that was joined on to the back of Lady Dreadnaught's by the outer stone staircase.

Down below in the hall we could hear the echo of policemen's boots, the cries of their voices, the questions of footmen and pantry maids, cooks and gardeners. After they had stopped tumbling over each other they would still have to find their way round the enormous house, or go down through the maze of the kitchens to find the quickest route to the gardens. Meanwhile, Joe and I had arrived at the curtain-covered door, the secret entrance to Frederick's Dreadnaught's room. Joe was throwing himself against this door as if that alone would breach the opening. I pulled him to one side and applied the little pen-knife I kept clipped to my father's fob-watch. When Bucket caught us up, I had already found the trip to the lock.

"So this is the secret room," Bucket said, panting, for he had followed on after us. "I wondered when you were going to share your discovery with me!"

There was no time for an answer. We passed the door in no time, racing through Frederick Dreadnaught's exotic chamber, running down past the outside of Lady Dreadnaught's room and then hurtling down the winding stone stairway to the outer world.

The moon was full and bright above us, swollen and yellow. It was the only light to guide us down the stone steps, through the night mist and onto the circular path that girdled the outer waist of Oblique House. Once on this path, Bucket and I stood in confusion. But Joe hurtled off without a word, sprinting onto the weed-infested lawns past the leaking outhouses and the sodden flower-beds.

"Won't the Beast be making for the stables, Inspector," I panted, "to make his getaway, I mean?"

"No, Will," Bucket panted in return, as we skidded along the slippery paths and through sludge-wet garden plots. "He'll know we've got Whelks waiting for us there. No, he's got another escape route in mind, I fancy. And Joe seems to know it!"

Joe seemed single-minded indeed. We could see him leaping ahead of us, and further ahead of him was the figure of the Beast himself. Bucket and I skidded and slithered around outhouses after them, until we emerged onto the sweeping lawn leading to the summer house. We were too exhausted for speech. Behind us, we could hear the voices of Sparrow and other constables struggling to keep up. It was the voices in *front* of us that now caught my ear.

As we ran on, panting hard and with hearts fit to burst, the mist cleared. I saw the outline of a black horse, probably the same one I had seen when I had shown the Dreadnaught gardens to Sparrow on his spying mission. But adjacent to the summer house, there was another horse and this one was attached to a dog-cart. The cart itself was half-fallen over, as if someone had driven it madly over rough roads to make the quickest way, and had abandoned it there. Bucket was completely out of breath by now and was forced to stop. I was relieved to take the opportunity to rest alongside him, but Joe hurried on, unrelenting. When I looked up again, I saw the shadows emerging from the cart and heard female voices calling out into the night air in fright. The figures were unclear, but the voices were not.

"Richard, no!" one screamed. It was the voice of Sarah Gavelstone.

The sound of this voice, and that name, spurred us on at once. I began to feel as if I was in a nightmare and might wake up at any minute, for next I heard a voice that I knew as well as my own: the voice of Phoebe Bucket. She had attempted to fulfil her duty in watching over Sarah Gavelstone and Richard Dreadnaught at *The White Lion*, but Richard, it seemed, despite Bucket's warnings, would not be confined and was determined to confront Frederick and his father at Oblique House. The women had at least persuaded him that they must go with him, and here they were. Hearing Phoebe's voice spurred me onwards to her aid.

As I came closer, I saw that there were two figures wrestling on the muddy earth. One of them was Richard Dreadnaught. The lone horse I had seen was for the Beast's escape, stabled for emergencies by the summer-house, where it could be ridden swiftly to the back of the Dreadnaught estate, and away, through a hidden gate that came out on quieter roads - the same way, of

355

course, that Richard Dreadnaught must have come in. The horse had been saddled up quickly by the Beast's bludger when he had run ahead. It was this thug that Richard Dreadnaught was struggling with in the mud. Richard had perhaps taken his opponent by surprise, for the blunderbuss he was carrying lay abandoned on the grass. Even so, the fight was uneven and Frederick's man had got the better of the smaller Richard Dreadnaught. From out of the shadows of the summer-house, Frederico, the Beast himself, appeared, calling shrilly, "Finish him off, Gibbons. Break his neck! Croak him!" As he spat out these deadly instructions, the Beast grabbed hold of the reins of the rearing horse. Sarah lurched herself forward, but she was cuffed brutally to the ground.

"You coward!" cried Richard and gave a fresh heave that knocked the brute he was struggling with over on to the mud. "You fiend, Rico!" Richard shouted again, scrabbling to his feet and helping Sarah to do the same. "You shan't escape! You have been the destruction of my father and the despoliation of my sister. You have driven her to madness and caused her child to be ripped from her, to languish in darkness. What hideous things you have done to other children, women and young girls I dread to guess at. Now it will end, even if I have to strangle you with my bare hands!"

The Beast simply laughed at this, a laughter that seemed to roll down towards me as I ran like a man running in a nightmare. The Beast had already turned away, ready to mount his horse. As he did so, Gibbons, the bludger, had come up behind Richard and, having reclaimed the blunderbuss, was aiming it at his head, poised to strew his brains across the grass.

I was helpless. I was not close enough to give aid, but Joe, who had been ahead of me all the time, was. Whatever torture there was in his decision, about whether to stop one or rescue the other, as he ran those final yards, it was evident in the shape of the leap he made. The choice itself contorted his body in mid-flight. He *seemed* to be leaping at the Beast, but with a cry of rage he twisted as he flew, and fell heavily upon the burly frame of Gibbons, just as the bludger's finger seemed to be on the trigger that would kill Richard Dreadnaught.

Gibbons gave a grunt as the full impact of Joe's flying leap hit him, and the blunderbuss flew from his hands. Richard Dreadnaught was struck by the flying bodies but not, mercifully, by the bullet from the blunderbuss - which shot harmlessly into the wilderness beyond, making the horse rear, tumbling the Beast to the earth, and galloping off rider-less into the night. Joe had drawn out his terrible hunting-knife as Gibbons recovered, and grappled for a hold. As if he were wielding a scimitar, he suddenly swept the blade in an arc, slicing Gibbons across the middle. The Beast's man was struck into silence for a second and then gave such a cry as might have awoken the city. He rolled to one side like a slaughtered bullock, blood gushing in a flood from the wound.

There were screams and cries of horror from women and men. The Beast's eyes shone in the moonlight, as he stared in astonishment at the bloodied figure of Gibbons and then down at the heaving breast of Mad Joe in the grass, twitching and frothing in the mud. In that moment, the Beast must have realised that the ripping blow from the hunting-knife had been meant for him, and that the blood spilt on the sod too, should have been his.

Joe lay quiet on the earth in a sort of sleep but Richard Dreadnaught had scrambled to his feet to face his step-brother. Bucket came up then, at last, and behind him Sparrow and the

357

other police officers, beginning to fan out in a semi-circle surrounding the Beast, who had retreated to the brink of the wilderness. There was no escape.

"You're finished, I think, Rico," said Bucket, his voice echoing. Phoebe was comforting the sobbing Sarah Gavelstone inside that circle at that moment and, even as Bucket spoke, the Beast made a sudden movement towards Phoebe. Before I was aware, and indeed like the nightmare I felt I had found myself in, he had hold of her. Whether she screamed or not I do not recall, for the night seemed full of screams. He had an arm around her shoulders and he was holding the terrible point of his stiletto against her naked neck. I might have leapt on him without consideration for the consequences, and so might Richard Dreadnaught, but Bucket had a cooler brain and held his arms out against us.

"Not finished *yet,* Inspector," said the Beast. "I think I have something here that we might barter with. I sense that this pretty morsel might have some currency with you and your friends. Perhaps you might want to *save* such a dainty." He pulled Phoebe back brutally, closer to the edge of the wilderness - to where it fell away into darkness behind him.

"Now *who* cares for her? I see *this* one does," he said, flicking his eyes at me. "And perhaps *you* do too, my dear Inspector." As he taunted us, he was inching back, pulling Phoebe with him closer, and closer still, to the edge.

"Stay where you are, Inspector," he commanded. "Come no closer. The earth is uneven here and I should not like anyone to slip."

He looked up at Bucket. His eyes glittered.

"We are similar, you and I, Inspector Bucket," The Beast said coldly. "We both love children, don't we?" Bucket seemed to shudder. "Yes. You see - though you have done *your* research on me, I have been interested by *you*. It is only a famous detective who may match a famous murderer, is it not? I have read about you in the press, Inspector." He pulled Phoebe still closer to him as he spoke, and again it was all I could do to restrain myself from charging at him. "*Reynolds' News*, for one, seems to have some special knowledge of you. I have heard reports, indeed, that you have no living children of your own. I believe the one child you and your wife *were* able to spawn died of some disease," he taunted. "What was it, Inspector Bucket? Influenza? Cholera? Or was it the smallpox?" There was a pause during which my pulse beat like a hammer in my temples. "*I* might have died of that too," the Beast pondered aloud. "But at least such a death is somewhat natural. What do you say, Inspector? You would not wish to lose *another* child, would you? This is one of your substitute children, is it not?"

The Beast gave Phoebe a shake.

"Now, Inspector, all you have to do for all our safety is to tell your constables to retreat. To retreat, shall we say, to the main house? I am sure there is something you could do there to tidy up," he sneered. "I doubt that you will bother with that depraved De Blarde. But there is the body of poor, dear Lord Dreadnaught to attend to and, of course, my dear Mama as well. Surely so. Then, when you have righted my step-brother's dog-cart for me, this young lady and I shall borrow it, and we shall trouble you no further. What do you say, Inspector? Is the agreement to your liking?"

Bucket stared at him impassively.

"Of course," added the Beast, "you may decline my offer if it is *not* to your taste, but I shall be forced to leave a parting gift for this sweet child who sits so meekly in my arms. And it shall be a

359

necklace with very fine red pearls and a tumble onto the rocks behind me. What do you say, Inspector?"

My head was swirling and I felt sick to the stomach, weakened by the Beast's words. But, as I stared at him, a strange and startled look came over him. He was gazing beyond me and beyond the row of policemen who stood mute as statues behind us. We all turned.

Like corpses who had climbed out of their graves, a woman and a man were hobbling towards us. They came on through the moonlight like spectres, their unearthly whiteness relieved only by gashes of red at their necks. The woman's silken dress was caught up by the night breeze. There was a pool of mist around the man's feet. He had a blunderbuss under his arm. It was the *other* hunting-gun that hitherto had been stored in the cabinet in Lord Dreadnaught's hall. Its sister weapon lay abandoned on the earth. The woman held gun in her hand: a pepperbox revolver. What tortures they had endured to crawl and hobble all this way was hard to imagine. The policemen scattered at such sights as if they were indeed ghosts that had materialised in front of them.

"Mama?" said Frederick Dreadnaught, stepping to one side of Phoebe so that he might see clearly. "De Blarde ...? But what ...?"

De Blarde raised the blunderbuss to his eye. Lady Dreadnaught lifted the revolver and, holding it in two hands, aimed at the Beast. In the same second there came a boom and a smart crack, like bones being split. Who it was that fired first I could not tell, for perhaps their new malice for Frederick Dreadnaught was of equal measure. He reeled but did not quite fall. As he swayed, I came out of my stunned trance and leapt forward, catching Phoebe on the lip of the wilderness. Her feet were almost gone - but she was safe in my arms.

The Beast staggered as if clubbed and yet he was still on his feet with the same look of astonishment in his eye. There were two gaping holes in his body, one to the forehead and one to the chest. He swayed for another sickening moment and at the same instant I heard a wild cry. A mad, red-haired figure, with a head too big for its body, launched itself even as the Beast fell and the two of them rolled together, crashing into the jagged rocks and the hard boulders. As they fell, I could not distinguish between the yells of triumph and the howls of agony as they tumbled to their ruin.

# Chapter 34

Of course, the papers were a sensation over the next few days. Fleet Street congratulated itself on how precipitate it had been at divining the true identity of 'The Beast'. They intimated that they had known from the very beginning. They had only been waiting for the monster to be captured to make the announcement that they had been correct in their suppositions all along:

'Murdering Aristocrat Tumbles to his Death', concluded *The Morning Post*; 'The Beast of London Town Revealed as Fiendish Footman', said *The Thunderer*; 'Wicked Master of Disguise Unmasked' *The News of the World* decided. And, of course, they were all correct in their own ways. However, the only tale of the event that could claim full veracity was the one that appeared in *Reynolds' Weekly News*.

The tale of Frederick Dreadnaught's demonic deceit was revealed here: the story of the calumnies committed by him on his stepbrother Richard; the narrative of the wicked plot by a scheming wife to murder a Lord of the Realm, as well as a full account of all his antecedents in tragedy; the tale of how that noble Lord, blinded by grief, learnt to see again and how he was shot down in cold blood in his moment of full sight; the story of how a wicked mother and a thwarted lover took courage, at last, to rid the world of the Beast. There, too, could be found the sorrowful narrative of Mr Merit, manservant to a Lord, and an account of how his son, poor Joe, fell to a desperate death with his skinner's knife plunged deeply into the heart of the hated Beast.

Of course, the main narrative was of a certain Inspector Bucket. I confess that there was something, too, about a brave girl, the fair ward of the Inspector, who did not flinch even with a knife at her throat.

The story of Frederick Dreadnaught's capture was in such demand that the first edition sold out and Reynolds was required to open up his presses in the afternoon to print another. The old Chartist was so pleased with the lucidity of the prose that the writer was offered a permanent appointment as crime correspondent.

Bucket himself retired at the end of the December in that year, to open his Private Inquiry Bureau - just like his friend Vidocq in Paris. He had asked me to be his amanuensis long ago, almost at the beginning of this narrative, but he meant, he said, an amanuensis *for life*, and for *after his life*, not just for *one* case. In addition, he offered me a permanent role as assistant in his new detective bureau.

"Not just to write up the cases," Bucket said, "though you're welcome to do that seeing as you won't put down that scribbling pencil and never have done since you first picked it up. No, I want you to actually *help* me in my investigations too, as you have done already."

In becoming a sort of detective myself, and writing stories about Inspector Bucket for *Reynolds* as crime correspondent, all my dreams seemed to come true.

However, as I have intimated elsewhere, there was darkness to come. This unhappiness was partly, indeed, due to the very reports I made of Bucket's exploits. For you see, I could not help myself but to talk of him always - as he will always be known – as *Inspector* Bucket. The truth, in point of strict actual fact, was that he had ceased to be an Inspector from the moment he had submitted his letter of resignation to the police force.

To their disgrace, Bucket's superiors complained about

Bucket's 'dishonest' use of the appellation 'Inspector'. It gave an 'erroneous impression' they claimed, an impression that he was earning his commission on false pretences. Furthermore, the Home Office concluded that Bucket had been engaged by Lord Montague Dreadnaught in a private capacity, and for payment, whilst still in the employ of the Metropolitan Force. In truth, of course, this cannot be denied - but the manner in which they ignored the fact that Bucket's commission had led to the capture of the Beast, a man who had terrorised London's rich and poor for almost two years, was disgraceful.

Having his name linked with *Reynolds* did not assist matters either. Reynolds had never lost his notoriety for being an early champion of the Chartists. *The Weekly* was seen by the government as the voice of the rising poor, the paper for the new town and city workers and the small tradesman classes, and hence was to be regarded with suspicion for fear of the rebellion it preached.

Bucket himself was always fighting on behalf of abused children and for the downtrodden classes. His reputation was assured in the streets and alleyways of Cripplegate and Seven Dials, and much further afield. But there were those in parliament who regarded such popularity with suspicion.

Thus, Bucket felt their barbs. He had, after all, offended their Lordships by exposing a scandal in Mayfair itself, at the heart of the London aristocracy. He had shone his bulls-eye on the shameful secrets of the gentry, the nobility and the bishops too. They felt that their noses had been put out. It was no surprise that those who might indulge in the depravity that Bucket exposed would take their chance to muddy Bucket's name.

In addition, there were many in the police service itself that were jealous of Bucket. The common constables continued to regard Bucket with affection and awe, but there were certain sergeants and fellow inspectors whom he had offended. One or two of these subsequently became inspectors or commissioners in their own right. They were only too glad to be able to repay Bucket with their malice when they could.

The shameful outcome of all of this was that Bucket's police pension was denied him due to his alleged misuse of the title of Inspector whilst working in a private capacity. In the end, though, good sense and proper gratitude was restored when Bucket's pension was at last reinstated by Sir George Grey.

Mr Richard Dreadnaught and Sarah Gavelstone were married and made their residence at Oblique House. This was another 'scandal in Bohemia', as *The Chronicle* described it. Society was in uproar at this union between a gardener's daughter and a Baronet. Lord Richard Dreadnaught, as he now was, continued to cause consternation amongst his neighbours, becoming famous at Drury Lane for his celebrated dramas.

More dismay was expressed by their Lordships when Caroline Dreadnaught, Richard's sister, recovered from her traumas, rebuilt and restored the erstwhile summer house at Oblique House as a home for orphaned children and distressed young women, paid for by Lord Montague Dreadnaught's estate. Her child, the baby that had spent its early days in Mrs Mason's baby farm, later founded a string of homes for orphans in her own right when she married the philanthropist, Dr Barnard. A good-looking young woman she became too, the image of her grandmother (as the older servants who came back to Oblique House said on their return) the first and truly beloved wife of the old Lord.

Mr Gavelstone was restored to his post as Head Gardener and, despite the fact that he spent most of his time asleep in his hut

365

and was a regular tyrant to his underlings, the pineapples flourished in Mayfair once more.

Ada was heart-broken that Alfred, for whom she had developed an inexplicable regard, had been the Beast. She was angry at having her emotions duped but she was too jolly a soul to mope for long. She was made housekeeper at Oblique House and struck up a romantic friendship with Constable Blakey, whom Bucket had put in charge of ensuring that none of Frederick Dreadnaught's contingent remained in Mayfair.

I met with my bosom friend, Archibald Sparrow, soon after and fulfilled my obligation to attend that long promised engagement party he had invited me to in Camden Town. The natural consequence of this was a wedding at St Giles, where I had the honour to be called upon to act as Sparrow's best man. The nuptials were held in the upper rooms of *The White Lion*. Mrs Beddows, the landlady, declared it would be a shame if they were to be held anywhere else, Alice having become almost a daughter to her. Mrs Bucket attended in all her finery and Bucket himself, of course, wearing his best diamond brooch and his top hat with the silken nap. He was in some respects, apart from the bride and groom, of course, the centre of attention. He seemed to be acquainted with everybody, moving amongst the guests as he had done through the beer houses of Seven Dials. It was no surprise that he happened to have a nephew or niece, uncle or aunt in exactly the same trade as whoever it was he was talking to, be it in haberdashery, millinery or manufacturing.

Even my old 'respecrable' landlady, Mrs Peckers, was in attendance, she and Sparrow now like mother and son. Nevertheless, she spent the entire evening staring at me and tutting or turning up her walnut nose or twisting her lemon slice of a mouth sourly as if she meant to have a word with Constable

Sparrow or Inspector Bucket about a certain notorious villain who had made an escape from Newgate Gaol.

The Naiskins were honoured guests of Mrs Alice Sparrow. John Naiskins was clearly uncomfortable at being in the same room as Bucket and a plethora of policemen, amongst them Coke, Cobb and Blakey, as well as Sergeant Mellors, to name but four. However, John Naiskins' discomfort was diminished by his proximity to the barrel of Old English Ale that was provided by no less a personage than Richard Dreadnaught, Baronet, of Mayfair.

Gertie Bucket and Nancy Naiskins were Maids of Honour. They clearly felt it their duty to dance and laugh throughout the whole event, their bouncing curls smothered in fresh ribbons tied on by Bucket himself. Gertie never failed to comment upon how silly I looked in my tails and top hat.

On the following morning, after a dream of rice and flour and church bells and dancing and kisses from the red lips of Miss Phoebe Bucket, I awoke with disappointment in my attic room to find that it was Buttons the cat whose kisses I was receiving. However, I recalled then a look and a wink that Sparrow had been giving me all the last evening whilst I was dancing with Phoebe. I sat up. I felt the blinding light of a revelation.

When I tumbled indecorously downstairs, Phoebe was sitting in the parlour. I was late down and Hetty was already collecting up the breakfast things. On the moment of my entry, Bucket, Ma Bucket, Gertie, and Hetty too, all rose as one and left the room. I observed that they wore broad smiles and that Gertie would not desist from giggling at the slightest opportunity - although in consequence of what, I was, at that moment, unable to say. Phoebe Bucket and I were left alone.

When we finally vacated the parlour, I was in an agony of

embarrassment and anticipation. Phoebe, as always, was calm and smiling. Ma Bucket returned the smile in equal measure, holding Gertie against her bosom and impeding any further taunts and teasing from that quarter with a hand placed loosely over her mischievous mouth. In this half-dream I floated towards Bucket's study.

He was at his desk holding a magnifying glass to his eye and reading over something written in the black notebook. He stood when he heard me come in and regarded me in that way he had that seemed to be measuring one for a suit of clothes.

"Ah, my lad," he said at last, for he had clearly seen that I was for the moment incapable of speech. "Well?" he asked, bringing his finger up and tapping me jovially on the collar.

"Excuse me, Inspector Buc…" I began with some hopelessness.

"Come on, lad!" he encouraged. "Is it done? Spit it out, won't you!" I was still tongue-tied but Bucket put me out of my misery.

"*Yes,* my boy," he said. "You have my permission. Why, I thought you'd never ask!"

At that, the door behind me flew open and three figures flew in with it. I was smothered by dancing, laughing females, all kissing and hugging me in delight. Bucket kept beating me on the back and was shaking my hand with such vigour that it was as if his intent was to make it come away at the joint. Patch ran in too, barking, to add his congratulations, leaping three times into the air - the highest he had achieved yet. Even Buttons completed a celebratory tour of my legs by way of an embrace, in and out, weaving her approval. But the longest embrace was with my own, my very own, Phoebe Bucket.